DEATH
BY
GASLIGHT

Available from Michael Kurland and Titan Books

THE PROFESSOR MORIARTY NOVELS

The Infernal Device
Death By Gaslight
The Great Game
The Empress of India
Who Thinks Evil

A
PROFESSOR
MORIARTY
NOVEL
DEATH
BY
GASLIGHT

MICHAEL KURLAND

TITAN BOOKS

DEATH BY GASLIGHT
Print edition ISBN: 9781783293285
E-book edition ISBN: 9781783293292

Published by Titan Books
A division of Titan Publishing Group Ltd
144 Southwark Street, London SE1 0UP

First edition: May 2014
1 2 3 4 5 6 7 8 9 10

A CIP catalogue record for this title is available from the British Library.

Printed and bound in Great Britain by CPI Group Ltd.

Did you enjoy this book? We love to hear from our readers.
Please email us at: readerfeedback@titanemail.com

To receive advance information, news, competitions, and exclusive offers online, please sign up for the Titan newsletter on our website:
TITANBOOKS.COM

DEATH
BY
GASLIGHT

Now entertain conjecture of a time
When creeping murmur and the poring dark
Fills the wide vessel of the Universe.
From camp to camp, through the foul womb of night...
WILLIAM SHAKESPEARE

PROLOGUE

When I consider life, 'tis all a cheat.
JOHN DRYDEN

The tall, thickset man in the gray frock coat walked slowly between the double row of headstones. He looked neither to the left nor the right, but stared at something ahead of him that the older man who walked beside him could not see. They stopped at a newly turned grave, not yet covered with sod, and the tall man crouched and placed his hands flat on the bare earth.

"This is it," he said, turning his vacant eyes on his companion. "This is where she lies."

"I'll take care of it, right enough," the old man said, squinting at the ground to note the number on the painted board that marked the place where the headstone would be. "Like she was my own daughter. My word."

"Flowers?"

"Every day. My word."

"She likes flowers." The tall man rose and turned to his companion. "I'll meet you at the gate," he said.

The old man stared at him for a second, and then said "A' course," and walked away.

The frock-coated man turned back to the bare earth. "I am here," he said.

The day was somber and the fog was dense. What light there was gladly fled before the encroaching dusk.

"I have discovered another one for you," he whispered. "Another death for your death. Another throat for the blade. It doesn't help. God knows it doesn't help. God knows—" The man's face contorted. "God!—God!" He fell to his knees, his hands twin tight-fisted balls before his eyes. "Someday I'll stand before the God who made what befell you part of His immortal plan; and then—and then—"

He stood up and slowly willed his fists to open. Semicircles of blood had formed where his nails had dug into his palms. "But until then, the men," he whispered, "the godlike men. One by one they shall fall like reeds before the avenging wind. And I am the wind."

He held out his hand and there was a bouquet of flowers between his fingers, which he placed gently down on the moist earth. Beside the bouquet he laid a small gold amulet with an intricate design. "Here is another," he said. "From the last one. The last murderer. The last to die before the wind. This is the sign by which we know them, you and I. The mark of Cain. The hell-mark of the damned."

Standing again, he brushed off his trousers. "I love you, Annie," he murmured to the bare earth. "I do not do this for you; I know you would not ask it, the killing. I do not do it for me; I have always been a gentle man, and it does not ease me. I do not like the blood, the moment of fear. But it is all I can do. I cannot stop myself. I have become the wind, and they shall all die."

He turned and slowly walked away.

ONE

NIGHT AND FOG

There was a Door to which I found no Key;
There was a Veil past which I could not see.
EDWARD FITZGERALD

Throughout much of March in the year 1887 the city of London was covered by a thick, almost tangible fog that swept in from the North Sea. It chilled the flesh, dampened the spirit, and oppressed the soul. It all but obscured the sun by day, and by night it occluded the stars, the moon, the streetlamps, and the minds of men. Things were done in that fog, in the night, that were better left undone.

In the early morning hours of Tuesday, the eighth of March, the fog blanketed the city; a moist discomforter that swallowed light and muffled sound. Police Constable William Alberts walked his rounds with a steady, measured stride, insulated from the enveloping fog by his thick blue greatcoat and the Majesty of the Law. The staccato echo of his footsteps sounded sharp and loud in the empty street as he turned off Kensington Gore into Regent's Gate and paced stolidly past the line of stately mansions.

P.C. Alberts paused and cocked his head. Somewhere in the fog ahead of him there was—what?—a sort of gliding, scurrying sound that he could not identify. The sound, perhaps, of someone trying to move silently through the night but betrayed by a loose paving stone.

He waited for the noise to be repeated, turning to face where he thought it had come from and straining his eyes to pierce the black, fog-shrouded night.

There! Farther over now—was that it again? A muted sound; could someone be trying to sneak past him in the dark? A scurrying sound; could it be rats? There were rats even in Regent's Gate. Even the mansions of the nobility had the occasional rats' nest in the cellar. P.C. Alberts shuddered. He was not fond of rats.

But there—another sound! Footsteps this time, good honest British footsteps pattering around the Kensington Gore corner and approaching the spot where Constable Alberts stood.

A portly man appeared out of the fog, his MacFarlane buttoned securely up to his chin and a dark-gray bowler pulled down to his eyes. A hand-knitted gray scarf obscured much of the remainder of his face, leaving visible only wide-set brown eyes and a hint of what was probably a large nose. For a second the man looked startled to see P.C. Alberts standing there, then he nodded as he recognized the uniform. "Evening, Constable."

"Evening, sir." Alberts touched the tip of his forefinger to the brim of his helmet. "A bit late, isn't it, sir?"

"It is that," the man agreed, pausing to peer up at Alberts's face. "I don't recollect you, Constable. New on this beat, are you?"

"I am, sir," Alberts admitted. "P.C. Alberts, sir. Do you live around here, sir?"

"I do, Constable; in point of fact, I do." The man pointed a pudgy finger into the fog. "Yonder lies my master's demesne. I am Lemming, the butler at Walbine House."

"Ah!" Alberts said, feeling that he should reply to this revelation. They walked silently together for a few steps.

"I have family in Islington," Lemming volunteered. "Been visiting for the day. Beastly hour to be getting back."

"It is that, sir," Alberts agreed.

"Missed my bus," Lemming explained. "Had to take a number twenty-seven down Marylebone Road and then walk from just this side of Paddington Station. I tell you, Constable, Hyde Park is not sufficiently lighted at night. Especially in this everlasting fog. I am, I will freely admit, a man of nervous disposition. I nearly jumped out of my skin two or three times while crossing the park; startled by something no more dangerous, I would imagine, than a squirrel."

They reached the entrance to Walbine House: a stout oaken door shielded by a wrought-iron gate. "At any rate I have arrived home before his lordship," Lemming said, producing a keychain from beneath his MacFarlane and applying a stubby, circular key to the incongruously new lock in the ancient gate.

"His lordship?" P.C. Alberts asked.

Lemming swung open the gate. "The Right Honorable the Lord Walbine," he said. He lifted the keychain up to his face and flipped through the keys, trying to locate the front-door key in the dim light of the small gas lamp that hung to the left of the massive oak door. "I served his father until he died two years ago, and now I serve his lordship."

"Ah!" Alberts said, wondering how the stout butler knew that his new lordship was still absent from Walbine House.

"Goodnight then, Constable," Lemming said, opening the great door as little as possible and pushing himself through the crack.

"Goodnight," Alberts said to the rapidly closing door. He waited until he heard the lock turned from the inside, and then resumed his measured stride along Regent's Gate. It was deathly quiet now; no more scurrying, no fancied noises, only the slight rustle of the wind through the distant trees and the echo of his own footsteps bouncing off the brick facades of the Georgian mansions that faced each other across the wide street.

At Cromwell Road, Constable Alberts paused under the streetlamp for a moment and peered thoughtfully around. He had the unwelcome sensation that he was being watched. By whom he could not tell, but the feeling persisted, an eerie, tingling sensation at the back of his neck. He turned and started back down the dark, fog-shrouded pavement.

From some distance away on Cromwell Road came the clattering noises of an approaching carriage, which grew steadily louder until, some twenty seconds later, a four-wheeler careened around the corner into Regent's Gate. The cab sped along the street, the horse encouraged by an occasional flick of the jarvey's whip. Entirely too fast, Alberts noted critically.

Halfway down Regent's Gate, opposite Walbine House, the jarvey pulled his horse to a stop. From where Alberts stood he could make out the form of a top-hatted man in evening dress emerging from the four-wheeler and tossing a coin up to the jarvey. The Right Honorable the Lord Walbine had obviously just returned home for the night. Lemming, Alberts thought, had been right.

The four-wheeler pulled away and rattled on down the street as his lordship let himself into Walbine House. All was quiet again. P.C. Alberts resumed his beat, the tread of his footsteps once more the only sound to be heard along the tree-lined street. He kept to a steady methodical pace as he headed toward Kensington Gore.

It took P.C. Alberts almost ten minutes to make the circuit along Kensington Gore, back up Queen's Gate, and then across Cromwell Road to the Regent's Gate corner. As he turned onto Regent's Gate again, from somewhere ahead of him there came a sudden cacophony of slamming doors and running feet. The faint gleam of a lantern wavered back and forth across the street. It caught Alberts in its dim beam. "Constable!" came an urgent whisper that carried clearly across the length of the street. "Constable Alberts! Come quickly!"

Alberts quickened his stride without quite breaking into a run. "Here I am," he called. "What's the trouble, now?"

The butler, Lemming, was standing in the middle of the street in his shirtsleeves, his eyes wide, breathing like a man who has just been chased by ghosts. An older woman with a coat misbuttoned over a hastily donned housedress peered from behind him.

"Please," Lemming said, "would you come inside with us?"

"If I am needed," Alberts said, taking a firmer grasp of his nightstick. "What seems to be the trouble?"

"It's 'is lordship," the old woman said. "'E just come in, and now 'e won't answer 'is door."

"His lordship arrived home a short while ago," Lemming explained, "and immediately retired to his room. Mrs. Beddoes was to bring him his nightly glass of toddy, as usual."

"'E rang for it," Mrs. Beddoes assured Alberts, "as 'e always does."

"But the bedroom door was locked when she arrived on the landing," Lemming said.

"And 'e don't answer 'is knock," Mrs. Beddoes finished, nodding her head back and forth like a pigeon.

"I'm afraid there's been an accident," Lemming said.

"Are you certain his lordship is in his bedroom?" Alberts asked, staring up at the one lighted window on the second story of the great house.

"The door is secured from the inside," Lemming said. "I'd appreciate having you take a look, Constable. Come this way, please."

P.C. Alberts followed Lemming up an ornate marble staircase and down a corridor on the second floor to his lordship's bedroom door. Which was locked. Alberts knocked on the polished dark wood of the door panel and called out. There was no response.

"Has his lordship ever done this before?" Alberts asked.

"His lordship has been known to secure the door on occasion," Lemming answered. "But he has previously always responded to a knock, even if it was only to yell, 'Go away!'"

P.C. Alberts thought for a second. "We'd best break it in," he decided. "Lord Walbine may require assistance."

Lemming sighed, the relief at having someone else make the decision evident in his face. "Very good, Constable. If you say so."

The two men applied their shoulders to the door in a series of blows. On the fourth, the wood around the lock splintered. On the sixth it gave, and the door swung inward.

Alberts entered the room first. It was a large bedroom, dominated by a canopy bed. The Right Honorable the Lord Walbine, twelfth baron of that name, was lying quietly in the center of that bed in a fresh pool of his own blood. Sometime within the past ten minutes his throat had been neatly sliced from clavicle to clavicle.

TWO

THE MORNING

Art in the blood is liable to take the strangest forms.
SHERLOCK HOLMES

Benjamin Barnett opened his *Morning Herald*, folded it in half, and propped it against the toast rack. "There's been another one," he said, peering down at the closely printed column as he cracked his first soft-boiled egg.

"Eh?" Professor James Moriarty looked up from his breakfast. "Another what?"

"Murder," Barnett said. "Another 'mysterious killing among the gentry,'" he read with evident satisfaction.

"Don't look so pleased," Moriarty said. "It might lead one to suspect that you had done it yourself."

"'The third outrage in as many weeks,' according to the *Herald*," Barnett said, tapping the headline with his egg spoon. "The police are baffled."

"If we are to believe the newspapers," Moriarty remarked, "the police are always baffled. Except when 'Inspector Gregson expects an early arrest.' Sometimes the police are 'baffled' and 'expect an early arrest' in the same paragraph. I can only wish that you journalists had a wider selection of descriptive phrases to choose from. It would certainly add an element of suspense to newspaper reading that is now grievously lacking."

"There's enough suspense in this story to keep even you happy," Barnett said. "A police constable broke down the victim's bedroom door, which was locked from the inside, to find him lying on his bed in a pool of his own blood, with his throat so deeply cut that the head was almost severed and the blood still flowing from the gaping wound in his neck. How's that for suspense?"

Moriarty sighed and shook his head. Taking off his pince-nez glasses to polish them with his linen napkin, he focused his water-gray eyes myopically on Barnett across the table. "Actually it's quite distressing," he said.

"How's that, Professor?"

Moriarty held up the thick paperbound volume that rested beside his plate. "This came in the first post this morning," he said. "It is the quarterly journal of the British Astro-Physical Society. There is more of mystery and suspense in these twelve-score pages than in ten years' worth of the *Morning Herald*."

"That may be, Professor," Barnett said, "but your average newspaper reader is not interested in what's happening on Mars, but in what's happening in Chelsea. He'd rather have a mysterious murder than a mysterious nebulosity any time."

"You are probably right," Moriarty said, laying the journal aside and replacing his pince-nez glasses on the bridge of his nose. "There is, nonetheless, some small comfort, some slight gleam of hope for the future of the human race that can be derived from current scientific theory. I read my journals and they comfort me."

"What sort of comfort, Professor?" Barnett asked, feeling that he had lost the thread of the conversation.

"I find solace in the theories expounded by Professor Herschel, among others, concerning nebulae," Moriarty said, pouring himself a cup of coffee from the large silver samovar which squatted at one end of the table. "They would suggest that the universe is larger by several orders of magnitude than previously imagined."

"This comforts you?"

"Yes. It indicates that mankind, confined as it is to this small planet in a random corner of the universe, is of no real importance or relevance whatsoever."

Barnett put his spoon carefully down on the side of his plate. He knew that Moriarty indulged in these misanthropic diatribes at least partly to annoy him, but at the same time he had never seen any sign that the professor was not totally serious about what he said. "I don't suppose you'd care to do a piece for my news service on that general theme, Professor?" Barnett asked.

"Bah!" Moriarty replied.

"I could probably get a couple of hundred American newspapers to carry the piece."

"The prospect of having my words read eagerly over the jam pot in Chicago is, I must confess, one that holds no particular charm for me," Moriarty said. "Having my phrases mouthed in San Francisco, or my ideas hotly debated in Des Moines, has equally little appeal. No, I'm afraid, my dear Mr. Barnett, that your offer will not entice me into a journalistic career."

"I'm sorry about that, Professor," Barnett said. "The world lost a great essayist when you chose to devote yourself to a life of, ah, science."

Professor Moriarty looked at Barnett suspiciously. "When I plucked you from a Turkish prison almost two years ago," he said, "you were as devoid of sarcasm as you were embedded with grime. I no longer detect any grime."

"*Touché*, Professor." Barnett smiled and poured himself a cup of coffee.

* * *

Benjamin Barnett had first met Professor James Moriarty in Constantinople almost two years before, at a moment when the professor was being chased down the Street of the Two Towers by a band of assassins in dirty brown burnooses. Barnett and a friend came to the professor's aid, for which he thanked them profusely, although he regarded the assault as a minor annoyance from which he could have extricated himself quite easily without assistance. Which, Barnett came to admit when he got to know the professor better, was most probably true.

Moriarty had reciprocated by rescuing Barnett from the dank confines of the prison of Mustafa II, where he was being held for the minor offense of murdering his friend and the major indiscretion of spying against the government of that most enlightened despot Sultan Abd-ul Hamid, Shah of Shahs, the second of that name. Both crimes of which he was equally innocent, and for either of which he was equally likely to be garroted at any moment at the whim of the Sublime Porte.

But Moriarty had exacted a price for his rescue. "What I want from you," he had told Barnett, "is two years of your life."

"Why?" Barnett had asked.

"You are good at your profession, and I have use for you."

"And after the two years?"

"After that, your destiny is once again your own."

"I accept!"

It had seemed like a good bargain at the time. And even when Moriarty had smuggled Barnett across the length of Europe and they stood face to face in the professor's basement laboratory in the house on Russell Square, it continued to seem so. Moriarty claimed to be a consultant and problem-solver, but he was strangely vague about the details. After extracting an oath of silence in regard to his affairs, he had put Barnett to work. Barnett had been a foreign correspondent for the *New York World*, living in Paris, when he had gone to Turkey to report on the sea trials of a new submarine and ended up in an Osmanli prison. It was his skills as a reporter that Moriarty wished to use. With Moriarty's assistance, Barnett opened the American News Service, a cable service to United States newspapers for British and European news. This gave Barnett a cover organization to investigate anything that Moriarty wanted investigated. To the surprise of both men, the service quickly began to make money, and soon took on a life of its own as a legitimate news organization.

Gradually it dawned on Barnett that Moriarty's ideas of law and morality were at variance with those of the rest of Victorian society. Moriarty, to put it bluntly, was a criminal. Sherlock Holmes, the brilliant consulting detective, considered Moriarty one of the most reprehensible villains in London as yet unhanged. This was, perhaps, an exaggeration. Holmes had been trying to catch Moriarty at some nefarious scheme or other for nearly a decade, and had yet to succeed. He had foiled one or two of the professor's plans, and apprehended a henchman or two; but he had never managed to link the crime in question to the quondam professor of mathematics now living in Russell Square. This had undoubtedly led to a certain pique, and a tendency to see Moriarty under every bush and a sinister plot behind every crime.

Professor Moriarty was not a simple criminal any more than he was a simple man. He had his own morality, as strict as or stricter than that of his contemporaries. But it differed in tone as well as in content from that smug complacency with which Victoria's subjects regarded "those lesser breeds without the law" unfortunate enough to be born in Borneo, or Abyssinia, or Whitechapel.

Moriarty had kept Barnett isolated from most of his criminal activities, finding Barnett more useful as an unbiased gatherer of information. As a result, Barnett had only hints of the organization that Moriarty commanded, or the activities that he directed. Barnett did know that whatever money Moriarty made from his activities, beyond that necessary to keep up his household, went into supporting his scientific experiments. Moriarty thought of himself as a scientist, and his other activities, legal and illegal, were merely the means of financing his inquiries into the scientific unknown.

* * *

Barnett stared at the tall, hawklike man across the breakfast table from him. Moriarty was an enigma: an avowed criminal, he had the highest intellectual and moral standards Barnett had ever known; an evident misanthrope, he quietly supported several charities in the most miserably poor sections of London; a confirmed realist, he showed an irrepressible inclination toward the romantic. It might not be that he sought out adventure; but however he might hide from it, it unerringly sought him out.

"You've always been interested in puzzles," Barnett said, breaking off his chain of thought as Moriarty noticed his fixed gaze. "Doesn't the image of a man murdered inside a locked room appeal to you?"

Moriarty thought over the question for a moment. "Not especially," he said. "I'd need more information than is given in the *Morning Herald* before I find it puzzling. The way they leave it, there are too many possible answers only because there are too many unasked questions."

"For example?"

"What of the windows, for example?"

"Locked. It says so."

"Of course. But what sort of locks? There are gentlemen, I believe, who can open a locked window from the outside."

"And then leave through the window, locking it after them?"

"In some cases, yes, depending upon the type of lock. Or, for example, the murderer could have concealed himself in a cupboard, or under the bed, and not left until after the body was discovered."

"I hadn't thought of that," Barnett said.

"I can list five other ways in which the supposed 'locked room' could have been circumvented," Moriarty said.

"I take it back," Barnett said, laying the newspaper face down on the table next to the chafing dish. "There is no puzzle. I was mistaken."

"There are, however, several items of interest in the account," Moriarty said.

"What items do you find interesting?"

"Ah!" Moriarty said. "More examples are requested. There is, for example, the question of motive. There are five motives for murder: greed, lust, fear, honor, and insanity. Which was this?"

"Scotland Yard is of the opinion that Lord Walbine was killed by a burglar."

"Greed then," Moriarty said. "But surely we have a most unusual burglar here: one who goes straight to the master bedroom when there are cupboards full of silver in the pantry; one who lays his lordship full length out on his bed and slashes his throat instead of giving him a friendly little tap on the head with a blunt object. And then one who disappears in a locked room."

"You just intimated that you knew several men who could have done it," Barnett said.

"Ah, yes. But again we come to the question of motive. Why would a burglar have gone to the additional trouble of closing the room after him? Why not just go out of the window and down the drainpipe?"

"I don't know," Barnett replied.

"And if it was indeed an interrupted act of burglary, what of the murder of Isadore Stanhope, the barrister, last week? Or the Honorable George Venn before that? All with their throats slit; all in their own bedrooms. One with his wife asleep in the adjoining bedroom, the other with a faithful hound lying undisturbed at the foot of the stairs. And nothing of value missing in any of the crimes. A singular burglar indeed!"

Barnett put down his spoon and stared across the table at his companion. Moriarty had not so much as glanced at the morning newspapers. Further, Barnett was willing to swear he hadn't seen a newspaper in the past three weeks. Moriarty scorned newspapers, and seldom opened them. One of Barnett's jobs was to keep a clipping file of current crime stories and other items that might interest the professor, but the last three weeks' clippings lay in a box, unsorted and unfiled, on Barnett's desk. Yet somehow Moriarty knew the details of the three linked murders, as he seemed always to know all that was happening in London and most of what was happening throughout the world.

"You have another theory, then?" Barnett suggested.

"One should never theorize with insufficient facts," Moriarty said. "It is a practice most destructive of the mental faculties. As I said, there are some obvious questions that should be asked. The answers should give one a clear picture of the murderer and his motive."

"Such as?"

Moriarty shook his head. "I don't understand your fascination with this," he said. "A mundane series of murders with nothing to recommend them to the connoisseur. Reminiscent of Roehm in Düsseldorf a few years back, or the notorious Philadelphia Fox murders in '78. The only mystery in such cases is how the police can be so inefficient."

"As I remember," Barnett said, "they never caught the Philadelphia Fox."

"My point exactly," said Moriarty.

"If the investigation were in your charge," Barnett asked, "what would you do?"

"I resist the answer which springs to my lips," Moriarty said, with a hint of a smile, "as the language involved is rather coarse. However—" The professor removed his pince-nez lenses once again and began polishing them with his napkin. As he did he stared absently across the table at the Vernet which hung above the sideboard, a three-by-five-foot oil entitled *Landscape with Cavalry*.

Barnett watched with interest as the professor polished his lenses and stared unseeingly across the room. He was watching Moriarty think, as impressive an event to Barnett as watching Norman-Néruda play the violin or watching W. S. Gilbert scribble. Something incredible was happening right there in front of you, and if you were very lucky there was always the chance that some of whatever it was would rub off on you.

"The question of motive," Moriarty said, readjusting his pince-nez on his nose, "would seem to be the most promising. Of the five I cited, we can eliminate but one: insanity. I would concentrate on the backgrounds of the three men to establish what they had in common, to try to find a common denominator for our killer."

"I don't know, Professor," Barnett said. "The way those three were killed seems pretty crazy to me. Slitting their throats in their own beds, then sneaking out past locked doors and sleeping dogs."

"Slitting their throats may be an action of insanity," Moriarty said, "but it seems to me that the subsequent innocuous departure was eminently sane."

Mr. Maws, Moriarty's butler, appeared at the dining-room door. "Beg pardon, Professor," he said in his gravelly voice, "but there is a gentleman to see you. An Indian gentleman. I took the liberty of placing him in the drawing room."

Moriarty pulled out his pocket watch and snapped it open. "And nine minutes early, I fancy," Moriarty said. "No card?"

"None, sir. He did mention the lack, sir. Apologized for not having one. Gave his name as Singh."

"I see," Moriarty said. "Tell the gentleman I shall be with him in a few moments."

"Nine minutes early?" Barnett asked, as Mr. Maws withdrew to reassure their visitor.

"It is nine minutes before ten," Moriarty said. "This also came in the first post." He extracted an envelope from his jacket pocket and flipped it across the table to Barnett. "What do you make of it?"

The envelope was a stiff, thick, slightly gray paper that Barnett was unfamiliar with, as was the paper inside. The address on the envelope, *James Moriarty, Ph.D., 64 Russell Square, City,* was done with a broad-nibbed pen in a round, flowing hand. The handwriting on the letter itself was more crabbed and angular, written with an extremely fine-pointed nib.

"Two different hands," Barnett noted. "Let's see what the note says":

James Moriarty, Sc.D.—
Will be calling upon you at ten of the a.m. tomorrow morning. Am hopeful to find you at home at that instant. Am hopeful to interest you in impossible but potentially lucrative endeavor. Have been informed by several that you are man most likely to talk to in this regard. With greatest hopes and much potential thanks, I am name of Singh.

"Very interesting stylistically, if not very informative." Barnett held the note up to the light. "I don't recognize this paper. No watermark. No crest. But it is a thick, expensive paper of the sort used for printing invitations, possibly. It's an odd size; almost square."

"What does all of this tell you?"

"Well," Barnett considered. "Nothing really beyond what it says. A gentleman named Singh will call at ten and he has some sort of proposition to put to you."

"A reasonable conclusion," Moriarty said, "confirmed by the fact that the gentleman has indeed shown up a trifle before the hour. Nothing more?"

"No, not really."

"Any suggestion regarding the distinctly different hands on the message and the envelope?"

"No. It is curious, I admit. But no ready explanation for it springs to my mind. What does it tell you?"

"That, and the unusual shape of the paper, do offer a field for speculation," Moriarty said, pushing himself to his feet, "but there is no point in indulging in that pernicious habit when the object of our speculation awaits us in the drawing room."

"You wish me to be present at the interview?"

"If you like."

"Thank you, but I think not. I really should get to the office."

"I thought the admirable Miss Perrine was handling the affairs of the American News Service."

"She is, and very well," Barnett said. "She controls a staff of nine reporters, four secretary-typists, three telegraphists, and assorted porters, page boys, errand boys, and the like with a hand of iron. A very exceptional young lady."

"She enjoys this position of authority?" Moriarty asked.

"Her only regret, or so she has informed me, is that her administrative duties leave her little time for writing."

"Well, you'd better leave, then," Moriarty said, "before the young lady discovers that you are dispensable. I will take care of the potentially lucrative Mr. Singh."

"I am going to put a couple of my reporters to work on those murders," Barnett said. "I am convinced that there's a story there."

"There well may be, Barnett," Moriarty said, smiling down at him, "but are you quite sure it should be told?"

THREE

221B BAKER STREET

Deceit, according to him, was an impossibility in the case of one
trained to observation and analysis. His conclusions were as infallible
as so many propositions of Euclid.

DR. JOHN H. WATSON

Sherlock Holmes waved his visitor to a seat. "Come, this is most gratifying," he said. "Welcome, my lord. I have sent the page boy down for some tea. In the meantime, what can I do for you?"

The Earl of Arundale looked with distaste around the cluttered sitting room of the world's foremost consulting detective. The basket of unfiled clippings on the desk, the jumble of chemical apparatus atop the deal-topped table to the right of the fireplace, the stack of envelopes affixed to the mantelpiece by a thin-bladed oriental knife; could genius indeed exist amid such disorder? He pulled the tails of his morning coat around him and gingerly sat on the edge of the aged leather sofa. "Gratifying?" he asked. "Surely a man of your repute has had noble clients before."

"I was referring to the problem that brought you, my lord," Holmes said. "It is gratifying to have a case that exercises the intellect. Those which have come my way for the last few months have indicated a sad decline of imagination among the criminal classes. As for my clientele, we entertain all sorts here. The last person to sit where you are sitting was a duke, and the person before that, if I remember correctly, was a woman who had murdered her first three husbands and was plotting the death of her fourth."

"Interesting," Lord Arundale murmured.

"Much more interesting than the duke," Holmes agreed. "The reigning monarch of a European kingdom has sat in the chair to your left, and a dwarf who does watercolors has sat in the seat beside you. The king was a boor; the dwarf is quite possibly a genius. How may I serve you, my lord?"

"Well, you would seem to know already," Lord Arundale said, nettled at Holmes's attitude. "You are gratified by the problem that brought me here before I've had a chance to tell you what it is. I was told that you had a sort of clairvoyance that enabled you to detect the actions of criminals in the absence of clues visible to the regular police. I was not, however, informed that you could predict the problem that a client would bring to you before he had the opportunity to elucidate it to you. Frankly, sir, the exercise strikes me as pure hocus!"

"No, no," Holmes said quickly. "I do apologize if I seem a trifle sharp. Put it down to the effects of the medication I am taking, my lord. My medical man, Dr. Watson, has prescribed a little something for my bouts of lethargy, and it sometimes has the effect of making me seem a bit testy."

"Then you don't claim to exercise clairvoyance, or other psychic abilities?"

"Not at all, my lord. Whatever abilities I have are founded firmly in a knowledge of the appropriate sciences, an extensive study of the history of crime, and a sharply honed faculty for deductive reasoning."

"Then," Lord Arundale pressed on, "you don't actually know what brought me here, and were merely making a general assumption that I would offer an interesting, ah, case?"

"On the contrary, my lord. I know exactly why you're here. You've come to consult with me regarding last night's murder in Regent's Gate. Ah, here's Billy with the tea. How do you like yours, my lord?"

Lord Arundale allowed his tea to be poured and milked and sugared while he thought this over. "You are right," he said finally.

"And if it's hocus, it's clever hocus indeed. For the life of me, I can't see how you know. You must admit that it smacks rather of clairvoyance, or the cleverer sort of conjuring trick."

"Not at all, my lord," Holmes said. "It is, after all, my profession to deduce hard facts from what would seem to others to be scanty evidence."

Lord Arundale sipped his tea thoughtfully. "What other deductions have you already made?" he asked.

Holmes leaned back in his armchair, his thin, sensitive fingers laced together under his chin. "Only the rather obvious facts that you've come from one or more officials of high government rank, probably cabinet ministers, to request that I take over the investigation; that you've been to Scotland Yard already and received the approval of the Commissioner of Police, although the detective inspector in charge of the case feels that I'll only get in the way."

"Astounding!" Lord Arundale said. "You must have agents in the police."

"I assure your lordship—"

Lord Arundale put his teacup on the tray and shook his head. "No need," he said. "Is there anything else?"

"Only that there is some fact or clue of major importance which has been withheld from the public that you have come to acquaint me with."

"By God, sir!" Lord Arundale said. "You must explain to me how you deduced all of that from the mere presence in your sitting room of a middle-aged peer in a morning coat."

"Every trade must have its secrets, my lord," Holmes said, rubbing his hands together. "I learned from my friend Dr. Watson, who shared these rooms with me before his marriage, not to reveal too easily how I attain these effects. The explanation moves them from the miraculous to the mundane. I would draw your attention, however, to the few additional facts that I noted."

"And they are?"

"First, I happened to notice the carriage in which you arrived; not your own, but one of those at the service of Scotland Yard. Next I observed the distinctive red-brown clay adhering to the instep of your right shoe. Surely acquired earlier today, since it seems unlikely that your valet would not see to it that your shoes are polished every night. There are several places around London where you might have picked it up, but the most likely is the east end of St. James's Park, across from the government offices."

"I begin to see," Lord Arundale said. "But I still think it's deucedly clever. Fancy knowing every bit of mud in London."

"In perpetrating a crime, the astute criminal strives to eliminate or disguise the facts surrounding his act," Holmes said. "Where he is most likely to go astray is in the small details, like the dirt on his shoes or the dust on his clothing. Therefore, my lord, you can see that the professional investigator must make a study of such details."

"Fantastic," Lord Arundale said. He picked up the small leather case that he had brought in with him and extracted an envelope from it. "How much do you know of the murder of Lord Walbine?"

"No more than what was in the morning papers, my lord."

"Here then is a précis of all the relevant facts," Lord Arundale said, handing the envelope to Holmes, "as prepared by the inspector in charge of the police investigation. Also included are accounts of the murders of the Honorable George Venn and of Isadore Stanhope."

"I shall read it immediately, your lordship," said Holmes. "I should also like to examine the rooms in which the three crimes were committed."

"Arrangements have been made," Lord Arundale said. "Inspector Lestrade said you'd want to, as he put it, 'crawl around the rooms on hands and knees with a reading glass.'"

"Ah, so it's Lestrade, is it?" cried Holmes. "That is somewhat helpful."

"You know Inspector Lestrade, then. I was favorably impressed with him. He seems to have a good command of his job. Claimed to be running down several promising leads, although he was rather vague as to what they were. Said that he thought arresting the butlers would produce results."

"What sort of results?" Holmes inquired.

"He didn't say. He did say that he thought that bringing you in on the case was quite unnecessary, although he admitted that you've been of some help to the regular force in the past. 'Special circumstances,' he put it. If it weren't that the P.M. feels that a quite out of the ordinary finesse is required in this instance, the Home Secretary and I would feel quite sanguine in leaving the case in his hands."

"Normally he is quite adequate," Holmes agreed. "But then the usual case is just that—usual. A crime of brute force committed without forethought, requiring neither specialized knowledge nor ratiocination to solve."

"Faint praise indeed," Lord Arundale said. "Don't you think Lestrade is capable?"

"As a bulldog, yes. The man is tenacious, unrelenting, brave, honest, and loyal. But as a bloodhound, I'm afraid the more subtle odors of crime escape his nose."

Lord Arundale held out his teacup to be refilled. "That is basically what the Prime Minister said," he told Holmes. "The Home Secretary is convinced that the Metropolitan Police can, and should, handle the problem, but the P.M. felt that it might be too sensitive for the bulldog approach. And you came highly recommended by, if you will excuse my being vague, a member of the Royal Household."

Holmes nodded. "Please thank her majesty for me," he said. "I gather that it is this 'special circumstance,' of which I am as yet unaware, that makes these crimes sensitive and commends me to the attention of Lord Salisbury, the Prime Minister."

"True," Lord Arundale said. "The Marquess of Salisbury is indeed concerned over these murders. He is concerned, to be more precise, with whether or not he has cause to be concerned."

"I see." Holmes looked thoughtful for a moment. "Am I to understand that the crimes may have some political significance, but it is not known at present whether they actually do or not?"

"Yes," Lord Arundale said. "That, concisely, is it. The crimes may, indeed, be the work of a madman, or someone with a long-festering hatred for the four murdered men because of some secret grievance. But they may also be part of an intricate plot by any of three great European powers against her majesty's government. And we must learn which of these possibilities is the truth. And we must know as soon as we can; every day's delay could be disastrous."

"Four men?" Holmes asked. "I know of but three."

"Lord John Darby was found dead about three weeks ago," Lord Arundale said. He stared down at his teacup for a moment, and then drained it and returned it to the tray. "Lord John was the younger brother of the Earl of Moncreith."

"I remember noting it at the time," Holmes said. "But it was reported as a natural death. Heart attack, I believe the newspaper report said."

"Lord John was found on the dining-room table in his flat in Tattersham Court. His throat had been cut. A silver serving platter had been placed on the floor by the table to catch the blood."

"Come now, that is a fascinating detail!" Holmes said, stretching a lean arm out for the cigarette box on the mantel. "May I offer you a cigarette, my lord? They are of a Virginia tobacco, made for me by K. K. Tamourlane & Sons. The weed is noxious, but I find it sharpens the mental processes."

"No, thank you," Lord Arundale said. "But if you wouldn't object to the smell of a cigar—"

"Not at all." Holmes lit a taper from the gas mantle and applied it to the tip of his cigarette while Lord Arundale took a long dun-colored cigar from a tooled-leather case and went through the ritual of preparing it for the match. "Pray continue with your recitation of the strange death of Lord John Darby," Holmes said, lighting Lord Arundale's cigar before tossing the taper into the fireplace.

Lord Arundale took a deep puff. "I usually reserve these for after meals," he said. "Where was I? Oh, yes. Lord John was lying on the table—a great big thing, could easily seat twelve. French, I believe. Turn-of-the-century piece. His arms were spread out to the sides, but his fists were clenched. Interesting how one remembers all the small details."

"You saw the body, my lord?"

Lord Arundale stood and walked over to the bay window. Pulling the drape aside, he stared down at the traffic below. "I *found* the damn thing!" he told Holmes.

"How long would you say Lord John had been dead when you found him?"

Lord Arundale turned to look at Holmes. "I couldn't really say," he said. "Finding corpses is not really in my line, you see. For what it's worth, my impression was that the incident was fairly recent. The blood seemed to be quite fresh."

"Was anyone else there at the time?"

"Quimby, Lord John's valet. He let me in. This was about seven-thirty in the morning. He'd been there all night. His room is off the front hall."

"Had he seen or heard anything during the night?"

"Nothing. He let Lord John in late the night before. He's not sure of the time, but estimates it at shortly before two. Then he went to bed. He had not yet gone in to awaken Lord John when I arrived the next morning, having received no instructions on the matter."

"No other servants?"

"None present. There are a maid and a cook, but they live two flights up in the servants' quarters. The building of flats is designed with a common servants' quarters on the top floor."

"I see," Holmes said. "What sort of nighttime security is there in the building?"

"There is a hall porter on each floor all night, and a uniformed commissionaire at the front door. There are two other entrances to the building, but both are locked and bolted from the inside at eight o'clock."

Holmes reflected silently for a minute. "I am amazed," he said, "that Lestrade has not already arrested the valet."

"Quimby?" Lord Arundale asked. "You think he could be guilty?"

"Not for an instant," Holmes said. "I am, however, amazed that Lestrade shares my opinion."

"The Metropolitan Police have not, as yet, been informed of the crime," Lord Arundale said.

Holmes leaped to his feet. "What?" he cried. "You have concealed a murder from the authorities? Come now, sir. Even a peer of the realm cannot be allowed such liberty with the Queen's justice."

Lord Arundale held up a hand. "Pray calm yourself," he said. "The Prime Minister has been notified; the Home Secretary, who, as you know, is in charge of the Metropolitan Police, has been notified; the Lord High Chancellor has been notified; and her majesty has been told. I think you will have to admit that the formalities have been observed—perhaps on a higher level than is usual, that is all."

"I see," Holmes said, resuming his seat. "And why was this unusual procedure followed?"

Lord Arundale returned to the sofa. "I shall explain."

"You have my attention, my lord."

"I will have to give you the complete background. I arrived at Lord John's flat that morning to take him to a special emergency meeting of the Continental Policies Committee. This is a group of some twelve men who advise the Prime Minister on matters affecting Britain's relations with the great powers of Europe. Only issues of great and immediate concern are taken up by the committee, which is composed of the leading minds in the government. The very existence of this committee is a closely held secret."

"I was not aware of it," Holmes commented.

"Your brother, Mycroft, is a member," Lord Arundale told Holmes.

"He is very close-mouthed about his work," Holmes replied.

"Just so," Lord Arundale said. "At any rate, Quimby asked me to wait while he awakened his master."

"In the dining room?"

"No, in the drawing room. But as I happened to mention that I had not yet broken my fast that morning, Quimby suggested that he have the cook prepare one of her French omelets for me while I waited. I was agreeable, and so I proceeded into the dining room, where I found Lord John."

"It all seems quite clear," Holmes said. "But why did you not notify the authorities? Surely the fact that the man was a member of the Continental Policies Committee is not, of itself, sufficient reason not to call the police when you find his blood-soaked corpse."

Lord Arundale pondered the question for a second, searching for the precise way to phrase his answer. "Lord John Darby had an older brother," he said finally, picking the words carefully, as one would pick the right gold shirt studs from a drawer full of almost identical gold shirt studs. "Midway in age between Lord John and the Earl of Moncreith. His name is Crecy. Lord Crecy Darby. It is an old family name."

"Yes?" Holmes said encouragingly, as Lord Arundale fell silent again.

"I went to school with Crecy," Lord Arundale said. "Hoxley and then Cambridge. We were determined to go into government service together. Crecy was—is—brilliant. He was going to be the first prime minister appointed before his fortieth birthday. I was to be his foreign secretary. We had the details carefully planned." Lord Arundale sighed and shook his head. "Perhaps it was hubris," he said. "But at any rate, Lord Crecy Darby went completely insane over a period of three years. Every specialist in England and on the Continent was called in, and none of them offered any hope."

"What form did this insanity take?"

"He imagined that intricate plots were being woven about him; that complete strangers on the street had been employed by some invisible agency to follow him about; that everything that happened anywhere in the world was somehow directed against him. He became extremely sly and cunning, and would listen in at doorways and stay concealed behind drapery hoping to overhear someone talking about him.

"His father had him sent away to a sanitarium in Basel that had a new treatment that was thought to offer some small hope."

"What sort of therapy?" Holmes asked.

"I was never too clear on that," Lord Arundale said. "Something to do with hot salt baths and encouraging the patient to run about and scream, I believe. At any rate, he escaped from the sanitarium. Nothing was heard from him for two years. Then, on Crecy's thirty-second birthday, as it happens, the old earl received a communication from an attorney in Munich. Lord Crecy Darby, under the name of Richard Plantagenet, was on trial for the brutal murders of two prostitutes."

Holmes flipped his cigarette into the fireplace. "I remember the case," he said. "Although the true identity of the man who called himself Richard Plantagenet never came out. There was no doubt as to his guilt."

"None at all," Lord Arundale agreed. "He killed two streetwalkers by slitting their throats with a razor, and then mutilated their bodies in a horrible fashion. Not, I suppose, that there is a pleasant way to mutilate bodies. The trial cost the old Earl of Moncreith a fortune. He was not trying to have Crecy found innocent, you understand, but merely to see that he was spared the death penalty and that the family name remained concealed."

"And what happened to Lord Crecy?"

"He was found guilty and totally insane. He was placed in the Bavarian State Prison-Hospital for the Criminally Insane at Forchheim for the rest of his life."

"I see," Holmes said. "And so when you saw his brother lying dead with his throat cut, you naturally assumed that Lord Crecy must have escaped and returned to England."

"That is correct."

"And to save the present earl and his family from the grief and disgrace—"

"I did not notify the police but went straight to the Lord Chamberlain."

"Who agreed with you?"

"Of course."

"Bah!" Holmes said. "You are not above the law, my lord—neither as a member of the nobility nor as a member of the government. Acting as you have done can only be destructive of the moral fiber of British justice. Nothing good can come of it."

"I have heard," Lord Arundale said, "that you do not always work within the structure of the law. Was I misinformed?"

Holmes gazed sternly at Lord Arundale. "I have on occasion acted outside the law," he said. "But that and setting oneself above the law are two separate and distinct things. If you act outside the law you are still subject to it through the possibility of apprehension. But if you act above the law—if a burglar, for example, could go and clear his crime with the Lord Chamberlain first—then there is no law for you. And if there is law for some but not for others, then there is no law. For a law that is unequally applied is an unjust law, and will not be obeyed."

"You have strong opinions, sir," Lord Arundale said.

"So I have been informed," said Holmes, "on more than one occasion."

Lord Arundale carefully laid his cigar on the lip of the large brass ashtray on the table before him. "I did not come here for your approbation, Mr. Holmes," he said. "Neither did I come here for your censure. I came for your assistance in apprehending a murderer."

"You telegraphed to Forchheim?"

"I did."

"Lord Crecy, I presume, had not escaped?"

"Indeed he had not. How did you know that?"

"Never mind that at the moment, my lord. So the deaths of Lord John and the others are again a mystery."

"Even so."

"And you suspect a possible political motivation. Were any of the other victims connected with the Continental Policies Committee, or otherwise involved in government activities?"

"Isadore Stanhope, the barrister, was an agent for the Austrian government," Lord Arundale said. "George Venn had no known connections to any government, but he is said to have taken frequent trips to Paris. The purpose of these trips is, as yet, unknown. It is being looked into."

"And what of Lord Walbine?"

"A quiet man of independent means. Seldom left London except to return to his ancestral estate near Stoke-on-Trent, and that but twice a year. The only thing of interest we've been able to find out about the baron is that he had a rather large collection of, let us say, exotic literature in a concealed set of bookcases in the library."

"What fascinating things one finds out about one's fellow man when one is compelled to search through his belongings," Holmes commented.

"Will you take the case?" Lord Arundale asked.

"I will," Holmes said. "As a problem, it is not altogether without interest. I was sure when I saw you arrive, my lord, that you would have something stimulating to offer. And so you do."

"Have you any ideas?"

"My dear Lord Arundale," Holmes said, chuckling, "I'm afraid that you have been given an exaggerated notion of my abilities. Even I cannot solve a crime before I have assimilated its details."

"Well, I wish you luck," Lord Arundale said. "Any assistance you require will be immediately forthcoming from Scotland Yard."

"That should prove to be a novel experience," Holmes said. "I will have to tell Inspector Lestrade and his people of the circumstances surrounding the death of Lord John Darby, you realize."

Lord Arundale rose to his feet. "I leave that to you," he said. "If you feel you must, then do so. As to your fee—"

"My fees are on a standard schedule," Holmes told him. "I shall send my bill to the Foreign Office."

"That will be satisfactory," Lord Arundale said. "There is one last thing you should know."

"And that is?"

"I have just received a second telegram from Forchheim. After being informed of his brother's death, Lord Crecy killed a guard and escaped from the asylum. That was yesterday. Presumably he is headed back to England, possibly to avenge his brother's death. Unless he is apprehended on the Continent, he should be here within the week."

"That," said Holmes, "should make things very interesting indeed!"

FOUR

MISS CECILY PERRINE

Small is the worth
Of beauty from the light retir'd...
EDMUND WALLER

In just under two years the offices of the American News Service had grown from one small room on the top floor of 27 Whitefriars Street to a set of chambers that encompassed the whole of the top floor and several rooms on the ground floor. The floor between was the ancestral home of McTeague, Burke, Samsone & Sons, who concocted and purveyed a variety of printing inks to the newspapers around the corner on Fleet Street. Benjamin Barnett had cast an occasional covetous eye on the frosted-glass door of McTeague *et al.* as he climbed the stairs to his overcrowded domain; but he knew that the inky firm would neither change locations nor cease to exist at any time in the foreseeable future. For, as the younger Samsone, a gentleman well into his seventh decade, had told Barnett in a characteristically loquacious moment: "It were a McTeague mixture which inked the pages of the first number of the *Daily Courant* in 1702. Thick, tarry stuff they used in them days. If you was to use it in one of them fine modrun-type rotaries now, it'd smear all abaht the paper. And it were McTeague inks what printed six of the eleven dailies what come out within three miles of this spot this very morning. Yes, young man; I tell you that as long as newsprint must be spread with ink, pressmen will trot up to the door to have it formulated."

And so, for as long as the Fleet Street presses continued to rumble, the copy desk and the dispatch desk of the American News Service would remain separated by untold demijohns of printers' ink. And whenever the little bell on the dispatch-room wall tingled, an errand boy would race up the two flights of narrow wooden stairs to pick up the precious sheets of copy and return them to the dispatch desk to be logged and turned over to the telegraphers.

Barnett noticed, as he climbed the stairs on this Tuesday afternoon, that no light was diffusing through the frosted glass on the ink merchants' door. They were closed for the day. McTeague *et al.* was a model of a modern Socialist employer, giving the whole day Saturday off and closing the shop for all sorts of obscure midweek holidays. The employees' delight in the abbreviated work week was perhaps mitigated by the McTeague custom of inviting Socialist speakers in to lecture during the lunch half hour.

At the top of the stairs, the door to his own offices was, as usual, wide open. Barnett dodged a descending errand boy and threaded his way toward the inner offices past the small, cluttered desks of those dedicated to creative journalism. The four secretaries—three gentlemen of varying ages and a young lady of severe demeanor—looked up and issued a variety of polite greetings as he passed. The reporters—two young, intense-looking gentlemen and an elderly lady named Burnside who was an authority on the Royal Family—all affected an air of being much too busy or too deeply sunken into the creative process to notice his passing.

Miss Cecily Perrine was at her desk in the inner office, staring intently at the half-page of copy in her Remington Standard typewriter. Miss Perrine had come to work for him the very day the American News Service had opened for business almost two years before. Her burning desire since early adolescence, for one of those inexplicable reasons that shape our lives beyond our control, was to become a journalist. Now, in the Merrie Land of England when Victoria was queen, and things were just about the best that things had ever been, a lady did not work for a newspaper. Oh, perhaps the society page would have a lady correspondent, but she would certainly never set foot in the actual offices of the paper. Even the secretaries and typists were traditionally male, and against tradition there is no argument.

So the American News Service, as far as it was from being a real newspaper, was as close to journalism as Miss Cecily Perrine could approach. At the beginning they wrote almost none of their own material; instead they bought stories that had already appeared in the London dailies, doing some minor rewriting to make them understandable to American readers. Then, once a day, one of them would walk over to the main Post Office on Newgate Street to have the stories telegraphed to New York.

Cecily Perrine proved to be innately brilliant at handling all the organizational details in running a business, a fact that surprised her as much as it pleased Barnett. She was calm and even-tempered, and much better at handling people than Barnett. And she was also lovely to look at.

Barnett observed her silently for a moment as she studied the page of copy in her typewriter, noting how the single shaft of sunlight, twisted by some prismatic effect of the ancient glass panes in the small window, highlighted the light-brown curls piled in artful disarray atop Cecily's attractive oval face. She was beauty in repose, a model of graceful elegance, even with her face screwed up in the awful concentration of creativity. Or so Barnett thought as he looked at her.

"Good morning, Miss Perrine," he said as she became aware of his presence behind her. "Busy little beehive we have out there."

"Good afternoon, Mr. Barnett," Cecily Perrine said pointedly, her clear blue eyes meeting his. "As you are the owner of this establishment, I shall not attempt to regulate your comings and goings, but I am bound to point out that when the employer arrives at the office at one-thirty in the afternoon, it is not conducive to creating a good work attitude among the employees."

"Ah, Miss Perrine," Barnett said, "let the staff believe that you are a hard-hearted harridan, capable of vilifying even your employer for an imagined tardiness. But to me, in private with the door closed"—he closed the door—"admit that you're tired of supervising others while they write the stories and get the acclaim and the bylines. Tell me that you desire to get out into the great city yourself and have doors slammed in your face, and suffer insults that a lady should never hear and epithets that a lady should not even understand."

"Why, Mr. Barnett," Cecily said, "you make it sound so attractive that I blush to admit that such might indeed be the case, for fear that people will think me nothing more than a dilettante!"

"Never, Cecily. You are too fine a woman for that!" Barnett said, going over to his desk and settling into his chair. "I may call you Cecily, may I not?"

"You may," Cecily said. "And I shall call you Benjamin, for that is your given name, is it not?"

"It is, and I should be proud to hear it from your lips," Barnett told her with a grandiloquent gesture that swept half of his morning mail from the desk to the floor.

Benjamin Barnett had an inordinate fondness for the theater. In his youth, in New York City, he had acted in many an amateur theatrical production of *The Drunkard*, or *His American Cousin*. Cecily Perrine had grown up in the theater. Her mother, Laura Croft, had been one of the great leading ladies of the melodramatic '60s. Her father had been a noted villain until, some ten years before, her mother had died and her father had quit the stage, devoting himself to his linguistic studies.

Barnett and Cecily frequently went to the theater together, usually chaperoned by Elton Perrine, Cecily's father. For their own amusement, they occasionally assumed the attitudes of the melodramatic stage in private conversation.

Barnett found the pastime satisfying for another reason. For roughly the past year he had been deeply in love with his office manager, the intelligent, perceptive, beautiful, talented, altogether wonderful Cecily Perrine. Not that love was a new emotion for him; indeed, he had been in love many times before. But his past loves had been light-hearted and evanescent, never deep, or serious, or meaningful, full of pleasant emotion and devoid of either thought or pain.

But this time it was real, and intense, and serious, and damnedly, irritatingly painful. And daily it grew worse and more intense instead of better. Barnett was in the unbearable position of being unable to declare his love to Cecily Perrine, and the need to do so was becoming overwhelming. Love is not normally a silent emotion. And the closest he could come to stating his feelings out loud was in the melodramatic banter that they exchanged. It gave him slight solace, but it was better than complete silence.

Barnett's reticence to speak to Cecily of his feelings lay in his contract with Professor Moriarty. As long as he was obliged to do the professor's bidding, and might at any time be required to perform a criminal act, how could he ask any girl, much less one as fine as Cecily Perrine, to marry him and share his life?

And so, except for the occasional histrionic outburst artfully disguised as melodrama, he kept his silence. He had never explained to Miss Perrine the exact nature of his relationship with Professor Moriarty, or the professor's strange attitude toward the law. How much of it she had deduced or assumed from the circumstances and events of the past two years he did not know. It was a subject that, by tacit agreement, they did not discuss. Nor did he know what Miss Perrine made of his strange ambivalent attitude toward her, and, being but a man, could not begin to guess.

"I've had a hard morning, but useful," Barnett told Cecily, leaning over to pick up his scattered mail. "And you, at least, should be pleased by the results."

"I am all ears, Benjamin; and my heart is aflutter with excitement!"

"John Pummery has been fired from the *Express*."

"The managing editor? When?"

"This morning. It was brewing for some time, he tells me. A political dispute with the new management. So, as of this afternoon, he is working for us!"

"Really?" Cecily said, her voice strangely flat. "That *is* nice."

Barnett caught the tone in her voice. "You are displeased," he said. "I thought the news would please you. Now tell me what the trouble is. Do you dislike the man? Are you peeved because I didn't consult you first? I felt that I had to act quickly, or I might lose the chance, and thus the man."

"I am not, as you put it, *peeved!*" Cecily said, tossing her head. "I am rather hurt. I thought I was doing a good job here."

"But you *are*, Cecily. An excellent job."

"If I am doing such a good job, why am I being replaced? Surely that is what Mr. Pummery will be doing here—my job!"

Barnett sighed. Why was it that he no longer seemed able to say the right thing to Cecily? She seemed to find some source of hurt or anger in everything he said and everything he did for the past few months. He didn't understand what had changed. He knew that he was so blinded by the strength of his feelings toward Cecily that he couldn't be sure whether it was his behavior or her attitude that was now different. But whatever it was, it created, not exactly friction, but more a sense of confusion in his dealings with her.

"I am sorry, Cecily," Barnett said. "I thought you understood. For the past year you have been berating me for keeping you behind a desk. This, you have observed, is not journalism. In hiring Mr. Pummery I was only attempting to free you from what you now do as office manager so that you can become one of the principal correspondents of the American News Service. You will be doing the same job I am myself—covering those stories that are most important to us, or that require a special understanding of the American market."

Cecily looked at him skeptically. "I am not, I trust, expected to devote myself to such 'important' stories as the charity bazaar of the Duchess of Malfi, or the favorite dinners of Our Dear Queen. Or am I?"

"Not at all," Barnett assured her. "Miss Burnside does those stories very well, and would feel quite put out if you were to take them over. 'From each according to her ability,' as Professor Moriarty is so fond of repeating."

"What is that supposed to mean?" Cecily asked.

"This fellow who used to spend the better part of each day in the British Museum said it all the time," Barnett told her. "Something to do with an outrageous economic theory he was developing. Professor Moriarty had many long arguments with the man in the Reading

Room before he went back to Germany or someplace."

"And what is my ability?" Cecily asked. "What sort of events am I to cover?"

"I have a subject in mind for you now that I believe you will find of interest," Barnett told her.

Cecily drew her legs up under her in the chair, tucking in the folds of her skirt, and gazed intently at Barnett. Some emotion that Barnett could not fathom sparkled in her eyes. "Elucidate," she said.

"Murder," Barnett stated, staring back into the sparkling pools of clear blue that were Cecily's eyes.

"Fascinating," she agreed. "And whom am I to kill?"

"You," Barnett told her, "are to report. Someone else has been doing the killing."

Cecily turned her head to the side and gazed thoughtfully through the glass window in the office wall. "Why?" she asked. "I appreciate the compliment, of course. But I can foresee many problems arising if I attempt to report on murder stories. I'm sure you must already have realized that."

"There will be difficulties," Barnett agreed. "Having a woman journalist following the course of a murder investigation and reporting on it will be an original idea to the authorities, and I'm sure they will react in an original manner. But I think you will do an excellent job with the story, if the gentlemen of the CID don't put too many obstructions in the way of your journalistic endeavors. I think it's worth giving it a shot, if you're willing."

"A shot?" Cecily smiled. "One of your American expressions? How apt in this instance. I am certainly willing to 'give it a shot,' if you think any good can come of it. But tell me, why do you suppose the readers of two hundred newspapers in the United States are going to be interested in a British murder?"

"The interest that the public—British or American—has for the sensational should not be underrated," Barnett told her. "And I, for one, am perfectly happy trying to fill that interest."

"Very good, Mr. Barnett," Cecily said. "Repellent as the idea is to us, we shall explore the sensational and examine the outré for the sake of our readers. I shall write a series of closely reasoned articles that fascinate by the compelling logic of their conclusions and the immense understanding of human nature so displayed. And I shall sign them C. Perrine, so that none of our readers will be shocked by the knowledge that a member of the fair sex has been delving into the sordid, seamy side of life in the world's greatest metropolis."

"I thought the idea would interest you, Miss Perrine," Barnett said. "But first, of course, we are going to have to go out into the world and catch our man."

"And what man, may I ask, are we looking for?"

"There have been three murders in London within the past month," Barnett told her, "that were, apparently, all done by the same man. The victims were all upper-class, and all three murders were committed in circumstances that were, if not impossible, at least highly improbable."

Cecily Perrine nodded. "Lord Walbine," she said, "and the Honorable George Venn, and Isadore Stanhope. Very interesting cases."

"That's them," Barnett agreed. "I've noticed that you have formed the practice of rewriting all the murder stories yourself, which is why I decided you would be interested in this assignment."

"I consider myself a competent writer, Mr. Barnett, as you know," Cecily said. "But I would not altogether affirm my competence to interview a Scotland Yard inspector in such a manner as to command his respect, and otherwise conduct the necessary investigation. This is my only hesitation."

"I'll assist you the first few times you conduct such interviews, until you get over your tentative feelings and the gentlemen at the CID get accustomed to your presence."

"I would appreciate such assistance," Cecily said.

"It will be my pleasure," Barnett told her. "I, also, am fascinated by mysterious murders."

"A fascination that I trust the rest of your countrymen share," Cecily said. "With both of us working on it, the stories are going to have to be carried by over three-quarters of our total subscription to pay for our time."

"We'll have over ninety percent," Barnett assured her. "This story has the one element that a purely American murder can never have: nobility. Two out of three of the victims were possessed of noble blood. You'll have to remember to play that up."

"Yes, indeed," Cecily agreed sweetly. "I shall research the lineage of Mr. Stanhope, the deceased barrister. Perhaps somewhere this side of the Domesday Book we can find the taint of noble blood running, in ever so diluted quantities, through his veins also."

"Not a bad idea," Barnett told her enthusiastically. "Put someone on that."

"Dear me," Cecily said. "I thought I was being humorous."

"Americans take British nobility very seriously," Barnett told her, "being deprived, as they are, of one of their own."

"It is of their own doing," Cecily said. "Had they remained loyal British subjects a hundred years ago, they could have their own nobility living among them now, and be as lucky as the Irish in that regard."

Their conversation was interrupted by a small person in a loudly checked suit with a spotless gray bowler tucked firmly under his left arm, who trotted between the desks in the outer office and rapped importantly on the inner office door.

Barnett pulled the door open. "Well," he exclaimed, "if it isn't the Mummer!"

"'Course it is," the little man replied. "Who says it ain't?" "Mummer" Tolliver was a fellow resident of 64 Russell Square, occupying a low-ceilinged room under the eaves and serving the professor as a general factotum and midget-of-all-work.

"Hello, Mummer," Cecily said. "My, you're looking natty today."

"Afternoon, Miss Perrine," the Mummer said, holding his bowler stiffly in front of his chest and giving his head two precise nods in her direction. "You're a rare vision of dainty loveliness yourself, Miss Perrine. S'welp me if you ain't!"

"Why, thank you, Mummer," Cecily said.

"I have a communication for Mr. Barnett from the professor," Mummer said. "'Into his hand,' the professor told me."

"Why, then, here is my hand," Barnett said, extending his hand.

Tolliver examined the appendage carefully. "Seems to be," he admitted, pulling a buff envelope from a hidden recess between two buttons of his checked jacket and passing it over to Barnett. "There. Now my duty is discharged, and I must be trotting along. Afternoon, Miss Perrine. Afternoon, all." Adjusting his bowler carefully on his slicked-down black hair, he did a neat shuffle-off to the front door and exited.

"What a charming little man," Cecily said.

"He is that," Barnett agreed, as the world's shortest confidence man and pickpocket disappeared around the door.

Barnett slit open the envelope and removed the sheet of foolscap within. *Railways*, the note said in Moriarty's precise hand, *with particular emphasis on the London and South-Western.* M.

"A task for us," Barnett said, slipping the note into his pocket. "Assign someone to research the London and South-Western Railway line. Bill it to the special account."

"What sort of research?" Cecily asked, looking curiously at him.

Barnett shrugged. "General," he said. "Whatever they're up to these days. I don't know. Tell them it's for a comparison of British and American railroads."

"Fine," Cecily said. "What *is* it for?"

"I don't know," Barnett said. "The ways of Professor Moriarty are mysterious. As you know, he is a consultant. Perhaps he has a commission from the railway, or perhaps from a rival railway. He is very close-mouthed."

"Hummm," Cecily said.

"Well," said Barnett, "let us go along to Scotland Yard and see whom we can speak to about these murders."

FIVE

SCOTLAND YARD

Mere theory is not encouraged at the Yard.
ARTHUR H. BEAVAN

The hansom cab passed under the arch and rattled along the ancient, well-worn paving stones of Scotland Yard. Swerving to miss a flock of off-duty constables heading across the road for a "quick 'un" at the Clarence before they went home for the night, it pulled to a stop in front of the dirty yellow brick building that housed the Metropolitan Police office.

"Here we are," Barnett said, helping Cecily Perrine down from the cab and tossing a coin up to the cabby. "The Criminal Investigation Department is in the building to the left here."

The constable guarding the narrow entrance to the CID nodded at Barnett's question. "That would be Inspector Lestrade." He checked a little pegboard on the wall by his side. "As it happens, the inspector is in at the moment. Room 109. You must wait here until I can get a uniformed officer to escort you upstairs."

"Why, Constable!" Cecily smiled sweetly. "We do not look dangerous, do we?"

"'Taint me, miss," the constable said. "It's the regulations. Ever since that bombing in the Yard three years ago by them anarchists, when all them policemen and civilians were blown about, with three of them dying, some constable stands here day and night, in this unheated doorway, and sees that all visitors are properly escorted upstairs. Them as are in authority were supposed to put a booth here for the constable's use, but it's been three years now and they ain't done it. Now as there's talk of a new building, I suppose they won't ever."

"I thought the bombing was outside," Barnett said.

"Yes, sir," the constable agreed. "Around to the right, there. By the public house. You can still see the damage to the bricks."

"But there's no constable on duty over there," Cecily said.

"No, miss."

"Then somebody could still chuck a dynamite bomb right where the last one was."

"Yes, miss."

"I don't understand."

"No, miss. Ah, here is someone now. Constable Hawkins, will you please escort these two people up to Room 109. Inspector Lestrade."

Room 109 was small, with one tiny soot-covered window, extremely cluttered, and, when they entered, apparently devoid of human life. Constable Hawkins, a small, taciturn man whose uniform looked as though it had been constructed for someone squatter and considerably more massive, obviously felt that he should not leave them alone in the room. So he stood fidgeting silently and uncomfortably, resisting all attempts to be drawn into conversation and turning very red in the face when Cecily spoke to him.

It was about ten minutes before Inspector Lestrade returned to the room, scurrying along the corridor with a sheaf of documents in a leather folder under his arm. "Ha! I know you," he said to Barnett, shaking his hand firmly. "Barnett's your name."

"You have a good memory, Inspector," Barnett said. "It's been almost two years since we met in that house on Little George Street."

"A den of anarchists it was, too," Lestrade said. "You gentlemen were lucky to get out of there alive." He looked around, rather puzzled. "There was someone here when I left."

"No one here when we arrived, Inspector," Constable Hawkins

assured Lestrade, standing at full brace like a little figure from a box of tin soldiers.

"Thank you, Hawkins," Lestrade said. "You can go." He turned back to Barnett. "And who is your charming companion?"

"Miss Cecily Perrine, may I present Detective Inspector Giles Lestrade of the CID. Inspector Lestrade, Miss Perrine is a valued associate of mine at the American News Service."

"A pleasure, Miss Perrine," Lestrade said, looking for all the world, as Cecily said later, like an eager bear as he took her hand and pressed it politely. "A sincere pleasure, I assure you."

"Charmed, Inspector," Cecily said. "Are all Scotland Yard inspectors so gallant?"

"You catch more flies with honey, miss," Lestrade said. "It always pays to be polite, and it costs you nothing. Or so I tell my men."

"And here I thought it was me," Cecily said, pouting, "and I find, instead, that it's regulation."

"Well, um, miss," Lestrade said, caught in the realization that his tact was not up to his manners, "I can assure you that in your case it is a pleasure to follow the regulations."

"Neat recovery, Inspector," Barnett said, smiling.

"Um," Lestrade said. "And what can I do for you? No problems, I hope?"

"Nothing for the police, Inspector," Barnett said. "No, we've come here on business, but it's our business rather than yours."

"Ah! And how is that?"

"We are planning an article, or a series of articles, on the murders you've been having here in London," Cecily said.

"Now that covers a lot of territory, miss," Lestrade said. "There've been a great many murders here in London during the twenty-six years I've been on the force."

"We had the recent ones in mind," Barnett said. "Lord Walbine—"

"Him!" Lestrade said. "Come, sit down. Just push the papers off that chair, Mr. Barnett. I'll have someone come along and file them. Should have done it weeks ago. The department is nothing but a maze of paperwork. It's a wonder that any of us ever get any work done, what with all the papers we have to fill out every time we take a step."

Cecily perched daintily on the edge of the old wooden chair that Lestrade thrust toward her. Barnett dropped into an ancient chair with a bentwood back, after taking Lestrade's advice and pushing the papers onto the floor. The chair creaked alarmingly, but it held.

"Now then," Lestrade said. "What do you want to know about Lord Walbine's murder? It *is* a puzzler, that I'll admit."

"And George Venn," Cecily said, "and Isadore Stanhope, the barrister."

"Well now," Lestrade said, "interestingly enough we think we have just solved the Venn and Stanhope murders."

"Is that right?" Barnett asked.

"It is," Lestrade said, looking exceedingly smug. "And, as it happens, arrests are expected momentarily in those cases."

"Congratulations are in order then, are they, Inspector?" Barnett asked. "You have solved a difficult case and brought a dangerous killer to justice. Who was the killer, then, and what was his motive?"

"Well," Lestrade said, glancing at the door, "this is confidential for the moment. The orders have gone out to arrest the culprits, but until I am sure they have been apprehended I would not want the news to appear in the press."

"You have our word, Inspector," Barnett said.

"Did you say *culprits?*" Cecily asked. "There was more than one person involved in the murders?"

"That there was," Lestrade agreed. "Each of the two murdered gentlemen was done in by his own butler!"

"The butler did it?" Barnett asked.

"Incredible, isn't it? But there's no telling to what lengths greed or fear will drive some people."

"What *was* their motive?" Cecily asked. "It was greed, wasn't it? They were each systematically stealing from their respective employer, and were about to be caught red-handed."

"Well, miss, we haven't found any indication—"

"Fear, then! They were both members of a secret society of

anarchists, and their evil captain had ordered them to kill their masters under pain of some horrible mutilation or death."

"We have given that theory some thought, miss," Lestrade said seriously.

"You have?" Barnett sounded surprised.

"Yes, sir. You see, there was a mysterious bit of newspaper in Lord Walbine's waistcoat pocket when he was killed."

"How fascinating!" Barnett said. "Was it a clipping from a London paper?"

"It was, we believe, from the *Morning Chronicle* classified section. What they call the agony column. But it wasn't exactly a clipping—more of a ripping," Lestrade said.

"What did it say?" Cecily asked.

"It was ripped from the middle of the classified pages. One column wide by about half an inch high. On one side it said, 'Thank you St. Simon for remembering the knights.' On the other side it said, 'Fourteen point four by six point thirteen: three-four-seven.' Written out, you know; not just the numbers."

"Two separate advertisements?"

"That is right, miss. One on each side of the paper, as you might expect. As far as we know, unconnected. Which one had relevance to poor Lord Walbine, I have no idea. But you must admit they are both odd. Put one in mind of some sort of secret society."

"How does this affect the two butlers?" Cecily asked.

"Well, you see, miss, they are both members of the same club."

"Club?" Barnett asked. "I didn't know there were clubs for butlers."

"There is a club for butlers and valets," Lestrade told him. "It is known as the Gentlemen's Gentlemen, and it is located off Oxford Street in Soho. Margery, who was the butler to the deceased Honorable George Venn, and Lizzard, who was the personal valet to the late Mr. Stanhope, are both members of the said Gentlemen's Gentlemen in good standing."

"Come now, Inspector," Barnett said, "you can't seriously believe that these two men murdered their employers simply because they are members of the same club?"

"That was merely the starting point for what I would like to refer to as a fine example of the value of good methodical police work. With that fact to work on, my men went out and knocked on doors and asked questions. No fancy staring at footsteps under a microscope or examining the dirt under the victim's fingernails or any of that nonsense. Very quickly we discovered that Margery spends his afternoons off at the racetrack, and that Lizzard has a lady friend in Wembley."

"Surely even valets are allowed to have lady friends," Cecily said. "I would have thought that having a lady friend was one of the indelible rights of man."

Lestrade smiled tolerantly. "Yes, but the lengths that a man will go to keep a woman have, on occasion, been known to approach the criminal."

"Oh, was he keeping her then?" Cecily asked.

"I meant that figuratively, miss," Lestrade said. "He was most assuredly trying to keep her interest. At any rate, he was spending far beyond what one would assume his means to be, as was Margery."

"So you think they killed their employers for money?"

"We don't think that they did it themselves," Lestrade said. "Not at all. The similarity of methods used in the two murders would seem to indicate that one man had done both. Our theory is that Margery and Lizzard each, either with the other's knowledge or without, hired the same man to do the killing. After we've picked them up, we should be able to frighten one of them into revealing who the actual killer was. And, when we have him, we may well have the killer of Lord Walbine."

"So you *do* think it was the same man," Cecily asked.

"Yes, miss. But not, if you take my meaning, part of the same conspiracy. We haven't been able to get anything on Lord Walbine's butler, one Lemming by name; and at the time of the murder his lordship was quite without a valet, the last one having left for Chicago to open a haberdashery with his brother-in-law two weeks before."

"Well, I'm glad to see that Scotland Yard is so efficient," Barnett said. "Miss Perrine or I will keep in touch with you as the case progresses. That is, if you don't mind having your name in print in two hundred American newspapers."

"Well, now," Lestrade said, "the Yard discourages personal publicity; but if it's to be in American newspapers, I don't see how there could be any problem. I will, naturally, be delighted to keep you and Miss Perrine fully informed as to the progress of the investigation."

"I thank you, Inspector," Barnett said. "Our American readers will be fascinated to read all the little details as to how a Scotland Yard investigation is carried out."

"I think I can give them a pretty fair example," Lestrade said, trying not to look too self-important. "It is not a matter of brilliance—I don't claim to be brilliant—but a matter of following established procedure and taking care that all the detail work gets done. That's what captures your murderers."

"Well, thank you very much, Inspector," Barnett said. "We shall be going along now. One or the other of us will be visiting you daily to hear the latest details."

"I shall be happy to oblige."

"Thank you. If it's all right with you, I think we shall go now to visit the scenes of the crimes, so that we can better describe them to our readers."

"Certainly," Lestrade said. "The Yard always tries to help out journalists, when it can. You won't let on now about the arrests?"

"My word, Inspector. Not a mention of either of their names until we hear that they are safely behind bars."

"It has been delightful meeting you, Inspector Lestrade," Cecily said. "It is comforting to know that our safety lies in such capable hands."

"We do our best, miss," Lestrade said, escorting them to the door and beaming at them as they left.

* * *

"You *are* an ass, Lestrade," a voice behind the inspector said as he gazed down the hall. He turned to find Sherlock Holmes sitting in the chair he had just vacated.

"Holmes! Where did you come from? I thought you had left."

"I got bored sitting there waiting for you to return," Holmes said, "so I started going through your files. When I saw your company approaching, I concealed myself between the filing cabinet and the wall, over there."

"I see," Lestrade said. "And why did you do a thing like that?"

"That young man, Barnett, is in the employ of Professor Moriarty, as you well know. It occurred to me that it might be a good idea to hear what he had to say when he thought himself unobserved."

"So? And what did he say?"

"Nothing. That imbecile of a constable never left them alone. What a shame—it might have been quite instructive."

"You still have that bee in your bonnet about the professor, eh, Holmes?" Lestrade chuckled. "Well, I don't fancy that he's your killer this time. I can't quite see him as an habitué of the Gentlemen's Gentlemen."

"Lestrade, you are incorrigible," Holmes said. "You really believe those poor butlers had something to do with the crimes?"

"I believe it well enough so that I'm having them held on suspicion," Lestrade said. "I don't take such action as a joke."

"Well, do that if it pleases you," Holmes told him. "But there is another action that I want you to take. You are obliged to follow my instructions, I believe?"

"We are," Lestrade said. "Orders is orders, whatever I think of them, and I have been so ordered. What do you want me to do?"

"I think those two came to pump you for information," Holmes said. "And, if that's so, then Moriarty is up to his neck in this in some way, and I intend to find out how. I want you to detail ten of your best plainclothesmen to follow Moriarty wherever he goes from now on, and report to you on his every move."

"If you say so, Mr. Holmes," Lestrade said. "Ten of my best it is. He won't make a move without our knowing of it."

"Nonsense," Holmes said. "Of course he will. I'm just hoping that this will annoy him sufficiently that he'll make a mistake. A small mistake, that's all I ask."

"Um," Lestrade said.

SIX

THE FOX

Was it a friend or foe that spread these lies?
Nay, who but infants question in such wise,
'Twas one of my most intimate enemies.
DANTE GABRIEL ROSSETTI

Old Potts had been with Moriarty from the beginning, and there were few around who knew how far back that went. Slowly, and with great love, over the course of many years, he had converted the upper cellar in the house at 64 Russell Square into a huge, well-equipped basement laboratory and workshop.

The old man had his bed in a corner of the workshop. He seldom came upstairs, and almost never left the house, except for occasional visits to the professor's observatory on Crimpton Moor. And he was happy thus. Professor Moriarty spent much time in the basement with old Potts. It was here that he designed the delicate apparatus with which he studied the cosmos and tested his physical and astronomical theories.

Within the past year, old Potts had helped Moriarty fabricate a mechanism which could determine the speed of light to better than three parts per thousand. Together they had experimented with a series of evacuated glass valves with sealed electrodes of various rare materials, and observed fascinating and as yet inexplicable results when an electric current was passed through. It may be that they also had constructed a device which would enable one to bypass an electrical alarm system without setting off the alarm, and an instrument which would allow one to hear the tumblers falling in the latest model wall safe. If so, it is perhaps reprehensible that such mundane practical engineering projects were necessary to support the professor's flights of pure science. But that is the way of the world.

When Barnett came down into the workshop a few days after his visit to Scotland Yard, he found Moriarty and old Potts working together on a new design of light-frame astronomical telescope, specially constructed to be carried high above the earth in a giant hydrogen balloon. The telescope was strapped into a great jig on the central table while Professor Moriarty, with his shirtsleeves rolled up, made final adjustments in a series of set-screws around the telescope's rim. Old Potts, with his lab smock wrapped around him, followed behind the professor and put little dabs of cement on each screw to lock it permanently in place.

"Well, it looks as if you've got it just about finished, Professor," Barnett commented, strolling over to inspect the intricate, spidery mechanism that held the highly polished mirror.

"It had better be," Moriarty said. "It lofts next week, if the weather on the moor stays clear."

"You are going off to Crimpton Moor, then?" Barnett asked.

Moriarty nodded. The estate he maintained on Crimpton Moor included a residence, a workshop, and an observatory housing his precious twelve-inch reflector. This was the site of most of his astronomical observations. "Prince Tseng Li-Chang is already in residence, preparing the balloon," he said. "His son claims to have perfected a new emulsion for the photographic plates that will more than double their sensitivity. If it performs as promised, we should get some fascinating pictures."

"What do you expect to learn from these balloon experiments, Professor?" Barnett asked. "And please don't just fob me off with your usual reply that you're furthering human knowledge. I'm sure you are. But as an answer, you will have to admit it is rather vague."

Moriarty snorted. "You, a journalist, are concerned about an answer being 'rather vague'? Truly the millennium has arrived."

"I ask purely out of my own interest, Professor," Barnett assured him. "The great newspaper-reading public will not concern itself with staring at Mars unless it feels that something up there is staring back."

Professor Moriarty made the final adjustment on the aluminum-bronze telescope mounting and put the tiny screwdriver back in its small case. He turned and regarded Barnett with interest. "Now that," he said, "is a truly fascinating notion!"

"How's that?"

"Ah, Benjamin, you know not what you say," Moriarty replied. "For some time I have been pondering ways to interest the common man in the abstruse sciences. You may have just given me a valuable suggestion: 'Something is staring back.' I like the sound of that! And, indeed, there is a good chance that something *is* staring back."

"I assume that you are not speaking religiously, Professor," Barnett said.

"Religiously? Indeed, no. Neither religiously nor metaphorically nor psychically nor figuratively. Somewhere out there, Mr. Barnett, there are intelligences greater than our own. How could it be else? And these beings might, even now, be watching us with the same diligence that a hymenopterologist studies a colony of ants. And for purposes as far beyond our understanding as the hymenopterologist's purposes are beyond the understanding of the ant."

"You really believe this?"

"I am forced to this conclusion by the inescapable logic of the universe," Moriarty said.

"But intelligences superior to our own?"

Moriarty smiled. "I am very afraid," he said, "that any intelligences we find—or who find us—will be superior to our own."

"You speak as a confirmed atheist," Barnett said as he sat on the wooden bench running along the great worktable.

Moriarty shrugged. "It is not that I disbelieve in God," he said, "it is merely that I see no need to drag some immortal being into the equation in order to explain the universe."

Moriarty's housekeeper, Mrs. H, appeared on the landing leading down to the basement. "I trust you are ready with your drayage, Professor," she said, folding her arms across the severe bosom of her stiffly starched black dress. "The dray awaits."

"Splendid, Mrs. H," Moriarty said, rolling his sleeves down and shrugging his arms back into his gray frock coat. "The instrument is ready, and the packing is prepared. It only remains to lower the telescope into the crate and nail it shut."

Mrs. H sniffed. "I shall inform the drayman that you will be within the hour," she said.

"I trust my instructions were followed?" Moriarty asked.

"Implicitly, Professor," Mrs. H told him. "The dray is around the corner on Montague Street, by the hotel. Mr. Maws awaited its arrival."

"Excellent!" Moriarty said. "Then this large crate, which will almost immediately contain the telescope, and these other five crates which are already nailed down, are to be taken out through the accommodation exit and loaded into the dray. Great care is to be taken; this is delicate apparatus."

"I shall see to it, Professor."

"I know you will, Mrs. H. You are a paragon of getting-it-done-properly. You run this household with an efficiency which amazes even me. It is a constant delight to be associated with you. Please send the Mummer down to me now."

"Very well, Professor." Mrs. H nodded and withdrew.

What Moriarty called the "accommodation exit" was a back way that led, through a twisting maze of alleys and two subtly concealed doors in separating walls, to the side entrance to the hotel on Montague Street. "Why are you going out that way, Professor?" Barnett asked. "Are you sneaking this equipment out?"

"I never sneak," Moriarty said firmly. "Since my business is nobody else's affair, I fail to see how my effort to avoid prying eyes can be considered 'sneaking.'"

"I take it back, Professor," Barnett said. "I wasn't aware that we had any prying eyes about. Whose eyes are they, and what are they trying to find out?"

"A good question," Moriarty said, "and one deserving of a factual answer. At the moment I have only conjecture, but I expect—Ah! Perhaps we can find out now; here is the Mummer."

"I didn't want to disturb you while you was at work down here, Professor," the little man said, bounding down the wooden staircase.

"Thoughtful of you, Mummer," Moriarty said. "Did you succeed?"

"'Course I did, what do you think?" the Mummer said, looking offended.

"With what result?"

"I buzzed the tall gent what's been mucking about outside keeping the admiral company, and found a rozzer in his poke."

"You see," Moriarty said, turning to Barnett. "It is as I suspected."

"What is?" Barnett asked.

"This house has been being watched for the past two days. Three men at least, at all times. Now Tolliver has picked the pocket of the tall gentleman who was loitering across the street by the statue of Lord Hornblower, and found a police badge in his wallet."

"'At's right," Tolliver agreed. "'Oo says I didn't?"

"This sudden interest in our doings corresponds with your visit to the CID," Moriarty told Barnett. "There may be some connection between that correspondence and the fact that Mr. Sherlock Holmes has been retained to assist the police in the matter of those murders that so fascinate you."

"How do you know that?" Barnett asked. "Sherlock Holmes certainly didn't tell you. He doesn't seem to have a very high opinion of you."

"Every time a purse is snatched anywhere in the greater London area, Holmes is certain that I am behind it," Moriarty said. "It gets tiresome."

"How do you know that he is helping Scotland Yard solve the murders?"

Moriarty chuckled. "I spoke to his landlady."

"His landlady?"

"Yes. Mrs. Hudson, by name. Charming lady. A bit deaf. I dressed myself as a nonconformist clergyman and went to Baker Street at a time I knew Holmes would be out. I told Mrs. Hudson that I needed the great man's services immediately. I was very put out that he wasn't at home. I told her I needed Holmes in relation to a case involving a politician, a lighthouse, and a trained cormorant. She told me that it was just the sort of thing that Mr. Holmes would be happy to take up, but that at the moment he was working with the police on the baffling murders of those aristocrats."

"I see," Barnett said.

"I told the charming lady how sorry I was to have missed Mr. Holmes, and that I was unable to wait. She begged me to stay, saying she was sure Holmes would want to talk with me. I said something to the effect that I thought so myself, but I really couldn't stay."

Barnett shook his head. "There is a certain justice in all of this, you will have to admit," he said. "While you are out with a false beard questioning Sherlock Holmes's landlady, he is having your house watched by Scotland Yard."

"There is indeed an elegant symmetry," Moriarty admitted. "But I assure you there was no false beard. Ecclesiastical muttonchops was as far as I went."

The Mummer hopped down from the bench, where he had been examining the telescope. "Quite a pickle you've got there, Professor," he said. "Is there anything else you need of me?"

Moriarty thought this over for a minute. "Yes," he said. "Go to that cupboard in the corner and open it up. Mr. Potts, please give the Mummer your key."

Tolliver took the key from old Potts and skipped over to the corner. He opened the cabinet, and for a second Barnett felt his heart rap against his chest and he caught his breath. There, inside the cabinet, was Professor Moriarty!

Barnett half turned to make sure that the professor was still, in reality, standing alongside of him, and then he approached the cabinet to figure out what he had just seen. It still, even from four feet away, appeared to be Moriarty closeted within the narrow confines of the small cabinet. He bent down to examine the apparition. "A dummy!" he exclaimed.

"Indeed," Moriarty said. "It was made at my direction some time ago. Amberly, the forger, did the face of papier-mâché, with the coloring accomplished with stage makeup dissolved in wax. Do you think it is good? You are a better judge than I, as my face is seldom visible to me except reversed in a glass."

"Good?" Barnett cried. "It is excellent! Remarkable!"

"I am glad to hear that," Moriarty said. "Because for the next two weeks, that dummy will be me." He turned to old Potts. "Do you think you can make a frame for it that the Mummer can wear on his shoulders?"

Old Potts looked reflectively at Tolliver and at the dummy. "Take a couple of hours," he said.

"Excellent," Moriarty said. "Then I leave with my telescope. Mummer, you will be me while I am gone. Follow Barnett's suggestions in that regard. That should keep the hounds away from Crimpton Moor while I complete these observations."

"I'll do my best, Professor," the Mummer said.

Moriarty turned to Barnett. "I leave you in charge of such of my activities as come within your purview in my absence," he said. "Do not get overenthusiastic. I shall see you in a fortnight."

"Goodbye, Professor," Barnett said. "Good luck!"

"Indeed?" Moriarty said. "Let us hope that luck plays small part in either of our endeavors for the next two weeks. For if you invoke the good, you may have to settle for the other. Goodbye, Mr. Barnett."

SEVEN

INTERLUDE: THE WIND

Thou wilt not with predestined evil round
Enmesh, and then impute my fall to sin!
EDWARD FITZGERALD

By ten-thirty in the evening he was done with his day's work, which had been his life's work; the daily repetition that had been his life, and was now but a senseless blur that marked the passing time. At ten-thirty he would be able to come to life; the new life that spread its endless days before him: days of seeking, days of hunting, days of revenge, days full of the infinite jest that had become his life, the jest that was death. At ten-thirty, with the sun safely down, the creature of the night that he had become could once more roam the streets of London and stalk its prey.

But he had to hunt out the right streets, for his prey was subtle; stalk silently through the ever-changing streets, for his prey was wily. And his prey was clever, for they went about disguised as gentlemen; but he knew them for secret devils by the mark of Cain, the hidden mark of Cain they wore.

He walked west on Long Acre, with a quick, gliding step, his great cape gathered about his stocky form, and considered where to go; where best to hunt for the hated men, the evil men, the doomed men.

It was the hunt that kept him alive. He did not want to live. His wish, his dream, his desire was but to die; to join his beloved Annie. But first there was this work to do. He was the wind.

This was Wednesday, the last Wednesday in March, and that was good. The fog, the all-enveloping fog, had returned tonight, and that was also good. Wednesday they were out, the men he sought. Wednesday they gamed, they drank, they did unspeakable things to innocent children. This Wednesday, with the help of a nameless god, another of them would die.

Frequently they changed the place at which they met, the building which housed them in their pleasures. Their horrible pleasures. They must have some means of communicating with each other, some devil's post office by which they could know when to change and where then to go. But although he had searched for some clue to what it was in the chambers of those he had already killed, and though he was skilled at reading such clues, he had not found it yet.

But he had his Judas goats, those he knew who would unknowingly be spared so that they could lead him to those he sought.

He quickened his step. It would not do to reach the Allegro after the evening performance had let out. The Allegro always ran a trifle late, trying to cram in fourteen turns where most houses were satisfied with twelve. But it served him well these nights. This Judas goat liked pretty girls, and the Allegro had a line of pretty girls. This Judas goat had a box at the Allegro, the closest box to the stage.

He stopped across the street from the Allegro, out of the actinic glare that curved around the theater entrance from the bright gaslights embedded in the ornate marquee overhead. From this shadowed position he could see all who left the theater through the lobby, without himself being seen. If necessary he could reach the cab stand in a few strides, if he had to give chase.

Five minutes passed, and then ten, as he stood in his dark corner, muffled by the creeping fog. And then the lobby of the Allegro began to fill, and the patrons of such of the arts as were represented by the evening's entertainments prepared to go home. Or elsewhere.

There he was—there! The dried-up little man with the German mustache, the latest baron of an ancient line, the evil man who joined with other men to practice pain, the Judas goat. The little man made no move toward the line of cabs; perhaps tonight he had come in his own carriage. And, indeed, there he was now, pushing his way through the throng, coming out to the curb and looking off down the street, stamping his feet with impatience because his carriage was not already there waiting for him.

And here came the private carriages, turning the corner in a line, fresh from some coop in the next block where the drivers waited until a page boy from the theater raced over to tell them the show was letting out.

The third one, the dull-black brougham with the red tracery, belonged to the little baron with the German mustache. The man who had become the wind stepped off the curb and approached the brougham from the far side, keeping out of sight of the driver, and straining his ears to hear what the Judas goat said.

"Wait here, Hackamore," the Judas goat told his driver. "I will have a charming young companion joining me in a few moments, then we will be going on to Brennen's for a late supper."

The listener who had become the wind slapped his fist into his open palm. So! The baron had an assignation with one of the show girls; there could be no other explanation. Another poor innocent was about to be drawn into his web. And if the baron was going on to a late supper at Brennen's, he would not be visiting his other friends this evening, and so he would be of little use as a Judas goat.

The baron's plans would have to be disarranged.

He went down the narrow alley to the stage entrance of the Allegro, where a pride of young gallants in evening dress were trying to talk their way past the stage doorman. "Evening, Tinker," he said, pushing past the young men to the gate.

"Ev'nin', Perfessor," the stage doorman said, releasing the catch for him. "Good to see yer again. You comin' back to us?"

"It could happen," he said. "You can never tell what's going to happen in this life. But for now, just a little visit."

He went up the circular iron staircase to the dressing rooms and knocked on the door to the girls' chorus. "One of you ladies supposed to meet a skinny gent with a walrus mustache out front?" he called.

The door opened and an attractive slender girl in a rose dressing robe came out. She had long brown hair which curled about her oval face in tight ringlets. "I am," she said. "Tell him I'll only be a couple of minutes more, please."

She must be fairly new to the chorus at the Allegro, he thought. He had never seen her before. He would have remembered. Annie had had hair like that. "I'm not from the baron, dear," he told her. "I've come to give you a warning."

"What?" The girl put her hands on her hips and glared up at him. "Listen, mister. I don't know who you are, and I don't care. But I want to tell you something. What I do is my own business, and I don't need no lessons in propriety, or any of the other social graces! So you can just get your bluenose out of here!"

"No, no, you misunderstand," he said, blocking her attempt to close the door. "Believe me, I have no interest in your actions, young lady, proper or improper. Do as you like with whom you like for all of me. It is your health and your career that concern me."

She stopped trying to close the door and looked up into his face. "That's what the baron told me," she said. "He's interested in my career. What's *your* interest?"

"I don't want to see you get into serious trouble," he said.

"What sort of trouble?"

"The wrong sort," he told her, improvising carefully. "The baron's wife has detectives following him."

"Detectives!"

"That's right. And she is determined to make trouble for him. She won't care about what happens to you in the process. If they catch you with him, it would ruin your career before it's rightly begun."

"Say, what's your interest in this?"

"Nothing," he told her. "I don't want to see you hurt. You remind me of my own daughter."

"Oh," she said. "Listen, I didn't know he was married, mister. Honest, I didn't."

"Of course not," he said. "*He* certainly wouldn't have told you."

"What should I do?"

"Don't go with him. Not tonight or ever, if you want to be safe."

"I won't," she said, looking sad. Perhaps it was the thought of all the fine dinners she would miss.

"You should warn the other girls," he said.

"I will."

"Write him a note. He's waiting out front."

"What should I say?"

"Tell him one of your chums is sick and you have to stay and take care of her. Have the page boy deliver it to him outside."

"All right, mister. Listen, I don't know who you are, but I suppose I should thank you."

"It is my pleasure, I assure you, miss," he told her. "Write that note now!"

"I will."

He tipped his hat and left her, whistling softly to himself. Once back outside he went around to the front, where the Judas goat was waiting by his carriage, impatiently tapping his feet and glaring at his pocket watch.

He crossed the street and stood by the small rank of hansom cabs that were left after most of the throng had already departed.

Here came the page boy now, looking about him for the man the chorus girl had described. He stared at the little baron for a moment, doubtfully, and then decided that it must be he.

He approached the baron and offered the note. The baron took it, and then glared at the boy, who was still standing alongside him waiting for a tip. The boy touched his cap and ran off.

Sweet little Judas goat, thought the man who had become the wind.

The little baron peered at the note, holding it close to his face. Then he stepped under the marquee to try to find enough light to read it. He stared at it intently for a minute, then, with a savage curse, he crumpled the paper into a little ball and threw it into the gutter.

The man watched his Judas goat stamp over to the black brougham, obviously quivering with rage to the roots of his mustache. The baron cursed out his driver and climbed up into the carriage, viciously slamming the door behind him.

The man who had become the wind approached the first hansom in line. "You see that brougham?" he asked the cabby. "I want you to follow it."

"What for, mate?" the cabby demanded, as the man climbed aboard.

"For an extra crown over your fare. A half-sovereign if you don't lose it!"

"A half-sovereign?" the cabby exclaimed. "Right on, mate, you've got it!"

The driver of the brougham flicked his reins, and the Judas goat started off down the dark street. Close behind him followed an avenging wind.

EIGHT

THE HOUNDS

*If once a man indulges himself in murder, very soon he comes to think
little of robbing; and from robbing he next comes to drinking and
Sabbath-breaking, and from that to incivility and procrastination.*
THOMAS DE QUINCEY

The itinerant street artist, a shabby, crumpled man with a hodgepodge
of broken colored chalks, chalk rubble, and chalk dust in an
ancient cap by his side, knelt to his work on the pavement at the Russell
Square corner of the British Museum, a short distance away from where
the guidebook hawkers were plying their dubious wares before the
museum's great marble facade. Quickly, and with a deft, sure hand, the
street artist sketched a row of pictures on the pavement squares in front
of him. His subjects were taken from the great city that surrounded him
and was his life. The Crystal Palace appeared in the first square, set in
the trees and with a line of carriages along the drive in the foreground.
The Houses of Parliament as seen from over Westminster Bridge were
the next subject, with one lone tugboat passing on the Thames. Then
the west front of Westminster Abbey appeared, and a parade of well-
dressed gentlemen and ladies were quickly chalked in, marching in a
stately fashion, two by two, toward the great doors.

A stocky man in a well-worn bowler hat who was lounging by the
Russell Square corner came over to stare down appreciatively at the

colorful chalkings. "Quite nice, that," he said. "Quite nice, indeed. Here you are!" And he tossed a twopenny bit into the artist's cap.

"Thank 'ee, gov'nor; thank 'ee indeed. Very good of your worship to say so," the artist said, sitting back on his heels. He tossed his chalks back in the cap and stared down at his work. "Is the professor in or out?" he demanded in an undertone.

"What?" The man started backward in surprise, seeming to almost choke for a second.

"Don't be so obvious, my man," the artist said. "Keep looking down at the pavement and answer my question, if you can."

"I don't know what you're talking about," the stocky man said indignantly.

"Don't be ridiculous," the artist said. "You are a CID detective named Gordon. I am Sherlock Holmes."

"Well, I'll be a—" Detective Gordon said, staring down at the grimy artist.

"Quite! Now, is the professor in or out?"

"He went out in his carriage about an hour ago. Macy and Stevens followed behind."

"First time out today?"

"Yes, sir."

"And last night?"

"In at four in the afternoon, and not out again until an hour ago."

"I expected no less."

"How's that, sir?"

Holmes stood up and stretched, stamping some of the stiffness out of his legs. "The body of Sir Geoffrey Cruikstaff, the Minister of Colonial Affairs for her majesty's government, was found this morning," he told the detective. "He was murdered in his study at some time between two and four in the morning, as closely as the autopsy surgeon can tell. It would be too much to expect that Moriarty was abroad and without an alibi to cover the time. And this time, damn him, the police are his alibi."

"Sir Geoffrey Cruikstaff?" Detective Gordon asked. "Why, sir, that is incredible!"

"I agree," Holmes said dryly.

"Why, Sir Geoffrey was under a twenty-four-hour guard. He claimed to have received death threats from some oriental secret society."

"That is correct," said Holmes. "At least his residence was under guard. Sir Geoffrey reserved the right to move about unwatched and unguarded outside his house. Which was, perhaps, foolish. He exercised that right last night, coming home no less than two hours before his death. Nevertheless, it was at home and not outside that he was killed. At the time of his death there were four constables outside the house and two CID plainclothesmen inside the house. And still he was found lying across his desk with his throat cut."

Gordon shook his head. "I had that duty myself a fortnight ago," he said. "Spent the night in his front hall for almost two weeks. And to tell you the truth, sir, I never took them death threats seriously. None of us did. Inspector Gregson just had us there because of Sir Geoffrey's position, you know."

"I know."

"Done in by an oriental secret society. What do you know?"

"It wasn't any oriental secret society," Holmes snapped. "It was the same hand that killed Lord Walbine, and Venn, and Darby, and Stanhope. It was an occidental hand. And, unless I miss my guess, whoever supplied the hand, it was Professor James Moriarty who supplied the brain."

"I can't speak to that, sir," Gordon said, "but I can speak to his location. The professor was in his house all night, and didn't go back out until an hour ago."

"That is when you saw him go out, at any rate," Holmes remarked. "Moriarty is a downy bird, and if he didn't want you to see him going out, why then he would go out without your seeing him."

"Begging your pardon, sir," Detective Gordon said with the apologetic air of one who has interrupted his superiors once too often with information they didn't wish to hear. "It ain't just that we didn't see him go out. We actually, so to speak, saw him at home."

"You *saw* him at home?"

"Yessir. At least, until about one in the morning when the interior lights was turned off in the house."

"I see," Holmes said. "That's good to know."

"Clears him of suspicion, does it, sir?"

"On the contrary," Holmes said. "It makes me more suspicious than ever. Far more suspicious. Exactly what do you mean when you say you *saw* him?"

"We did, sir. Just that. At his window."

"I see. Which window was that?"

"Ground floor, Mr. Holmes. Facing Russell Square. To the right of the door."

"The study window?"

"If you say so, Mr. Holmes. Never having been inside the house, I couldn't rightly say. What we could see from outside looked like it might be a study."

"What, exactly, did you see? His shadow on the blinds?"

"No, sir. The blinds were drawn aside. We could see right into the room."

"Strange," Holmes said. "And tell me, just what did you observe in the room?"

"We saw the professor. He was sitting behind a desk, or some such. I wouldn't swear it was a desk because of the angle, you know."

"And what was he doing?"

"He seemed to be looking at something. We couldn't see what."

"Looking at something? Something on his desk?"

"Not exactly, Mr. Holmes. Something off to one side. There was a part of the room that was not visible from the window, and he was looking over in that direction. Something on the wall, perhaps. Or something in the air."

"In the air?"

"Well, you know, sir. Held up by somebody."

"There was someone else in there with him?"

"Not that we could see, sir. Mr. Barnett came into the room several times, but he didn't stay."

"But there might have been someone else?"

"Yes, sir."

"And Professor Moriarty was looking at something that might have been on the wall or been held up by this possible person whom you could not see. He was staring at this object, whatever it was, the whole time?"

"Well, it may not have been the same thing the whole time," Detective Gordon said. "He would shift his gaze from time to time, as though he were looking at one thing, you know, and then at another."

Holmes stuffed his chalk-filled cap into one of the side pockets of his bulky jacket. "There is something unnatural-sounding in your description," he said. "I wish I had been present to see for myself."

"How do you mean, Mr. Holmes?"

"I'm not sure. Moriarty was sitting at his desk, looking at first one thing and then another."

"That's right."

"For a long time?"

"From nine in the evening until about one or so."

"He didn't leave the study at all in this time?"

"I wouldn't swear to that, sir. But if he did, then it weren't for more than a few minutes. Say ten at most."

"What a strange image," Holmes said. "Moriarty was in his study with the drapes open, sitting behind his desk and looking at something on the wall or in the air in front of him. And he did this for four hours."

"When you put it that way, Mr. Holmes, it does sound strange. But at the time it looked perfectly natural."

"I am sure it did," Holmes said.

"Well," Detective Gordon said, "here he comes now, so if you have any questions, you can ask him yourself."

Holmes dropped to his knees instantly as Moriarty's carriage came into sight down Montague Place. "I prefer to watch without being watched," he told Gordon, pulling the chalk-filled cap out of his pocket and starting on another picture.

Detective Gordon drifted away to lounge on the museum steps, and Holmes began an enthusiastic rendition of St. Paul's Cathedral in pink chalk as Moriarty's four-wheeler passed in front of the British

Museum and pulled to a stop at 64 Russell Square. A hansom cab loaded down by two large men in black bowlers who were doing their best to look invisible pulled off into Montague Street right before Moriarty's carriage stopped.

The carriage door opened, and the hulking figure of the professor emerged, his black greatcoat buttoned up to the neck. Holmes stared at the familiar figure. It was Moriarty, all right; there was no mistaking the massive forehead under that top hat, the slightly bulging eyes, the beak of a nose. But there was something wrong; something Holmes couldn't put a name to. Moriarty moved up the steps to his front door with a rapid walk, taking curiously short steps. The door opened as he reached it, and he disappeared inside.

What was wrong? Holmes went over in his mind what he had just seen. Something—

Holmes fell backward to a sitting position on the pavement and threw the piece of chalk in the air. "Perfect!" he yelled. "Oh, perfect!" He burst out laughing.

Detective Gordon came up behind Holmes, trying to look casual. "What is it, Mr. Holmes?" he asked out of the side of his mouth, staring earnestly down at the pink dome of St. Paul's.

"You saw it, didn't you?" Holmes gasped. "You saw Moriarty go into the house."

"I did," Gordon said, sounding puzzled.

"You did!" Holmes broke out laughing again. "Oh, that is rich. I have to give him credit for this one."

Detectives Macy and Stevens, the two bulky gentlemen who had been in the hansom following Moriarty's carriage, came trotting down the street, ready to take up their observation posts. "Those must be your friends coming," Holmes said. "Call them over here, Detective Gordon. Call them over here."

"But Mr. Holmes," Gordon said, "Professor Moriarty might see us together. It is very bad for an observation team to allow the subject to see them all bunched together."

Gordon looked puzzled when this statement also caused Holmes to laugh. He shrugged and signaled Macy and Stevens to join them, and explained to them who the ragged-looking street artist was while Holmes stood up and dusted himself off.

"Gentlemen," Holmes said after shaking hands with the two policemen, "no need to worry about Professor Moriarty seeing us together. No need to keep watching his house, for that matter. The professor has made fools of the three of you. He has almost made a fool of me."

"What's that? What do you mean, Mr. Holmes?" Detective Gordon asked.

"Why, man, you saw it. You just don't know what you saw."

"Saw what, Mr. Holmes?" Detective Stevens asked.

"The gentleman who just left that carriage, Mr. Stevens. The gentleman whom you have been following about for the past few days. It isn't Professor Moriarty at all!"

"What?" Stevens asked.

"But," Gordon protested, "how could you mistake that face? He is a very distinctive-looking man, the professor."

"Indeed he is," Holmes agreed. "And that has been your downfall. You have been so preoccupied with his face that you never noticed his feet!"

"His feet?" Gordon asked.

"And his arms. You really should have noticed his arms. I should say that the motions of his arms were quite worthy of notice."

"But, Mr. Holmes," Gordon protested, "as I remember, his arms didn't move."

"True. They did not. And was that not quite remarkable?"

"I'm afraid I don't understand, Mr. Holmes," Gordon said.

Stevens and Macy looked uncomfortably away, as though wishing to disassociate themselves from this madman that the Commissioner of Police had temporarily placed over them.

Holmes looked from one to the other of them, and then burst out laughing again. "Why, men, don't you see? It wasn't Moriarty at all. It was a wax dummy. That's what you saw last night, and that's what we just saw emerging from the carriage."

"A wax dummy, sir? Walking?" Gordon asked.

"Judging by the stride, I should say it was being carried on the shoulders of a midget," Holmes said.

Gordon looked stricken. "A midget!" he exclaimed. "Mummer Tolliver!"

"Exactly!" Holmes said. "Why, man, didn't you see that short stride? It shouldn't have fooled us for a second."

"Well, sir, what do we do now?" Gordon asked.

"We call for some more men to surround the house," Holmes said. "Subtly, very subtly. And then, acting on information received, we get an order from the Home Secretary and proceed to search the house from top to bottom."

"Information received? From whom, sir?"

"From me, Detective Gordon, from me!" Holmes said firmly.

NINE

THE CHASE

As I was going up the stair
I met a man who wasn't there.
He wasn't there again to-day.
I wish, I wish he'd stay away.
HUGHES MEARNS

Amass of burly policemen in ill-fitting civilian clothes burst through the front door of 64 Russell Square when Mr. Maws answered the bell. Five of them grabbed the powerful butler and were struggling to subdue him and clap handcuffs on him when Barnett, in a mouse-gray dressing gown, armed with a large revolver, ran out of the dining room to see what the commotion was about. "What's this?" he yelled. "Unhand him, you men, and put your hands up! Mrs. H, run outside and whistle for a policeman."

"Come, come, now, Mr. Barnett," Sherlock Holmes said, appearing in the front doorway. "You know quite well that these men are policemen. Now put down that horse pistol and behave like a gentleman."

"Mr. Holmes!" Barnett exclaimed. "Is this your idea? Will you please tell me what it is that's happening? If you are responsible for the hoard of burly savages in this hallway, will you make some attempt to get them to behave in a civilized fashion? Have you a warrant for Mr. Maws's arrest? If so, on what charge?"

"Nobody is attempting to arrest your butler," Holmes said. "It merely seemed to us that the element of surprise might be useful. We do have a warrant to search this house. And we intend to do so, immediately."

"That's fine," Barnett said. "Show me the warrant and, if it is in order, go ahead and search the house. There is no call to manhandle the butler."

"Where is your master?" Holmes asked, signaling the policemen to release Mr. Maws.

"I have no master," Barnett said. "I am an American. George the Third was the last man to consider himself our master, and he's been dead these past sixty-seven years."

Mr. Maws dusted off his jacket and trousers. "If any one of you gentlemen would like to step outside," he said, his voice a study in exaggerated politeness, "I would be delighted to give him a lesson in proper manners. Or any three of you?"

"I do apologize, Mr. Maws," Holmes said lightly. "These gentlemen were merely overeager, having heard of your reputation as a pugilist, I'm sure. No harm done."

"Lucky thing, that," Mr. Maws said. "Busting in here like that. Grabbing a man and tussling about with him. Where do you think you are, France?"

"The police would like to ask some questions of Professor James Moriarty," Holmes said. "Where is he?"

"Not at home at the moment," Barnett said. "Had you sent word that you were coming, I'm sure he would have stayed around to greet you."

"Where has he gone?" Holmes asked. "And when did he leave?"

"Why?" Barnett asked.

"What do you mean, why?" Holmes demanded, eyeing Barnett closely. "Exactly which of the words did you fail to understand?"

"I mean, why do you want to know?" Barnett said, glaring back at Holmes, his arms crossed across his chest and his voice even. "What right have you to burst in here, attack a resident of the house, and demand to know anything at all about Professor Moriarty? Why did you bring fifteen policemen? On what basis did you get a warrant to search this house? Mr. Holmes, I think perhaps you have gone too far."

"I think not, Mr. Barnett," Holmes said, brandishing a folded-up document at him. "Here is the warrant. On information received, the police are to search the premises at 64 Russell Square, and any surrounding adjacent area. They are to look for any items, objects, personal possessions, dunnage, household furnishings, weapons, or other articles not specified herein, which would serve to connect Professor James Moriarty or other persons as yet unspecified in this instrument with the murder of Sir Geoffrey Cruikstaff, or with other crimes relating to or growing out of the specified murder."

"Murder?" Mr. Maws sniffed. "So now it's murder you are accusing us of!"

"Dunnage?" Barnett asked. "Dunnage? Why not flotsam and jetsam?"

"You may laugh," Holmes said, "but you will also stand aside while we search the house. And where is Professor Moriarty? We would very much like to speak to him in regard to this murder."

Barnett unfolded the paper and glanced at it. "So this is what a warrant looks like," he said. "I suppose it is in order, I've never seen one before. It certainly looks official, with a red seal in one corner and a blue seal in the other. Done at her majesty's order, eh? Why, I'll bet that if I were to ask her majesty right now, she wouldn't know anything about it. What exactly is this squiggle down here, this ink blot?"

"That is the magistrate's signature," Holmes told him. "I assure you it is quite in order. And stalling us will get you nowhere. The house is completely surrounded and nobody is going to get in or out until we have completed our search."

"Go ahead," Barnett said. "I've already told you to go ahead. But this paper had better be legit. I intend to send it to Professor Moriarty's solicitor, and if he informs me that this thing is a phony, or that you have in any way exceeded your authority under it, we shall certainly see what sort of legal trouble we can cause you and your friends of the police." He turned. "Mrs. H!" he called.

The housekeeper appeared in the dining-room door, her fingers laced together at her waist. "Yes, Mr. Barnett?"

"Would you please show Mr. Holmes and his friends whatever

they would like to see in the house," Barnett told her. "Discourage them from making more of a mess than is absolutely necessary."

"Very well, Mr. Barnett," Mrs. H said, her face expressionless.

"Have Lucille clean up the breakfast things," Barnett added. "I shall go up and dress now."

Mrs. H nodded, and then turned and focused her gaze on Sherlock Holmes. "Mr. Holmes," she said.

"Mrs. H," Holmes said.

"One cannot expect gratitude in this life," she told the detective, "but one has a right to expect civility. I consider this sort of behavior most ungracious and uncivil."

"I owe you no gratitude, Mrs. H," Holmes said, "nor any more civility than is common between the sexes in this day and age."

"I was not speaking of any debt to myself, Mr. Sherlock Holmes," Mrs. H said, "but to the debt of gratitude that it might be thought you owe to your old friend and mentor, Professor James Moriarty— the man who took you in and treated you like a son. The man whose house you are now so rudely invading and ravaging."

"Ravaging, Mrs. H? Hardly ravaging, I daresay."

"No? What else do you call knocking poor Mr. Maws about? And look at all those men with their muddy boots grinding the dirt into the carpeting."

"Well, call it what you will, Mrs. H," Holmes said. "Anything that happens to this house, or to Professor Moriarty, for that matter, he has brought on himself. In his pursuit of crime to further his own secret desires, in his delight in evil, he has placed himself and his associates outside the human pale. And any ill results that he suffers, he brought on his own head with his own hand."

"What are you talking about, Sherlock Holmes?" Mrs. H asked. "Never in fifteen years has Professor Moriarty so much as lifted a finger to harm you, and yet you continue this senseless vendetta past all reason. And now you bring in the police on some kind of trumped-up warrant! I rather think that is going too far, and I'm sure that the professor will think so also."

"What Professor James Moriarty thinks is of no concern to me,"

Holmes said. "Not now, and not ever again. Will you show us around, Mrs. H, or shall we find our own way?"

Mrs. H sniffed. "This way," she said. "Mind your boots on the rug."

The search began on the top floor, where Mummer Tolliver slept under the eaves, and slowly worked its way downstairs. Large policemen were stationed at each landing of both the front and rear staircases to make sure nothing was removed in one direction while the searchers looked in the other.

Nothing of interest was found on the top floor.

On the second floor Mrs. H protested loudly when Holmes's minions stamped their big feet into Professor Moriarty's bedroom. Barnett merely watched with interest as the search proceeded. He thought that Moriarty would be more enraged at the coming invasion of his laboratory than at the search of his bedroom.

Sherlock Holmes directed the endeavor, and kept himself busy tapping on walls and measuring the space between closets in search of hidden passageways or secret panels. The search seemed thorough and complete, but Barnett became more and more convinced, watching Holmes, that the detective's heart was not in it. Holmes went through the gestures with the regard for minutia that was his hallmark, having every drawer pulled out and looked under, peering under rugs, thumping at cracks in the flooring, sending someone down the dumbwaiter to see what might be concealed in the shaft. But somehow Barnett sensed that he knew he was beaten before he began; that the professor was not lurking about the house and that there was nothing in the dunnage to connect Moriarty with any crime.

The search of the house took most of the day. Holmes himself spent two hours in the basement laboratory, poking into retorts, peering into dusty jars and canisters, looking through stacks of photographic plates, and otherwise searching for clues.

The Mummer insisted upon following two of the policemen about, telling them that they were getting warmer or colder at random until they finally tried to chase him away. At which he indignantly reminded them that it was his house, after all, not theirs, and he would go where he liked. Mr. Maws settled down to ostentatiously count the silver service in the pantry after the policemen had finished searching in there. Mrs. H stayed ahead of the group, pointing out things they should examine and sniffing with disdain when they did. She kept warning them to mind their feet, and not brush things with their shoulders, until she made one constable so nervous that he knocked over a four-foot Tseng vase while trying to avoid an armoire.

There was a flurry of excitement when one of the policemen discovered the bust of Moriarty in the study. Holmes went over and examined with interest the arrangement of straps that enabled Mummer Tolliver to wear the device on his shoulders. Then he called Barnett over. "What, exactly, is this doing here?" Holmes asked, pointing an accusatory finger at the offending object.

"It doesn't appear to be doing much of anything," Barnett replied.

"That may be," Holmes said, "but we both know what it has been doing for the past few hours. It and Tolliver. Exactly how long has he been parading about with that device on his shoulders?"

"Ask him," Barnett said.

The Mummer was called for, and the question was put to him. "Blimey!" he said. "Ye've discovered me secret. I goes about in me professor disguise all the time."

"And for how long?" Holmes demanded.

"Oh, years and years."

"I see," Holmes said. "To give Moriarty an alibi while he is off committing some deviltry, no doubt."

"None of that!" Tolliver said. "'Ow dares you talk about the professor that way!"

"Then why do you wear the dummy?"

"It gives me stature," Tolliver explained. "'Ow would you like to go about being barely four feet high all the time?"

"Bah!" Holmes said.

"Exactly the way I feels about it," the Mummer agreed.

Three hours later, Holmes, having found nothing of official interest, gathered his minions about him in the front hall and prepared to leave.

"I hope you are quite satisfied," Mrs. H said, her voice frigid.

"Not entirely," Holmes told her. "But then, we are not yet done with the investigation."

"What now?" Barnett asked. "Are you going to tear the house down brick by brick?"

"Not at all," Holmes said. "We are done with this house. But I have a second warrant, which I am now going to execute. I was, as you see, prepared for this!"

"What are you talking about?" Barnett asked. "What second warrant?"

Holmes pulled another piece of official-looking paper from inside his jacket and flourished it. "To search the premises and outbuildings of Moriarty's holdings on Crimpton Moor!" he exclaimed, a note of triumph in his voice. "Didn't think I knew about that, did you?"

"In truth," Barnett said, "the question had not occurred to me."

"There is a special train awaiting us at Paddington to take us to Crimpton," Holmes said. "We should be there at dusk. And if we have to spend the whole night and all of tomorrow searching, why then we shall do so." He turned and stalked out the door, followed closely by the Baker Street regulars.

Barnett turned to Mrs. H as the door closed behind the last burly man. "The professor is not going to be pleased," he said.

TEN

DRAWING THE COVER

On approaching a cover, one whip should go on in advance and station himself on the lee side of it, where he may often see a fox steal away as soon as the hounds are thrown in.

E.D. BRICKWOOD

Sherlock Holmes studied the map of Devon which lay open across his knees as the special police train sped west. In the orange-yellow beam of a bull's-eye lantern borrowed from one of the constables to counter the approaching dusk, he peered through his four-inch glass at the web of black lines and crosshatches on the stiff paper. Inspector Lestrade, who had joined Holmes at Paddington, contented himself with sitting silently in the opposite corner of the carriage.

"Bah!" Holmes said finally, casting the map aside. "This is useless."

Inspector Lestrade stirred himself and eyed Holmes. "Useless?" he asked. "I could have told you that before you opened the map. What do we need a map for? We know where we're going."

"As you say," Holmes said. "But you have your ways and I have mine. I would give five pounds right now for a large-scale ordnance map of the area."

Lestrade viewed Holmes tolerantly. "Professor Moriarty's holdings are at Crimpton-on-the-Moor," he explained patiently, as one would to a bright eight-year-old. "For which we detrain at Mossback Station.

The only possible confusion is with Grimpon, a hamlet on the other side of the moor, which one gets access to through Coryton Station. The house is called Sigerson Manor locally, apparently after the family which built the house and occupied it for some two hundred years. The last Sigerson passed on some fifteen years ago, and the property stood deserted until Professor Moriarty took it over."

He smiled a smile of quiet satisfaction, and added, "We research these things at the Yard."

"I know all that," Holmes said.

"You know?" Lestrade leaned forward and tapped Holmes on the knee. "Your obsession with Professor Moriarty is quite impressive," he said. "You must spend all your spare time and money following him around. I tell you, Mr. Holmes, I only hope you're right this time. You have made us look foolish before, acting on your accusations."

"I have known of Sigerson Manor all my life," Holmes told Lestrade. "The Sigersons were distant relations of mine. I knew of Moriarty's purchase of the property when it happened five years ago. And as for what you call my 'obsession' with Moriarty"—he paused to blow out the lantern—"the fact that that man is not breaking stone at Dartmoor right now instead of living in luxury in a townhouse in Russell Square and a country estate at Crimpton-on-the-Moor is testimony to his genius, not his honesty. Moriarty is everything foul, Lestrade; inside that vulturelike head is the mind of a fiend incarnate. And I am his nemesis."

"That's all very well, Mr. Holmes," Lestrade said. "But you can't prove a word of it. We found someone murdered in an empty house, and you muttered, 'Moriarty!' But it wasn't. A girl was kidnapped, and you would have had us clap the professor in irons. But it was some Russian did it, not the professor at all. Now, the professor may be everything you say he is and more, but I, for one, am getting extremely tired of apologizing to him. If you can't get him convicted of a crime, Mr. Holmes, if you can't even get him held on suspicion, then don't it make good sense to just leave him be?"

Holmes folded up the map and moved over to the window seat, where he stared out at the bleak Devonshire countryside. "I cannot," he said. "As I am his nemesis, so he is my passion, the focus of my energies. Without Moriarty, Sherlock Holmes is merely a detective." He raised his right hand and balled it into a fist. "But mark this: without Sherlock Holmes to dog his steps, to intercept his secret communications, to apprehend his henchmen, to deduce his intentions and thus to foil his plans, Professor James Moriarty would by now control the largest criminal empire the world has ever seen. He would make the infamous Jonathan Wild look like a bumbling amateur!"

"So you say, Mr. Holmes. So you have been saying for the past seven years. And yet the fact is that if you were to say the same aloud in any public place, Professor Moriarty would have an action of slander against you. And if your friend Dr. Watson were to write one word defamatory of Professor Moriarty in any of the accounts of your cases that he has been writing for the magazines, he could be held for libel."

"No fear of that, Lestrade," Holmes said. "I have requested the good doctor not to so much as mention Moriarty in any of his little cautionary tales during my lifetime, unless it is to record his immediate sojourn, at her majesty's pleasure, in some penal institution."

"Well, let us hope that this is the time," Lestrade said. "When you were acting on your own, so to speak, as an unofficial detective, running about dogging the professor's footprints was your affair. But now you are acting with official sanction, and that brings Scotland Yard into it. The Home Secretary is not going to be pleased if a distinguished scientist brings an action against the Yard for false arrest or harassment."

"It was the Home Secretary who brought me into the case," Holmes reminded Lestrade. "He cannot hold the Yard culpable for my actions."

"Home Secretaries have very selective memories," Lestrade said. "If you succeed in apprehending the killer, he will be very pleased with himself for having appointed you. And the press and the House will hear, in detail, how clever he was. If you fail, he will certainly vocally reprimand the commissioners for their laxness in this important matter."

"A policeman's lot," Holmes quoted, "is not an 'appy one."

"That is so, Mr. Holmes," Lestrade agreed. "And it ain't the felons which make it so, but the sanctimonious bloody politicians."

"Very insightful, Inspector," Holmes said.

"Thank you, Mr. Holmes," Lestrade replied. "You learn a few things in twelve years on the force."

The sun was still above the horizon when the special pulled into Mossback Station. The local constable, who had been alerted by telegraph, had managed to assemble three open wagons to transport Holmes, Lestrade, and the fifteen plainclothes constables from the Yard. The wagons, ancient vehicles that had certainly conformed to some standard pattern of design at one time, had, over decades of hard use and random repair, taken on unique characters. They sat on the road outside the station like a trio of rustic old drunks, clearly willing to do whatever was required of them, but doubtful as to whether they could negotiate the first bump under any sort of load. The three horses were obviously great-grandmothers, and any member of the R.S.P.C.A. who had happened by and seen them hitched up to wagons would certainly have called the nearest policeman.

The nearest policeman, a thickset village constable named Wiggs, stood proudly next to the drooping head of the forward horse. "'Taint often we gets a call to cooperate with Scotland Yard out here," he told Lestrade, "but we're right pleased to do our bit."

"What is this?" Holmes asked, encompassing horses and wagons with a wave of his hand.

"Wot does yer mean, sir?" Wiggs asked, pulling his shoulders back and glaring at Holmes. "Transportation fer fifteen ter twenty officers, that's wot we was asked ter pervide, and that's wot we has pervided. 'Taint easy roundin' up transportation fer twenty officers at a moment's notice, like that."

"That's all right," Lestrade said. "You have done very well. I'm sure Mr. Holmes meant no offense."

"Mr. Holmes?" Wiggs asked. "Mr. *Sherlock* Holmes?"

Holmes acknowledged the fact.

"Well, I am truly proud ter make yer acquaintance, Mr. Holmes. I have read yer monograph on identifying cigarette ash."

For the first time in Lestrade's memory, Holmes looked astonished. "You have?"

Constable Wiggs nodded. "'Twas in the circulatin' library of the Southern Counties Constabulary. Not many people smoke cigars er cigarettes out here; mostly they smoke a pipe er chew. But if a criminous offense is ever committed hereabouts by a geezer wot is puffin' on a Trichinopoly cigar, why, I'll have him cold."

Holmes glared suspiciously at Wiggs, but the constable did not seem to notice. He shifted his glare to Lestrade for a moment, and then turned back to Wiggs. "I am sure you will, Constable," he said. "We had best mount these, ah, wagons, and proceed. The sun is about to dip behind the western hills."

"How far to Sigerson Manor?" Lestrade asked Wiggs.

"No more 'n three miles," Wiggs told him. "Off that way. Is that where yer headed?"

"That's right," Lestrade replied. "Anything of interest happening out there to your knowledge?"

"Aye. Strange and wonderful things indeed. They is constructin' an aerostat, the professor and them people wot lives out there with him."

"A what?"

"An aerostat. Like a balloon. These modrun times wot we live in are truly times of progress and invention. They been fillin' it with hydrogen all day wot they makes themselves."

"A balloon!" Holmes exclaimed. "Come, Lestrade, load your men aboard these wagons. We must get out there quickly."

"Very well, Mr. Holmes," Lestrade said. He turned and, with a crisp series of commands, divided his men among the three wagons.

Holmes clambered up into the forward wagon next to Constable Wiggs, who gathered the reins and prodded the ancient mare into motion. "Where is this aerostat?" Holmes asked. "In the lower field, I suppose. Or the east lawn, past the formal part, where it slopes away to the drive in front of the house? I understand that Moriarty has built an observatory. Where is that? I would have placed it on the old stone foundation for the granary."

"Yer must be right familiar with ther property, Mr. Holmes,"

Wiggs said. "Have yer been out this way before?"

"Not for many years," Holmes said.

"Well," Wiggs told him, "ther observatory is where ther ruined granary was, like yer said. And ther aerostat is bein' filled on ther lawn in front of ther manor house. A great many of ther young people from ther area have gone over ter watch ther event."

"Do you hear that, Lestrade?" Holmes demanded, bending over to speak to the inspector, who was sitting in the wagon with his back to the driver's seat. "What nerve, what consummate nerve that man has."

"I fear that I don't follow that," Lestrade said.

"Why, man, he's making his getaway!"

"By balloon? I can't see it, Mr. Holmes. Where would he go?"

"France. He must know we have men on the lookout for him at the channel ports, so the clever devil is going to float right over their heads! Once he reaches Dieppe, the whole of the Continent is open to him."

"I still don't see it, Mr. Holmes," Lestrade said. "The French coast must be five hundred miles from here."

"What is that to someone being wafted along by the currents of the upper atmosphere?" Holmes asked. "I tell you, Lestrade, Moriarty is escaping us!"

"But why?" Lestrade persisted. "We have nothing against him."

"Ah, but he doesn't know that," Holmes said. "The guilty flee when no man pursueth.'"

"That'd be ther wicked," Constable Wiggs said over his shoulder. 'Ther wicked flee when no man pursueth: but ther righteous are bold as a lion.' Proverbs."

Holmes turned to glare at the imperturbable Wiggs. "Thank you, Constable," he said.

The upper tip of the sun disappeared behind a low-lying hill to the southwest. "It will be pitch-dark in twenty minutes," Lestrade said. "How is this balloon going to navigate in the dark?"

"It will be in the hands of the man who penned *The Dynamics of an Asteroid*. Do you really think that determining in which direction the French coast lies will be too much for him?"

"I suppose not," Lestrade said.

"Can't we go any faster?" Holmes demanded. "It will be dark before we get there!"

"Yer said transportation fer fifteen," Constable Wiggs said. "Yer didn't say nothin' about racin'."

"Confound it, man, I could run faster than this," Holmes said.

"That yer could," Wiggs agreed.

"Then I shall!" Holmes cried, and he leaped off the side of the wagon and rapidly disappeared down the road ahead.

Over the next twenty minutes the last of the daylight gradually dimmed and vanished. The horses, undeterred by the dark, continued stoically plodding along down the center of the dirt road.

About ten minutes after the last of the twilight had disappeared they came upon Holmes standing in the middle of the road waiting for them. "Thank God you're in time," he said. "Moriarty and his men are right over that hill. The whole lawn is lit up bright as midday with electrical lighting. There is a great black balloon tied down in the center of the lawn, and Professor Moriarty is just about ready to ascend, as far as I can tell. A crowd of locals with picnic baskets have gathered at the far end of the lawn, where the road curves about, and they are sitting there, gnawing on chicken bones and watching the spectacle. I tell you, Lestrade, that man has more gall than the Prince of Wales, assembling a crowd to watch his getaway. We must hurry!"

Lestrade climbed down from the wagon and gathered his men about him. "We are at your orders, Mr. Holmes," he said.

"There is no time for finesse," Holmes said. "We will go straight over the hill and apprehend Moriarty and all of his henchmen. He must not get away in that balloon. And unless I miss my guess, the evidence of his crimes will be in the balloon with him. Are you armed?"

"As you instructed," Lestrade said, "we checked out five handguns before we left. I have given them to the five men who can account themselves best with them."

"That should be sufficient," Holmes said. "I expect that we have a large enough force so that there will be little resistance. Come now, we must arrive before the balloon goes up."

Lestrade and his men struggled up the hill in an irregular line behind Holmes. As they worked their way up they could see the glow of yellowish light that spilled over from the far side. At the top of the hill, beside an irregular jumble of massive stones that were the remains of some Neolithic temple, Holmes gathered his troop. A few hundred yards ahead of them, down a shallow, brush-covered slope, lay the wide expanse of flat, well-rolled land that was the east lawn. Beyond that, almost invisible past the illuminating circle of electrical lights, sat the massive east wing of the manor house. Built over two hundred years before of large blocks of the native stone, this was the original house, which had been added to over the centuries by generations of Sigersons until it represented less than a third of the present structure.

At the back of the lawn, toward the house, two low sheds had been erected. One housed the electrical generating plant, to judge by the cluster of wires coming out of the top and leading to the array of electrical lights strung on the surrounding trees and poles. The other held some sort of machinery. A pair of long hoses emanating from the second shed curled across the lawn to the center, where, held to the earth by several thick cables, floated the giant aerostat. The device consisted of three great gas bags separated by a large metal ring, in which was suspended a fabric-covered gondola. The whole was painted black, and it rose perhaps ten stories in the air. The top disappeared into the dark sky above the electrical lights, and was visible only as an inky presence, blotting out the stars.

Even as they watched, the hoses from the shed were being disconnected from the couplings to the gas bags. Suddenly two flares, like great skyrockets, shot up into the night, leaving a stream of white light behind them as they climbed.

"Look at that!" Lestrade exclaimed. "It must be some sort of signal."

"Quickly!" Holmes cried. "There's no time to lose!" Leaping up, he led his little force scurrying and sliding down the hill to the lawn below. As they reached the edge of the lawn two of the tethering cables fell away and the balloon flew skyward, trailing a third cable below it like an umbilical cord.

"There he goes!" Holmes yelled, running forward like a demented man to reach the gondola before it was too high. "We must stop him!" He leaped for the bottom of the gondola and managed to grab it with his fingers, but there was nothing to cling to and he fell away.

"Stop! Stop!" the constabulary yelled, racing across the lawn. One of them drew his pistol and fired at the ascending balloon.

"Come back down here!" another one yelled, stopping to take aim at the rapidly rising gondola, "Come back in the name of the law!"

Once the shooting had started it was contagious, and within seconds a fusillade of small-arms fire was directed at the great black object, which was rapidly disappearing into the great star-filled bowl of the night sky. Two of the policemen reached the one cable which, rising from layers of coils on the ground, was still attached to the ascending gondola. One of them leaped for it and was fifteen feet in the air before, realizing the folly of what he was doing, he let go and fell to the ground.

Moriarty's men dived for cover under whatever was available as this strange armed band appeared in their midst and began shooting at their precious aerostat. The locals, who were mostly sitting together on the side of the lawn nearest the road, began shrieking and howling. Most of them ran off into the night, but a few sat stolidly watching, perhaps suspecting that this was all part of the entertainment.

Gradually the shooting and yelling died away, until, within two minutes, the small group of Scotland Yard men were clustered silently in the middle of the lawn together, staring at the sky.

* * *

"What is the meaning of all this?" a firm, didactic voice suddenly asked from close behind them. "Inspector Lestrade, have you taken leave of your senses?"

Lestrade jerked around like a man on a string and gaped at the tall, dark-clad figure. "Professor Moriarty!" he gasped.

"I refuse to believe that you didn't expect to find me here," Moriarty said. "Now, what exactly is the meaning of this charade?"

"I—we—thought you were in that balloon."

"I see," Moriarty said. "Anytime you see an aerostat ascending into the sky, you naturally assume that I am aboard. And this, of course, explains why you were shooting at it."

"Ah, well, not precisely—"

Sherlock Holmes came striding toward them across the lawn. "Moriarty!" he yelled.

"Holmes!" Moriarty said, turning and shaking his fist at him. "Now I understand. This moronic escapade was your doing."

"I have a warrant, Moriarty," Holmes shouted, brandishing the document over his head, "to search this property, house and grounds."

"And fire upon any aerostat that you happen to find ascending when you arrive?" Moriarty demanded. "Really, Holmes—"

"There was a murder in London last night," Holmes said, "and I have reason to believe that you were involved."

"There are about three murders in London every week, if the statistical abstracts are to be believed," Moriarty said. "And you believe that I am involved in each and every one of them. Is that any reason to go about shooting revolvers at perfectly innocent teen-age boys?"

"What boys?"

"There are two teen-age boys in the aerostat to work the equipment," Moriarty told him. "And if either of them is hurt, you will answer for it!"

"We thought you were on the balloon, Professor," Lestrade said in what he hoped was a conciliatory tone. "Mr. Holmes said you were escaping."

"Escaping? From what? The aerostat is tethered, as you can see for yourselves if you'd bother to look." Moriarty indicated the one cable which was still uncoiling from the ground and following the balloon into the heavens.

A Chinese gentleman in dark robes and a close-fitting cap came scurrying across the lawn from the house. "They are unhurt," he called to Moriarty. "My son wishes to be informed as to what is going on down here, but neither of them was injured by the cannonade. What is going on down here?"

"Gentlemen," Moriarty said, "may I introduce my friend and colleague, Prince Tseng Li-Chang, fourteenth in line for the throne of Imperial China. His son, Low, at whom you were shooting in the aerostat, is fifteenth in line. They are here in exile, under the personal protection of her majesty, Queen Victoria. Prince Tseng, let me present Inspector Giles Lestrade of Scotland Yard, and Mr. Sherlock Holmes."

"You were shooting at my son?" Tseng demanded, glaring alternately at Lestrade and then at Holmes. "Why were you doing this? Are you agents of the Empress Dowager?"

Lestrade sighed. "I am afraid we have made a mistake," he said. "Please accept my apologies, and the apologies of the Yard."

"Mistake!" Moriarty snorted. "You'll be back in uniform tomorrow, Lestrade, if Prince Tseng complains to her majesty. You'll be lucky not to lose your pension."

"In my country," Prince Tseng interjected, "they would suffer the death of a thousand knives for shooting at a royal heir."

"Let me try to explain, Professor," Lestrade said.

"I can't imagine any possible explanation for what just went on here," Moriarty said, "but it will be fascinating to hear you try. Unfortunately I have no time now. We have a lot of work ahead of us, Prince Tseng and I and the two lads, and we cannot take the time right now. We are commencing a night of astronomical observations by a specially constructed aerostat-carried telescope."

"So you say," Holmes said, "but then what are you doing down here?"

Moriarty turned to glare at him. "The lads are up there to expose photographic plates. They send them down on small parachutes attached to the tethering cable, which also contains a telegraphic wire. We stay down here to develop the plates. Now please leave us alone for the remainder of the night. You have a warrant—go and search the house. Try to refrain from shooting up the furniture."

"Assassins!" Prince Tseng exclaimed.

"I think we'd better go," Lestrade said. "We don't have to search the house. We'll just go back to the city now. Can we talk about this sometime, Professor? I mean, without bringing her majesty into the discussion?"

"Monday," Moriarty said. "Come by and see me at Russell Square on Monday. I'll speak to the prince."

"I have a warrant," Holmes said. "I intend to search the house."

Lestrade looked from Holmes to Moriarty to Prince Tseng, who was glowering at them with unconcealed hostility. "Come along, Mr. Holmes," he said. "We'll go now."

ELEVEN

THE GENTLEMEN'S GENTLEMEN

*Thus in the beginning the world was so made that certain signs
come before certain events.*
MARCUS TULLIUS CICERO

Upper Sedgwick Lane ran for two blocks south of Oxford Street, terminating abruptly at the high brick wall to the rear of Good Sisters' Hospital. Despite the best efforts of the residents and shopkeepers, the lane degenerated into shabby disrepute as one traveled the two-hundred-yard length of that final block.

The blame, if any, could be laid at the door of Good Sisters' Hospital. A massive rear door sheathed in heavy iron plate, studded with spikes and crusted with layers of muddy green paint, it was the only acknowledgment that Good Sisters gave to Upper Sedgwick Lane. And it was never used.

The front door of the hospital was on Beverton Street, a three-and-a-half-block semicircle from the lane. It was there that the carriages came and went, and there that the attentive doctors smiled and nodded at their respectable patients.

This sealed door was the subject of much speculation in Upper Sedgwick Lane. Rumor had it that in the darkest hours of the blackest nights, the green door opened.

In the dark of the moon, so the whisper went, mysterious carts, their wheels muffled with rags, would thump slowly over the ancient cobblestones and back up to the green door. Then the door would be opened by unseen hands, and corpses, wrapped in white linen, would be whisked inside. Why the carts were said to be delivering bodies to the hospital instead of taking them away was never discussed. That is what happened, everyone knew it. They hadn't seen it themselves, but they could name two or three who had, if they hadn't promised to keep their mouths shut.

Then there was the matter of the epigraph circumscribed around the hospital wall, which was always referred to by the lane's residents as "them words." The full and proper name of Good Sisters' Hospital was "The Hospice and Sanitarium in Holy Charity of the Good Sisters of the Miraculous Scars of the Bloody Body of Our Lord and Savior Jesus Christ." The architect and builder of the hospital, one Matthew Creighton, had wrapped a frieze around the upper story of the structure with this title deeply chiseled thereon, intended to last until the final trumpet should make hospices redundant. And the portion of this full and proper name that happened, by some malicious chance, to come around on the Upper Sedgwick Lane side, two feet high and five stories up, in deep relief, was: ARS OF THE BLOODY BODY.

Upper Sedgwick Lane had never recovered from this indignity.

"It is by such fortuitous happenings," Mr. Nathaniel Palmar told Barnett, "that the destinies of men and nations are determined. Were it not for Matthew Creighton's infantile sense of humor—for there can be little doubt that the placement of the lettering on that infamous frieze was deliberate—then Upper Sedgwick Lane might not have slowly degenerated over the past hundred years. Had that not happened, then this fine old mansion, once the home of Admiral Sir George Tallbouys, would never have been available at such a remarkably reasonable price. And had it not, then the Gentlemen's Gentlemen, through lack of a proper home, could never have come into being."

"That would have been a shame," Barnett said, running his hand over the dark mahogany woodwork of the entrance hall, with its patina of a hundred years' polishing and waxing.

"It would," Mr. Palmar agreed, "it would indeed." He led the way into the guests' parlor: a large room with a scattering of armchairs toward the front balanced by an ancient, well-used billiard table at the rear. "Yes, we owe a lot to Matthew Creighton. 'For his work continueth,' as the poet says, 'far beyond his knowing.' Were it not for the whimsical builder and the inadvertent benefactor, we would not be here."

"The inadvertent benefactor?"

Mr. Palmar indicated a large oil portrait on the wall behind them. Done in the whimsically realistic style of the '40s, it showed a portly gentleman with a choleric expression, wearing hunting tweeds and carrying a shotgun in the crook of his right arm and a brace of dead birds in his left hand.

Barnett peered at the brass plate under the portrait. "'Sir Hector Billysgait,'" he read. "He was your benefactor?"

"It is a complex story involving an unexpected predeceasing, a residual legatee, and a gentleman whose taste for practical jokes extended even to the grave," Mr. Palmar said.

"Fascinating!" Barnett said sincerely. He took out the small notebook that was his reporter's disguise. "If you don't mind telling me about it..."

"In brief," Mr. Palmar said, "Sir Hector, though knighted for a service to the Crown, was merely the impoverished younger son of a baronet. Impoverished only in terms of his family and class, you understand. It was a constant struggle for him to maintain his flat in the city and his various shooting boxes and fishing rights and the like. He hardly ever killed as many creatures in a year as he would like to have done. And his income ceased upon his death, the principal reverting to the entailed estate which progressed from eldest son to eldest son."

"I see," Barnett said. "The man had no money."

"None to call his own," Mr. Palmar agreed, "beyond the value of those possessions which he had acquired over a lifetime—rifles, shotguns, fishing tackle, framed oils of men killing animals in a variety of ways, and a remarkable variety of clothing for tramping through the woods and shooting at things or wading in mountain streams with a fishing rod."

"So," Barnett said.

"Over the long years of their relationship," Mr. Palmar continued, "Sir Hector grew more and more in debt to his valet, Fellows. It was a gradual process—a couple of pounds borrowed here, a quarter's wages unpaid there—but eventually the total grew to in excess of two hundred pounds. Which, although a comparatively small sum to someone of Sir Hector's class, was a fortune to Fellows.

"Now Sir Hector was something of a practical joker. He promised Fellows, who was his junior by some twenty years, that he would leave him everything in his will. 'Every penny I have,' as he put it."

"But," Barnett interjected, "I thought he had no money of his own."

"True," Mr. Palmar agreed. "And when he died his income would cease. But his possessions remained part of his estate—those things he had bought over the years. And several of the firearms were of themselves worth well into the hundreds of pounds. Sir Hector did not stint himself."

"I see," Barnett said. "It still doesn't sound like enough to purchase a building and endow a private club."

"Ah," Mr. Palmar said, "but here is where the hand of fate takes over, and a strange chain of events turns a practical joke into a legacy. May I offer you a glass of sherry?"

Barnett accepted the sherry, which proved to be a particularly fine Garrett d'Austine '67. He sipped it, savored it, commented on its quality.

"Butlers and valets," Mr. Palmar said, "are particularly well-placed to develop a fine palate for wines, especially fortified wines." He sipped from his own glass and continued with the story he never tired of telling.

"Sir Hector died quite suddenly one morning in September, 1878. And he proved to be as good as his word. Exactly as good, and no better. Fellows was made residual legatee, meaning he was to have whatever was left over after all the specific bequests had been fulfilled. What quickly became apparent as the will was read was that the specific bequests would consume all of Sir Hector's real and personal property. The only thing left for Fellows was the bit of actual money that Sir Hector had on his person and in his flat at the moment of his decease. It amounted, if I remember aright, to a trifle over thirteen pounds. Fellows was rather disappointed."

"I can understand that."

"But then it transpired that Sir Hector's youngest brother, Sydney, who had been shooting in Bengal, had met with an untimely and very fatal accident. He was staking out a goat to attract a tiger when the goat, sensing perhaps that what was about to happen was not to his best interest, butted Sir Sydney in the stomach. Ruptured his spleen. It took a while for news of this to reach England. It actually happened several months before Sir Hector died."

"I see," Barnett said. "And Sir Hector was Sydney's heir?"

"Sydney was still youthful enough to be unaffected by intimations of mortality. He never made a will. But they both had an elderly aunt named Agatha, who passed on about a week before Sir Hector. And thus, you see, a month or so after Sydney, although nobody realized it at the time."

"Yes?"

"Dame Agatha had left her considerable private fortune to Sydney, long her favorite, to sustain himself with and to use for whatever good works he deemed appropriate. But as Sydney predeceased Dame Agatha, her estate went to Sir Hector. He died without ever knowing that he was a millionaire."

"And the valet?"

"As residual legatee, Fellows suddenly found himself a man of considerable wealth. Since his unwitting benefactress, Dame Agatha, had wished part of her fortune to be used for good works, Fellows endowed the Gentlemen's Gentlemen as a club for butlers and valets in service in London, along with a generous fund to take care of former or retired men of these professions who have fallen on hard times."

"A fine gesture," Barnett said, looking up from his notebook. "Is Fellows in residence here himself?"

"No longer," Mr. Palmar said.

"I see," Barnett said. "Has he, ah, passed on?"

"In a sense. He has moved to Paris. Having reverted to a family name which I am not at liberty to tell you, he has taken up painting in oils. Now, is there any other way in which I can be of service to you?"

"I think so," Barnett said. "What brought me here in the first place, Mr. Palmar, was a Scotland Yard report that the two gentlemen's gentlemen who were arrested on suspicion of murdering their employers this past week are both members of this club."

"Ah!" Mr. Palmar said. "Lizzard and Margery. Yes, they are indeed. Let me point out, purely in the interest of accuracy, that they are both butlers. In current usage, the phrase 'gentleman's gentleman' properly applies only to a valet."

"I understand," Barnett said. "Thank you for making that distinction. In my profession we strive for verbal accuracy, of course. But we need all the help we can get. Do you know Lizzard and Margery? Can you tell me anything about them?"

"I actually don't know either of them too well," Palmar said. "As club steward, of course, I am acquainted with all of our members, but both Lizzard and Margery were noticeably reserved with their confidences. Which is not unusual, you must understand; their vocations tend to encourage habitual reticence. I believe, however, that I can introduce you to someone who knows them both quite well."

"I would appreciate that," Barnett said.

"I shall go and see if he's here." Mr. Palmer excused himself and went off down the dark wood-paneled hallway. Barnett sipped his sherry and considered multiple murder. He composed his thoughts and began to construct the lead paragraph for the article he would write for the American News Service. A bit of philosophy to lead off. It would make the reader feel as though he were exploring the human condition instead of merely indulging a morbid curiosity.

As *ripples in a pond*, Barnett scribbled in his notebook, *radiate from every stone, no matter how casually flung, so do unforeseeable consequences emanate from every human action, no matter how seemingly minor.*

Barnett paused to chew on his pencil and stare down at the page.

It read fairly well, he decided. After all, as an unforeseen result of this series of murders, Professor Moriarty, who was completely unconnected with the crimes, had been seriously inconvenienced by the unwarranted attentions of Sherlock Holmes and Scotland Yard. But surely any of the victims would rather have been seriously inconvenienced than have had his throat cut.

Barnett decided to work on the text of his article later, make a few notes first, and try to produce something that was actually worth saying. *NOTE:* he wrote large on the rest of the page, *Murder is the worst crime of all. Why? Because it is the only one which cannot be taken back and cannot be apologized for.*

Not a bad thought, Barnett decided, folding his notebook and sticking it back in his pocket. With a little work he should be able to get five hundred to a thousand words out of it.

Palmar came back down the hall. With him was a slender, stoop-shouldered man, whose intelligent brown eyes peered out of a face that was habitually set in a serious mien. "Mr. Barnett," he said, "permit me to introduce Mr. Quimby. Mr. Quimby was, until recently, the valet for Lord John Darby. He has been staying with us since his lordship's unfortunate demise, and has had occasion to become reasonably well acquainted with both Lizzard and Margery."

"A pleasure," Barnett said. "Please, sit here. You don't mind if I ask you a few questions? I trust Mr. Palmar has explained what I'm here for."

"A journalist," Quimby said, continuing to stand.

Barnett sensed hostility. "That's right," he said, trying to look as open and honest as possible. "I'd like to talk to you about your friends Lizzard and Margery."

"Why?"

"I am trying to gather information on the events surrounding the murders of their employers."

"They were not responsible."

"I am convinced of that also," Barnett said.

"Scotland Yard does not seem to be. They have been placed under arrest."

"I know. I believe that Inspector Lestrade was acting hastily."

"That's so," Quimby agreed. "And it was the newspapers that made him do it. Long stories about how nobody was safe, not even the nobility. Not even in their own homes, or in their own beds. The people were becoming agitated, and the Home Secretary had to do something. Scotland Yard had to arrest somebody, and right quick, too, just to show they was doing their jobs."

"There may be something in what you say," Barnett admitted. "And if journalistic outcry caused your friends to be incarcerated, then perhaps a renewed outcry can get them released again."

"The authorities will have to let them go soon anyway," Quimby said, nodding with satisfaction. "Five killings all committed the same way, and the last while they were already locked up. It stands to reason."

"Five?" Barnett asked, surprised. "I know of only four."

"Five," Quimby said. "And I'm the one who should know."

"Let's see," Barnett said, counting on his fingers. "There's Venn and Stanhope and Lord Walbine and Sir Geoffrey Cruikstaff—"

"And my late master," Quimby said. "Lord John Darby."

"He was murdered?" Barnett asked. "I don't remember hearing of it. When did it happen?"

"His body was found early in the morning of Tuesday, the fifteenth of February."

"By you?"

"No, sir. By the Earl of Arundale."

"In his bedroom?"

"No, sir. In the dining room."

"I see." Barnett leaned back in his chair, which creaked alarmingly. He shifted forward again. "What makes you think that your master's death is related to the others?"

"His throat was cut. And there was no way for anyone to have got in or out. An impossible crime, Mr. Barnett. The only one who could have committed it was me."

Barnett nodded. "I take it you didn't kill Lord John," he said.

"No, sir," Quimby said. "He wasn't a particularly easy man to work for, but I had no reason to wish to do myself out of a position.

Besides, I can't stand the sight of blood."

"I see," Barnett said. "If, then, for some reason you *had* wanted to do his lordship in, you would have used poison."

Quimby shook his head. "I couldn't do that to good food," he said. "No, sir; if I ever decide to do anybody in, I fancy I shall use a very large, very blunt instrument."

Barnett pulled out his notebook. "May I ask a few questions regarding your late employer and your two friends Lizzard and Margery?" he said.

"I will assist you," Quimby said, "because I live in fear that Inspector Lestrade will decide to add a third manservant to the two he already has in quod."

"That is one of my questions," Barnett said. "Why hasn't he? That is, why haven't I read anything about the death of Lord John Darby?"

Quimby poured himself a glass of sherry from the decanter and then seated himself gingerly on one of the hardback chairs beside the upholstered armchair Barnett had settled into. "That I cannot tell you, Mr. Barnett," he said. "Lord Arundale is a powerful enough man to have the news of the murder quenched, and he has done so. But what his motivation is, I do not know."

"Do the police know of the murder?"

"I am not sure. I would think not. There is a private inquiry agent working with the police—a Mr. Holmes—who does know about it. He has questioned me extensively. He also thinks Lizzard and Margery are innocent; he told me so."

"What did he ask you about?"

"Everything you can think of. He asked me how long I had been employed by his lordship, whether his lordship had any enemies that I knew of, what sort of books his lordship liked to read."

"Books?"

"Yes, sir. That's what he asked."

"And what did you reply? What sort of books *did* Lord John like to read?"

"I can't recall ever seeing his lordship with a book in his hands, unless it was Bradshaw."

"He restricted his reading to the railway timetables, eh?"

"His lordship did take a newspaper, sir. The *Daily Gazette*."

"I see. Can you remark on anything else of note, either in Mr. Holmes's questions or in your responses?"

"It's hard for me to tell, sir. Being interrogated is a novel experience for me."

"Well then, did Mr. Holmes seem particularly pleased or distressed at any of your responses?"

"No, sir. He did compliment me on my powers of observation at one point."

"When was that?"

"He asked me if anything was missing from the house or from his lordship's person. I replied in the negative, with the possible exception of a thin gold chain that his lordship wore on occasion around his neck. I said I couldn't be sure it was taken, as his lordship didn't always wear it."

"Did you check where it was kept when Lord John wasn't wearing it?"

"Mr. Holmes asked me that, also. I told him that I couldn't say, because I have no idea where his lordship kept it. His other personal jewelry was kept in a box on the dressing table, but I never saw the chain in there. It was when I mentioned that to him that Mr. Holmes complimented me."

"Was the chain found among his lordship's effects?"

"I don't believe so. I was present at a preliminary inventory, conducted by the family solicitor, and it was not found at that time."

"Did Lord John have anything suspended from this chain?"

"Yes, but I cannot tell you what. He always kept it beneath his shirt, next to his skin."

"I see," Barnett said. "An interesting idiosyncrasy, although probably bearing no relationship to the crime. The object cannot have been very large, and if it had been of great value, I'm sure its existence would have been known of by some other member of the family."

"That is probably so," Quimby agreed.

"What I find most interesting is the secrecy," Barnett said. "I can see why the murderer wouldn't wish to advertise, but why the Earl of Arundale would want to suppress knowledge of a murder I don't know. But I will do my best to find out. I suppose there is no chance that this earl did your boss in?"

"Did him in? No, sir. The homicide assuredly occurred before the arrival of the earl."

"Pity," said Barnett, with the heartlessness of a true newspaperman. "Now, about Lizzard and Margery. How well do you know them?"

"Fairly well," Quimby said. "As well as one can get to know somebody in a short time. We are all in the same boat, so to speak, and it gave us a strong community of interest. We were possessed of a great desire to discover who committed the murders, and how they were accomplished, even before we discovered that we ourselves might be blamed for them."

"Did you come to any conclusions?" Barnett asked.

"No, sir, unfortunately not. Of course, it is not a field that we are particularly competent in. That is why I was so pleased to discover that Mr. Holmes is taking an interest in the problem. He is highly thought of."

"In your own mind there is no chance that either of your friends might actually have had a hand in the, ah, crimes?"

"No chance, sir. Neither of them had a motive. On the contrary, they both lost good positions upon the deaths of their employers."

"Scotland Yard contends that they were paid off by some third person to either commit the deeds themselves or allow someone else access to the bedrooms."

"I cannot believe that, Mr. Barnett. Neither of them is the sort of man who would murder his employer. Also, neither of them was in a position where a desire for immediate financial gain would outweigh the need for security of employment."

"I understood that Margery was an inveterate racecourse-goer."

"Yes, sir. He has what I believe is called a 'system,' sir. Has put away quite a little nest egg with it."

"You mean he wins?"

"Not invariably, but certainly more than he loses."

"And what about Lizzard? Word is that he has a lady friend in Wembley."

"Mr. Lizzard is seeing a lady who lives in Wembley, sir. That's true enough."

"Was his butler's salary sufficient for his, ah, needs in this regard?"

Quimby pondered this for a moment. "Actually, sir," he said, "the size of Mr. Lizzard's salary is not relevant in this case, the lady in question being the sole owner and proprietress of a public house. She has asked Mr. Lizzard to come into the business as her partner, feeling, as she says, that the presence of a man about the establishment is desirable."

"It sounds like a subtle proposal of marriage," Barnett commented.

"I have no doubt that matrimony is in the lady's mind," Quimby said, "but the offer is a straightforward business offer. I would assume that she's waiting for Mr. Lizzard to do the proposing."

"An enviable position for the gentleman to be in," Barnett said, "if he is fond of the lady. And it would certainly seem from that as though Lizzard was not in any desperate need of funds."

"I would say that was so," Quimby said.

"Thank you for your assistance in this," Barnett said. "Is there anything else that has come to your attention during these past weeks that I have neglected to ask about that you think might have any bearing, however slight, on the question of the murders of your employers?"

"Well, sir," Quimby said, "as I declared before, the field of criminal investigation is out of my provenance; I really can't say what would be of interest to the trained investigator." He paused. "There is one thing, however, which I find interesting."

"And that is?"

"Well, sir, it's possibly only indirectly related to the murders themselves, but it is curious just the same. There has been another gentleman here asking questions. And despite the lack of publicity given to the subject, he seemed to know the details of the killing of my master, Lord John Darby."

"That is curious," Barnett agreed.

"Not only that, sir, but there's something even more curious about it."

"Yes?" Barnett urged.

"Well, sir, he called himself Mr. Plantagenet, but he was the spitting image of Lord John. Could have been his brother."

TWELVE

INTERLUDE: NOT TO BE

The fever called "Living"
Is conquered at last.
EDGAR ALLAN POE

The night had been long and physically exhausting; but his sport was the game of life, the game of truth, the devil's game, the only game worth the playing. And this night the game had been piquant and especially fine. Desmond Chauvelin had been loath to leave the squalid building wherein lay concealed his very private club.

Two girls this time, the older a hardened street-wise moll, coarse and foul-mouthed. But the younger—no more than sixteen, slender, with pale, unblemished skin and a fair, frightened face. A delicate flower to find among the street weeds with whom they usually practiced their arts. Where did the Master Incarnate find such a girl? Better, he realized, not to wonder. And, in truth, Chauvelin was really not interested in the girl's antecedents. It was her slender, unmarked body, her youth, her innocence, and her capacity for terror that he found so supernaturally exciting. There is a special quality in tortured innocence—a pain-heightened wide-eyed terror; fear mingled with disbelief, and the constant hope of surcease—that is highly valued by the connoisseur.

The rose-trimmed ebony brougham coursed through the deserted streets of the West End of London, its steel-shod wheels pounding an allegro along the pavement. Chauvelin stretched his plump body across the wide cushioned seat and idly watched the gaslights pass in orderly procession outside the coach window, which was rolled up against the predawn chill. For all that life was tedious and dull, he mused, there were brief moments that blazed out with a hellish fire.

He sometimes thought that at a certain point in the intricate, prolonged ceremonies of this game of games, the slaves became truly aware. He could see it in their eyes; he could watch the comprehension grow with the careful repetition of pain, the measured torment, until it surpassed the fear, and transcended the weak flesh. So it had been with this girl; knowledge had grown under the screams. The knowledge that was greater than wisdom: that all was hopeless and that there was no escape; that life had no more meaning than death, and that pain—physical pain—endless pain—sensual overwhelming pain—was the closest one could come to reality. They all said they were grateful, of course; he made them say it. It was one of the rules. Humble appreciation for the pain that gave them meaning and assured them that they were still alive.

The brougham turned off Old London Road onto Bentham Way, and the coachman slowed up as they approached the gate to Infant Court, the small, private circle on which fronted three residences: that of a duke, another of an exiled queen, and his own.

Chauvelin was roused sufficiently from his reverie by the brougham's slowing and stopping before the gate to watch as two guards—in the comic-opera uniforms of the deposed queen's household troops—opened the gate and waved the coach through. He chuckled as they closed the gate behind him. Guarded like royalty, he was. Buttoning his waistcoat and the top button of his jacket, he allowed the coachman to swing down and open the brougham's door for him and then stepped gingerly out and waddled across to his own front door. The coachman, wise in the ways of his master, clambered back up to the driver's seat and swung the brougham away without pausing for further instructions. Chauvelin expected his servants to behave like automata, without prompting, without recognition, without gratitude. When he stretched his hand out for his evening snifter of brandy, it had best be there. How it arrived there was not his concern.

The butler was neither required nor expected to man the front door after midnight; Chauvelin trusted no man's discretion save his own. He let himself in with his own two keys, lit a taper with a wooden safety match, and thumped his way up the broad staircase to his bedroom.

His bedroom was a rectangular room, much longer than it was wide. The ancestral four-post canopied bed crouched at the far end, away from the windows. Across from the door were three matched chiffoniers and a specially built triple-size wardrobe closet. Desmond Chauvelin did not believe in being far from his extensive collection of costumes and accouterments. Whatever one does, one must be correctly garbed for the occasion; and one might be called upon to do the strangest things on the shortest notice.

To the left of the door, by the large casement windows, stood his dressing table; and it was to this that he repaired, casting his garments to the right and left as he entered the bedroom. He paused only to light the gas mantle on the wall and the two beeswax candles in simple porcelain holders on the dressing table. The plum velvet jacket he hung on a drawer handle, the gold brocade waistcoat he draped over the back of a chair, the cravat he suspended from a brass hook on the gas fixture. The night's exertions had left Chauvelin happy. When he was depressed he was excessively neat.

He investigated his face in the large looking glass on the dressing table. He had heard it said that the health of the body and the soundness of the spirit could be determined by examining the eyes. Opening his eyelids wide, he stared through the glass at himself. The pupils seemed to have an unnatural luster, he thought, suggestive more of putrefaction than of health. He shook his head as if to clear it of the unnatural thought. It must be an effect of the candlelight, or the lateness of the hour. He examined his cheeks. They seemed red and puffy to him, and he could make out the tiny blue threads of broken veins beneath the skin. He pushed away from the mirror. *I lead an unhealthy life*, he thought. The idea seemed to amuse him.

What was that? A motion in the mirror? Something behind him, some great black object, flickered across his field of view in the shadowy light of the gas lamp.

There was someone in the room with him. He had not heard the door open or close, but nonetheless—

Chauvelin did not believe in ghosts, but it was with an almost supernatural dread that he leaped to his feet and turned to face the unknown intruder. He clutched at the hardbacked chair he had been sitting in and raised it chest-high, thrusting the chair legs aggressively out in front of him, examining the room through the cane bottom.

At first he thought he had been mistaken, so hard was the man to see, but after a few seconds the man's actions made him visible. It was not one of his servants, Chauvelin realized, but a tall, hulking man he had never seen before, dressed in what seemed to be evening clothes covered by a full black cape that swirled in a full circle around him, his face shrouded beneath a wide-brimmed hat of a strange design. The man appeared to be going through the pockets of Chauvelin's discarded jacket. It was incredible! Right here in Chauvelin's own bedroom, with Chauvelin fifteen feet away waving a heavy chair at him!

"Who are you?" Chauvelin demanded, noting with some pride the calmness of his voice. "How did you get in here? And what in the name of all that's holy do you think you are doing?"

The man cast the jacket aside with a grunt of annoyance, and began deftly going through the pockets of the waistcoat. The presence of Desmond Chauvelin, who was advancing slowly toward him with the wooden chair held waist-high, did not seem to deter him in the slightest.

It was certainly a lunatic, Chauvelin decided, escaped from some local asylum. Any burglar would have run at his presence, and anyone with designs on his person would not pause to rifle his jacket pockets. Chauvelin debated calling for assistance. It seemed a good plan, except for the fact that almost certainly nobody would hear him. If he could get past the man to his bed, he could use the bellpull. There was nobody presently in the butler's pantry to hear the *ting* of the bell, but in four and a half hours, when the butler came downstairs to start his day he would see the little telltale flag on the call board and come to investigate.

The man dropped the waistcoat and for the first time turned to Chauvelin. "Where is it?" he asked, in the measured, reasonable tone of one who sees nothing unusual about his question. It might have been "What is the time?" or "Unreasonably chilly, isn't it?" from an acquaintance at the track. But it wasn't. It was a cloaked stranger, in his bedroom at four o'clock in the morning.

"Where is it?" the man repeated.

"What?" Chauvelin asked. "Look, my man." He took two steps forward and prodded at the apparition with his chair. "I don't know how you got in here, or what it is you think you're doing, but I am not amused. Come to think of it, how did you get in here, anyway?"

The man knocked the chair aside as a thing of no consequence and grabbed Chauvelin by the shirtfront with his left hand. "The bauble," he said, forcing Chauvelin to his knees. "Where do you keep it?"

Chauvelin's bowels knotted with fear. He felt a great desire to be calm, to be reasonable, to keep the conversation with his uninvited guest on a friendly level. "Bauble?" he asked. "What's mine is yours, I assure you. You have but to ask. What bauble? I don't go in for baubles. I have an extensive collection of cravats—"

"The bauble," the man repeated. "The device, the signet, the devil's sign."

"Devil's—" A strange look crossed the face of Desmond Chauvelin; a look of comprehension, and of fear. Of its own volition his right hand reached down and touched the fob pocket sewn into the top of his trouser waistband.

"So!" the man said. Slapping Chauvelin's hand aside, he reached into the small pocket and pulled out a circular gold locket designed like a miniature pocket watch. He flipped open the lid and looked inside, and the devil, arms akimbo, stared back at him. Spaced evenly around the outside of the engraving, circling and confining the devil, were the capital letters D C L X V I.

"Oh, that bauble," Chauvelin said.

The man picked Chauvelin up and threw him across the room.

Chauvelin hit the floor and slid and tumbled, coming up hard against the high oaken sides of the four-poster bed. He felt something wrench and snap inside of him, and an intense pain centered itself on the left side of his chest. He did not lose consciousness, but the bubble of reason popped inside his brain and he began to whimper like a frightened baby.

There was, deep inside Chauvelin, a point of awareness, an observer that remained detached, and quizzical, and faintly amused, while his body retched with fear and curled into a tight little ball on the floor. That was interesting; he had always surmised that it would be so.

"I am going to kill you," the dark man said, striding across the room. "Don't vomit; none of the others have vomited."

Chauvelin raised his right arm defensively before his face.

From somewhere the tall dark man produced a cane. He looked down at Chauvelin almost compassionately. "I must do this, you understand," he said. "I am the wind."

Chauvelin gagged and puked all over his white shirtfront.

The tall man twisted the cane and pulled out a slim knife with a razor-sharp nine-inch blade. "The wind," he said. He bent over Chauvelin.

THIRTEEN

THE PROBLEM

Laws were made to be broken.
CHRISTOPHER NORTH

For the past five days, since the evening of his return from the observatory, Professor Moriarty had remained in his room. Surrounded by a great pile of books, mostly on loan from one of the libraries of the British Museum, he spent each day wrapped in his blue dressing gown, stretched out on his bed reading, or pacing back and forth across the small rectangle of floor between the bed and the dressing table, drinking tea, and smoking a particularly acrid brand of Turkish cigarettes.

"It is the cigarettes I object to mostly," Mrs. H told Barnett over breakfast the next Friday. "It will take months to get the smell out of the drapes and bed curtains. And when he is not smoking the wretched things himself, he cannot abide the smell."

"I find these periodic retreats of the professor's to be very trying," Barnett said. "This is the fifth time in the two years I've been here that he has disappeared into his bedroom for an extended period, and it always happens at the most awkward times. Everything has to grind to a halt around here while Moriarty takes to his bed and reads about aardvarks."

"You misunderstand," Mrs. H said, leaning forward and waving a buttered muffin in Barnett's face. "He is not retreating, no indeed! The professor is working this time. I've been with him for a good many years, and I can tell. It's his smoking those cigarettes that makes the difference. When it's lethargy or lassitude, Mr. Barnett, he smokes a pipe. When it's work, it's those vile cigarettes. And then he's asking for specific books to be brought to him. When he's in one of his sulks and in seclusion from the world, he merely works his way alphabetically through the collections in the Grenville Library or the King's Library of the British Museum."

"So the professor's hard at work up there, pacing back and forth," Barnett said.

"'At's right enough," Mummer Tolliver said from his perch in the large armchair at the head of the dining table, where he was gorging himself from the platter of fresh, hot muffins and the stoneware jug of marmalade. "And it's a fine thing to see. Not that you can see the process—the wheels turning, so to speak—it's the results! Professor Moriarty is in his room, thinking; and the world had better watch its step!"

Barnett poured some fresh cream into his coffee and stirred it with one of the delicate lace-pattern Queen Anne spoons from what Mrs. H insisted upon referring to as "the old service." "What do you suppose he spends his time thinking about while he's pacing back and forth and puffing Turkish smoke?" he asked.

"Once it was about gravity," Mrs. H said. "About how it keeps all the stars and planets circling in their proper places. He was watching this asteroid through his telescope, what he calls a 'bit of rock flinging itself around the sun,' and it was just the slightest bit late in getting to where it was supposed to be. Well, the professor went up to his room and stayed there for weeks, pacing up and down and thinking about it. Other scientists might have just decided that their observations had been faulty, but not the professor! He wrote a paper on it when he came down that tells how all the parts of the universe relate to each other. Just from watching this tiny ball of rock out in space."

"*The Dynamics of an Asteroid,*" Barnett said. "I've seen it."

"Another time he designed a safety gas mantle that would shut off the gas supply if the flame blew out. And then once he composed an epic poem in classical Greek in honor of a German archaeologist named Schliemann."

"Was it any good?" Barnett asked.

Mrs. H smiled. She carefully chewed and swallowed a bite of buttered muffin before replying, "It was Greek to me."

Tolliver chortled. Barnett frowned.

"It's when 'e 'as a real problem that the professor, 'e goes off like this," Tolliver offered. "Why, I remember one time when 'e figured out 'ow to make a whole building disappear without a trace."

"Why would he want to do that?" Barnett asked.

"It were a bank," Tolliver explained.

"Ah!" Barnett said. "I wonder what sort of problem it is this time—a heavenly equation or an earthly conundrum."

"I think it's something what might be considered in the line of business," the Mummer offered. "That Indian gent, says 'is name is Singh, has been to see the professor two afternoons this week. He's the only bloke what the professor *will* see."

"Oh, yes," Barnett said. "The author of that strange note. What sort of fellow is he? Do you think he has a commission for Professor Moriarty?"

Mrs. H rose from her seat, sniffed, murmured, "I must get about my work now," and left the room.

"*She* doesn't like to hear about that sort of thing," Tolliver commented, pointing a silver spoon at Mrs. H's retreating back. "*She* likes to suppose as 'ow we is all living off wealth what we 'as inherited from deceased uncles. The fact that we occasionally break the law in pursuit of our 'ard-earned nickers is a consideration upon which Mrs. H don't like to dwell. A right proper lady, she is."

"There are those of us who don't like to be constantly reminded of our iniquities, Mummer," Barnett said. "No matter how righteous we may feel about our particular morality, and no matter how strong a logical case we can build up for our actions, if that morality or those actions differ too strongly from those in which we were reared to believe, the struggle to convince ourselves fully will never be completely won."

Tolliver looked up at Barnett with his head cocked to one side and his mouth opened, a pose that he firmly believed connoted awe. To Barnett it looked more as though the little man had just swallowed something that had unexpectedly turned out to be alive. "You talk pretty sometimes," the Mummer said. "Like the professor."

"Your speech has a certain fascination also, Mummer," Barnett said. "You have the strangest mixture of dialects and street cant that I've ever heard."

"That's 'cause of where I were brought up," the Mummer said. "Which were everywhere. My folks was traveling people, they was. Longest we ever stayed in one place, that I can remember, were about three months. And that were when my dad broke 'is arm. We missed the whole steeplechase circuit in the north of England that season."

"Your father wasn't a jockey, was he?" Barnett asked.

"Naow, 'course not. 'E worked the crowds, same as my mum. Real elegant-looking 'e were, too, when 'e were working. 'E were the best dip I ever saw. Didn't work with nobody, neither. Cleaned out the mark all by 'imself. 'Lightfingered Harry Tolliver,' they called 'im."

"I see," Barnett said. "Then you were just carrying on the family tradition when you became a pickpocket."

"My dad taught me everything I know. 'E were better than what I ever been. 'Course 'e 'ad a natural advantage over me, being somewhat taller in stature."

"I should think being short would be more desirable. You can sort of melt into the crowd and disappear while the hue and cry is being raised."

"It don't work that way," Tolliver said. "Consider the respective sizes of the fox and the fox hunter."

"At first glance," Barnett said doubtfully, "that appears to make sense."

"'Course it were great while I looked like a little innocent," Tolliver said. "Being pushed about in my pram, dipping into hip pockets as we passed the toffs. I mean, even if anyone had caught a glimpse o' the action, who would have believed it? I can hear it now: Lord Cecil turns to his neighbor and 'e says, 'I say, Colonel, did you see that?'

"'What?' asked the colonel.

"'Sir Henry just 'ad 'is pocket picked!'

"'By Jove!' says the colonel. 'What a rum show! And where's the blighter what did it?'

"'There's the blighter, there,' says Lord Cecil, pointing into the pram.

"'What, the little bloke with the sunbonnet what can't be more than three years old?' asks the colonel. And pretty soon, you see, the subject is changed by mutual agreement."

"You must have been a charming baby," Barnett said.

"I was," Tolliver agreed. "For years and years."

* * *

Barnett finished his coffee and then went upstairs to see Professor Moriarty before leaving the house. He was meeting Miss Cecily Perrine for luncheon at Hempelmayer's. He had a question to ask her that could make this one of the most important occasions of his life, but there were some details to be taken care of first.

Moriarty was up and dressed for the day, to Barnett's surprise. His tweed suit suggested a venture into the outside world, and probably in a direction away from the city. Moriarty described clothing as "mere costume," but nonetheless he was usually correctly attired. "One should always be in the right disguise," he had said. And since gentlemen did not wear tweeds to town, the professor was probably headed toward the country.

"I was just coming down," he told Barnett. "There is a lot of work to be done in a short time. I have spent many years assembling, from among London's criminal classes, a talented and able crew of assistants. What Sherlock Holmes calls my 'henchmen.' These are men and women who, had they been better born or been given any sort of chance in life, would be serving England proudly now as statesmen, soldiers, or artisans. But they have had no such chance, so instead they serve me. And here is the job that is going to require all the talents, all the skills, all the brains that I have so painstakingly assembled."

"I gather there's a job on," Barnett said.

"A job!" Moriarty rubbed his hands together and looked satisfied. "My dear Barnett, we are going to commit the crime of the century, you and I."

"I see, Professor," Barnett said. "Just the two of us?"

"I fancy we will need a little assistance," Moriarty said. "Twenty-five or thirty people should suffice. And the artifices of all my skilled artisans. I have a task for Benlevi that should appeal to him; and old Roos the chemist, and Gilchester, the mummers' gaff. And I need to find someone who makes uniforms."

"It sounds extensive," Barnett said.

Moriarty gathered together some drawings on sheets of foolscap that were loose on his bed and put them, together with some drafting and surveying instruments, in a small portfolio. "I venture to say that no other organization but mine could attempt this," he said. "And certainly no other brain than mine could have conceived the plan necessary to penetrate the interwoven nest of formidable defenses guarding our prize."

"Which is?"

Moriarty picked up the *Morning Herald* and tossed it to Barnett. "Examine page one," he said.

"I thought you never read the newspapers," Barnett said.

"Only in the way of business," Moriarty told him. "Never for pleasure."

Barnett unfolded the *Herald* and looked over the stories on the front page. "'Police Baffled at Latest Slasher Outrage,'" he read.

"No doubt," Moriarty commented.

Barnett looked at him, and then back at the paper. "That's not it, then." He studied the headlines. "'French Official Detained by Germans in Alsace—Boulanger Protests.'"

Moriarty strapped the portfolio closed without looking up.

"'Home Rule Bill Will Face Parliament Again.'"

Moriarty chuckled.

"'Lord East Arrives on *Drakonia*.'"

"Ah!" Moriarty said. "You might further peruse that article. It has certain points of interest."

Barnett read: "'Lord East, Viceroy of India until relieved February last by Sir Harry Wittington, arrived in Liverpool yesterday afternoon aboard the Anglo-Indian Line steam packet *Drakonia*. His lordship will proceed directly to London to make arrangements for the reception and transportation of the justly famous Lord East collection of Indian artifacts.

"'The collection, a vast assemblage of archaeological material, artwork, and precious metals and gems from all over the Indian subcontinent, has been placed by Lord East on indefinite loan to the Crown for display at selected locations throughout London on the occasion of her majesty's impending Golden Jubilee.

"'The Lord East Collection is due to arrive at Plymouth aboard Her Majesty's Battleship *Hornblower* for transport by rail to the five museums in London which have been designated custodians for the duration of the Golden Jubilee, after which a permanent exhibition site will be picked and proper housing for the collection constructed.

"'The special train which is planned for carrying Lord East's priceless treasure is to consist of twenty cars—ten goods wagons for the collection, and ten special troop cars for the military escort. Unusual precautions are being taken to safeguard the treasure, which our correspondent is given to believe has been threatened by an Indian secret society dedicated to the overthrow of the British raj.

"'Lord East has held the title of Viceroy for the past six years, and is generally considered to have been most effective in spreading British rule throughout the subcontinent and bringing the civilizing influence of British law and custom to every corner of this vast land.'"

"He has also," Moriarty said, interrupting Barnett's reading, "succeeded in looting a five-thousand-year-old civilization of such items as were gaudy or valuable enough to catch his fancy, and in the process has damaged, defaced, or utterly destroyed everything he touched that he didn't covet or understand. The man is a vandal."

Barnett put the paper aside. "I have an intimation of what the problem is that you have been pondering for the past few days," he said. "Considering this article, paired with the fact that a gentleman of Indian background has been visiting you of late."

"Ah, Barnett, there is something of the investigator in you after all. Which is to the good, as that is what I've been principally employing you for during these past two years." Moriarty left the room and preceded Barnett down to his study. "I assume you wish to speak to me," he said, settling into the leather chair behind his massive desk.

"A few words, Professor," Barnett said. "I have to leave the house shortly, but I thought I'd better apprise you of a decision I've made."

Moriarty silently studied Barnett for a few seconds. "You have my approval and my blessings, for what they're worth," he said. "The state of matrimony is not for me. By its nature it cannot be an equal relationship, and I would take neither part of an unequal relationship. But I think you, if I may use a metaphor, are the sort of ship that needs a rudder."

Barnett's face turned bright pink. "Come now, Professor," he said, staring down at Moriarty, "how can you possibly know what I intend to ask you before I have done so?"

"An elementary problem, my dear Barnett. Our agreement terminates in a little over a month, I believe?"

"That is so."

"Yes. And it has been preying on your mind. You have made several oblique references to the fact over the past weeks. Usually during dinner. So, after two years of harmonious association, you wish to go your own way."

"How do you know I don't wish to extend the contract for another year or two?" Barnett asked.

"It seems clear that in that case it wouldn't occupy your thoughts. You know that I find our association satisfactory, so you can't be concerned as to whether I am preparing to throw you out. It must be that you are preparing to sever the connection. But by the same token, if you had already definitely decided to leave, you would certainly have informed me shortly after making the decision. You would, as you might say, get it off your chest."

"Probably," Barnett admitted.

"So, when my observations and deductions had taken me that far, I was faced with the following question: here is my trusted associate planning to leave my service. But his plans aren't definite, or he would certainly have informed me. Therefore, his leave-taking is predicated upon some future event that might not happen as anticipated. At first, I will admit, I contemplated the possibility that you had received an offer from some other organization; something perhaps entirely inside the law, something offering more remuneration or more interesting and varied assignments."

"Professor—"

Moriarty held up his hand. "But upon reflection," he said, "I realized that that could not be. You are not unhappy here. You are one of those who finds a necessary vitality in the practice of our endeavors. Quick thinking, fast response, the ever-present scent of danger; these things serve as anodyne and stimulant to you."

"I admit to feeling more alert, even more vital, when I'm risking my life and liberty in your employ," Barnett said. "But I am not altogether sure that it is the most sensible way to achieve that result."

"So far my logic took me," Moriarty said. "Some further reflection made it evident that you were preparing to propose marriage to Miss Cecily Perrine. If she accepts, you will wish to leave my employ, it being unchivalrous to ask her to wed someone who might conceivably be convicted of a felony."

"That is so," Barnett said.

"Therefore I offered you my approval and blessings."

"It is pointless to try to keep a secret from you, Professor," Barnett said. "I am meeting Miss Perrine for luncheon, and I expect to broach the subject to her at that time."

"I doubt whether you will surprise the young lady, either," Moriarty commented. "In my experience, although the man does the proposing, he is often the last to know."

"I'm afraid that I shall have to give up my services to you, except for those which come through the American News Service," Barnett said. "This Indian venture will probably be the last effort in which I am directly involved."

"Are you sure you desire to take part in this one?" Moriarty asked. "After all, with only a month left, and a marriage impending—"

"The lady hasn't accepted me yet," Barnett said. "I certainly hope she will, but if not I will surely need something to keep my mind off her refusal. And if she does accept, well, I'm sure the marriage will be several months off. And, after reading the newspaper description—" He paused. "Well, let me put it this way. If you are planning to remove a treasure shipment from either the *Hornblower* or a troop train, that's something I wouldn't miss for the world!"

FOURTEEN

THE ART OF DETECTION

And lo, between the sundown and the sun,
His day's work and his night's work are undone;
And lo, between the nightfall and the light,
He is not, and none knoweth of such an one.
ALGERNON CHARLES SWINBURNE

"If you are not satisfied with my reports, or with the progress I've made in the investigation," Sherlock Holmes said, rising from his caneback chair and fixing his sharp, piercing gaze on the man across the desk, "then by all means get another investigator. I shall consider myself off the case from this moment, and I shall submit no bill. Please call your clerk and ask him to retrieve my overcoat."

"No, no, Mr. Holmes, you misunderstand," the Earl of Arundale said, leaping to his feet and placing a placating hand on Holmes's arm. "We are all distressed that this murderer has not been apprehended, but I am satisfied that no man could have done more than you in the attempt. Your reports are, indeed, full of detail that was overlooked or unseen by the regular police."

Holmes dropped back onto the brocade-covered seat of his chair and stared glumly across the desk. "I apologize for taking offense so easily, my lord," he said. "But this is a vexatious problem with which you have presented me. With each subsequent murder our killer manages to make himself more obscure. This is contrary to my experience. There is something—some essential fact—which connects these killings, which I am failing to grasp. I'm certain that it is there, in those documents, staring me in the face. I have gone over them for countless hours, both the police reports and my own notes. I sense that the answer is there, sometimes I feel that I almost have it, and yet it eludes me."

"You have given us a description of the murderer," Lord Arundale pointed out. "Something that the regular police have been unable to do. And that without anyone's having seen the man."

"Bah! A description that would fit thousands of men walking about London at this moment." Holmes hit his fist against the side of the desk. "I tell you, my lord, it is maddening!"

Lord Arundale's butler, an ancient retainer in red velvet knee breeches and a swallowtail jacket, knocked on the study door and pulled it open. "The Count d'Hiver has arrived, my lord," he announced, pronouncing the name "Deever."

"Show him in, Threshampton," Lord Arundale said. He turned to Holmes. "The name is pronounced 'd'Hiver,' he explained, giving it the full value of its French ancestry. "The count is interested in this affair. He has what we would call in legal terms a 'watching brief' from the Lord Privy Seal. Her majesty herself is quite concerned. She does not, for obvious reasons, wish this concern to become known. D'Hiver regularly travels abroad for the Home Office, I am given to understand, on assignments of a confidential nature. He is considered quite perceptive and quite able. Some people find him rather abrasive—I give you warning."

"I understand, my lord," Holmes said, sounding thoughtful, "but surely—"

"What is it?"

"Nothing—nothing important. But tell me—the Count d'Hiver? Certainly that is not a British title, neither in style nor name."

"The title is French," Lord Arundale said, "but the d'Hivers are English for the last hundred years. The present count's great-grandfather, or some such, came over one jump ahead of Robespierre. Got out of revolutionary France by a neck, if you see what I mean."

The count was a slight, delicate-looking man with a precisely trimmed beard that made his face look angular. His family's hundred years in England did not show in his taste in clothing; his double-breasted blue foulard suit jacket covered a white flowered waistcoat with just a touch of lace along the collar. The effect was so un-British, so Parisian, as to skirt the bounds of taste for a proper London gentleman. But Count d'Hiver bore it well. His every move reflected an air of panache and a manner of self-assurance that made it clear that he valued no man's opinion save his own. He strode into the room and stopped in the middle of the carpet, his gaze darting about like that of a predatory animal in search of its lunch.

The Earl of Arundale rose and performed the necessary introductions. "Mr. Holmes was just about to discuss with me some of the conclusions he has reached," he said.

"I have read your reports," d'Hiver said, looking down his aquiline nose at Holmes, "and those of the police. The police are bunglers. You show a little imagination, Mr. Holmes. But still, we don't seem to be any closer to apprehending our killer."

"That is, unfortunately, the truth," Holmes admitted. "There has been very little to work on so far. The first four killings took place before I was called in. Thus I was unable to examine the scenes of the crimes until well after the most suggestive evidence had been handled and tramped over by a dozen other people. Three of the murder rooms had been cleaned before I got to see them. Nonetheless several facts of interest have been uncovered. I have initiated several lines of inquiry, but so far they have all proved fruitless."

"In your last report there is a description of the man you claim is the killer," d'Hiver said. "How much of it is guesswork?"

"I never guess," Holmes said. "And if I were prone to guesswork, I certainly wouldn't do it in my reports. What I have given you is my considered opinion, based upon investigation and deduction. It may prove to be wrong in one or two particulars, but on the whole it is accurate."

Count d'Hiver perched himself on one of the caneback chairs, his body rigidly erect and tilted slightly forward, his hands crossed over the massive gold knob on his ebony cane. "Accurate it may be," he snapped, "useful it is not! Your description is as vague as the fortune-teller's fabled 'tall, dark man.'"

"Sketchy, perhaps, Count d'Hiver," Holmes said, "but hardly vague. The man is between five feet ten and six feet tall, weighs about twelve stone, is neither adolescent nor aged—I estimate his age at forty to forty-five, but there I could be off. He has light-brown hair of medium length, dresses like a gentleman, is not obviously disfigured, and is probably Eastern European. If so, he speaks English fluently."

"Really?" D'Hiver said, his voice showing aristocratic doubt. "And this description of a man who has not been seen is pieced together from your examination of rooms where the experts of Scotland Yard can find no clues. Tell me, is there anything else that has eluded the professionals?"

"A few items," Holmes said, apparently oblivious to d'Hiver's sarcastic tone. "The man is in good physical condition, athletic and robust. He picks his victims carefully, not at random. All of the murdered men have—for the killer—something in common."

D'Hiver leaned forward in his chair, his eyes like dark gimlets peering at Holmes. "And that is?"

Holmes shook his head. "That I cannot tell you. That is the point which has succeeded in eluding me."

"Then this is not the work of a lunatic?" Lord Arundale asked.

"On the contrary, my lord," Holmes said. "This is clearly the work of a lunatic. But the killings are not random. This lunatic has a pattern, a goal, a fixed purpose. And he knows something that we do not."

"What do you mean?" Lord Arundale asked.

"Look at it this way, my lord. Let us say that the killer hates the color red, and is killing everyone he sees dressed in red. Well then, the pattern should be obvious, but we don't see it. We are colorblind. We cannot solve this hypothetical case until someone who is not colorblind happens to mention that all of the victims have been clad in red."

"You believe these victims are tied together in some fashion?" Count d'Hiver asked.

"Yes, I would say so. Something definite and precise, beyond the obvious similarities of sex and class."

"Why? What evidence have you of this?"

"Evidence? I have nothing so strong as to be called 'evidence.' I have, rather, hints, suggestions; nothing better. However, I also have my knowledge and experience, and upon that I base my conclusion."

"You have found nothing that would support my fears of a foreign connection?" Lord Arundale asked.

"None," Holmes said. "It was in following that possibility that I got led astray some days ago and ended up at the country estate of my old friend Professor James Moriarty."

"I read of that," Lord Arundale said. "The police report of the raid did not go into much detail. I had the feeling much was left out."

"It doesn't matter, my lord. It was a mistake. Sometimes specialized knowledge can lead one astray. The knowledge that there is one great villain yet unhanged can temporarily blind one to the fact that other villainy can coexist. I am not yet totally convinced that Moriarty is not involved, but I must admit that the preponderance of evidences would so indicate."

"These 'hints' of a common tie between the victims," Count d'Hiver said. "Upon what sort of facts, of clues, are they based?"

Holmes turned to face the count. "I would rather wait until I have had a chance to assemble a few more facts," he said. "I dislike presenting my conclusions piecemeal in this fashion. I agreed to keep you informed as to my progress only because of the unusual circumstances, and because her majesty is interested. This is not my usual way of proceeding, and I don't like it."

"My dear Mr. Sherlock Holmes," Count d'Hiver said, "we don't have time for you to assemble. There are decisions that must be made now, and to make them intelligently we must have all the available information. I'm sure you understand." He smiled. His teeth were even and white, and gave the impression of being sharp.

"Let *us* tell *you* what is happening, Mr. Holmes," Lord Arundale said. "There have been six men murdered in London in the past six weeks. All gentlemen of the upper classes. All apparently murdered by the same hand while they were in their own home—in some cases in their own bedrooms. The police have been powerless to stop these attacks."

"It is difficult to stop what you are unable to anticipate," Holmes commented.

"Mr. Holmes," Lord Arundale said, "the people are getting restless."

"The people," Holmes said, "only know of five of the six killings."

"And a good thing, too," Count d'Hiver said.

"Considering how selective our murderer is," Holmes commented, "it is clear that the great majority of the citizens of London would be better off worrying about being run down by a horse tram. Unless one is a male, over thirty-five, has an income in excess of twenty thousand pounds a year, and has some pretensions to aristocracy, one is almost certain not to find himself on our killer's little list."

"The point is," Lord Arundale said, "that if a mysterious killer can take these six lives without our being able to stop him, then nobody in London is safe. And the people, even the common people who are admittedly not targets, are beginning to sense that. There is a certain nervous tension building in the city."

"I concede that," Holmes said.

"The last major riots in London were over twenty years ago," Lord Arundale said, "but this could provoke the sort of feeling that leads to riots."

Holmes tapped his finger on the desk. "The feeling that leads to riots," he said, "is more easily provoked by the sort of behavior the police are currently indulging in. At, I believe, the instigation of the Home Office."

"We must keep them busy," Count d'Hiver said. "Let them feel that they are accomplishing something. It is necessary for their morale."

"Rounding up everyone who has ever been arrested for a crime in the past fifteen years?" Holmes asked. "Scotland Yard doesn't have the manpower for that sort of job. As a result the people they are rounding up are bullied and harassed merely because the police do not have the time to do the job right. You are making the criminal classes apprehensive, which is not a good way to maintain law and order."

"Doubtless," Count d'Hiver said. "But expediency is not the best basis for a standard of law enforcement. Tell me, what evidence have you found that indicates to you that the victims of these murders share some specific connection?"

"Aside from the dramatic evidence of their common *fate?*" Holmes leaned back and laced his fingers together. "I'll tell you," he said, "but I warn you that you won't be as impressed by it as I am. It is a delicate skein, only seen by the experienced observer. And right now these clues are tentative, since I don't know where they lead. I need more time. I must have additional evidence."

"You think a few more murders will provide you with the evidence you need?" Lord Arundale asked.

"Most certainly, my lord. And since there is no indication that the killer is planning to stop, I imagine the necessary clues will soon be forthcoming."

D'Hiver frowned. "A heartless viewpoint."

"If I could catch the killer now," Holmes said, "I would. On the other hand, if he were to stop the killing now without having the grace to identify himself, I should consider that preferable to his committing the one last murder that traps him. I am not heartless, merely rational."

Lord Arundale sighed. "I am glad this doesn't seem to be a political crime," he said. "I would not like to be charged with deciding which of the great European powers is killing off the English aristocracy. I would enjoy even less having to take some action against such a power or accuse it in some public forum of such a vile act."

"Accuse?" Count d'Hiver snorted. "Talking never got anyone anything but hoarse. Retaliation, that's the key to international affairs. An eye for an eye." He tapped his cane impatiently on the hardwood floor. "Come now," he said to Holmes, "tell us your theory about the connecting link between the murders."

Holmes considered. "Certain similarities point in the direction of a common cause," he said. "For example, either the room or the body of each of the victims was searched by the murderer."

"That sounds perfectly normal," Lord Arundale said. "Not that

I have any great knowledge of what is normal for a murderer; but I should think that if one is going to go to the trouble of killing someone, one would want to gain something out of it."

"Robbery was not the motive for any of these killings," Holmes said.

"Quite so," Count d'Hiver said. "That much is clear from the reports. Not the primary motive, certainly. But a quick search for some extremely portable wealth? I mean, a man who commits a murder is quite probably willing to steal."

"Lord Walbine had a pocket watch on his person," Holmes said, "crafted by Pronzini and Wilcox. The cloisonné inlay work on the case alone should have made it a national treasure. I can't think of anything more portable. Even the meanest fence would feel guilty at offering less than five hundred pounds for it."

"The villain, whoever he is, might have missed it," Lord Arundale said.

"Isadore Stanhope had a ruby stickpin the size of a robin's egg," Holmes said. "George Venn had fifty pounds in Bank of England notes on the table by his bed. Sir Geoffrey Cruikstaff had a solid gold cigarette case in his pocket and an extensive coin collection in the top drawer of his secretary. None of these was disturbed."

"Then nothing was taken?" d'Hiver asked.

"I believe," Holmes said carefully, "that *something* was taken. The murderer searched for and found some small object at the scene of each of his killings. That object is what he took away with him."

"What object?" Lord Arundale asked.

"That I don't know," Holmes said. "Inferential evidence suggests that it was small, unremarkable, easily concealed on the person, and of little intrinsic value."

"You say the killer took something from *each* of his victims? What sort of thing do you suppose it could be?" Count d'Hiver asked.

"A key, perhaps," Holmes said. "Or a medallion or signet of some sort."

"Key to what?" Lord Arundale asked.

Holmes smiled. "I would welcome ideas as to that, my lord. The only thing I would suggest is that whatever the object is, it was an identical object for each of the victims."

Count d'Hiver stared silently at Holmes, his thoughts clearly somewhere else. Lord Arundale tapped his fingernails on the polished surface of his desk thoughtfully. "Some small object," he said, "taken from each of the victims, and identical in each case. Why do you feel that it's the same object in each case?"

"The murderer was certainly looking for some specific object," Holmes said. "Such insistence would indicate that the object, whatever it was, must be in some way part of the motive for the crime. Surely it would be stretching the bounds of credulity to suggest that it was a different object in each case."

"I don't know about that," Count d'Hiver said. "Perhaps our killer is some sort of fetishist. Perhaps he merely wants some small memento from each of his victims. Something to wear on his watch chain."

"Perhaps." Holmes stood up. "Is there any further way in which I can assist or enlighten either of you gentlemen at the moment? No? Then I shall get back to my investigations. It may be that with luck I can prevent another killing. But I am not sanguine, my lords. I am afraid that there will be more blood shed before we reach the bottom of this."

"Keep us informed," Lord Arundale said.

"I shall, my lord," Holmes assured him.

FIFTEEN

A MODEST PROPOSAL

When Chloris to the temple comes,
Adoring crowds before her fall:
She can restore the dead from tombs,
And every life but mine recall.
I only am by love designed
To be the victim for mankind.
JOHN DRYDEN

When one is in the grip of a powerful emotion, small events can hold magnified significance. Benjamin Barnett paused at a flower stall on his way to lunch with Cecily Perrine and purchased a bunch of violets. Then, as he walked the last few blocks to the restaurant, he found himself staring at the flowers and thinking what a paltry, inappropriate gift they were for the woman one intended to marry. This thought grew into a conviction, and so he paused at a confectioner's and selected a pound of mixed chocolates, which were wrapped in fancy paper and tied with a bow. But then, after he had paid for the chocolates, the indecision returned, and he found himself unable to choose between the flowers and the chocolates.

The problem, Barnett realized, was not with the gifts. He would have liked to have given her something major, something important—a ring, a pendant, a brooch speckled with precious gems—but he couldn't very well do that. It would be in very bad taste until after he had asked her father formally for her hand. But under the circumstances, limited to a token gift, flowers were nice. Chocolates were acceptable. It was the imminent proposal itself that was making his hands go clammy and his heart beat triple-time against his chest. He certainly wanted to ask her—more than anything in the world he wanted Cecily Perrine to be his wife. He fully intended to ask her. But he wasn't sure that he actually could. He felt his heartbeat increase in speed and pressure as he just walked along with a bunch of flowers under one arm, a pound of chocolates under the other elbow, and *thought* about proposing to Cecily.

What if she turns me down? he thought. *What if she smiles at me gently and says, "Benjamin, you know that I do love you—but it is like a brother. I've never thought of you the other way!"* After all, it could happen. He knew she was fond of him, but he had no assurance that it went beyond that. What if she *laughed* at him?

On the whole, Barnett decided, women had it much better in this society than men did. Men had to do the asking. Everything from "May I have this dance?" to "Will you marry me?" If a woman was rejected it was indirect, by not being asked; and if no one knew that she expected to be asked, then it remained a private, personal grief. Romantic traces of such past opportunity lost could be seen as a secret anguish in love-haunted eyes. A man was rejected as a public act, a direct holding up of one's innermost desires and most private feelings to the jeers of the crowd, a humiliation that could be felt as a physical wrenching, like a knife in the pit of the stomach.

When Barnett reached the front door of Hempelmayer's, he still had to choose between the chocolates and the flowers. Walking in with both, he was convinced, would make him look ridiculous. And if there's anything a man in love cannot stand, it is to look ridiculous. Especially since he realizes that in word and deed, he is already sufficiently ridiculous with no external aid. Or so Mr. Wilde, the American News Service's favorite epigrammatist, would maintain. But then, Mr. Wilde didn't seem to like women very much.

Barnett looked at his two purchases and realized that he would have to make an arbitrary decision.

"Are you married?" he asked the elderly doorman who pulled open the ornate brass-on-glass door for him.

"For these past twenty-eight years, sir," the doorman told him. "Nine little ones. Some of 'em nary so little anymore."

"Well then, here," Barnett said, handing the man the elaborately wrapped box of chocolates. "A present for your wife."

"Thank ye, sir." The doorman touched the brim of his uniform cap with his knuckle. "Thank ye very much."

Cecily was perched like a princess on an overstuffed plush couch in the anteroom, waiting for Barnett. "About time you arrived," she said. "You are a quarter of an hour late."

"I'm sorry," Barnett said. "I didn't realize the time. My watch must be slow. I stopped to get you some flowers. Violets. Here." He thrust the bunch at her.

"Well, that's very nice," Cecily said in an insincere voice. "Quite thoughtful of you." She rose and took the tissue-paper-wrapped bunch, holding them at arm's length, as though they had a bad odor. "I'll just leave them in the cloakroom until after our meal."

"I'll do it," Barnett said, retrieving the vegetation. "I have to hang up my topcoat anyhow." He disposed of his coat and the flowers in the cloakroom and returned. A short, fussy man with a prim mustache showed them to their table, presented them with their menus, and pranced off. Barnett looked across the table at Cecily. "Would you have preferred chocolates?" he asked. "It will just take me a second to switch with the doorman."

Cecily looked up from the menu. "What's that?" she asked. "Switch what?"

"The violets. I didn't know you disliked violets. Very few people have a natural antipathy to them. It's just my misfortune that you are one of them. Well, live and learn, I always say. Now that I've learned, I shall never offend your delicate nostrils with the scent of violets again."

"Benjamin, my dear, I like violets," Cecily said, looking over her menu at him. "I assure you I am very pleased that you have brought me violets. I shall put them in water as soon as I can, and carry the vase about with me everywhere until the poor things wilt and the petals fall off. I *love* violets."

"The way you treated the poor things when I handed them to you, I had formed quite a contrary opinion," Barnett told her.

"I am sorry," Cecily said. "I was distracted. I was angry. I still am, if it comes to that. But I do apologize for taking it out on you."

"Angry?" Barnett asked. "Why are you angry? Listen, Cecily, if someone has offended you, tell me about it and let me be angry too."

"Circumstances conspire to offend me, Benjamin," Cecily said. "This most recent circumstance has, I fear, provoked a reaction quite out of relation to its cause. The fault, I believe, lies in the fact that I was raised by my father. And my father is a man most intolerant of the stifling stupidity of convention and the rigid imbecility of custom."

"I see," said Barnett, who didn't at all. "Some custom has angered you? What sort of custom?"

"Have you ever stopped to realize how unequal is the relationship between men and women in our society?" Cecily asked, staring intently across the table at Barnett. "Have you ever considered how much freedom men have in everyday discourse and commerce, and how stifling it is to be a woman?"

"I am not sure what you mean," Barnett said, taken slightly aback by the intensity with which his loved one was speaking on a subject to which he had never given much thought.

"I arrived at this restaurant fifteen minutes before you did," Cecily said.

"I told you I'm sorry—"

Cecily raised a hand to stop him. "Not you," she said. "I asked to be seated when I arrived. The manager informed me that unescorted women are not seated in his establishment. The way he said 'unescorted' was, of itself, an insult. I told him my escort would be along shortly. He replied that when my escort arrived he would be pleased to seat us both."

Barnett thought about this for a moment, and then his face turned red and he started to rise, but Cecily reached across and put her hand on his shoulder. "Please don't make a scene," she said. "That would accomplish nothing except to make me feel worse."

"Someone should teach a boor like that to have proper respect for a lady!" Barnett exclaimed.

"Perhaps," Cecily said, "but an altercation in a public place will not accomplish that end. If I thought it would, I would have started one myself."

Barnett relaxed on his seat. "Yes," he said, "I guess you would have."

"This is merely a symptom of the condition of women in our society today," Cecily said. *"That's* what makes me angry!"

"Now, I don't think that's fair," Barnett said. "This boob, this scoundrel, is obviously *non compos mentis.* Anyone who is capable of confusing a lady like you with a, ah, woman should not be in a position where he has to make such fine discernments."

"That is not my point," Cecily insisted. "It's the inequality of the situation that frustrates and angers me. If a man wants to eat in here alone, and is reasonably well dressed, the manager doesn't ask to see proof of his gentle birth. If a woman, no matter how well dressed, wishes to eat lunch but is not currently in possession of an escort, the manager feels free to assume that she's 'no better than she ought to be.' In the first place, what authority has he to assume any such thing? In the second place, even if it were so, is that any reason to deprive her of the right to eat lunch?"

"Now, Cecily," Barnett said. "Women in this society are protected, guarded; all in all, they are treated far better than men."

"Protected from whom?" Cecily demanded. "Guarded from what?"

"You are an intensely independent person, Cecily, quite determined to have your own way in everything. And I admire you for it," Barnett said. "But most ladies enjoy the protection of their special status."

"You think so?" Cecily asked. "Try asking some of them. You might be surprised."

Barnett realized that now was not a propitious time to propose marriage. He should probably postpone the question until another day. But he had spent all morning building up the courage and it would probably be even harder another time. He decided to wait until dessert.

They spoke of many things during the course of the meal. One of the hallmarks of a good journalist is a wide and searching curiosity. The conversation ranged from the possibility of a new war in Europe to the claims of a Scottish inventor that he was perfecting a machine that could fly. The question of the rights and indignities of women gradually faded into the past, although Barnett was sure that it was not forgotten. He would have to give it some thought.

Toward the end of the entrée they reached the subject of the series of murders. Cecily was quite wrapped up in the articles she was doing about the murders. "There must be something that connects these crimes," she insisted to Barnett. "The poor man is obviously in the grip of some overpowering compulsion that causes him to seek out these particular victims."

"By 'the poor man,' I assume you are referring to the mysterious individual who has been slitting the throats of perfectly innocuous middle-aged men in their own bedrooms," Barnett said.

Cecily poked thoughtfully at the remains of a poached whitefish on her plate. "A man who commits a heinous crime," she said, "has put himself outside the bounds of common human intercourse. This is not an easy thing to do, not an easy decision to make. To choose to be isolated from the rest of humanity, there must be a compelling need. One can feel a revulsion at the deed, and at the same time pity the man who felt compelled to commit it."

"I'd rather save my pity for the victims," Barnett said. "The frightening thing about a murderer like this one is that he *isn't* isolated from society. We could breathe easier if he were. He is embedded in our midst, and hidden by the camouflage of assumed innocence. There is nothing about his appearance or manner to proclaim him as a secret slitter of throats. He probably discusses each murder with his friends, and shakes his head in wonder that anyone could commit such a horrible deed."

"A man like this has no friends," Cecily said. "That is one of the signs of the type of abnormality that causes a man to feel impelled to commit this sort of crime."

"How can you be so sure about that?" Barnett asked. "He may be the most popular man in his club. He may have to employ two social secretaries to respond to all his invitations."

Cecily put down her fork and pushed her plate aside. "I don't think so," she said. "I've been doing some reading, you might say research, on the background and antecedents of the killer type, and I would say that almost certainly he is a very lonely man."

One waiter returned to hand them dessert menus, while another sneaked in behind the first and removed the fishy remains from in front of Cecily.

"Now," Barnett said, after the waiter went off to have vanilla soufflés constructed for their desserts, "what have you found in your research that indicates our murderer is such a lonely man? You think he is driven to commit these crimes out of simple boredom?"

"No," Cecily told him. "You have it the wrong way around. I believe this man is so driven by his need to commit these crimes that he has no time for normal human desires like companionship, or love, or recreation."

"What about eating?" Barnett asked.

"I would say he eats as an animal eats," Cecily said. "He ingests food to give him the necessary energy to keep going. I doubt if he cares what he eats, or is even aware what the dish in front of him contains."

"And upon what do you base this stark image of a man driven by forces stronger than himself?"

"On my study of similar crimes committed in the recent past," Cecily said. "The Düsseldorf Slasher of fifteen years ago was a man named Roehm. When the police apprehended him he was living in a bare, unfurnished room with only a couple of blankets on the floor to sleep on. The only clothing he possessed was several changes of undergarments and one extra shirt. And this was a formerly respectable, middle-class man."

"Who was he killing," Barnett asked, "and why?"

"He killed three magistrates, two clerks of the court, two bailiffs, and a man that drove the prison wagon before he was captured."

"He must have had it in for the courts."

"His wife was arrested and convicted of a homicide and sentenced to the mines. Three years later it was discovered that she was innocent, and she was released. It was too late; the hard labor and terrible conditions at the mines had weakened her until she was beyond medical help. The state gave her thirty gold marks for recompense. She died six months later. A year after that the murders began."

"I'd say the man had a just grievance," Barnett commented. "Imagine what emotions must have been bottled up inside of him. It's not surprising that they came out as a series of slashings."

"He was certainly acting under the influence of a powerful compulsion," Cecily agreed. "As was the Mad Bomber of Paris in 1878, who went around leaving infernal devices in the left-luggage rooms of railway stations. As was Mr. Pinkley of Chicago, who made it his practice to give bonbons laced with arsenic to ladies of the street."

The soufflés were delivered at this moment, and Barnett stared down at his. It was very attractive, rising a full three inches off the top of the dish. "Arsenic, eh?" he said.

Cecily laughed. "Don't worry," she told him. "I've heard of its being sprinkled into omelets, but never a soufflé."

Barnett looked up and grinned at her. "You can't be too careful," he said.

"So I've been led to believe," Cecily said.

They ate their desserts in contemplative silence. The time, Barnett realized, had come. He took a deep breath. "Cecily," he said, "there is something I'd like to ask you."

"Yes, Benjamin?"

He took another deep breath. "I, ah, would like to ask your father for your hand in marriage."

Cecily put her fork down carefully on the side of the plate and nudged it with her finger until it was in the perfect position. The silence stretched on.

"Say something, Cecily," Barnett finally blurted out.

For another long moment there was no response. Cecily's eyes darted around as though she felt trapped at the table and was looking desperately for a way out. Then she turned to Barnett and pointed a finger at him. "I'm certain you don't realize this," she said, "but that proves my point, what you just said. It's so typical. And you're not even aware of what you did."

"What do you mean, 'not aware'?" Barnett demanded, his voice cracking slightly with the effort to suppress both his anger and his bewilderment at this reaction. "I just proposed marriage to you, that's what happened."

"No, it isn't," she said. "You just informed me that you were going to ask my father. Is it my father that you wish to marry? If not, then why are you going to ask him?"

This, Barnett decided, was not his day. Perhaps there was something to astrology after all. "It is the custom," he said. "What I'm actually doing is asking you, you know that. But your father has to give you away."

"Why?" she asked. "Supposing Father says no?"

"I, ah, hadn't thought of that," Barnett said. "Frankly, if you say yes, I don't give a damn what your father says."

"That is courageous of you," she said.

Barnett dropped his fork onto his plate with a little silver clatter. "All right!" he said. "I'm not asking your father, I'm asking you. Cecily, will you marry me?"

"I don't know," she said.

"What?"

Cecily leaned forward and took his hand. "I would like to marry you," she told him. "But I'm not sure you'd really like to be married to the sort of wife I'd be."

"Cecily, I love you," Barnett said. "This table's too wide for me to hold you properly, but I love you more than anything and I want you to be my wife. I know that's trite, but there it is. I have loved you for some time. Since the day you first knocked on the door of the American News Service, as a matter of fact."

"It took you long enough to get around to declaring it," she said.

"I had commitments," Barnett said. "There were reasons."

"No, never mind that," she said. "That was unfair of me. I've been aware for some time of how you feel about me. And I'm honored."

"Honored," Barnett said. "Which means that you don't love me."

"No, it doesn't," Cecily said. "Benjamin, dearest, I do love you. I even wish to marry you. I just don't think you *really* want to marry me."

"With all my heart," Barnett said.

"You want me to be your wife."

"Yes."

"You want to set up a home for me."

"*With* you."

"You want me to quit work."

"Of course."

"Well, I want to marry you, Benjamin, but I have no desire to give up my career. I want to be a reporter. I don't want to just sit home and tend the babies—if we have any babies."

"Why not?" Benjamin asked. "What's wrong with tending babies?"

"I'll tell you what," Cecily said. "I'll keep my job and *you* stay home and tend the babies."

"Cecily!" Benjamin said, sounding positively shocked.

"Those are my terms," Cecily said. "Have you a counter offer?"

"Don't be ridiculous," Barnett said.

"You think it's ridiculous, do you?" Cecily demanded. "All my life I've wanted to be a reporter. And now, when I've just begun to make it, when I'm doing a series that's picked up by our whole list, when I've been offered a job in the city room of the *Chronicle*, you think I should give it up just because you happen to love me and I happen to love you. Well, I tell you, Mr. Barnett, it won't wash. It just won't wash!"

"You love me?" Barnett said.

"Of course I love you," Cecily replied. "What do you think I've been telling you?"

"Oh," he said. "But—now let me see if I understand this correctly—you don't want to marry me because then you'd have to stay at home and tend the babies, if we had any babies, rather than being free to pursue your career as a journalist."

"That's right," Cecily said. "Although you make it sound horrible. What is so wrong with a woman's wanting to do something with her life?"

"I, ah, don't know," Barnett confessed. "I've never given it much thought. I mean, basically I see nothing wrong with it at all. I think women should certainly be as free as men to do—most things. But when I think of my wife, I must confess that I picture her at home running the household while I battle the outside world."

"I agree it is a lovely image," Cecily said. "And there are undoubtedly many women who would dearly love to occupy the position you imagine. Which is why I think that although I might love you, we should not marry. It would be stifling to me and dreadfully unfair to you. I must be free, Benjamin, to take advantage of whatever life has to offer!"

"Well," Benjamin said, "if you must..." He stared into his coffee. "I will admit that I have not given much actual thought to what I want or need from a wife. What I have is mostly half-formed images involving you and me sitting around a fire and holding each other in various, ah, postures."

"I am sorry, Benjamin," Cecily said.

Slowly Barnett raised his eyes to meet hers. "The *Chronicle*?" he asked.

"I meant to tell you about that," she said.

SIXTEEN

THE GAME

In a contemplative fashion
And a tranquil frame of mind,
Free from every kind of passion
Some solution let us find.
W.S. GILBERT

Int is commonly believed that work is anodyne of sorrow. Benjamin Barnett reminded himself of this as he focused his energies on the work at hand. First there was the necessary rearranging of the staff of the American News Service in the absence of Cecily Perrine. Then there was the detail work for Professor Moriarty, as he perfected his plans for the impossible crime. But the sorrow remained. There seemed to be nothing he could do that did not, in some tortuous way, remind him of Cecily. She had left the American News Service office to take a feature reporter's position with the *Morning Chronicle*. He did not begrudge her that. It was the sort of experience she could not get at the Service. And she was very sincere in wanting the experience. She had taken a cut in salary on accepting the new position.

The American News Service had not actually lost Miss Perrine as a writer, since they were free to buy her stories from the *Chronicle* for the American wire. But the office was certainly empty without her. Through a conversation with the *Chronicle's* general manager, who was simultaneously resentful and apologetic about acquiring Cecily Perrine, Barnett found out how and why the job offer was made. The *Morning Chronicle* suddenly realized that it was in great and immediate need of a female reporter. This discovery was the direct result of Lord Hogbine's having left the sixty-year-old newspaper to his wife in his will. And Lady Hogbine, who had already used much of the unentailed Hogbine fortune to endow an undergraduate ladies' college at Oxford, a home for unwed mothers in Stepney, and a trade school for female typewriter operators in Bethnal Green, was shocked to discover that there were no ladies on the reporting staff of the *Morning Chronicle*. Cecily Perrine was one of the few experienced reporters who also happened to be a lady.

"She does love me, you understand," he told Moriarty in a confidential conversation in the privacy of the professor's study. "It is the prospect of matrimony that she finds unacceptable. She is not willing to give up her freedom to become any man's wife."

"A sensible girl," Moriarty said. "Wife is the only position of involuntary servitude left in the civilized world since Mr. Lincoln's Emancipation Proclamation."

Barnett snorted and left the room. He had felt the need to confide in someone, but this was not what he wanted to hear.

Moriarty sent Barnett to Plymouth to meet the *Hornblower* when she docked. "My plans are nearly complete," he said. "But there is certain information that is sketchy or absent. You are a reporter. You have unquestioned access to the various officials and a historical right to ask stupid questions. Find out everything you can about the transportation of the treasure."

"What, exactly, do you want to know?" Barnett asked.

"Details," Moriarty told him. "I want all the picayune, unimportant little details. Everything, no matter how small or seemingly insignificant, is of interest to me."

"Supposing they don't want to tell me anything?" Barnett said. "After all, they will be transporting a priceless treasure. The police and the army may be smart enough to want to keep their exact plans a secret."

"Don't go to the military or police authorities," Moriarty said.

"Interview Lord East. He is the sort of busybody who will insist upon knowing every facet of the plan. Actually, he probably formulated the plan himself. He fancies himself awfully clever."

And so Barnett arrived in Plymouth the day before the battleship *Hornblower* was scheduled to tie up to the military dock. That evening, in his hotel, Lord East allowed himself to be interviewed by the gentlemen of the press. He and his entourage occupied an entire floor, and they seemed to have brought along enough furnishings and paraphernalia to outfit an expedition to Tibet. Lord East was a short, fat man whose once-fair complexion had turned beet-red from years of exposure to the Indian sun. He dressed in the best Savile Row approximation of an oriental potentate, and carried a swagger cane of dark-brown wood, traced with a delicate ivory inlay.

"Always glad to talk to you newspaper wallahs," Lord East told the score of fidgeting reporters who had gathered in his receiving room. He climbed up onto a rattan footstool, which one of his Hindu servants placed carefully in front of his feet. "The average Briton doesn't know nearly enough about the empire we've been carving out for him for the past hundred years. The Indian subcontinent is a vast and fascinating region, more than ten times the size of these little islands. And we have made it ours; sent forth the best we breed, our sons and brothers, and made it ours. We have unified some two hundred petty kingdoms under the British raj. I am proud of my small part in this great achievement."

A stocky man with a great walrus mustache who stood in the left-hand lobe of the flock of reporters raised his hand. "Tell us, your lordship," he called out, "would you say it has been as rewarding for the natives as it has been for the British?"

Lord East looked down at him in annoyance. "What was that?" he asked.

"This conquest," the man said with a slight, undefinable mid-European accent. "These unifications—would you say they have been on the whole good for the native peoples in question? Educational, perhaps?"

"Who are you, sir?" Lord East demanded.

"Heinrich von Hertzog, your lordship. *Berliner Tagenblatt.*"

Lord East struck a pose on his footstool that would have been the envy of many a piece of heroic statuary. "Welcome to England, Mr. Hertzog," he said, his voice carrying a burden of frigid disapproval that is only achieved at the better public schools. "It is certainly a pleasure to have you among us. To answer your question, what's good for Britain is good for the empire. That should be self-evident."

The *Berliner Tagenblatt* correspondent noted down the answer, and seemed satisfied with it. Even pleased. Perhaps he was picturing how it would sound to his two million Anglophobic German readers. "Thank you, your lordship," he called.

Lord East looked around. "Anything, ah, else?" he asked.

"The treasure, your lordship," called a beefy gentleman in a broadly checked jacket that would have looked more at home on a racecourse tout than a reporter.

Lord East peered down at him. "I didn't know the 'pink 'un' was represented here," he ventured, and smiled broadly when he got the laugh he had been trying for.

"Jameson, your lordship. *Daily Telegraph*," the beefy reporter said, joining in the general chuckle. "Excuse the inappropriate attire, but I was called here from a rather different assignment."

"Indeed?" Lord East remarked. "I trust you backed a winner." Satisfied that his reputation as a wit was secure, his lordship now struck another pose. "The Lord East Collection," he said, "how can I describe it to you?"

There was a rustling from the crowd, as reporters pulled out their notebooks and licked the points on their pencils.

"India is a land of unbelievable contrasts," his lordship began. "The grandeur of past ages surrounds one in India hidden under the filth and squalor of the present. When I first arrived in Calcutta twelve years ago, as resident director of the Northeastern and Southern Indian Railway, I determined to make it my job to rescue as much of the rapidly disappearing storehouse of irreplaceable knowledge and archaeological beauty as possible. My concern was for the instruction and pleasure of all the people of the empire, and especially the people of India itself, so that they could know their own past before it was eradicated brick by brick. I also strove for the future, so that those who come after us can have some knowledge of those who came before. I have not stinted of my own time or fortune in making these acquisitions, and the result, twenty tons of unique and irreplaceable archaeological treasure, is arriving tomorrow aboard Her Majesty's Battleship *Hornblower.*"

As Lord East paused for breath, the man standing to Barnett's right, a gentleman named Higgins who was a correspondent for the *Pall Mall Gazette*, leaned toward Barnett and whispered, "He stole it all, you know."

"Stole it?" Barnett whispered.

"Exactly. Oh, there are other words. One item was 'sequestered,' another was 'confiscated,' columns and friezes were 'salvaged' from where they'd stood for twenty centuries. The Indian treasure was not purchased with Lord East's personal fortune, the Indian treasure *is* Lord East's personal fortune. He's not giving it to the Crown, you know, only loaning it."

Barnett nodded. "I'm not surprised," he whispered. "They say history is written on the backs of the losers."

Higgins stared at him. "I don't think that's *exactly* what they say," he said, "but I suppose it's close enough for a wire service."

"It must make you nervous, Lord East," one of the reporters suggested.

"Very little makes me nervous, young man," Lord East said. "To what were you referring?"

"Safeguarding all that treasure," the reporter said. "Seeing it safely back to England. Taking it overland to London."

Lord East leaned back with his arms on his hips, and managed to look exceedingly smug. "One of the guiding principles of my viceroyship, and before that of my tenure as resident director of the Northeastern and Southern Indian Railway, was that a well-armed militia is more than a match for any group of brigands. Another is that rigorous planning and preparation before the battle pay for themselves many times over when the battle begins. No, young man, I am not nervous. I am confident."

"Beg your pardon, my lord, but isn't there some native Indian secret organization that has threatened to recover the Lord East treasure and return it to the Indian people?" Higgins called out.

"I have received threats from such a group," Lord East admitted. "But I do not take them seriously. Hàtshikha nà Tivviha, they call themselves. It means 'the Seven Without Faces.'"

"Romantic," one of the reporters commented.

"Barbaric," Lord East said.

"Have they made any attempts on the treasure yet?" Higgins asked.

Lord East snorted. "They wouldn't dare *do* anything," he said. "Talk is cheap. Letters pinned to my pillow in an attempt to frighten me do not achieve their desired effect. But I doubt whether they have actually gone any further than that."

"Then I take it that you are not worried about this Indian group, your lordship," Barnett said.

"Not at all. I am more concerned about common thieves. The Lord East Collection would make a tempting target."

"But Lord East," Higgins said, "how far could a thief, or even a group of thieves, get with a ten-foot statue, or a twenty-five-foot column?"

"Quite true," Lord East agreed. "But the smaller pieces are vulnerable. The Rod of Pataliputra, twenty-two inches long, crusted with diamonds and rubies, said to be the symbol of authority given by Alexander the Great to Chandra Gupta, known to the Greeks as Sandrocottus, King of the Prasii. The Káthiáwár Buddha, carved out of one single piece of red carnelian, fifteen and one-quarter inches high. The dagger of Allad-ud-din Khalji, a gift to him from Malik Kafúr, who is believed to have had a precious stone set into its hilt or sheath for every Hindu priest he murdered. It contains over six hundred gems. I have over two thousand such items; small, highly portable, of great historical interest, and valuable out of all relation to their size."

"Can you describe the safeguards you have taken, your lordship?" Higgins called.

Barnett nodded agreement. "Yes, please do. That is the sort of detail that will fascinate our American readers."

"Unless you are afraid that a published description of your security measures will attract the very brigands you seek to avoid," von Hertzog suggested, tamping the tobacco down in an oversized pipe he had produced from an inner pocket.

Lord East glared at the German. "My security measures are designed to discourage any attempt at theft," he said. "And such criminals as are not discouraged will either be thwarted or apprehended."

"Very wise, your lordship," Higgins said.

"You will remember that I have some experience with railways and railway equipage," Lord East said. "Let me describe my plan.

"When the *Hornblower* docks tomorrow, I shall go aboard to inventory the collection. This will take three days, as I intend personally to inspect each item and check it against my list. In the meantime a special train is going to be assembled and prepared."

"Will you describe the train for us, your lordship?" Barnett asked.

"A Drummond engine pulling twenty-one cars," Lord East said. "Ten specially prepared goods wagons for the collections; seven troop-carrying cars for two companies of Her Majesty's Bengalese Foot; three drop-side wagons for the one platoon of the Twenty-third Light Horse, who will ride with their mounts; and one guards' van bringing up the rear, which will hold a few selected crack marksmen along with the usual railway guards."

Lord East paused for breath, and to wait for the hastily scribbling reporters to catch up with him. "The ten goods wagons will be fitted in as a unit between the Bengalese Foot," he continued, "and all of the wagons from the coal tender to the guards' van will be wired together with a special electrical wire designed to set off a loud alarm if it is broken anywhere along its length. This will prevent any attempt to shunt one or more wagons to a side track while going around a curve and then reconnect the remaining cars. A method that was actually attempted some years ago in the Punjab, let me say.

"The goods wagons themselves are being prepared now to receive the treasure. This preparation is in two parts. The first is an inspection of the wheels, axles, coupling mechanisms, and the entire exterior body, sides, bottom, and top. The second is lining the interior of each car with a layer of seamless white muslin."

Featherby-Ffolks of the *Manchester Register* raised his pencil from his notebook page and looked up, his finely trimmed mustache twitching suspiciously. "White muslin?" he asked. "You are having the sides covered with fabric?" Ever since he had scooped the London papers with the story of the successful cross-Channel flight of the Quigsly Ornithopter, only to discover that it was all an elaborate hoax, he twisted each new coin between his teeth, examined all notes under a reading glass, and twitched his mustache at the slightest unusual or unexpected detail in any story.

"Yes, that's correct," Lord East said. "One can have trapdoors or secret panels in wooden walls or metal framing, but it is difficult to conceal a panel or a door in seamless white muslin."

Featherby-Ffolks considered this for a moment, and then nodded. "I see, your lordship," he said.

"Each goods wagon will have three triangular frames constructed of metal pipes placed equidistant down the center line of the wagon floor. Large objects, such as marble columns and stone statuary, will be placed on special supporting harnesses atop these frames. The treasure trunks will, likewise, be placed on metal rods running almost the length of the wagons, which will be fitted onto the triangular frames, leaving just enough room to get around them."

"Your lordship," Barnett interrupted, "excuse me, but what exactly is the advantage of this arrangement?"

"It prevents the use of a whole bag of tricks of the sort common to brigands and thieves. This is the way the treasure was safeguarded as it was moved about India, and if it foiled the brigands of India, my good fellow, rest assured it will succeed here.

"The triangular frames serve to support the treasure three feet from the floor of the wagon, and at least two feet from either side. There is no place of concealment, as all is visible. What is more, from the time the treasure is placed upon these supports until the time it is removed, it will be impossible for any man to achieve entrance to any of the wagons."

"Ingenious," Barnett said.

"Indeed so," Lord East agreed. "You have to get up very early in the morning to pull the wool over my eyes!"

SEVENTEEN

THE CANDLE

Oh, East is East, and West is West, and never the twain shall meet,
Till Earth and Sky stand presently at God's great judgment seat;
But there is neither East nor West, Border, nor Breed, nor Birth,
When two strong men stand face to face, though they come from the
ends of the earth!
RUDYARD KIPLING

Benjamin Barnett arose and packed his kit-bag at five o'clock the next morning. The earliest train to London left Plymouth at 6:08, and he had the whole first-class compartment to himself. He stretched out across the seat and caught an additional two hours' sleep, and then used the next three hours to go over his notes and write them up into a comprehensive account and analysis of Lord East's philosophy of acquiring and guarding Indian treasure. By the time the train arrived at Waterloo Station, he had two versions of the Lord East treasure story prepared, one for the American News Service, and one for Professor James Moriarty.

"Hm," Moriarty said, reading Barnett's account of the interview, "it is as I assumed. Lord East does not venture into the unknown. He continues to use the same rituals to safeguard his hoard that he practiced while he was acquiring the loot in India."

"I imagine one comes to trust those techniques that have worked for one in the past," Barnett commented.

"Easily understandable and very human," Moriarty admitted. "I certainly cannot fault him for that. Furthermore, it does simplify my task."

"If you say so," Barnett said. "Although I can't see how you intend to get near the train. It's never going to stop from the time it leaves Plymouth until it reaches London, not once. And if you somehow do manage to halt it, a regiment of very large guardsmen with loaded rifles will have the train surrounded in seconds, and a troop of light horse will be leaping off of their wagons to chase anyone who appears in their way."

"The military escort will not affect my plan one way or the other," Moriarty said. "It makes no difference whether there is a company of men or a field army guarding the treasure, it shall be removed."

"Are you saying that the treasure will leave Plymouth, but it won't make it to London?" Barnett asked.

Moriarty smiled. "To paraphrase a former Lord of the Admiralty," he said, "I don't say the treasure will not arrive in London, I merely say it won't arrive in that train."

Mr. Maws opened the study door. "Beg pardon," he said. "There is a delegation to see you, Professor. Six gentlemen. They have no cards."

Moriarty looked up. "Gentlemen, you say, Mr. Maws?"

"In a manner of speaking, Professor. Gentlemen of the night, gentlemen of the mask, gentlemen of the Hidden Ways. I believe all these appellations have been applied to our guests, Professor."

Barnett smiled at the butler. "Well, Mr. Maws, you astound me," he said. "You have hidden depths."

"Yeah? 'Oo says?" Mr. Maws demanded, his face remaining expressionless.

"Do we know any of these gentlemen, Mr. Maws?" asked Professor Moriarty.

"Yes, sir," Mr. Maws replied. "There's the Snoozer, and Twist, and Upper McHennory, and the Twopenny Yob, and Colonel Moran, and Percy the Painter."

"Well, well," Professor Moriarty said, rubbing the side of his nose, "an impressive gallery of rogues. What could have brought them all together; and what on earth could have brought them here to see me?" He adjusted his pince-nez glasses. "Well, the best way to find out is to bring them in here and let them tell me. Mr. Maws, if you would."

"Would you like me to leave?" Barnett asked, as Mr. Maws silently closed the door behind him.

"Not at all," Moriarty said. "You already know one or two of these gentlemen, I believe. You would be doing me a favor if you sat quietly in the corner and, ah, observed."

"My pleasure, Professor," Barnett said, and he was speaking no less than the truth. It sounded like a fascinating meeting from any point of view. "Let's see—Twist I've met, of course; head of the Mendicants' Guild. I'm an honorary member, I believe."

"That's so," Moriarty said. "And the Snoozer's a sneak thief. Got his name from his favorite method of operating, which is to pretend to be asleep in railway terminals or hotel lobbies and then wake up and calmly walk off with a few pieces of luggage. Upper McHennory you met briefly two years ago; he gave you a couple of lessons in opening the simpler sort of tumbler locks."

Barnett nodded. "Tall, sandy-haired fellow," he said.

"Quite right," Moriarty said. "Expert at his craft. Specializes in the smaller wall safes, of the sort found in private houses or small businesses."

"And the Twopenny Yob?" Barnett asked.

"'Yob' is reverse slang," Moriarty said. "The Twopenny Yob, now a man in his fifties, dresses and looks like the younger son of an earl. His precarious but quite remunerative occupation is crashing parties in the West End or other haunts of the rich and going through the pockets of all the coats in the cloakroom."

"You can really make a living doing that?" Barnett asked.

"One can," Moriarty said, "if one happens to have the appearance of an earl's son and the morals of a guttersnipe. He also makes friends with chambermaids to get into houses while the owners are away." Moriarty removed his pince-nez and thoughtfully polished the lenses. Barnett could tell that the usually unperturbable professor was as curious as he was about the purpose of the impending delegation.

"Colonel Sebastian Moran," Moriarty continued, "is probably the most dangerous man in London. I have used him for a couple of assignments, and he has performed well. The colonel is intelligent, diligent, and obeys orders, but he is as unstable as a bottle of nitroglycerine. Someday someone is going to jar him the wrong way, and he's going to do something unfortunate. He has the cool courage of a man who singlehandedly hunted man-eating Bengal tigers in India, but he was cashiered out of the Indian Army for an incident involving a young native girl and his very violent temper.

"Percy the Painter, now, is a meek, gentle man who runs a small, very exclusive gallery for *objets d'art* and antiques. He dislikes associating with riffraff, but is known to pay good prices for the odd bits of gold or lapis lazuli one may happen upon in the course of one's earnest endeavors."

"A fascinating group," Barnett commented. "It sounds as if we're going to be entertaining the cast of characters of a medieval morality play. 'Enter Malice and Cupidity; exit Avarice and Lust. Jealousy speaks to Everyman.'"

Moriarty looked as though he were about to comment on this, but Mr. Maws's triple knock on the study door interrupted him. "This way, gentlemen," the butler said, opening the door and stepping aside to allow the strange assortment of guests to file into the room.

Twist, in the lead, scurried across the carpet and hopped up into a red leather chair to one side of Moriarty's large oaken desk. "Morning, Professor," he said, his eyes shifting about the room. "Morning, there, Araby Ben. Been a while, it has."

"Araby Ben?" Moriarty asked, with an amused look at Barnett.

"My, ah, nickname in Mr. Twist's guild," Barnett said, trying not to look embarrassed.

"It's 'is moniker in the Maund Book," Twist said. "Which I signed 'im in personal-like these two years ago. 'Cause 'e took such an interest, you see. Gives 'im the right to beg on any street corner in London what ain't otherwise occupied."

"A singular distinction, Mr. Barnett," Moriarty said. "And one that might, in some strange circumstance, come in useful. One never knows where the vagaries of life will lead."

Twist, a misshapen little man with a patch over his right eye, grinned up at Moriarty. "There's many as do worse," he said.

Barnett examined the others as they entered, and found that he had no trouble telling them apart. Upper McHennory he remembered: a tall, serious-looking man, dressed like a superior artisan, which he was. Snoozer had the appearance of a soft-goods drummer from Manchester, who had somehow misplaced his sample bag. The Twopenny Yob, a tall, pale man with almost no chin, had a sort of insubstantial, vague, aristocratic look, as though he had wandered into the room by mistake, and was hoping his valet would appear and tell him where he was supposed to be. Colonel Moran was the image of the hale, bluff colonial officer in mufti. With his wide shoulders and solidly planted feet, he had a look of carefully controlled power. His bushy mustache could not disguise the hint of sadistic cruelty that showed in the twisted corners of his thin-lipped mouth. Percy the Painter was a small, fleshy man with altogether too many gold rings on his chubby fingers and an air of determined petulance.

The six distributed themselves about the study, each according to his preference. Barnett noted that they all kept instinctively clear of the front windows. Moriarty rose to greet them. "Good day, gentlemen," he said. "This is my colleague, Benjamin Barnett. To what do I owe the honor of this visit?"

"It's on the way of being a consultation, Professor," Upper McHennory said.

"We is here to ask you to help us, Professor," the Snoozer said.

"To put it concisely," said Colonel Sebastian Moran, shouldering his malacca walking stick and giving an automatic twist to the corners of his precise mustache, "we are a delegation, sent here by our comrades-in-crime, to solicit your aid."

"You never were one to mince words, Colonel," Percy the Painter said approvingly. "'Comrades-in-crime.' Yes; within the confines of this lovely room—I particularly admire that Berkman oil to the left of the door—I admit to the justice of that description. Lovely."

"Beg pardon," the Twopenny Yob said, "but I believe we are creating sound without facilitating the exchange of information." He turned to Moriarty. "Professor, we have come to see you on behalf of the Amateur Mendicant Society. We are a specially formed committee of that society empowered to represent the entire membership in our discussions with you."

Moriarty sat back down in his chair and leaned forward, peering with his intense gaze at each of his visitors. "The Amateur Mendicant Society," he said finally. "I don't believe I am acquainted with it."

"It's a brand-new organization, Professor," Upper McHennory said. "A group of us from the different corners of the snide decided we had to get together and discuss subjects of mutual benefit—"

"Such as what it is what we is going to be telling you about," Twist interrupted.

"There are things happening in London," said the Twopenny Yob, "that are against the common interests of us artisans of the underworld. So we decided to get together and discuss these things. But you can see the problems an attempt on the part of our collective brethren to assemble would cause. The authorities would not encourage such a gathering. Particularly at the present time, they would frown upon it. They would do their best to discourage it."

"The present time?" Moriarty asked.

"You bloody well said it there, Professor," Twist said. "The present times is different from other times, 'cause of some bloody bastard what is going about knocking off the toffery."

"Ah! The murders," Moriarty said.

"Indeed," the Twopenny Yob agreed. "And so we formed a club. It was Percy the Painter's notion—"

Percy shrugged modestly. "It comes of employing a competent solicitor," he said. "Expensive, but well worth it in times of need. My solicitor pointed out that gentlemen's clubs were quite legal, quite common in London, could have anyone they wished as members, and could exclude nonmembers from attendance if they wished. So we formed a club. The Amateur Mendicant Society. We rented the ground floor and vault of a furniture warehouse, and fixed it up quite nicely."

"Vault?"

"For private discussions," Snoozer explained.

"Ah!" Moriarty said. Barnett, who had come to know his moods quite well over two years, could tell that he was doing his best not to look amused. Since the average person couldn't tell when the professor *was* amused, his attempt at concealment worked quite well. "So now there is a club—no doubt with billiard tables and a reading room—for gentlemen purse snatchers, pickpockets, panderers—"

"Sir!" Colonel Moran said sharply, his face flushing. "We may indulge in occasional activities which are technically on the wrong side of the laws of this effete country, but we are none of us lacking in respect for the ladies. There are no panderers welcome in our group!"

"Accept my apologies, Colonel," Moriarty said. "I was carried away by the lure of alliteration. So, at any rate, you have discovered that it is possible to make a den of thieves respectable by giving it the facade of a gentlemen's club."

"Well," Upper McHennory said, smiling, "it has worked so far."

"Can we get back to the purpose of this visit?" Colonel Moran said, impatiently slapping his walking stick against the side of his shoe.

"Very well," the Twopenny Yob said. "Professor Moriarty, in the name of the collective membership of the Amateur Mendicant Society, we request your assistance. We must see to it that this vile murderer who has been haunting the West End is apprehended."

"I see," Moriarty said. "And why this interest? A sense of civic duty, perhaps?"

"Pah!" Twist exclaimed, scrunching forward in his chair. "The rozzers 'as been 'arassing us sumfing awful. Knocking my boys off the street corners, chasing blind and lame beggars up the street. I tells you, it ain't good."

"I believe you," Moriarty said. "Seeing a lame beggar outrun a bobby must stretch your customers' credulity."

"You wouldn't think it humorous," Percy the Painter commented, "if it was your men being harassed and arrested by the police anytime they enter a swank neighborhood. And keeping them out of swank neighborhoods is not sensible. Stealing from the poor goes against ancient English tradition; it's in bad taste and it's unremunerative."

Moriarty raised an eyebrow. "What about the great and growing body of the middle class?" he asked. "Surely you can still steal from shopkeepers, factory owners, salesmen, innkeepers, bank clerks, and assorted merchants, tradesmen, and professionals?"

"You doesn't grasp the magnanimousness of the situation," Twist said. "Strangely, when the rich are struck at, it is the middling classes what feel most threatened."

"It's the truth," the Twopenny Yob said. "Now, with this madman going around and murdering the aristocracy, you could clearly see where it would make my profession difficult. The swells are just naturally going to be more cautious as to who they let into their mansions. Even during the wildest soirées, they are not going to suffer the chance of having their throats cut merely for the privilege of having their pockets picked."

Very nicely put, Barnett thought, and made a note to use it in a future article.

"But the odd thing about it," the Yob continued, "is the reaction of your bourgeois shopkeeper. He feels personally threatened, and writes letters to the *Times* about it. The public uproar causes the police to cancel all leaves and bring in auxiliary men, and get a visible patrol on every street. Calms down the masses, don't y'see."

"And, just for the raw fun of it, 'cause they ain't got nothing else to do," Snoozer added, "the rozzers arrest everybody in sight for 'suspicious loitering.' Now I tell you, Professor, it's a sad day when a chap can't do a bit of suspicious loitering without getting thrown in quod for his troubles!"

Moriarty leaned back in his chair and pursed his lips. "An interesting scene you are painting, gentlemen," he said. "And a sad tale it is, indeed, that this one unknown murderer is putting the entire criminal class of London out of business. What, exactly, is it that you want me to do about it? Help you compose a letter to the *Times*? Get the police off your collective backs? What?"

"They're on your back too, you know," Percy the Painter said, and then put his hand to his mouth, as if frightened by his own audacity.

Moriarty turned his head slightly and inspected Percy speculatively for a moment. "Pray tell me, Percy, whatever are you talking about?"

"One of my customers, you know," Percy said. "Collector of Georgian china. Which I can't imagine why, for the life of me. Ugly, hideous, gross chamber pots they are, too. But he likes them. Lestrade is his name."

Professor Moriarty laughed. "Giles Lestrade, a collector of Georgian chamber pots! The man has untold depths."

"You know him then? Scotland Yard inspector. Always makes me a bit nervous when he visits the shop, if the truth be told. Well, last time he came in, about three days ago, it was, he had one of his Scotland Yard buddies with him, and they were having a conversation, which I couldn't help overhearing, while they looked at the china."

"And what did they say?" Moriarty asked.

"Inspector Lestrade said that Sherlock Holmes—he's—"

"I know who he is," Moriarty growled. "Go on."

"Well, Inspector Lestrade said that Sherlock Holmes was still convinced that you, Professor Moriarty, are responsible for these murders. The chap with him—named Gregson—said it was Holmes's *idée fixe*, and there wasn't anything to be done about it. And he hoped they wouldn't have to keep too many men away from their other duties for too long, while Holmes has them following you about. It seems that Mr. Holmes is in some position of authority over at Scotland Yard, at least insofar as this investigation is concerned."

Moriarty nodded, and allowed his gaze to rest briefly on each of his guests. They were silent while he prepared to speak. "You're telling me that my interests coincide with yours on this matter," he said. "I will not dispute that; it is partly so. But not wholly. When the murderer is finally apprehended, and the level of police activity once more falls to normal, you gentlemen are free to resume or continue your nefarious activity. But it will not free me of the attentions of the master sleuth. Sherlock Holmes will inevitably suspect me of whatever heinous crime comes to light next."

"He will certainly lose his official status when this case is solved," Percy the Painter said.

"That's so," Moriarty admitted. "Which will once more lower his nuisance value to a more tolerable level. Is this what you wish me to do—solve the crime? Apprehend the murderer?"

The six of them shifted uncomfortably, all looking vaguely unhappy, except for Colonel Moran, who looked pugnacious. Barnett was briefly puzzled by this, but he suddenly realized: to these men, asking Professor Moriarty to solve a crime was like asking the Archbishop of Canterbury to commit one. It was the antithesis of the ordinary.

"Not *necessarily*, Professor," Snoozer said.

"What we want is that you should get the rozzers off our backs," Twist said. "Catching the gent what's committing these outrages seems the easiest way, but if you come up with another, that'd be jonnick with us."

Professor Moriarty stood up and removed the pince-nez from the bridge of his nose. "It is an interesting situation, and an interesting problem," he said, polishing the lenses with his pocket handkerchief. "If I agree, and I apprehend this killer, what would you have me do with him?"

"Whatever you think best. If you want to turn 'im over to the rozzers, that's jonnick," Twist said. The others all nodded agreement, looking even more uncomfortable.

Moriarty looked up sharply. "Even if he's one of yours?" he asked.

"He isn't," Upper McHennory said firmly.

"But if he is?"

"The agreement holds as stated," Percy the Painter said. "Do whatever you want with the bloke, as long as you get the forces of law and order to direct their attentions elsewhere."

"I see. No complaints from you gentlemen, or your colleagues, no matter who the killer turns out to be?"

"None!" said Colonel Moran, with unnecessary force. The others nodded.

"And what," Moriarty asked, "is to be my remuneration for removing this obstacle from the paths of the unrighteous?"

"What do you want?" Upper McHennory asked.

Moriarty thought about it for a moment. "I want from you—from the Amateur Mendicants—just what Sherlock Holmes is getting from the government."

"That don't sound too unreasonable," Twist said. "'Er majesty's paymasters, from what I understand, is not known for their largess."

"How much, precisely, would it be?" Percy the Painter asked. "Just for the record, you know."

"I'll have to find out what Mr. Holmes's monetary arrangement is," Moriarty said, "but as Twist says, it's certainly not excessive. Be aware, however, that there's another half to that. I want the sort of support from your people that Holmes is getting from the Yard."

"Support?"

"That's correct. You will be my eyes and ears. You will assemble information for me, interview people, follow people, lurk in doorways, pounce upon clues and bring them here for my perusal. I will tell you what I require done as the tasks come up. How you divide the labor is up to you, except that I shall expect you to be very careful to select the right men for the job."

"The London Maund is yours for the calling," Twist said. "Every stook-buzzer, thin-wire, prop-nailer, thimble-screwer, sneaks-man, till-frisker, bluey-hunter, and tosher in the book."

"Fine," Moriarty said. "I expected no less. What about the rest of you? And what of the various and assorted Amateur Mendicants?"

Colonel Sebastian Moran stood up and tucked his walking stick firmly under his arm. "They'll go along, Professor," he said. "I shall see to that! And if you should happen to need my services, it happens that I find myself at liberty at the moment. A liberty, let me say, that will end when you apprehend this contemptible maniac and get the rozzers off our backs."

"Ask and you shall receive," Moriarty said. "Such assistance as I do require will be paid for at my usual rates, so the requests should not seem too onerous. These expenses will be passed on to your membership along with my bill."

Percy the Painter clasped his palms together. "We shall, of course, expect you to use judicious restraint in the matter of expenses," he said. "Some of the members will be dunned at a higher rate than the others."

"I'll keep that in mind," Moriarty promised.

"We thank you," the Twopenny Yob said, rising and buttoning his

Chesterfield overcoat. "On behalf of the membership, we thank you for what we are about to receive, as the bishop said to the lady of the chorus. As one of those whose livelihood is most directly affected by the overly ambitious attempts of Scotland Yard, I, personally, thank you. When will you begin?"

"I have something on right now that will keep me fully occupied for the next few days," Moriarty said. "But if Colonel Moran wouldn't mind waiting in the library for, let us say, two hours, I will prepare a list of the various reports and investigations that I will require you to undertake immediately, so that the information will be awaiting me when I return."

"I shall run across the street to the British Museum," Colonel Moran said. "I should have no trouble keeping myself amused for a few hours in the Mausoleum Room."

"Very good," Moriarty agreed, ringing for Mr. Maws. The six Amateur Mendicants solemnly shook hands with the professor, and then allowed themselves to be escorted from the room.

"A fascinating gathering, Professor," Barnett said when the room was clear. "It's hard to believe that those people are professional criminals. They're very well mannered and polite."

"You saw them on their best behavior," Moriarty said. "A circus lion may seem quite tame as it jumps from place to place with no more than a gentle urge from the trainer. Had you met these men in their native environment, they might well have behaved more like the wild animals they are. Snoozer would have stolen your suitcase, Percy the Painter would have removed your gold cufflinks, the Twopenny Yob would have picked your pocket, and Colonel Moran would have cut your throat."

Barnett considered. "That may be so, Professor," he said. "But nonetheless it was quite a meeting, and I'm glad to have sat in on it."

"So," Moriarty said, turning his gaze toward the corner where Barnett was just rising from his chair. "And what was your impression of the event?"

"Well, Professor," Barnett said, "I think they have you suckered in right good, as we'd say at home. Scotland Yard's been after this bird for a month, and they haven't come anywhere near him. He doesn't seem to leave any clues behind—just corpses. Even Sherlock Holmes has gotten nowhere with his investigation. And you're coming to a very cold trail, which has already been stomped over by every detective, amateur sleuth, and journalist in London. I don't see how you're going to get a handle on it. Tell me, Professor, are you really going to try solving this thing, or did you just agree to look at it to keep your friends happy?"

"I doubt whether these people would stay happy if I failed to get results," Moriarty said. "But it is not quite as hopeless as your analysis would indicate."

"You mean you have some clue as to who the murderer is?" Barnett asked.

"Not at all," Moriarty said. "But I discern seven separate and distinct approaches to the problem. However, that must all be put aside for now. We have an appointment with a baggage car."

EIGHTEEN

RICHARD PLANTAGENET

Don Desperado
Walked on the Prado,
And there he met his enemy.
CHARLES KINGSLEY

Quincy Hope was dead. His body, throat gashed open from ear to ear, lay supine on the floor in his consultation room, arms stretched out cruciform, feet, curiously, raised neatly up onto the seat of the leather couch. He was still in his evening dress, just as he had been when he arrived home a half hour before he was found, missing only his hat and shoes.

"I haven't touched a thing, sir, I assure you. Not a thing. I couldn't," Gammidge, the valet, told Mr. Sherlock Holmes. A tall, skinny, stoop-shouldered man whose garb appeared too large for his frame, Gammidge stood right inside the room, hovering by the door, and seemed on the verge of tears. "Everything was exactly like this when I found the master, and no one has entered the room since that moment. I only left long enough to go outside and whistle for a policeman. What a dreadful thing, sir."

"You did right, Gammidge," Holmes said soothingly. "What sort of room is this?" It was a long, rectangular room on the ground floor, to the right of the main entrance of Quincy Hope's large, luxurious house.

Across from its paneled door was the comfortable leather couch upon which rested the legs of the corpse, from the black-trousered knees to the black silk-stockinged toes. To the left, a low table and some chairs were by the front windows; to the right, a massive flat desk and chair, flanked by a tall glass-front cabinet and a wooden examination table.

"It's Hope's consultation room, Mr. Holmes," Inspector Lestrade said. "Mr. Hope would appear to have been some sort of medical man."

"What sort?" Holmes inquired.

"Why, he was—I don't really know," Lestrade said. "Gammidge?"

"I couldn't say, gentlemen," Gammidge told them. "I served only as Mr. Hope's valet. There were several persons who came in during the daytime and aided the master with his medical practice. I really know nothing about it."

"What about the other servants?" Lestrade asked.

"Well, sir, Frazier, the butler, may know more about the master's affairs."

"Right enough. Bring him down here, then. Tell him Scotland Yard wants to talk to him."

Gammidge shrank back slightly. "I'm sorry, sir," he said, with the air of one who knows that whatever happens, it's all his fault, "but Frazier isn't here this evening. He and the other servants have the night off. They have all, I believe, gone home to various relatives."

"All gone, eh?" Lestrade asked, sticking his head forward pugnaciously.

"I believe so, sir," Gammidge said, twisting his hands together nervously as he talked. His eyes darted about the room like a caged bird who thinks that an invisible carnivore has somehow entered his cage. "I'll go and check, if you like."

"What's the matter with you, Gammidge?" Lestrade asked suspiciously. "Something on your mind?"

"No, sir; only..."

"Yes, yes; only what, Gammidge?"

"Only, Inspector, I'd like to leave this room, if I may. It's making me quite faint, really it is; being in here with the master's body and all. It's not the sort of thing I'm used to, you see, and I've always had a weak constitution."

Lestrade stuck his nose square in front of the poor valet's face, making him inadvertently leap backward. "Are you *sure* that's all, Gammidge? Are you *sure* you don't know something more about this? You'd better speak up now, you know; it will save you a lot of trouble later."

Gammidge turned white. "I don't feel so good," he said, and fainted dead away on the floor.

"Very clever, Lestrade," Holmes said sharply. "You've managed to render unconscious the only man who was here while the crime was committed; the only one who might be able to tell us anything of what happened here."

"So you say, Mr. Holmes," Lestrade said, looking down unsympathetically at Gammidge, who lay crumpled on the rug. "*I* say he's faking; and *I* say he could probably tell us a good deal of what happened here; and *I* say it's a most peculiar circumstance that the rest of the servants have the night off, but this here one remains."

"Let us be honest, Lestrade," Holmes said. "You like finding the servants guilty of crimes because you still suffer from an inborn reverence for the upper classes. Every time you hear someone speaking who clips his vowels, you instinctively want to tug your forelock. If the criminal classes would take elocution lessons, Scotland Yard's arrest rate would be cut in half."

"Now, Mr. Holmes, that isn't hardly fair," Lestrade protested, following after the consulting detective as he dropped to his hands and knees and began examining the floor in the murder room with his magnifying lens. "We usually end up arresting the lower orders because most crime comes from the lower orders. Which only makes sense, after all. No call for a duke with an income of a hundred thousand clear every year to cosh someone for his wallet."

"I'll grant you that, Lestrade, but murder knows no social boundaries. Would you turn up those gas mantles on the wall? I need more light."

"Um," Lestrade said, doing as he was bidden. "I don't know what you expect to find, crawling about on the rug."

"Truthfully, Lestrade, I don't know what I expect to find, either. That's why I look."

The valet sat up, looked around for a second, a puzzled expression on his face, and then pushed himself to his feet. "Is there anything further I can do for you gentlemen?" he asked weakly, holding onto the doorframe for support.

Lestrade turned around and advanced on the valet, raising a hectoring finger.

"Why, yes, Gammidge," Sherlock Holmes said, looking up from the rug and cutting Lestrade off as he was about to speak, "I'd appreciate it if you would go up to your master's bedroom and have a look about. See if anything has been disturbed, and especially see if anything seems to be missing."

"Very good, sir," Gammidge said, and he fled up the stairs.

"Bah!" Lestrade said. "You expect something to be missing? What?"

"I expect nothing," Holmes said. "But I would like to know."

"But Holmes, how do you expect to learn anything from what *isn't* here?"

"What *is* here," Holmes said, carefully extracting a bit of brown matter from the green rug and inserting it into a small envelope, "is suggestive, but what *isn't* here is even more suggestive, and I expect, with any luck, to learn a great deal from it."

"What *isn't* here?" Lestrade looked around, baffled. "What on earth are you talking about, Holmes? What isn't here?"

"The victim's shoes, Lestrade. They are missing. Along with his top hat. I have great hopes for the victim's shoes, although, frankly, I don't expect as much from the hat."

"You think the missing shoes are important?"

"Very!"

Lestrade shrugged. "If you say so, Mr. Holmes. But we'll probably find them under the couch, or in the bedroom."

"I've looked under the couch, Lestrade. And he never got up to the bedroom."

"Then why send that valet up there?"

"The murderer may have got to the bedroom."

"Oh." Lestrade thought that over. "Nonsense!" he said. "Missing shoes. Missing hat. I'd say that all that shows is that he had a new pair of shoes. The murderer probably took them for himself."

"Could be, Lestrade," Holmes said. "That's good thinking. Only..."

"Only what, Holmes?" Lestrade asked, looking pleased at the compliment. "Just you ask me. I'll be glad to give you the benefit of my years of professional experience. What's troubling you about this case?"

"Only, Lestrade, if he took Hope's shoes, then what did he do with his own?"

"Well—carried them off with him, I suppose."

"Come now, Lestrade. You think our murderer has developed an acquisitive instinct for his seventh killing? What about all the fine jackets and waistcoats and cravats and assorted men's furnishings at each of the previous victim's abodes?"

"It's just possible the fellow needed a pair of shoes," Lestrade insisted. "Perhaps he suddenly developed a hole in one of his own, or the uppers separated from the lowers. And he didn't leave his own behind because he was afraid of our finding some identifying mark on them."

"So he took them off with him to discard unobtrusively?"

"Right, Mr. Holmes. Like that."

"I don't think so, Lestrade. I think he took the victim's shoes because he wanted the victim's shoes; but not to wear. I think he wanted the shoes themselves, or something concealed in them. But with any luck we may soon find out whether you're right or I'm right. Lestrade, have your men scour the area for ten blocks in every direction. Have them carefully examine gutter drains and dustbins, and any other place of concealment. Instruct them to bring back any article of clothing they find, most especially shoes or parts of shoes."

"Certainly, Mr. Holmes. Whatever shoes they turn out to be, I agree that it will be useful to find them. I'll send to the division station for some large bull's-eye lanterns and put some men right on it."

"Very good. Where is that medical examiner? We've been here half an hour already."

"Dr. Pilschard doesn't like coming out after midnight, Mr. Holmes. We'll have some of our men bring the body in to St. Luke's in a death wagon, and he'll examine it in the morning."

"Is that his standard practice? Well, send somebody after Dr. Pilschard and inform him that I want the body examined *in situ*, and I want it examined soon. The man gets a two-guinea fee for every body he cuts up; let him do something to earn it!"

Lestrade shook his head. He didn't see what difference a few hours would make, but the commissioners, in their infinite wisdom, had seen fit to put Sherlock Holmes in charge of this investigation, and orders is orders. He left the room and whistled up a pair of his plainclothesmen, and sent them on their way. When he returned to the room, Holmes had reached the victim's head in his crawl across the carpet, and was concentrating his attention on it. It was not an attractive sight, jaws gaping open, eyes staring, lying in a pool of half-clotted blood.

"Help me move the couch, Lestrade," Holmes said, carefully placing the corpse's feet on the floor. "I didn't want to touch the body until the medical examiner had seen it, but time passes and the killer gets farther away. I'll disturb it as little as possible. Let's just take the couch over to the left, along the wall. That's the way. Careful where you step!"

They put the couch down, and Holmes examined the great pool of blood that was now revealed. "As I thought," he said, kneeling and peering through his glass. "The poor man was certainly killed right at this spot. The paucity of blood under and around the head had me worried, considering the depth of the wound. But a slight slope of the floor explains that. It all ran under the couch."

"It certainly did," Lestrade agreed.

There was a disturbance at the front door, and one of the constables stationed outside came in and stopped smartly in front of Inspector Lestrade. "Beg pardon, sir," he said, "but there's a gentleman outside, just pulled up in a carriage, who demands access."

"Ah!" Lestrade said. "Friend of the victim?"

"No, sir," the constable said. "Says he's a friend of the commissioner, sir."

"Is that right?" Lestrade said. "How curious, at one in the morning. Fellow must have a powerful interest. What's his name?"

"He says he's the Count d'Hiver, sir."

Sherlock Holmes looked up from the corpse. "D'Hiver?" he asked. "Show his lordship in, Constable!"

"And just who is 'his lordship'?" Lestrade demanded, as the constable retreated to the front door.

"As it was described to me," Holmes said, "he has a watching brief from the Privy Seal. I'm not sure what that actually signifies, but I assume it covers visiting the scene of the crime."

"He may have a 'watching brief,'" Lestrade said, "but how did he know there was anything to watch? How did he find out about the crime so quickly, and at such an unlikely hour?"

"We shall ask him," Holmes said, getting to his feet. "I myself am curious as to how—and why."

The Count d'Hiver burst through the door with that excess of energy that seems to possess many people who are of less than normal stature. "What's happening here?" he demanded of the empty hall. "Who's in charge? I want to see—Oh, there you are, Holmes. My God! He certainly is dead, whoever he is. Who would have known the human body had so much blood in it?"

"I assume the question is rhetorical, my lord," Holmes said. "Let me introduce Inspector Lestrade, who is in charge of the investigation for Scotland Yard."

"Lestrade," d'Hiver said, nodding slightly. "I have heard the name. You are well thought of."

"Thank you—"

"Which, frankly, I consider astounding: seven corpses and no arrests, barring the idiotic detention of a brace of servants."

"We do our best, my lord, We can't all be Sherlock Holmes," Lestrade said, his face suffusing with the red tint of suppressed anger.

"It seemingly wouldn't be of any great help if you were," d'Hiver commented coldly, fixing his gaze on Holmes. "Well, have you made any progress, Mr. Holmes? Have you found any clues?"

"I have been here only for some thirty minutes, my lord," Holmes said calmly. "The hunt for information—for clues, if you will—is painstaking and time-consuming. Perhaps, if you wish to converse, we had best go out into the entrance hall. It is better to disturb the area immediately around the body as little as possible, for fear of destroying possible evidence."

"Destroying evidence?" D'Hiver sniffed. "How can my mere presence in the room destroy any evidence?"

"A hair can be evidence, my lord," Holmes said, rising and stalking into the entrance hall himself, so that d'Hiver was forced to follow. "Or a bit of fluff, or a speck of dirt lying on the carpet. Just by walking over such a minuscule object, you may remove it; or you might inadvertently leave behind a hair or a few grains of dust yourself, thus confusing the real evidence."

D'Hiver stared at Holmes, trying to decide whether the famous consulting detective was serious. "Preposterous," he said uncertainly.

"Not at all, my lord," Holmes assured him. "The smallest trifle can be of the utmost importance, to one trained to observe and practiced in making logical deductions from what he observes. I once cleared up an obscure murder by winding a watch; and another time I discerned a dreadful secret because I noticed the depth to which the parsley had sunk into the butter on a hot day. Then again, I once cleared a man named Estermann of the charge of murdering his wife because of noting something as fragile as a cobweb."

D'Hiver pursed his lips thoughtfully, continuing to glare up at the hawk-nosed consulting detective. "If you can make so much of so little," he said, "why don't you have more on this case? Seven murders so far, Mr. Holmes."

"I am aware of the body count, my lord," Holmes said. "This is only the second opportunity that I have had to arrive in time to try to rescue some of this small detail before it is ground into the dust by hordes of police inspectors, Home Office officials, reporters, curiosity seekers, and cleaning women. I have hopes of developing something from what we find here." Noting Lestrade's frantic signaling from behind Count d'Hiver's head, Holmes continued, "May I ask how it happens that you are here, my lord?"

"Come now, Holmes, you know of my position and my interest."

"Indeed, my lord," Holmes said. "It is your information that I question. How did you know to come here?"

"Ah!" d'Hiver said. "Now I comprehend. You wonder how I popped up so mysteriously at the opportune moment at the—what do you call it?—scene of the crime. Is that it?"

"Yes, my lord."

"It is not so strange. The commissioner notified the Earl of Arundale when word came in, and Arundale notified me. And here I am. I confess I rather fancied the chance to view the actual site of one of these senseless killings so soon after it happened; but I was not prepared for the appearance of that corpse. It makes death look very unappealing. One would just as soon not see such a thing soon after a meal."

The soft footsteps of Gammidge, the valet, coming down the stairs, interrupted the conversation. He looked startled as three pairs of eyes turned to watch him descend. "I could find nothing amiss, Mr. Holmes," he said. "As far as I can tell, no one has been in the master's bedroom since he left it this evening."

"And the hat and shoes?" Holmes asked.

"Not in evidence, Mr. Holmes."

"Come now," Count d'Hiver said, "this sounds interesting. Hat and shoes?"

"Missing, my lord," Lestrade said. "I have sent some men out looking for them."

"The victim's?"

"Yes, my lord," Holmes said. "Evening dress: a black silk hat and black patent-leather shoes."

"Taken by the killer? How very fascinating. Whatever for?"

"Mr. Holmes knows," Lestrade said, "but he's not saying."

"I have a theory, that's all," Holmes said. "The recovery of the shoes will tell whether I am right."

"And if they're not recovered," Lestrade said, "it will show that *I'm* right: they were taken to replace the killer's own shoes."

"It does seem an odd thing to do," Count d'Hiver said, "taking the victim's shoes and top hat."

The door of the library, down the hall from where they were standing, opened, and a team of two plainclothesmen emerged. "We have checked all around the ground floor, Inspector," the taller of the two told Lestrade. "As far as we can tell, there is no way that the murderer could have entered or left the premises. All windows are securely fastened; the rear egress is double-bolted from the inside; the stairs to the cellar, which emerge in the butler's pantry, have a door which is closed and bolted at the upper end. It is a flimsy bolt, but nonetheless it has not been violated."

Lestrade nodded. "What we expected," he said. "Just on the off chance, MacDonald, check around upstairs, also."

"Yes sir!" MacDonald said, making a perfunctory gesture that somewhat resembled a salute, and the two plainclothesmen turned and headed up the broad stairway.

"If you don't mind, my lord, I would like to go back to my examination of the victim and the murder room," Holmes said.

"If you don't mind, Mr. Holmes," Count d'Hiver replied, "I'd like to watch." He held up a hand to cut off Holmes's retort. "I'll stand in the doorway," he promised, "and I will not disturb you, except, perhaps, with a very occasional question. I know you think me overly critical, but it may be because I do not grasp the complexities of your task. I begin to see that this is so from the conversation we have just had. Perhaps if I am permitted to observe, it will instill in me a proper appreciation for the difficulties of your profession."

"Perhaps, my lord," Holmes said dryly. "At any rate, if you wish to observe, silently, from the doorway, you are welcome to do so."

One of the constables guarding the portals came into the hall. "Beg pardon, sir," he said to Lestrade, "but there's a reporter outside who wants to speak with someone in charge."

"A reporter?" Lestrade swiveled around.

"*Morning Chronicle*, sir."

"Tell the *Morning Chronicle* to return in the morning," Holmes said. "We can't be bothered with that now. Tell him we'll have a complete report of the crime available to the press in the morning. Say seven-thirty."

"Beg pardon, Mr. Holmes, but it's a young lady."

Holmes looked irritated. "*What's* a young lady?"

"The reporter, sir."

"A young lady?" Lestrade was clearly scandalized. "The reporter for the *Morning Chronicle?*"

"Yes, sir. There is a gentleman with her, a sketch artist. They would like to see the, ah, room, Inspector. Where the victim is, you know. And she says that she is put to bed at three, so she would really like the information now."

"She is put to bed at three?" Count d'Hiver asked, looking vaguely amused. "By whom?"

"No, no," a musically feminine voice said from the front door, and the reporter for the *Morning Chronicle*, Miss Cecily Perrine, entered the hall. Behind her trailed a small man with a brown bowler hat, a wide walrus mustache, and a sketchpad. "It is the newspaper that is put to bed at three," Cecily Perrine explained, unfastening her wide brown sealskin cape and folding it over her arm. "Which is why I would like some details of the crime now, so that my readers will have the opportunity of learning all about it over their morning kippers."

"Miss Cecily Perrine, isn't it?" Sherlock Holmes said. "I thought you were a valued employee of the American News Service."

"Life is change, Mr. Holmes," Cecily said. "Good morning, Inspector Lestrade. I see you're wondering what I'm doing here. My editor sent a boy with a carriage around for me and my colleague here when he received word of the murder. He would not allow the late hour, nor the fog, nor the chilling weather to interfere with his reporters getting a good story."

"And just how, if you don't mind my asking, did he get word of the murder?" Lestrade asked.

"I have no idea," Cecily Perrine said. "I imagine he has a friend at the Yard. You'll have to ask him."

The Count d'Hiver stepped forward and took Cecily's hand. "Allow me to introduce myself," he said, bending forward at the waist with what was almost a parody of a Continental bow. "The Count d'Hiver at your service."

"Charmed," she said. "Miss Cecily Perrine, crime reporter for the *Morning Chronicle*. And this is Mr. William Doyle, sketch artist for the same paper."

At this moment the outer door slammed, and one of Lestrade's plainclothesmen rushed into the room, past Miss Perrine and Mr. Doyle, and stopped, panting, in front of the inspector. "We've got it, sir!" he declared, brandishing a bundle wrapped in oilcloth. "And a fortunate thing it was, too, us spotting it in this fog. It was all wound up in this piece of scrap oilcloth, just like it is now, and tossed down one of these stairwells that leads to a cellar door around the side of a manor house on Pettigrew Court in the next block."

"Very pleasing work, Thompson," Lestrade said, taking the bundle. "Now we'll see." He turned to Holmes. "Well, Mr. Holmes, would you care to attempt a description of the contents of this oilcloth before I open it?"

"Certainly, Lestrade," Holmes said. "One black silk top hat; one pair of black patent-leather shoes."

"Is that all?"

"I think you'll find that one or both of the shoes have been cut or ripped apart. And you'll certainly find bloodstains on both shoes."

"Bloodstains!" Lestrade ripped open the bundle. "Here's the hat. The shoes—yes, they're inside." He gave the hat a cursory glance, and then put it aside and held the shoes up to the light. "Yes, they do seem to be splattered with some sort of stain. Blood! I believe it is blood. Amazing, Holmes; how ever did you deduce that? But they would seem to be whole." He held the pair of shoes out to Holmes. "No ripping or slicing appears to have been done on either shoe."

Holmes took the shoes and examined them, one at a time. He sniffed, he peered, he pried, he took his magnifying glass to them. "Ah!" he said. "Lestrade, look here! There was no need for the killer to destroy the shoes. The matter is self-evident!" He took the left shoe and, with Lestrade peering over his arm, and the rest of his audience gathered closely behind, sharply twisted the heel. It rotated a half turn, revealing a meticulously cut-out compartment in the leather. "This is what the killer was after," Holmes said. "The contents of this compartment. Which, I note, he now has."

"You expected to find that?" Lestrade asked.

"Something like it," Holmes said. "The killer was searching for something, as he was in each of the other murders, and somehow he discovered that it was concealed in one of the shoes. Probably the victim told him, hoping to be spared a few moments longer. This business is grotesque."

"Then why did he take the top hat?" Lestrade demanded. "Was there something concealed in it also?"

"Yes, Inspector, there was."

"What?"

"The bloody shoes. The killer didn't want to wait in the victim's house to discover the secret of the shoes. Perhaps he heard the valet descending from upstairs. He also didn't want to be seen on the street carrying a pair of bloody shoes. So he concealed his own hat under his outer garment—probably a collapsible topper—and borrowed the victim's."

"Why not conceal the shoes under his own hat, or his top-coat or cloak or whatever?"

"All that blood, Lestrade. Remember, the blood was a lot fresher when he departed with the shoes."

"That's so," Lestrade admitted.

"Fascinating!" Cecily Perrine said softly, making obscure scratches with her pencil in her small notebook.

"Indeed a remarkable bit of deduction," the Count d'Hiver agreed.

"Elementary," Holmes commented. "The real question is, what was the object which was once concealed in this shallow space?"

Lestrade took the shoe and stared into the hollow heel. "Precious gems?" he suggested.

"That is a possibility," Holmes said. He took out a slender ivory rule and carefully measured the cavity, making a sketch of it in his pocket notebook and jotting down the measurements.

"Well," the Count d'Hiver said, "this has all been very interesting. I thank you for your patience, Mr. Holmes. And you, Inspector. I will not stand in your way any longer. I only hope that the unfortunate demise of Mr., ah, Hope brings us to a solution of these damnable—excuse me, Miss Perrine—murders. I will await with interest your report on this affair." And with that, he nodded abruptly to each of them, carefully adjusted his top hat on his head, and strode through the door.

"*Au revoir*, Count," Sherlock Holmes murmured, staring after the departing nobleman with a bemused expression on his face.

Once outside, the Count d'Hiver buttoned his topcoat, nodded to the two constables at the door, and hurried down the steps to the sidewalk. He stared up and down the street for his carriage. The fog had settled in, and it was hard to see more than a few feet in any direction. The brougham was not in evidence, but it could have been no more than four or five yards down the block and been completely invisible. He could have asked one of the constables where his driver had settled in to wait, but it seemed somehow demeaning not to know where one's own brougham had gone.

He headed off to the left, the direction the vehicle had been heading when they stopped. It would, he realized with a wry internal chuckle, serve him right if his driver had taken the brougham around the block and pulled up a few feet before the Hope mansion. Then the two constables would see him backtracking, the very image of a man who didn't know where his own carriage was. He could always go back into the house for a moment, as though he had forgotten something; then, perhaps, they wouldn't notice. The Count d'Hiver was a man who couldn't stand to be embarrassed, and he found the potential for embarrassment in every trivial act.

There was a carriage ahead. Was it his, or the young lady journalist's? A few more steps and—

An arm, a muscular right arm, appeared from nowhere and hooked around his throat, forcing the chin up, cutting off the windpipe, stifling any attempt to cry out, to breathe. "Greetings, gov'nor," a soft, deep, curiously familiar voice said behind his ear. "Let's go over this way, shall we?" And he was dragged, effortlessly, his heels clattering along the pavement, into a small alley beside the Hope mansion.

"What?—who?—why?—" He forced the words out as the pressure around his windpipe was ever so slightly relaxed.

"Well," the deep voice said, "quite a little journalist we're becoming, isn't it, Count? Who, what, why, when, where; all questions that will shortly cease to concern you."

"My wallet is in the breast pocket of my suit jacket," the Count d'Hiver gasped. "Take it. There are forty or fifty pounds in it. Only for God's sake let me breathe!"

"Your wallet, d'Hiver?" the voice persisted. "Now what would I want with your wallet? Fifty pounds is of no interest to me. It's you I want."

"Me?" The count struggled to turn around in the iron grasp, suddenly realizing the import of his attacker's use of his name. This was not a random street crime; he was not an accidental victim. "Who are you? What do you want with me? What do you think you're doing?"

"You may call me Richard Plantagenet," the voice said. "And I want vengeance." Somehow the mild, soft insistence of that voice was more frightening than a thousand screaming fanatics would have been.

"Vengeance? Vengeance upon whom?" D'Hiver rasped the question out with the little air permitted him. "And what has it to do with me? You cannot get my assistance by choking me to death!"

"Vengeance on you, d'Hiver," the voice said, mildly, calmly, rationally. "And you can't help. You could, however, assuage my curiosity by explaining just why you are killing these gentlemen off, before I cut your heart out."

"I?" The Count d'Hiver could feel his heart pounding against his rib cage as though it were trying to break through. "I have done nothing! I have killed no one! You are making a horrible mistake! Do not do this thing! Let us reason this out. Plantagenet? I know no one called Plantagenet." And yet he had a horrible feeling that, from somewhere, he knew that voice.

"That is so," the voice admitted, a hot, horrible breath in his ear. "You do not know me by this name. But I know you! I know you by all your various names: the Count d'Hiver; Clubmaster; Hellhound; Master Incarnate of the Ancient and Evil Order of Hellfire. I know you!"

D'Hiver felt a momentary shock almost greater than the physical pain. He had not expected that. He twisted his arm around and thrust his heel backward in a swift kick, making a sudden desperate attempt to break free. He felt the heel connect hard against his captor's leg. But despite his twisting and kicking, and the grunt the kick drew from Plantagenet, the arm never loosened from around his neck.

"You're making some sort of mistake," he insisted, giving up the struggle. "I have no idea what you're talking about!"

"No?" the soft voice of Richard Plantagenet breathed. "Pity. Then you'll die for nothing. For whether or not you tell me why you are killing the others, I shall still certainly kill you. And within the next few minutes, too. I will lift my arm"—he applied just a little upward pressure, and a great knot of pain thrust itself through the back of d'Hiver's neck and up into his brain—"and you will be quite uncomfortable. And then you will be dead."

"Wait, wait; listen," d'Hiver croaked. "Let me talk."

"Talk."

D'Hiver took a few deep breaths, to try to calm himself. There was always a way to turn any situation to your own advantage, if you were smart enough. Even this one.

The pressure increased on his throat. "Waiting for someone to come by and save you? Won't happen; you have my word it won't. Talk."

"I am who you say I am," d'Hiver gasped, squeezing the words through his compressed windpipe.

"I know you are," the other said reasonably. "Did you think I was guessing? Is that what you have to tell me?" The pressure increased again.

"Wait! Wait! Think! If you know who I am, if you know who the men who died were—then how can you think that *I* killed them? I was their master; I was their guide. I was not their enemy. Whoever is committing these murders must surely be after me, too. You can see that, whoever you are."

"We are brothers, as are all men," the whisper sounded in his ear. "I am your brother, and you are my brother; you have killed my brother, and I must kill you. Simple, isn't it?"

"Not so simple," d'Hiver insisted. "I did not kill your brother."

"Who did," the soft voice asked, "and why?"

"I am trying to find out who is behind these killings," d'Hiver said. "You think I am not? Who is your brother?"

"Was," the voice corrected. "My brother was Lord John Darby; now he is dust."

"*Crecy!*"

The arm tightened around his throat. "You may call me Richard Plantagenet," the man who had once been Lord Crecy Darby said.

"Of course, of course! I'm sorry. Plantagenet it is. Where have you been, Cr–Plantagenet?"

"Away. I have been performing experiments. Remember how we used to experiment, d'Hiver? I have done more—much more. But someone murdered my brother, and so I have come back. To speak with you; perhaps to kill you."

"Not me, Plantagenet. Help me catch the man who is really doing this. I need your help."

"If I am to believe you."

"Listen, you know who I am. You know where I live. You know how to find the club. If I'm lying to you, you can kill me later."

"That is so." The grip around his throat lessened, but did not release. "I want to find the murderer of my brother. This is distracting me from other work."

"I will help you," d'Hiver insisted. "It is to our interest to find the killer, and to eliminate him before Scotland Yard gets to him."

"So?"

"His motive must intimately concern us, since everyone so far identified murdered by this maniac has been one of us."

"Someone within the group?"

"I do not think so. Come home with me; my carriage is over there. We will discuss the possibilities."

"Fair enough." The hold around his throat was released.

Together, they moved out of the shadows.

There was the clicking sound of high heels on the pavement, and a cloaked figure rapidly headed back up the street.

"How long was she standing there?" d'Hiver demanded.

"I don't know. I didn't hear her. Who is she?"

"A girl reporter. She must have heard too much. Grab her—silently. I'll pull my carriage up."

The large figure disengaged from d'Hiver and raced silently up the street. There was a strange sound that could have been the beginnings of a girl's scream, suddenly choked off. The two constables outside the front door heard it and ran down the street, flashing their lanterns about.

The Count d'Hiver descended from his carriage and helped them look about. They found nothing. Nobody thought to look in the Count d'Hiver's carriage.

NINETEEN

THE GREAT TRAIN ROBBERY

Beyond (51½ M.) Beer (or Bere) Ferrers we cross the Tavy and skirt the E. Bank of the Tamar (p. 151). 55¾ M. St. Budeaux (for Saltash, p. 151); 57 M. Ford; 58 M. Devonport & Storehouse (see pp. 150, 151). We then pass the suburban stations of North Road and Mutley and enter the Friary Terminus at (62½ M.) Plymouth.

BAEDEKER'S *Great Britain*

It took Barnett and Professor Moriarty the better part of two days to reach Plymouth. Moriarty left the train repeatedly, to confer with an odd assortment of agents who were awaiting him in such places as Weston-super-Mare, Taunton, Newton Abbot, Totnes, Dawlish, Teignmouth, Paignton, Okehampton, Tavistock, and nine other, even smaller, towns. It seemed to Barnett, who tagged along, that the professor was pleased with the results of these conferences.

Barnett listened to the usually brief conversations, but they told him very little, and Moriarty volunteered no additional information. "Are the pit reinforcements holding?" Moriarty asked the short Welshman who had rented a house in Dawlish for himself and his crew. "With nary a shiver," the Welshman told him. "Are the false cross-ties completed?" he asked the skinny Cockney who had opened a workshop in Teignmouth. "Work like a dream," he was informed. "How is Toby's nose?" he asked the slender man in the well-worn tweeds who awaited them at the Totnes Station. "His nose, his lungs, his voice, and his fightin' heart are all waitin' on your needs," the tweedy man told him. At each stop Moriarty passed an envelope to the person awaiting him. "Here are your instructions from this moment; take every care," he told each.

At Plymouth, Lord East's preparations were well in hand for the loading of the treasure train, which was scheduled to take place the next morning. The two companies of Her Majesty's Bengalese Foot, which had been encamped in a park by the west wall of the Citadel, had moved to the railway assembly yard and were busily patrolling the area between the H.M.S. *Hornblower* and the line of railway goods wagons, which had been meticulously prepared to receive the treasure. The Twenty-third Light Horse were occupying themselves by cantering about Plymouth, giving the citizenry an exhibition of precision horsemanship.

Barnett and Moriarty took rooms at the Duke of Clarence, an ancient and venerable inn some blocks from the scene of the Lord East activity. When they arrived, Barnett went to his room and collapsed for several hours, exhausted by the inactivity of train travel. Then he gave himself a quick sponge bath and put on, among other things, a fresh collar. Moriarty awaited him in the gentlemen's reading room on the first floor, a long, narrow room with a low beam ceiling, which went across the front of the hotel, overlooking the street. It had been completely outfitted, according to a plaque on the wall, with furniture and fittings from the admiral's cabin, the captain's cabin, and the wardroom of the 96-gun ship of the line H.M.S. *Indefatigable*, which had carried Admiral Pellew to Egypt in 1803, salvaged when she was turned into a hulk in 1836.

"Damned fine history," Moriarty said, when Barnett insisted upon reading him the plaque, "damned uncomfortable furniture."

"Which is probably why the admiral left it behind," Barnett said, going over to the window and staring down at the street below. "What time is it, Professor?"

"Ten past seven," Moriarty said, snapping open his pocket watch, consulting it, and then snapping it shut again. "Have you an engagement?"

"No," Barnett said. "However, the thought of food has crossed my mind. I was just wondering why there are so many people on the street at this hour. But now that I take a good look at those passing below, it seems to me that about one out of four is a policeman."

Moriarty came over, polished his pince-nez, and glanced out the window. "I believe you're right," he said. "There's no mistaking the peculiarly heavy regulation shoe leather, and the special flatness to which a plainclothes policeman chooses to adjust his bowler."

"You don't suppose that our presence here has anything to do with their presence here, do you?" Barnett asked. "I should have thought that Lord East would regard the various military units as sufficient guard for his treasure."

"I'm sure he does," Moriarty said. "The police are here to protect tomorrow's crowds of onlookers from having their pockets picked. Every gang of dips in England is probably here tonight."

"Ah," Barnett said, continuing to stare thoughtfully out the window. "So you don't think the presence of these flat-footed gentlemen with the bowler hats will interfere with your plans?"

"No," Moriarty said. "Is this a subtle interrogation? You realize that there are some things that it would not do to print, even in an American newspaper."

"No, no," Barnett said hastily. "I was just wondering."

"Nothing could interfere with my plans now," Moriarty told him, "except a major flood. Which I do not anticipate. Shall we dine here at the hotel, or have you a better suggestion? Perhaps some establishment where your compatriots of the press will gather."

"Well," Barnett considered. "The Railway Arms commercial hotel is probably where most of the London reporters will be staying. But I doubt if the restaurant is very good; reporters' expense accounts are not up to first-class bills of fare."

"Nevertheless," Moriarty said, "it might behoove us to dine in that establishment, if they serve so late."

"I believe the dining room is open quite late," Barnett said. "They cater to the traveler."

"Well then, let us travel!"

The Railway Arms served a buffet dinner until ten, and was, as Barnett had anticipated, full of reporters come to witness the next morning's activities. Much to Barnett's surprise, the usually antisocial Professor Moriarty was quite pleased to meet Barnett's associates and seemed fascinated by the stories they had to tell. Barnett's surprise lessened when he realized that the professor was artfully turning each of the stories to extract the last bit of information about Lord East, the treasure, and the train ride. Which, since that is why they were all there—in one way or another—was not hard to do.

"I say, Barnett," said Harry Inglestone, a *Morning Chronicle* staff reporter who had just come straight down from London, pausing at their table, "Caterby-Cahors is rather perturbed at your young lady."

Barnett stifled the remarks that sprang to his lips at Inglestone's innocent use of the phrase "your young lady." A forced smile creased his face. "What is your editor concerned about?" he asked. "If you are referring to Miss Perrine, formerly of the American News Service staff, she is one of the most competent reporters I have ever known, aside from possessing sufficient organizational skills to run an office single-handedly."

"Which is what makes it so puzzling," Inglestone commented, sitting himself down at their table and happily accepting Moriarty's offer of a glass of something. "A nice after-dinner claret," he told the waiter.

"What?" Barnett asked.

"I beg your pardon?" Inglestone said, looking totally confused.

"What is so puzzling?"

Inglestone thought over the recent conversation, trying to pick up the missing thread. "Oh, yes; Miss Perrine's disappearance. Thought I mentioned it, old man."

"What do you mean, her 'disappearance'?" Barnett demanded. "When did she disappear? What are you talking about?"

"Sorry again, old man. I should have realized that you'd be concerned. Ex-employer, and all that. Should have occurred to me that you didn't know. Well, I tell you, just between us, if she doesn't turn up quickly, she's going to lose her job, Lady Hogbine or no Lady Hogbine.

Ah! The claret; thank you, Binns. It is Binns, isn't it? I shall mention you in the dispatches. Binns of the Railway Arms. A lifesaver."

"Disappearance," Barnett prompted.

"Oh, yes. Well, it's this way, old man. The lady went out on an assignment last night. No, it would be night before last, now. Doyle went with her. Artist fellow. Fine work. Well, Doyle left to take the carriage back to the Warren." He turned to Professor Moriarty. "That's what we call the lovely common room maintained for the reporters, 'the Warren.'"

"How clever of you," Moriarty murmured politely.

"Yes, well, Miss Perrine never showed up at the carriage. Doyle finally decided that she was chasing up some information or other, and returned to the Warren by himself. And, well, to make a long story short, she never did come back."

"Never got back? To the office, you mean?"

"Yes. Caterby-Cahors sent someone around to her house, and her pater was quite concerned at her absence. Claimed that she hadn't been there, either. And it certainly wasn't her custom to stay out all night. But if a lady is going to choose to be a reporter—well, you know, exigencies of the job, and all that. At any rate, Caterby-Cahors was furious. He can't even stand tardiness, so you can imagine how he feels about unexcused absence. He was ready to fire her outright until the note came."

"The note?"

"Miss Perrine was considerate enough to send a note. She said she was after a very hot lead, and not to wait the story for her, but to write it as it stood. She might be a few days, she said. Well, Caterby-Cahors was fit to be tied. Had to get the information on the murder she was covering from Doyle. Nice fellow, Doyle; good sketch artist, but no reporter. Caterby-Cahors has given Miss Perrine three days to turn up with story in hand, and it had better be a dilly. That was Caterby-Cahors's term, 'a dilly.'"

Barnett turned to Moriarty. "Something's happened to her," he said.

Moriarty considered. "I believe you are right," he said. "She has been covering that series of murders?"

"Yes." Barnett felt the blood drain from his face. "My God! You don't think—"

Moriarty put out a restraining hand. "No, I don't," he said. "Stay calm."

Inglestone looked from one to the other of them. "I say!" he said. "You don't suppose something has happened to Miss Perrine?"

"Something has definitely happened to Miss Perrine," Moriarty said. "Even my rather sketchy acquaintance with her over the past two years tells me that she didn't run off. And she certainly isn't skulking about on some London street, following a suspect. If she were, she would have found a better way to communicate than a brief note. And she certainly would have informed her father."

"But—"

"On the other hand, Mr. Barnett, the pattern of this murderer we're dealing with shows that he doesn't attack women; that he doesn't make the sort of mistake that would have enabled Miss Perrine to walk in on him; and that he doesn't conceal bodies. So, as no body has been found, we must conclude that whatever happened to Miss Perrine, it was not the doing of our multiple killer."

"That's very reassuring," Barnett said. "She may be lying bleeding on some street, sliced up by some maniac, but at least it's a *different* maniac! I've got to get back to London!"

"What for?" Moriarty asked.

"What do you mean, what for? To find Cecily. Nobody else seems even to be looking."

"I shall remedy that," Moriarty said. "I'll put a telegram in at the desk, and there will be five hundred people out looking for her in an hour."

"I say, you chaps really do seem to be taking this thing seriously," Inglestone said. "You don't actually suppose that anything nasty has happened to the young lady, do you?" He chuckled. "Well, if it has, it would serve old Caterby-Cahors right, I'll tell you."

Barnett stared incredulously at Inglestone for a second, not sure he had heard right. How callous it was possible to be about someone one didn't know very well. And Inglestone didn't seem to think he had said anything at all strange.

"I'd better pass the telegram in now," Moriarty said, rising and heading for the door. "Meet you in the lobby, Barnett."

Barnett also rose. "Very good chatting with you, Inglestone," he said. "We must do it again sometime. You don't mind paying, do you? There's a good chap!" And with that, he slapped Inglestone on the back and hurried after Moriarty.

"I say!" Inglestone exclaimed.

"I really think I should go back to London," Barnett told Moriarty, catching up to him in the lobby.

"I have given a telegram to the porter," Moriarty said. "It will be clacking its ways over the wires in ten minutes and will be delivered to 64 Russell Square within the hour. It is now ten o'clock. Before midnight, five hundred people will be searching for the young lady. By tomorrow morning the first report on the search will be awaiting me at the desk of this hotel. If there is any definite word on her whereabouts earlier, I will be immediately notified. Believe me, Barnett, I know how you feel; but no more could be done if you were present, and I need you here."

"I appreciate that," Barnett said. "I certainly don't want to desert you. But we both know that any of fifty men could do what you would have me do tomorrow. I am not in any way essential to your plan. I should get on the next train to London."

Moriarty put his hand on Barnett's shoulder and peered at him intently. "Understand me," he said. "I am not an unfeeling man. If there were anything that you could do in London that would further the search for Cecily Perrine, I would hire a special for you and put you on it. If there were any way in which my presence would help, I would join you."

"Thank you, Professor," Barnett said. "I'm sure you're right; and I appreciate what you say more than I can tell you. It's just that—"

"Furthermore," Moriarty said, "whatever your opinion of yourself, the fact is that I *do* need you here. You are not irreplaceable, but you are intelligent, competent, and resourceful, and the man with whom I would have to replace you might lack one or more of those virtues.

"I pledge you this, Barnett: if any word comes of Miss Perrine—at all—and it seems desirable for you to go to London, I'll have that special put on for you immediately. In any case, we shall both be on the next regular train for London. I shall leave it midway, but you will go on through."

"The next train?" Barnett asked.

"Yes. There are no more trains scheduled tonight, and the first train out tomorrow morning is the, let's see"—he pulled out his schedule—"the 6:08 doesn't run on Saturdays, so we shall be on the 7:42. Will that suffice?"

"I suppose," Barnett said unhappily, "that it will have to."

He slept fitfully that night. If asked, he would have sworn that he slept not at all. Complex images kept springing into his mind, unbidden. Images of the myriad ways in which Cecily, by chance or by design, could have discovered the mysterious murderer. And then the image would unfold and become horrible, as the murderer, in turn, found Cecily. Barnett's mind rebelled from the worst possibilities, but even the ones his mind would accept did not bear dwelling upon.

The loading of the treasure was set to begin an hour before sunrise, which, according to *Whitaker's Almanack*, would occur at 5:42. And so at a little after four in the damp, chilly morning of the first Saturday in April, Barnett found himself dressing by candlelight so that he could go to watch large, heavily guarded boxes being loaded onto goods wagons in the predawn blackness for transport to London. And do his small part in seeing that they did not arrive.

The reporters, sketch artists, and such of the idly curious as could drag themselves out of bed at such an hour, were to be assembled on a three-tiered grandstand specially erected in the goods yard for the event. This would give them a splendid view of the proceedings and yet keep them out of the way. The real crowds would gather later in the morning, when the military guard was added and the treasure train prepared to leave.

Barnett had wondered how they were going to move treasure from the ship to the goods wagons in the dark; even with the route marked with a line of lanterns, it would not seem a prudent procedure from the standpoint of security. And indeed, when he and Professor Moriarty arrived and took their seats in the front row of the grandstand, the brightest object around was the conductor's lantern, which was carried by the railway guard. There was no line of lanterns, and no apparent motion from what Barnett believed to be the direction of H.M.S. *Hornblower*, a quarter mile away at Stonehouse Basin. "Are we early?" he whispered to the guard, looking around at the ten or fifteen other people already in the stands.

"No sir, you'm jest a'time," the guard told him in a broad north-counties accent. And as if merely waiting for his word, the entire goods yard was suddenly bathed in an intense white light.

Barnett blinked, squinted, and shielded his eyes from the intense glare. "What on earth is that?" he asked no one in particular.

"They appear to have four Drummond apparatuses mounted in towers," Moriarty said. "We are now bathed in a light as bright as the sun, if rather more limited in scope."

"Drummond?" Barnett peered out from between his fingers. His eyes were starting to adjust now, and he could see slightly between his fingers as he shut off most of the light with his hands. The professor was right; except for the bizarre shadows cast by the four light sources, it could have been daylight within the limited area of the goods yard.

"The light is generated by application of a flame of hydrogen gas burned in a stream of oxygen to a core of calcium oxide. You should be intimately familiar with the principle, fond as you are of attending the music halls."

"Music halls?" Barnett asked.

"Calcium oxide is perhaps better known as lime," Moriarty explained.

"Limelight!"

"Correct. The same light that illuminates your favorite singers, jugglers, and acrobats, done on a much larger scale. This sort of Drummond apparatus is usually found in lighthouses, where the beam can be seen from twenty miles away. The only difference is the shape of the mirrored reflector; parabolic in lighthouses, and, I would assume, conical here. It covers a much wider field, you see."

"I see," Barnett said. And he was beginning to. He took his hands away from his face and looked around. "It's quite a shock, going from pitch-black to daylight in an instant. I'm not sure that the human eye was built to take that sort of transition."

The grandstand was now filling up rapidly with the gentlemen of the press. The area before them, a loading platform with one of the specially prepared goods wagons pulled up before it, was curiously devoid of life and motion. It reminded Barnett of a stage setting in the moments before the curtain went up on the first act. Which, he realized, was probably a fair assessment. Lord East had arranged this show for the press, and he was going to see that they got their money's worth. For whatever motive, Lord East craved the public eye, and he had spent thirty years learning how to stay in it.

A line of red-coated soldiers marched into the limelight from the left, the direction of the *Hornblower*, and the Lord East treasure. Leading them, astride three spirited chargers, were a colonel, a brigadier, and Lord East. It was, as it had been contrived to be, an inspiring sight.

As the reporters fell silent at Lord East's approach, Moriarty leaned over to Barnett and whispered, "Ready?"

"Yes," Barnett replied, feeling his heart beat faster.

Moriarty nodded. "We have one thing to thank that mysterious murderer for," he commented.

"We do? What's that?"

"Were it not for him, Sherlock Holmes would even now be sitting behind us disguised as an itinerant colorman, breathing down our necks."

"He did have three Scotland Yard men following you about," Barnett reminded Moriarty.

"Yes, but we were able to divert them with little trouble. Holmes would have been much more difficult to get rid of. Even now he must be spending whatever time he can spare in wondering where I've got to. It is these small things that make life worth living."

"You are a vindictive man, Professor," Barnett said.

"Nonsense!" Moriarty whispered. "I would gladly be willing to relinquish the childish pleasure I get in thwarting him if he would give up following me about and spying on me. I think East is about to speak."

"Welcome!" Lord East bellowed to the assemblage on the grandstand, maneuvering his horse in close to the railing. "I apologize for getting you all up at such a ridiculous hour to witness the loading, but we want to have a clear run to London during the daylight hours. I'm sure you can understand." As he spoke, his horse began walking around in a small circle. His lordship, trying to ignore this, gradually twisted around in his saddle until he was speaking over the animal's rump. Then, in a sudden fit of anger, he put his spurs to the animal to make it obey the reins. The horse responded by kicking up sharply with its hind feet, causing his lordship to lose his stirrups and almost fly head over rump to the earth below. He caught himself, barely, by grabbing onto the saddle with both hands, pulled himself up, and savagely yanked the horse around to face the group. "Military mount," he said in an annoyed undertone that carried across the field. "Always give the best of everything to the military!"

The soldiers had now formed a double line leading from somewhere to the left of the limelit area to the loading platform. The shifting of the Lord East Collection from the battleship to the railway train was about to commence. "It should take a bit over two hours to transfer the entire collection into the ten goods wagons," Lord East explained, having regained control of his mouth. "But you must understand that this is, metaphorically speaking, only the tip of a vast iceberg. Hundreds and hundreds of man-hours have already gone into the preparations. Wafting the collection ashore and loading it onto the baggage carts which will bring it here was a process which began yesterday evening and was not completed until but a short time ago."

"'E don't want us to think it was easy," someone behind Barnett muttered.

"Where is the official photographer?" Lord East fretted. "I

wanted the whole process captured on glass plates. History is being made here!"

The first baggage cart appeared, pushed between the twin rows of soldiers and onto the loading platform by an octet of workmen who, judging by their appearance and dress, must have been brought back from India by Lord East. It held twelve large statues of different ancient gods and goddesses of various Indian religions, deities that would have been very surprised to have ended up on the same small cart. The workmen rapidly and efficiently prised the statuary off the cart and into the goods wagon, tying the pieces into place with a complex of ropes and scaffolding.

There was a pause in the loading now, and a certain amount of backtracking, while the official photographer bustled up and set up his apparatus to the side of the grandstand. Lord East and his entourage assumed a variety of poses that were supposed to suggest the earlier stages of the operation before continuing with the job.

The next cart held what looked like a load of bricks. Lord East's audience broke into a subdued chattering at the sight of it, as the reporters tried to guess the history and purpose of the load. Some of the suggestions as to the uses to which the bricks could be put were rather imaginative. "Sun-baked bricks," Lord East explained, "forming a lovely frieze that went around the wall of a four-thousand-year-old temple. Quite beautiful. A pair of hunters accosting a lion, I believe. The bricks were all numbered with Chinese chalk when we took it apart, but many of the numbers seem to have rubbed off during the journey. Or perhaps during the five years in storage. I hope we can reassemble it, nonetheless; it really was quite striking."

Barnett's brief but essential part in Professor Moriarty's master plan for the acquisition of the Lord East Collection was to be enacted as the third treasure chest was being loaded. What he was to do was clear, and not overly difficult, given the known habits of his brother reporters. Why he was to do it was another matter. Moriarty was not communicative with his plans. It was enough for one to execute his part; one was not called upon to understand what he was doing, or why. Barnett gave a mental shrug as he prepared to move.

The third wagon was loaded now, and sealed; the fourth was about to be rolled into its place before the platform. Lord East rode over to the loading platform to supervise as his most precious cargo was installed in its place.

Barnett unostentatiously moved up one row in the grandstand and over toward the middle. His colleague Inglestone was sitting a few seats over from where Barnett now found himself, doing his best to ignore Barnett's existence. He must be still smarting from having to pay the bill the night before, Barnett decided. He would serve well as Barnett's unwitting ally.

Barnett slid over along the bench and slapped Inglestone on the back. "How are you, friend?" he asked solicitously. "Sleep well?"

"As well as could be expected, old man," Inglestone said frostily. "You owe me fourteen bob."

"Do I?" Barnett leaned back, his elbows on the seat behind. He pitched his voice just loud enough so that the reporters in the seats surrounding could overhear. "Well then, I'll tell you what: I'll give you a chance to get even."

"How's that?" Inglestone asked, sounding annoyed. "It wasn't a question of a wager, old man; this was cold, hard cash."

"Ah, yes," Barnett said. "But there's wagers and there's wagers." He indicated the first treasure chest, now being loaded into the wagon. "I'll bet you five quid on the nose that there's nothing in that there box."

Inglestone turned to stare at him. "What do you mean?" he asked. "The treasure chest?"

"You've got it," Barnett said. "Five quid says that the so-called treasure chest is empty."

"What are you saying, Barnett?" the columnist for the *Evening Standard* demanded, his mustache twitching.

The first chest was now in place in the goods wagon, and the second was being brought up. "I say they're empty," Barnett said.

"That's ridiculous!" the *Morning Intelligencer-Whig* declared. "Do you know what you're saying?"

"Have you seen inside any of those chests?" Barnett demanded. "I'm saying there's a reason. I say they're empty!"

Heinrich von Hertzog, British correspondent for the *Berliner Tagenblatt*, nodded his head sagely. "It could be," he said. "It makes sense."

Barnett was glad to hear that, because the one thing that had worried him was that his accusation made no sense whatsoever, as far as he could tell. "Of course it does," he agreed.

"What sort of sense?" Jameson of the *Daily Telegraph* demanded.

"Lord East creates all this excitement, all this preparation, all this display, to draw attention to the treasure train," von Hertzog explained. "But the real treasure is sent otherwise. A clever man, Lord East."

Barnett nodded. "I'll up it to ten quid," he said. "Any takers? Ten quid says those boxes are as empty as an editor's heart."

"That's nonsense!" Inglestone said. "It certainly doesn't make any sense that I can see. Do you know what you're talking about, Barnett?"

The second chest was now in place. "Ten quid says I do," Barnett said.

"Come on, Barnett," Jameson said. "Don't try to make money on your friends. If you know something, spill it. Don't just sit there looking smug."

The cart with the third chest on it was being pushed up onto the loading platform. "Easy enough to check," Barnett said. "Any takers? Ten quid; easy money."

"How would you establish the contents of the chests?" von Hertzog asked.

"Open one," Barnett said.

"You're on!" Inglestone said, coming to a decision. "Ten pounds says that you're mistaken; that those chests are, indeed, full of the pieces in the Lord East Collection. But understand that this wager has nothing to do with the fourteen bob you owe me."

"Fair enough," Barnett said. "You can deduct it from my winnings. Well, shall we go find out? His lordship can't object to a reasonable request to open one of the chests. We'll all promise not to touch; won't we, boys?"

Now that the suggestion had been advanced, the reporters were unable to leave it alone. It became imperative to them to discover whether a possibility that none of them had even considered five minutes ago, that was unlikely in the extreme, that was actually none of their business, was true. In a body they left the grandstand and advanced toward the loading dock, the treasure chest, the goods wagon, and Lord East.

The four plainclothes policemen who were guarding the grandstand moved to stop the cluster of them as they advanced. "Gentlemen, gentlemen, please!" one of them cried, opening his arms wide, as if to encircle the group himself.

"'Ere now, what's this?" a second barked, running around to the front of the group. The other two also raced around to the front to place themselves uncertainly between the reporters and the platform.

Lord East heard the disturbance and turned to see the cluster of correspondents advancing on him. For a second he looked nonplussed, but then he gathered himself and guided his horse over to the group, placing himself and his horse between the reporters and the platform. "You gentlemen were requested to remain on the grandstand," he said sternly. "You must realize that we cannot compromise our security arrangements, even to oblige the press. Please return immediately whence you came."

The third chest was now inside the goods wagon, placed carefully on its supporting frame, and the Indian carters were emerging from the wagon as the fourth chest was pulled up in its cart. "If you don't mind, my lord," Barnett called up to him, "we'd like to see inside that box."

"Box?" Lord East looked uncertain for a moment. "You mean the treasure chest, sir?"

"Yes, my lord," Higgins, of the *Pall Mall Gazette*, called. "There seems to be some doubt as to whether the treasure is actually in the chests, or whether this is merely a ruse."

"A ruse, gentlemen?" Lord East looked shocked. He had just been accused of doing something un-British.

"The suggestion is, my lord," Inglestone said, "ridiculous as it sounds, that you have spirited the treasure away by some alternate means, while encouraging us to believe that it is still in those chests. Thus supposedly foiling possible criminal attempts upon the collection."

Lord East considered for a second. "And just why should I do that?" he asked. "The treasure is quite safe where it is. Certainly safer than any other place I could put it. I do not like these devious methods you speak of, nor do I resort to them. They are unnecessary."

"Then, my lord, the treasure is, indeed, in the chests?" Inglestone asked, looking inordinately pleased. "You affirm that?"

"There is my seal," Lord East said, pointing with his riding crop to the lid of the fourth chest, now being inserted into the goods wagon. He indicated the strip of ribbon that went across the lid's opening, sealed above and below. "It has not been broken."

"You will permit us to check?" von Hertzog asked.

"I most certainly will not!" Lord East said sharply. He waved the chest on into the wagon. "Gentlemen, this is outrageous! How dare you question me! The chest will be opened at the Royal Albert Museum, in the presence of a representative of her imperial majesty, and not a jot before. Please return to your seats."

The reporters, muttering uncertainly, returned to the grandstand. Barnett watched as Lord East checked the inside of the goods wagon and then ordered it closed and sealed from the outside.

Barnett's part of the job, whatever it had accomplished, was done. Now there was nothing to do but wait for the train that would take Moriarty to Hampermire Station and himself through to London. How the little act he had just put on would further the cause, he didn't know, and at the moment he didn't care. Somewhere in London, Cecily Perrine had disappeared; somewhere in London she was at this very moment. In what state she was, Barnett did not care to speculate. How he would find her, he had no idea. But if she was still alive, find her he would.

The sun was coming up, and the area outside the limelight was just beginning to be visible. Moriarty and Barnett left the grandstand

and returned to the hotel. There was a telegram waiting for Moriarty when they arrived. He opened it and read it in a second. "Nothing," he said. "Sorry, Barnett. No trace of the lady yet."

"I'll find her," Barnett said.

"Of course you will," Moriarty told him.

TWENTY

ALWAYS DARKEST

I had a dream, which was not all a dream.
The bright sun was extinguished, and the stars
Did wander darkling in the eternal space,
Rayless, and pathless, and the icy Earth
Swung blind and blackening in the moonless air;
Morn came and went—and came, and brought no day...
GEORGE GORDON, LORD BYRON

Cecily Perrine awoke. Slowly, dimly, her awareness returned, and she was amazed to realize that she had been asleep. She had no idea how long she had slept; there was no way to mark the passage of time in her pitch-black surroundings. She rose from the ticking full of dank straw that was her mattress on the cold stone floor, and felt her way around the smooth stone walls. She did not know what she hoped to find, and in any case her groping fingers encountered nothing but damp stone. The cell she was in was approximately six feet square, and higher than her fingers could reach with her arms fully extended. It contained the straw-filled ticking, a chamber pot, and Cecily. The door in the corner of one wall was no more than a foot wide and four feet high, and held neither a peephole nor a doorknob.

She was not sure how, or why, she had arrived where she was. She remembered leaving the Hope mansion and walking toward her carriage. She had passed an alley where the Count d'Hiver was engaged in earnest conversation with some tall man. She remembered wondering who the man was, and where he had sprung from at such an hour. Then, on an idle whim, she had turned to hurry back to the mansion; she had thought of an unimportant question she wanted to put to Mr. Holmes. It would wait, but after all, she was there now. Rapid footsteps had sounded behind her, and a large, powerful man had grabbed her from behind. She had instinctively started to cry out, but her assailant had instantly clamped one great hand over her mouth, cutting her scream to no more than a loud gasp. He had then carried her a short distance, where some other person draped a sweet-smelling rag across her face. It must have been dosed with chloroform or some similar substance, for the next thing Cecily knew she was in this chamber.

It *must* have been Count d'Hiver and the man he was talking to who had done this thing to her; so she decided once again, as she had a dozen times before. But it made no sense. Why would the count, the representative of the Privy Seal and thus of the Queen, abduct Cecily Perrine? Why would he abduct anyone, for that matter? What did he want with her? Why had no one come to her cell—except the man in black—since she had been there?

The man in black! Four times since she had awakened from her drugged sleep to find herself in this featureless stone cell, the man in black had entered. He had given no warning; suddenly she had heard the bolts being thrown back and the door had opened. The cell had been bathed in a bright light—how bright she could not tell, since in her darkness a candle would have seemed the sun—and a man dressed all in tight-fitting black garments, even to a black hood and black mask, had stepped in.

She had, at first, tried speaking to him, reasoning with him, pleading with him, screaming at him; but to no avail. Four times he had put down bowls of rancid-smelling gruel and cups of water. Three times he had turned and left, wordlessly, gesturelessly. The fourth time he had reached out a hand and touched her on the arm; briefly, probingly, experimentally. And this had been the most horrible thing of all. He had not touched her as a man touches a woman, not even the gloating, possessive touch of a captor for his captive. This was immeasurably worse. There had not been even the humanity of lust in that touch. He had touched her as a farmer might probe a prize pig, to test the firmness of its skin, to feel its muscles, and how well fatted it was.

She could not tell how long she had been held a prisoner. She had been fed four times, but at what intervals? She had eaten but little of the gruel, and was still not hungry; but this was no indication. She felt wretched and afraid and alone, and such feelings would keep her from hunger for weeks, not merely days.

Cecily shrank back into the corner; there was that sound now, the *snick-snick-snick* of three bolts being thrown. The narrow wooden door was pulled open, and light flooded into the tiny cell. The tall man in black had once again come to visit. This time he brought no gruel. This time he took her by the arm and propelled her, as though she were a rag doll, out into the narrow stone corridor beyond the door. She resisted an impulse to cry out, feeling obscurely that it would give him satisfaction, and maintained a passive silence as he pushed her ahead of him down the corridor. He did not appear to notice her silence, any more than he had heeded her crying and pleading on his previous visits.

Cecily tried to prepare herself for whatever might happen. Her mind was in turmoil, and she realized that she had no idea what to prepare herself for. This was so far outside her experience as to be a succession of unbelievable happenings, one long nightmare from which she was unable to wake.

The light, which had seemed so blinding from within the black cell, proved to come from a row of gas-mantle fixtures set high in the corridor wall. From the way that the pipe ran along the outside of the wall, right below the ceiling, it was evident that the stone corridor and its row of cells had been constructed long before the coming of gaslight. She was captive in the ancient cellar of some great house, the house of a man important enough to plan on keeping captives in his own basement, back in the days when influential noblemen might expect to have a few captives of their own. And now the present owner of the house was using his inherited cellar for purposes that nineteenth-century authorities would frown on, if only they knew. That was a fact to be filed away. Probably useless, but a fact nonetheless. Collecting and sorting facts kept her mind busy and active, and that in itself was helpful.

The man in black paused at the end of the corridor to unlock a thick wooden door, and then to lock it behind him. Just habit? Or were there other prisoners in that hellish black dungeon?

After three more locked doors and a twisting iron staircase, they came at last to a room, a well-appointed study, the floor deeply carpeted and the walls lined with bookcases filled with leather-bound books. For all its fine appointments, there was something strange about the room, and it took Cecily a minute to figure out what it was: there were no windows.

Behind an ancient, ornately carved oak table in the middle of the room, perched on a chair that would have served as a throne in many lesser kingdoms, was a small man clad in a black velvet lounging suit, his face concealed behind a great harlequin mask. Cecily thought it looked suspiciously like the Count d'Hiver—the size and build were about right—but she couldn't be sure.

The man in black brought Cecily to the front of the table, facing the harlequin, and released her. The harlequin stared intently at her, his blue eyes peering through the mask's eye slits, and said nothing.

Cecily felt a mixture of strong emotions all trying to surface at once; fear, astonishment, hatred, and rage boiled inside of her, causing her heart to thump loudly in her chest, her face to flush, her hands to feel alternately hot and cold. She wanted to cry, to scream, to beg, to hit out with all of her might at the man in black, to throw herself across the desk and throttle the smug harlequin. And so she did nothing. She felt that the harlequin was waiting for her to speak, perhaps to beg, to entreat, to demand; and so, mustering all the self-control she had available in her weary, frightened body, she remained mute.

"Welcome!" the harlequin said at last, in a deep voice. (Artificially deep? The voice of d'Hiver, lowered for effect or disguise? She couldn't be sure.) "Do you know why you are here?"

"What?" The single syllable was drawn out of Cecily involuntarily, so shocked was she by the question. "Listen, you," she said, putting her hands flat on the table in front of her and leaning aggressively forward toward the masked man. "I've been kidnapped, drugged, locked up in a black, dank cell, fed some kind of repulsive gruel, ministered to by this ape behind me, and you want to know if I know why I'm here! I'm here against my will, obviously at your behest, and you shall suffer for this. You can't expect to get away with a thing like this in the middle of London in 1887, as though you were some sort of feudal lord. My friends are looking for me, and you will live to regret this. Don't think they won't find me!"

The man in black grabbed her by the hair and lifted her straight up and back away from the table, actually raising her off the floor with one hand. The suddenness of the act, the shock and surprise, and the almost unbearable pain made her scream and brought tears to her eyes. She grabbed for his hand just as he released her hair, causing her to fall heavily to the floor. "Stand!" he commanded—the first word he had spoken in her presence.

Cecily struggled to her feet, tears stinging her eyes. "You bastards!" she screamed across the desk. "If Benjamin were here—"

"You are here as an acolyte, a supplicant, a slave," the harlequin said, precisely as though nothing had just happened, as though she had remained respectfully silent. "There was some discussion at first about what you might know, or not know; but it was realized that it does not matter. What will grow in you, what will become of paramount importance, is your own knowledge of your condition. And that will change from day to day, from moment to moment."

She gaped at him. "What are you talking about?" she demanded. "Do you know what you're doing—what you've done? You must be insane!"

"I am the Master Incarnate," the harlequin continued, ignoring her outburst. "In the course of time, you will come to know other masters. You are to be removed from here, and taken to the place of your service. You will learn what it means to be a slave."

"Listen!" Cecily yelled, anger at this man, so smug behind his silly mask, outweighing her fear. "You—"

The harlequin turned to the man in black. "Is it time, Plantagenet?" he asked.

The man in black nodded.

The harlequin smiled. It was not a pleasant smile. "Take her!" he commanded.

"Now, look—" Cecily said.

The man called Plantagenet wrapped his right arm around her body, pinning her arms to her side. She tried to fight, but was unable to move in his iron grip. His left hand came up to her face, and there was a sweet-smelling rag in it.

"No!" she cried...

TWENTY-ONE

INSIDE OUT

In the still air the music lies unheard;
In the rough marble beauty lies unseen;
To wake the music and the beauty needs
The master's touch, the sculptor's chisel keen.
HORATIUS BONAR

After an uneventful journey through some of England's most beautiful countryside, Lord East's treasure train arrived in London shortly after four o'clock, Saturday afternoon, and came to rest at a specially designated siding in Hampton Court. It remained there, sealed and surrounded with its military escort, until two o'clock next afternoon, Sunday, when her imperial majesty's personal representative, the stern and splendidly choleric Duke of Denver, eighty years old and ramrod-stiff in the saddle, trotted officially over to accept delivery of the Lord East Collection, as an indefinite loan, in her majesty's name.

The seals on each of the special goods wagons were now broken, and the great doors rolled aside, one at a time. The contents of the first three wagons—statuary, pillars, walls, friezes, and great stone urns—had passed the trip in fine condition. The fourth wagon, holding the five great treasure chests, appeared to be as it was when it was sealed. With a flourish, Lord East himself opened the first chest—

—which was empty.

In a haste approaching frenzy, the lids of the other four chests were pried off, revealing the impossible: each chest contained nothing but air, and dust, and one small seed pearl which was found wedged in a crack on the bottom of the third chest.

All the color drained out of Lord East's face, and, were it not for the instant aid of his two faithful Indian companions, he would have fainted dead away on the wagon floor. "It's impossible!" he screamed to the Duke of Denver, as his aides helped him over the side of the wagon and down to the ground. "I tell you, the thing's manifestly impossible! They *can't* be gone!"

The Duke of Denver wheeled in his saddle and turned to his escort, the Captain Commander of the Household Guard. "Get me Sherlock Holmes!" he ordered.

* * *

Benjamin Barnett did not return to the Russell Square house until late Sunday night, having spent every moment since he arrived back in London on Saturday afternoon doing his best to find out what had happened to Cecily Perrine. As far as he could discover, she had left the Hope mansion slightly after two o'clock the morning of Thursday, the thirty-first of March, and then disappeared off the face of the earth. He could seem to get no further.

When he entered the house, Professor Moriarty was in his study, reading a late-edition *Evening Standard*. "Ah!" Moriarty said, waving him into the room. "The wanderer returns. You look exhausted. Have you eaten? Take a glass of sherry."

"No, thank you," Barnett said, dropping onto the leather couch and pulling off his shoes. "I haven't sat down in, it must be, twenty-four hours. I confess, I don't have much energy left."

"Not surprising," Moriarty said. "You have been quite busy, although it has been the purposeless busy-ness of a headless chicken. You scurry here, you scurry there, you accomplish nothing."

"You've been having me followed!" Barnett accused.

"Nonsense!" Moriarty responded. "But most of the places you've been, most of the people you've spoken to, are being covered by my agents, who are just about ubiquitous at the moment. I told you I'd have five hundred people on the street. In addition to the minions usually in my employ in such cases, every member of Twist's Beggar's Guild is now keeping his eyes open for Miss Cecily Perrine. I have offered a hundred pounds reward for any word. More would be counterproductive."

"That's very nice of you," Barnett said. "But what good will it do? How would they know her if they see her?"

"Mr. Doyle, the sketch artist, was kind enough to do a portrait from memory, which I have had reproduced on a small letterpress." Moriarty lifted a piece of paper from his desk and, with a flip of his wrist, skimmed it across the room to Barnett. "A good likeness, I think."

Barnett stared at the picture on the four-by-five-inch card. "Amazingly good," he agreed, trying to ignore the lump that rose in his throat. "They should certainly recognize her if they see her, with the aid of this. But supposing they don't?"

"Always possible," Moriarty said. "I have taken certain other steps which might lead to Miss Perrine. I don't want to raise false hopes—"

"What are they?" Barnett demanded. "Please tell me what you're doing."

Moriarty shook his head. "They may lead to nothing," he said. "But then, if so, I will think of something else. Perhaps some slender shred of information, some slight indication, will come in; that's all I need, a slender thread. I have been known to accomplish wonders with a slender thread."

Barnett stared morosely at Moriarty, and then shook his head. "I know you're trying to cheer me up," he said. "And don't think I'm not grateful. I am. I've never known you to go to such trouble before over someone else's problem; and I know you probably consider it weak of me to be so emotional about it—"

"Not to have emotions is to be less than human, Mr. Barnett," Moriarty said. "The trick we British learn is not to display them. Perhaps I have learned that trick better than most. But you are not

British. And your emotions are entirely understandable. You should not, however, allow them to cloud your reason, which will be of much greater use in actually recovering Miss Perrine."

"She may already be dead," Barnett said, speaking aloud for the first time what had been preying on his mind for the past day and a half.

"I doubt it," Moriarty said. "If whoever abducted her wished her dead, he would have merely killed her. It is, after all, so much less trouble."

"Perhaps—" Barnett paused. "A fate worse than death..."

"Don't torture yourself, Mr. Barnett," Moriarty said. "Besides, despite the Romantic writers, there is no fate worse than death. Any pain, indignation, or horror that Miss Perrine may experience at the hands of her abductors will fade away with time—and love. Death, Mr. Barnett, will not fade away."

Barnett sat up. "I suppose you're right, Professor," he said. "It's doing nothing—at least, nothing useful—that's driving me crazy. If there were only something I could do!"

"Get a good night's sleep," Moriarty said. "Get your mind off this thing, at least as much as possible. I promise you that tomorrow you will start useful activity."

Barnett stood up and stretched. "Your word's good with me, Professor," he said. "I guess it has to be. I'll do my best. Tonight I sleep. Tomorrow I follow your instructions. If the blisters on my feet allow me to walk at all."

"Have Mrs. H give you a basin in which to soak your feet," Moriarty said. "She has some sort of concoction that works wonders on abused feet."

"I'll do that," Barnett said. He pointed to the *Evening Standard* that Moriarty was holding. "I read about the great mystery," he added. "Two tons of precious jewelry disappears from a locked goods wagon. The mystery sensation of the age. I was part of it, Professor, and I confess that I have no idea of how you managed it."

"Let us hope that the authorities remain as puzzled as you are," Moriarty said. He reached to the side of his desk and picked up a small bronze statuette that Barnett had never noticed before. "May the luck of Uma stay with us."

"Uma?" Barnett asked.

"A Hindu goddess," Moriarty told him. "Consort of Shiva. A fascinating, complex religion, that."

"That's not part of the, ah, loot, is it?" Barnett asked, looking alarmed.

"Never mind," Moriarty said. "It's not important. Go to bed."

"Tell me how you did it," Barnett said.

"Did what?"

"The robbery. Tell me how you removed two tons of jewelry from a locked wagon while it was surrounded by armed guards."

Moriarty considered. "Briefly," he said.

Barnett nodded.

"Like most things that seem impossible," Moriarty said, "it was actually quite simple. I'm afraid that telling you will ruin the effect."

"Please, Professor," Barnett said. "After all, I was part of it."

"True," Moriarty admitted. "And a very important part, although you knew not what you did."

"What did I do?"

"The problem was," Moriarty said, "to get someone into that sealed wagon."

Barnett nodded. "That was indeed the problem," he agreed.

And you did it," Moriarty said.

"*I* did?"

"With a brilliant bit of misdirection. You see, I already had an agent in place: one of the Indian porters was my man. He arranged to be among the crew who carried the third treasure chest into the wagon."

"And then?"

"And then, while you drew the momentary attention of everyone with your clever little wager, he merely stayed behind in the wagon while the others left."

"But that's impossible," Barnett said. "Lord East inspected the wagon after it was loaded, and there was no place for anyone to hide. The walls were even covered with fabric."

"Indeed," Moriarty said. "And an interesting quality of any such solid-color material is that from more than two feet or so distant, you cannot tell how far away you are from any piece of identical fabric without an external referent."

"What does that mean?" Barnett asked. "I confess that you've lost me."

"Picture a table, placed, let us say, five feet in front of a fabric curtain," Moriarty said. "You are staring at the table with the curtain behind it. Wherever you look you see the curtain—above the table, to the right of the table, to the left of the table, between the legs of the table. Correct?"

"I guess so."

"I know, it sounds too obvious to be worth stating. But now, supposing I take a piece of fabric that is identical to the curtain and fasten it between the back legs of the table, from the rim of the table to the floor. When you look at it, you'll think you see the back curtain, but in reality you'll be staring at a piece of fabric that is five feet closer to you."

"I see," Barnett said.

"And between that fabric and the actual curtain," Moriarty said, "I could hide a man, a donkey, a small cannon, or anything else that would fit, and you'd be willing to swear that you could see the whole area clearly, and there was nothing there."

Barnett thought this over. "So that's how you did it," he said.

"That's how *you* did it," Moriarty replied. "You distracted the crowd for long enough for my agent to drop a fabric curtain that he had rolled around one of the carrying bars for the chest. There he was, crouched down, in the supposedly empty area between the chest and the wall. Lord East thought he could see the far wall, but he couldn't."

"So the wagon was sealed with the man inside."

"Just so."

"But how did the man get the treasure out?"

"One piece at a time."

"And the guards?"

"It was invisible to the guards."

"You mesmerized them?"

Moriarty chuckled. "Listen, and I shall describe the rest of the operation," he said. "The agent in the goods wagon waited until the train was in motion. Then he pried up a one-foot-square section of the sheet-metal floor with a device that I had fabricated, which looks a great deal like an oversized tin opener. After which he took a small keyhole saw and leisurely cut out the underlying boards. For this task he was allowed two hours.

"The next step was to stop the train at a precisely predetermined point."

"A snap," Barnett commented.

"Indeed it was," Moriarty agreed, "if I correctly interpret that barbaric expression. Especially a 'snap' if you consider that the engine driver was almost certainly not going to overrun a danger signal on the semaphore repeater. And if you consider that the railways use a 'positive' system of signaling, which assures that the normal condition of the signal arm will be 'danger.' This means that if any natural misfortune occurs to the semaphore apparatus, it assumes the 'danger' position rather than the 'safety' or 'caution' positions."

"A natural misfortune?"

"Correct. In this case, a severely corroded cable accidentally snapped. The maintenance division must be sternly spoken to. A 'snap,' as you say. There are substances known to chemists which can incredibly speed up the corrosion of any metal object."

"And the signal swung to 'danger'?"

"Just so. And the engine driver of Lord East's caravan stopped the train. What else was he to do?"

"And then?"

"A hatch opened between the metals—what you would call the rails—in the track bed. Carefully disguised as two wooden sleepers and the space between, the hatch covered a specially constructed chamber buried in the embankment. The hatch was so placed as to be directly beneath the hole in the floor of the wagon when the train halted at the signal."

"That simple?" Barnett marveled. "And the treasure was just handed out?"

"No, no, the stop would not be nearly long enough for that," Moriarty said. "I estimated three minutes. As it happened, they took seven, but even that would not have been nearly long enough for the transfer of that bulk of boodle. No, Mr. Barnett, what happened at this carefully prearranged pause was that certain materials were handed up into the wagon. And then a second man joined the one who was already there.

"This second man was an expert in the ancient craft of reproducing seals. And he brought with him the needed equipment—to wit, a spoon, a candle, and a loaf of bread."

Barnett sat back down on the couch. Moriarty had obviously succeeded in his attempt to distract his assistant from his troubles, at least for the moment. "A loaf of bread?" Barnett asked.

"The best way to duplicate a wax seal in anything like a reasonable length of time," Moriarty said, "is to take an impression of it with moist bread which you have kneaded between your palms. Done by an expert, it's as effective as any other method. What the expert does in this case is to use a hot wire to separate the seal from the treasure chest, first making a bread impression of it in case it breaks while being removed."

"Yes, but why bother?" Barnett asked. "Why not just break open the chests?"

"It adds an extra element of confusion," Moriarty said. "It is my experience that a crime should be either so simple that there is no place to look for a solution, or so confusing that there are too many places to look. In this case, I chose the latter."

"How do you mean, Professor?"

Moriarty thought for a second. "In a simple crime," he explained, "you know all the elements, but they take you nowhere. A man is hit on the head, and his purse is taken. When he comes to, there is nobody around. You know everything that happened, but unless he recognized his assailant, it is virtually hopeless to try to recover the purse.

"In a complex crime, there are so many factors to trace down that much time is lost before you find out which are pertinent. The seals are broken on the chests, and they are found to be empty. But you don't know when the treasure was removed. Before the chests were loaded on the train? After the train left Plymouth? After it arrived at Hampton Court? Each of these must be investigated. It confuses things, you see."

"What did happen?" Barnett asked.

"After the train started up again, my agents opened the treasure chests, removed all the baubles, and closed and very carefully resealed the chests. Then, immediately after the train passed through Hampermire Station, they spread newspaper on the floor, and carefully immersed each article in a basin containing an oily solution, with just a hint of creosote, which dyed the item a dingy brown. Then they tossed it through the hole. The jewelry was spread over six miles of track, and quite invisible unless you were looking for it. Even then it would be easy to miss."

"You were at Hampermire," Barnett said.

"True. And Toby was waiting for me."

"Toby?"

"A hound I borrowed from a friend. Quite a nose, Toby has. I believe he could follow the scent of creosote through a windstorm in a peppermill."

"Ah!" Barnett said.

"The rest is obvious," Moriarty said. "The two in the wagon cleaned up, leaving no trace of themselves, and tossed the detritus onto the track, where other agents immediately removed it. Then they themselves went into a carefully prepared hole when the train was forced to stop for a herd of cows which had unaccountably broken through their fence and wandered onto the track. They pulled a specially prepared metal patch over the hole in the floor and, by igniting a thin strip of magnesium which came out the bottom, caused it to solder itself into place."

Barnett thought this over for a while. "Very neat," he said. "They'll never catch on to it. It will be one of the mysteries of the century."

"I doubt that," Moriarty said. "The authorities will, sooner or later, discover how it was done. Especially if, as I suspect, they call in Sherlock Holmes. But by the time they figure it out, the back-trail will be so cold that all their leads will peter out into dead ends. Your little bit of misdirection, I believe, will elude even Mr. Holmes."

"I sincerely hope so," Barnett said. "I have developed a distinct aversion to prison food." He got up and, taking his shoes in his hand, hobbled out of the study and started up the stairs.

TWENTY-TWO

TETE-A-TETE

*"He knows that I know, and I'm sure he knows that I know he
knows. But for all of that, can I assume that he knows I know he
knows I know he knows?"*
*"I don't follow that," the baroness replied. "And I wish you'd stop;
you're giving me quite a headache!"*
D'ARCY ST. MICHEL

At ten o'clock the next morning, Sherlock Holmes was at the front
door of 64 Russell Square, yanking on the bellpull. "Tell your
master I wish to see him," he announced when the butler opened
the door.

"Yes, sir," Mr. Maws replied, bowing and stepping aside in a
parody of butlerian stiffness. "Alone today, are you, sir? Please follow
me into the study. The professor is expecting you. I shall inform him
that you're here, and he will be down directly."

"Expecting me, is he?" Holmes asked, stalking into the study and
glaring around at the furnishings.

"Yes, sir," Mr. Maws said. "So he told me, sir."

Ten minutes later, when Moriarty came downstairs and entered the
study, he found Holmes crouching in front of the desk, unabashedly
going through the third drawer down. "Looking for something?"
Moriarty demanded, reaching around his desk and slamming the drawer.

Holmes jerked his hand aside. "Always, Professor," he said. "And someday I'll find it." He retreated to the black leather armchair on the other side of the desk. "I have this insatiable curiosity about you, Professor Moriarty. Every little thing you do is of interest to me. Every little scrap of paper in this room helps, in some small way, round out my picture of you and your activities."

"Would you care to go through the bottom drawer?" Moriarty asked. "I assume you've already been through the upper two."

"Very kind of you," Holmes said. "Some other time, perhaps."

Moriarty settled into the chair behind his desk and regarded Holmes unblinkingly. "You have lost all shame, Holmes," he said. "It was but a few weeks ago that you and a squad of cloddish policemen went through this house from attic to sub-basement, examining the contents of every drawer, scratching furniture, bending lampshades, ripping curtains, breaking porcelain, and no doubt stealing the silver. After that farce it will be a long time before you get any judge to issue you another warrant against any of my property. And yet here you are again, going through my desk."

"Your butler had me wait in here," Holmes said mildly. "I was merely amusing myself while I waited."

"I admit I should have locked the drawers and cabinets before you arrived," Moriarty said. "But I keep forgetting, Holmes, that you are capable of such appalling manners."

Holmes chuckled. "Perhaps you are right," he admitted. "But only in my dealings with you, Moriarty. I assure you that when it comes to the rest of humanity, I am considered urbane and civil, and my manners are irreproachable. There is something about our relationship that brings out my worst qualities. I think it is, perhaps, the fact that every time I see you sitting there in your sack coat and your striped trousers and your impeccably knotted cravat, with a painting worth ten thousand pounds hanging on your wall and a library filled with rare books and a wine cellar filled with rare vintages, I cannot help reflecting that were there any justice in this world, you would be wearing gray cloth and occupying your time by walking the treadmill at Dartmoor."

"Justice, Holmes? Were there any justice, you would be forced by the state, whose rules you admire so greatly, to spend your time in some profession more fitting to your talents, such as giving diverting lectures in music halls, and identifying the occupations of ten random ticket holders. Instead you spend your days following me about and annoying me at every opportunity."

"Your butler said you expected me," Holmes said.

"And so I did," Moriarty replied.

"Why? I had no appointment with you."

"There was a major crime yesterday, was there not?" Moriarty inquired. "An 'impossible' crime, one of the newspapers called it. Surely it was not a wide leap of logic to assume that you would be called in. And even more surely, you would immediately scurry around to see me. Hoping, no doubt, to find a great pile of stolen artifacts on the rug."

"Indeed," Holmes agreed complacently. "Almost startled not to. You don't object, I suppose, if I look *under* the rug?"

Moriarty sighed. "Understand, Holmes, that I am somewhat honored that you suspect me of committing every crime in London that you can't solve. However, it does get to be wearing after a time."

"Not the crimes I can't solve, Professor," Holmes said, smiling tightly. "In several instances I have solved them to my satisfaction, I have just been unable to provide enough proof to bring the case before a jury. That is where you have shown yourself so infernally clever, my dear Professor Moriarty. *I* know you for the rogue you are, but I can't prove it. However, you and I know that I shall not stop trying; and one of these times, I shall succeed. And then you will exchange your black sack coat for prison gray. But enough of this cheery conversation; I wish to speak to you of trains and treasures."

"Curiously enough, Holmes, I also wish to speak to you, although on another subject. Shall we discuss the fate of the Lord East Collection first, and then get on to more consequential matters?"

There was a knock at the door. "That would be Mr. Barnett," Moriarty said. "I have asked him to sit in our little tête-à-tête, if you don't mind?" Then, without waiting for Holmes's response, he called for Barnett to come in.

"Good morning, Professor," Barnett said, coming through the door with a cup of coffee in his hand. He looked rested. "Good morning, Mr. Holmes." He sat down on the leather couch and sipped his coffee.

"It has all the markings of a Moriarty crime," Holmes said, ignoring Barnett. "I can sense your hand in this undertaking just as an art connoisseur can recognize a work of Goya or of Vernet, whether or not the canvas is signed. And then when I learned that you were actually present at the loading of the goods wagons, how could I doubt further? Moriarty was present; a fortune was stolen: *Quid hoc sibi vult?*"

"I was there," Moriarty said. "I make no apologies for my presence. It was mere vulgar curiosity. And as a matter of fact, it was not gratified. We did not get to see the treasure, as I'm sure you know."

"That's true," Barnett commented. "I mentioned it at the time. Loudly. How were we to know it was even in those boxes? Why wouldn't Lord East open them? What was he hiding? It is my duty as a journalist to ask these questions."

Holmes turned and favored Barnett with a scowl, then he returned his gaze to Moriarty. "I have indications of the method already," he said. "I believe the floor of the goods wagon has been tampered with. I have discovered that the train stopped twice on the way to London—both times briefly, both times accidentally. It is, perhaps, a flaw in my nature that I distrust such accidents."

"So?" Moriarty demanded. "Would you like to drag me off to prison now, or wait until you get some sort of proof that I was actually involved?"

"Don't ask me what I'd like to do, Professor," Holmes said, his long fingers tapping restlessly on the arm of his chair. "You know very well what I'd like to do."

"Pshaw!" Moriarty said. "Let us turn from the fanciful to the pertinent, Mr. Holmes." He reached down and, opening the bottom drawer of his desk, pulled out a thick handful of file folders. "I would like to discuss with you the seven murders which have taken place since the twenty-second of February."

Holmes stood up and pointed at the folders. "Those," he said, with a slight quaver in his voice, "are the official files!"

"Not quite," Moriarty said. "They are merely accurate transcripts of the official files. Certified duplicates of all the material contained in the files."

"Where did you obtain them?" Holmes demanded.

"From Giles Lestrade," Moriarty said. "There's no secret about it. I am, after all, working on the case."

"You're what?"

"I have offered my services to Scotland Yard, and have been accepted. Without a fee, of course. I have a private client, but there is no conflict of interest since my client's only concern is to have the murderer apprehended."

Holmes stared at Moriarty with fascination. "I don't believe it," he murmured.

"Why not?" Moriarty asked. "I am, after all, a consultant."

"Let us not discuss what you are, for the moment," Holmes said. "What I'm trying to figure out is what you'll be getting out of this."

"Paid," Moriarty said. "I will be collecting a fee from my private client."

"There is that, of course," Holmes said. "Frankly, Professor, I had just about concluded that you were not involved in the killings when I heard about the robbery. Then I was sure. Since you are so clearly involved in the robbery, you wouldn't really have had time to take part in the slaughter of the upper class."

Moriarty tapped the pile of folders in front of him. "I've been reading these reports, Holmes," he said. "And I would like to see how your conclusions compare with mine."

Holmes leaned back in his chair and laced his fingers together. He stared thoughtfully at Moriarty over his cupped hands for a minute. "Go ahead," he said.

"We'll start with basics," Moriarty said. "One murderer."

"Agreed."

"Male."

"Agreed."

"Early forties."

"Most likely."

"Average to slightly above in height."

"That's all in my report!" Holmes said. "All you're doing is reading my own report back to me."

"What report?" Moriarty asked. "There is no such report in these files."

"Ah!" Holmes said. "I gave that report directly to Lord Arundale. I suppose he never bothered returning it to the Scotland Yard files."

"I have noticed this regrettable tendency myself," Moriarty said. "It would seem that the aristocracy has little regard for record keeping. Except tables of genealogy, of course. Tell me, what other observations about the murderer have you detailed on this absent report?"

Barnett, watching this exchange with interest, could see how speaking civilly to Moriarty, how volunteering information to this friend and mentor that he had turned into an enemy, caused the muscles in Holmes's jaw to tighten, forming his lips into an involuntary grimace. But Holmes, with an effort of will, conquered his feelings. "I believe he is a foreigner," the detective said. "Probably Eastern European."

"A logical interpretation," Moriarty agreed. "But if so, he almost certainly speaks English like a native."

"I truly dislike interrupting, and I wouldn't doubt either of you for the world, but from where are you two getting these notions?" Barnett asked. "I've been following these killings, as you know, and you lost me a while back, right after you decided it was a man. For me, even that would still be conjecture."

"Oh come now, Mr. Barnett," Holmes said, swiveling around to look at him. "These crimes all take place late at night, for one thing. A woman skulking around at such an hour would certainly be noted."

"A woman in man's clothing?" Barnett suggested, just to keep up his side of the argument.

"Then there is the matter of simple physical strength," Moriarty said, tapping his fingers on the desk. "Each of the victims would seem to have been easily overpowered by his assailant."

"Drugs," Barnett suggested.

"There is no sign that any of them ate or drank anything prior to their demise," Holmes said. "With several of them, it is certain that they didn't."

"All right," Barnett said, giving up on that point, "but what about the rest of it?"

"We presume a single murderer because the killings are idiosyncratic, each like the others down to fine detail," Moriarty said. "More than one person would surely have more than one opinion as to how to properly knife a man, at least in some small detail. And then, you note how easily our killer assumes a cloak of invisibility? Hard as it is for one man to vanish as easily as our killer has, it is at least twice as hard for two."

"The age is more of a probability," Holmes said. "Not an old man, because of the required physical strength in the murders and physical dexterity in the disappearances—however they are contrived. And yet not a young man because of the care taken in the crime, and the economy of savagery in what are clearly murders of passion."

"Passion?"

"Probably revenge," Moriarty said. "Which is why we put it to a foreigner."

"Englishmen, I take it, are incapable of acts of revenge?" Barnett inquired.

"Not at all," Moriarty said. "But they would usually use their fists, or some handy weapon, and do it immediately and in public. Englishmen do not believe, as do the Italians, that revenge is a dish best eaten cold."

"And your hot-blooded Latin races would probably not commit such a surgical murder as each of these has been," Holmes said. "This, of course, is not conclusive, it merely indicates a direction for investigation."

"I'm not convinced," Barnett said.

"Luckily, that is not essential," Moriarty said.

"What about Miss Perrine's kidnapping?" Barnett asked. "How do you fit that in?"

Holmes pursed his lips. "That is a problem," he said. "It certainly doesn't coincide with the murderer's pattern, and yet it would be

stretching the bounds of credulity to suggest that it could be unrelated."
He chuckled. "Lestrade thinks it was the murderer returning to the
scene of his crime. It makes one believe in competitive examinations
for the rank of detective inspector."

"Have you any information that is not on these reports, Holmes?"
Moriarty asked.

"On the killings or the disappearance?"

"Either," Moriarty said. "We are interested in both."

"Only the possibly relevant fact that, for the past few days, someone
has had me followed about by a gang of street ruffians. However, I
strongly suspect that the someone is you."

Moriarty nodded. "I admit it," he said.

"An unpardonable liberty," Holmes stated.

Moriarty chuckled. "Not at all," he replied. "Indeed, it is strange
to hear you say that, considering that you have a substantial portion
of the plainclothes police force following me about on every occasion
when they are not otherwise occupied. Turnabout, Holmes."

Holmes smiled grimly. "Revenge, Professor?"

"On the contrary, Holmes. It occurred to me that whoever
removed Miss Perrine from the public eye might not be satisfied with
this one triumph, but might go after bigger game. If so, I wanted to
have my agents at hand when he did. Unfortunately, the idea seems
not to have occurred to him. I take it no murderous attacks have been
made on your person in the past few days that I do not know of?"

"You think someone might be after me?" Holmes asked, clearly
astounded at the notion.

"I think it possible," Moriarty said. "I don't think it probable, but
I decided it would be worthwhile to keep an eye on you."

"Well!" Holmes said. "You suspect that Miss Perrine might have
been kidnapped because of something she knew? But she knew nothing
that wasn't published the next day in ten morning newspapers."

"Perhaps the kidnapper was not aware of that," Moriarty said. "Or
perhaps she discovered something of which we are unaware."

"Really, Moriarty," Holmes said. "I profess, I dislike this role
reversal, whatever your excuse. Let us keep things in their proper

perspective: you are the criminal and I am the detective."

"One of the first things you must realize about categories, Holmes," Moriarty said, lecturing the detective in the dry, didactic tone he was so fond of, "is that they are not immutable."

"Come now, Professor," Holmes said. "As a scientist, you surely cannot maintain that the truth is not a fixed quantity."

"No, sir, but I can and do maintain that our perception of the truth is ever changing. What was regarded as 'truth' in science but a generation ago is laughable now. And human affairs, Mr. Holmes, change even more rapidly. Also human beings are far more complex than you give them credit for. It is not enough to read the calluses on a man's fingers and know that he is a cork-cutter. To understand him, you must also be able to read his soul: to know his fears, his needs, his ambitions, his desires, and his secret shames."

"All of which you, undoubtedly, perceive at an instant, eh, Professor?" Holmes said smugly.

"I do not claim to be a detective, Holmes. The hearts of stars are, to me, far more transparent than the hearts of men."

"Are you going to persist in having me followed?" Holmes demanded.

"Not if it bothers you," Moriarty said. "I wouldn't dream of it. Are you going to persist in having me followed, Holmes?"

"Of course," Holmes said. He stood up. "If you can name this mad killer, or locate Miss Perrine, I shall be the first to applaud. But I still intend to establish your complicity in the treasure-train robbery."

"You'll understand if I don't wish you luck," Moriarty said dryly.

"Is there any other action which you have taken in regard to these killings that you have failed to mention?" Holmes asked.

"One obvious measure," Moriarty said, "in an effort to precipitate some sort of reaction." He handed a folded copy of the *Morning Telegraph* to Holmes. "I placed a small boxed advertisement in several dailies. Here is its first appearance."

Barnett stood up and read over Holmes's shoulder.

LOST—several small medallions. Identical designs.
Apply 64 Russell Square. REWARD.

"Interesting idea," Holmes said. "If it is, indeed, a medallion that the murderer has been taking from his victims."

"That's the most likely word to describe whatever the objects are," Moriarty said.

"You don't think the killer is going to answer your advertisement?" Barnett asked. "I mean, he's going to a lot of trouble to collect these things, whatever they are. He's not likely to hand them over to you."

"That's so," Moriarty agreed. "But strange things happen in this world, especially if one encourages them. He may have an avaricious landlady who wonders why he is collecting so many identical artifacts. Or he may just leave them somewhere after using them for whatever he does use them for. Or a sneak thief may by some great chance filch them from his bureau drawer, where he has them secreted. One can never tell, can one, Holmes?"

Holmes put down the newspaper. "I must go," he said. He reached out for the small bronze statuette of Uma that stood on a corner of Moriarty's desk. "I shall borrow this for a while if you don't mind, Professor."

"You'll *what?*" Moriarty demanded, leaping to his feet. "Now look here, Holmes—"

"I hold in my hand," Holmes said, raising the object to eye level, "a small bronze statuette inlaid with precious and semiprecious stones, obviously of Indian origin. It was not here the last time I visited. Indeed, I can safely say that it was nowhere in the house. And now, shortly after a vast Indian treasure has been stolen, I find it here on your desk. Surely, knowing of my suspicions, you want me to take this statuette away with me and compare it against all the items on Lord East's list, don't you, Professor? You want to show me up, prove that my suspicions were for naught, have the last laugh—don't you, Professor James Moriarty?"

Moriarty glared at his thin, intense antagonist. "I am tempted to say no," he said. "The impulse to annoy you as strongly as you annoy me is almost irresistible. You know you have no right to remove that bronze without my permission unless you get a warrant, showing probable cause. Which would be stretching the truth, something you would not consider in other circumstances. I am strongly tempted to make you step outside and whistle up a policeman, and force the poor fellow to scurry off in search of some complaint magistrate who is unaware of your vendetta against me and might possibly issue such a warrant. But then I'd have to put up with your sitting here glaring at me for half the day, clutching the bronze to your breast, wondering whether the warrant had been issued or not.

"And so I won't. I haven't the time for such fancies. Take the thing, Holmes. Give me a receipt for it. And when you're forced to return it, I shall frame the receipt and hang it next to the ten-thousand-pound Vernet you object to so much."

Holmes brought out his small notebook and scribbled a receipt on a page, which he ripped out and handed to Moriarty. "I shall be back within two days, Professor," he said. "Either to return the bronze, or to take you away. Which do you suppose it will be?"

"I expect an apology," Moriarty told Holmes, "when you return the bronze."

"I expect a confession," Holmes replied, "when I take you to prison. Do you suppose either of us will be satisfied with what we actually get? But enough! Much as I am enjoying our little chat, I really must be off."

"If you must—" Moriarty said.

Holmes turned to Barnett. "Dealing with Professor Moriarty creates in me an attitude that is destructive of my manners and my sentiments," he said. "I want you to know that I am aware of your attachment to Miss Perrine, and I fully sympathize with the sense of loss that you must be feeling now."

Barnett nodded his thanks. "It is more a sense of futility," he replied. "There is little I can do that is useful. I can keep busy, which keeps my mind off the problem but brings me no closer to finding Miss Perrine."

"I and my temporary associates of Scotland Yard are doing everything we can to locate and rescue the girl. I pray we will be successful." Holmes nodded to Moriarty. "Don't bother showing me out."

With a final glance around the room, Holmes stepped purposefully to the front door and threw it open. "*Au revoir*, Professor," he called, striding through the door and slamming it behind him.

"A unique man," Barnett commented.

"True," Moriarty agreed. "For which I am profoundly grateful. More than one Sherlock Holmes on this planet at the same time is an idea that I do not wish to contemplate."

"Tell me, Professor," Barnett said, "*is* that statuette from the robbery?"

"Yes," Moriarty said.

"Can Holmes prove it?" asked Barnett.

"That remains to be seen," Moriarty replied.

A loud clattering sound came from the street outside the house, followed almost immediately by a great crash. Moriarty and Barnett jumped to their feet. Before the sound of the crash had died away, the voices of several people yelling and the shrill sound of a woman screaming joined the cacophony.

Barnett rushed to the front door and ran outside, with Moriarty right behind him. There on the pavement in front of the house a large poultry cart had overturned; its wheels were still spinning in the air. The horse had apparently broken free, and was racing off in a maddened frenzy down the road. Right behind it raced a small covered chaise, its driver whipping its horse to even greater effort.

"'Megawd!" an elderly woman screamed, pulling her shawl about her as bystanders started to gather around the scene. "I ain't never seen nothing like it. "'E done it on purpose, 'e did. Rode right up on the pavement, right at the poor man. 'E never 'ad a chance! It were murder!"

"Calm down, woman!" Moriarty ordered. "Who murdered whom?"

"The Johnny what were atop of the cart," the old lady sobbed. "The Johnny what leaped into that other gig and ran off after 'e'd started the cart toward the pavement. 'E deliberately aimed the cart right for that poor gentleman there!" She pointed. On the ground, almost buried under crates of terrified geese, lay the unconscious body of Sherlock Holmes.

TWENTY-THREE

THE POSSIBLE

Truth, like a torch, the more it's shook it shines.
SIR WILLIAM HAMILTON

With the assistance of the curator of the Egyptian Collection of the British Museum and a retired sergeant of marines, both of whom were passing at the moment of the accident, Moriarty and Barnett carried Sherlock Holmes up to the front bedroom and placed him gently on the bed. Holmes's face was bloody, but his breathing was regular and even. Moriarty checked his pulse and pulled an eyelid back to examine the eye.

"How is he?" Barnett asked.

"Alive," Moriarty replied. "Unconscious—perhaps suffering from concussion. No broken bones that I can tell. My expertise in medical matters goes no further." He pulled out his handkerchief and dabbed tentatively at Holmes's bloody face. "Thank you gentlemen for your assistance," he said to the sergeant and the curator. "You'd best leave your names, as the police may wish to question you about the incident."

The two men both protested that they had not actually observed what happened, but allowed Barnett to write down their names before bustling off downstairs.

Mrs. H appeared in the bedroom doorway with a basin of warm water and a sponge, and shooed Moriarty and Barnett aside. "I'll take care of him," she said. "I have sent Mr. Maws off to Cavendish Square to fetch Dr. Breckstone."

"I don't know what I'd do without you, Mrs. H," Moriarty said.

She sniffed. "I don't either, Professor, and that's the truth!"

"A wonderful woman," Moriarty told Barnett as they headed downstairs to the study. "She is both secure and humble in her certain knowledge of her proper place, which is most assuredly on God's right hand." He took the bronze statuette, which he had retrieved from where it had fallen alongside of Holmes, and replaced it on the corner of his desk. "Very curious," he said. "Very curious, indeed."

"Mrs. H?" Barnett asked.

"No, no; the, ah, incident."

"It certainly is," Barnett agreed. "Who could have done a thing like that? I don't imagine that there is any doubt that it was deliberate?"

"I wouldn't think so," Moriarty said dryly. "One doesn't usually prepare a getaway from an accident. The question is, why was Holmes assaulted, and why at this peculiar place and time?"

"I'm sure the man has many enemies," Barnett said.

"I am amazed that he has any friends," Moriarty commented. "There is always his faithful hound, Dr. Watson, of course; but you'll notice that Holmes has never married."

"Neither have you, Professor," Barnett said.

Moriarty glared at Barnett for a minute, then he nodded. "Touché!" he said. "But, nonetheless—" He broke off and stared, musingly, at the windows for a minute.

"What is it?" Barnett asked.

"It occurs to me that we have probably just had the first response to our advertisement," Moriarty said slowly.

"We have?"

"Indeed. It came in the form of an attack on Sherlock Holmes."

"You think that was the killer out there?"

"No," Moriarty said. "That's what had me puzzled at first. It's not his method. Curiously enough, I believe we have taken a tree with more than one apple. Someone else was frightened by the advertisement, frightened enough to feel the need for direct and drastic measures. He must have come along to see if the advertisement meant what he feared it meant. Perhaps he meant to come inside, but that proved unnecessary. He found out what he needed to know from the outside, and he was prepared to take instant action."

"But why against Holmes?" Barnett asked.

"That was his clue," Moriarty said. "The presence of Holmes must have signified something to him—clearly something that it does not signify to us. He recognized the detective as a part of the menace."

"Farfetched," Barnett said. Moriarty merely smiled.

The front door slammed, and Mummer Tolliver came limping into the room. "'E got away," he announced.

"Too bad," Moriarty said. "Who?"

"The bloke what I was following. The bloke what drove that cart against poor Mr. Holmes."

"You were following him?" Barnett asked, surprised.

"Well, I were out there to follow Mr. Holmes. But when that cart 'it 'im, I didn't think as 'ow 'e were going anywhere for a while. And I thought the professor might be interested in the bloke what did it. So I 'opped aboard the trunk rack on the rear of the chaise what 'e jumped into. I tell you, Mr. Barnett, that were a ride!"

"I'll bet it was, Mummer," Barnett said, picturing the little man clinging to the trunk rack, inches off the roadway, as the chaise careened down the road behind a galloping horse. The experience had deprived the usually nonchalant Tolliver of his painfully acquired aitches.

"How did you lose him?" Moriarty asked.

"I fell off," the Mummer said belligerently. "But it weren't my fault. 'E went around a corner like no carriage has any right going around a corner, and then bumped against the curb in the process. But it ain't no big deal, on account of I got 'is name."

"You have his name?" Moriarty patted the little man on the back. "Very good, Mummer. Indeed, excellent work. I am proud of you. What is it?"

"I 'eard 'is driver call 'im 'Deever,'" Tolliver said.

"Deever?" Barnett repeated doubtfully.

"D'Hiver," Moriarty said. "The Count d'Hiver. How very odd.

You're sure, Tolliver? You heard him say d'Hiver?"

"Right as a puffin. Deever it were."

"Not *Count* d'Hiver?"

"No."

"Curious. But it must be he; coincidence can only stretch so far. That is very valuable information, Tolliver; you have done well. Now I have another job for you. Notify the Amateur Mendicants that I wish the Count d'Hiver to be followed from this moment on, wherever he goes; and I want his residence and any other place he frequents to be put under constant surveillance. Tell Colonel Moran that he is in command, and that I will hold him responsible for any slip-ups." Moriarty scribbled on a slip of paper. "Here is the count's address. Tell Moran that those who follow the count are not to be seen. I want him to send me reports every three hours, or more often if the situation warrants."

"I got it, Professor," Tolliver said. "I'm on my way. I won't even stop upstairs to change my suit, which 'as suffered somewhat in the past 'alf 'our—I'll be off!"

Moriarty shook the little man's hand, and Tolliver limped rapidly from the room.

"The Count d'Hiver?" Barnett asked. "The man who was at the Hope mansion the night Cecily disappeared?"

"That is my assumption," Moriarty told him.

Barnett stood up. "Do you suppose—"

"I try never to suppose," Moriarty said. "We shall find out."

"I must help," Barnett said. "What can I do?"

"As it happens," Moriarty told him, "I have another task for you. One more particularly suited to your talents and abilities."

"Please, Professor, don't try to fob off some meaningless job on me just to keep me busy," Barnett said.

"I wouldn't think of it," Moriarty said.

* * *

And so Barnett found himself in a hansom cab, commencing an afternoon of investigation. His objective: the lower end of the Strand, with its appendage streets and lanes, and the theatrical agents and managers whose offices were clustered about the area.

"What, exactly, am I supposed to be looking for?" he had asked Moriarty before the professor hustled him toward the door.

"You are seeking truth," Moriarty explained. "You are trying to identify a murderer."

"In a theatrical agent's office?"

"There are very few possibilities," Moriarty said. "Very few facades beneath which our killer could be lurking. I have had most of them investigated already: locksmiths, burglars—"

"You said some time ago that it wasn't a burglar," Barnett interrupted.

"I said some time ago that it was not someone intent on burglary," Moriarty replied. "We are not now looking for motive, but training and ability. There are few people as knowledgeable and competent in the field of surreptitious entry as our killer has shown himself to be. This is an acquired skill, not an innate ability. Most of those who are known to have acquired such a skill have already been investigated, either by my own men or by Holmes's official minions, without turning up a possibility."

"And so?" Barnett asked.

"When you have eliminated the impossible," Moriarty told him, "it is time to take a hard look about and see what's left."

The first offices Barnett visited were those of Simes & McNaughten, Theatrical Agents, Specialty Acts, Bookings for London and the Provinces. He spoke to Mr. Simes, a man who looked as though he could have been the model for the puppet Punch.

"Magicians, you say?" Simes asked. He went to a cabinet and pulled open a dusty lower drawer. "I'd say we've handled a fair number over the years. None recently. They used to be very popular as a music-hall turn. Drew top money, top billing. Kind of died out now, though. Some really big names there were, back in the sixties and seventies. Manders, the Modern Merlin, was a top draw for, maybe, twenty years. Retired to Sussex. Still around, I believe. Keeps bees."

"Have you handled any in the past few years?" Barnett asked.

"I specialize in animal acts now," Simes said, waving his arm to indicate the posters on the surrounding walls. "Seals, dogs, bears, doves. No magicians. They're too temperamental. Most of them these days are foreigners. Italians and such."

"Thanks for your time," Barnett said.

He visited three more theatrical agencies with similar results. But then he arrived at the offices of Ditmar Forbis, Theatrical Representative—All Major Cities.

Ditmar Forbis was a tall, thin man with deeply set, searching eyes, who was dressed immaculately and tastefully in a hand-tailored black sack suit. Barnett's impression was that the man was miscast as a theatrical agent. He was much too somber and far too elegant. Barnett decided that by appearance and inclination, Forbis should be an undertaker to royalty. "You say this is for a newspaper article, Mr. Barnett?" Forbis asked.

"That's correct," Barnett told him. "Probably turn into a series of pieces on music halls and vaudeville."

"Vaudeville, Mr. Barnett, is an American phenomenon."

"I write for an American news agency," Barnett told him.

"I see," Forbis said. "Magicians, you say. As it happens, I handle most of the magical gentlemen working London today."

"Well," Barnett said, relieved that he had finally come to the right place, "is that so?"

"Yes, it is. They are mostly foreign gentlemen, you know. Largely Italians or Frenchmen. Even when they're not Italians or Frenchmen, they tend to take French or Italian names. Signor Gespardo, the Court Card King, for example; he is really a Swede."

"The Court Card King?"

"Yes. He does tricks with playing cards, but he only uses the king, queen, or jack—the court cards."

"Strange," Barnett commented.

"They are that—all of them." Forbis reached for a wooden box on his desk. "I've got cards on all the magicians who are currently active. Must be twenty or thirty of them. I don't imagine you want to see them all. How shall we sort them for you?"

"I'd like to concentrate on escape artists," Barnett said, taking out his notebook and flipping it open to a blank page. "People who are expert at picking locks and the like."

"That's not what they do, you know," Forbis said. "Or, at least, that's not what they admit they do. It's supposed to be some sort of miraculous power they have; nothing so mundane as a lockpick."

"What sort of things do they do?" Barnett asked. "Can you give me an example?"

Forbis shrugged. "Anything you can think of. And if you think of something they haven't done, why one of them will try it." He groped behind him and came up with a handful of handbills. "I'll show you a few examples of the sort of stuff they advertise. Here—here's one." He waved it across the desk.

The four-color illustration on the handbill portrayed a man in evening dress with his arms stretched out in front of him, hands clasped. He was shackled by every variety of handcuff and chain imaginable, but there was a confident glare in his clear blue eyes. Across the top of the print was the semicircular legend KRIS KOLONI THE HANDKUFF KING.

"He does challenge escapes," Forbes said. "You name it and he'll get out of it. Last year he escaped from a patented strait-waistcoat used at the Beaverstream Lunacy Asylum."

"That's the sort of chap I'm interested in," Barnett said enthusiastically, writing the name on the top line of his notebook. "Can I get in touch with him?"

"I'm afraid he is in Paris at the moment. In jail, as it happens."

"Jail?" Barnett was now definitely interested. "For how long and for what crime, do you know?"

"For the past four or five months, I believe. Refuses to pay alimony to his ex-wife."

"Ah," Barnett said, drawing a line through the name. "I assume you're reasonably sure of your facts—that is, that the fellow is still in jail?"

"I received a letter from him just last week," Forbis said. "Pleading for money, as it happens. Performers are just like children—totally incapable of handling their own affairs, most of them. Here's another chap." Forbis pulled a handbill free of the pile. "Moritz the Wonderful Wizard, he calls himself. His specialty is escaping from locked steamer trunks. Actually a very boring act. For twenty minutes the audience has nothing to look at save this trunk in the center of the stage. Then all at once Moritz pops out, waving his arms about as though he's done something clever. You understand that if you were a theater manager from the Midlands, that isn't how I would describe the turn. But just between us, that's the effect."

"Doesn't sound precisely like what I had in mind," Barnett said.

"Don't blame you," Forbis said. "Let's see, what else have I?" He riffled through the card box. "There's Professor Chardino—the Invisible Man. That's the way he bills himself. Works with his daughter; has a very interesting stage presentation. It's a sort of challenge to the audience. Gets them involved. He escapes from things people bring with them to the theater. Trunks, boxes, canvas bags, leg irons, handcuffs, animal cages, anything you can think of. It may sound superficially like Moritz the Wonderful's act, but I can assure you that the effect is entirely different. The man has a wonderful grasp of stage presence and stage personality. He makes the audience *care* what happens to him."

"How so?" Barnett asked.

Forbis frowned in concentration, his right hand grasping the air for the right word. "Let me describe it," he said. "Chardino is locked into the restraint—whatever it happens to be—usually by a committee of spectators. Through his conversation with the committee and the audience he has established the difficulty of what he is about to attempt and won the sympathy of his audience. Then his daughter covers him, and whatever he may be locked into, with a large drop cloth. There is now a period of waiting. The daughter, after standing expectantly for a minute, commences to pace nervously, obviously worried. There is a muted conversation about 'air supply' or something else possibly relevant. The audience are on the edge of their seats. Then it happens! Sometimes he appears from under the cloth; sometimes she whisks the cloth aside and he has disappeared completely. Sometimes she raises the cloth up to cover herself also, and then it drops and Chardino has taken his daughter's place, and it is she now locked inside the restraint. Once a society of undertakers in some provincial town brought along a coffin, and they took him to a local plot of land and buried him in it. After a while, when nothing happened, they dug the coffin up and opened it to find him gone. He beat them back to the theater."

"Why does he call himself the Invisible Man?" Barnett asked.

"Chardino specializes in getting in and out of impossible places—often without being seen."

Barnett made another entry in his notebook. "What sort of places?"

"Well, let me see." Forbis referred to his card. "He was locked in the tower room of Waldbeck Castle and escaped while two companies of guardsmen were surrounding the building. They saw nothing. Another time he was locked in the vault of Bombeck Frères, in Paris, and was found to be gone the next morning when the time lock permitted the manager to open the door. The man is a great showman."

Barnett nodded slowly. "I would very much like to meet Professor Chardino," he said. "He sounds like just the sort of person I have been looking for."

"Fascinating to talk to," Forbis agreed. He flipped over a few more cards. "Then there's the Amazing Doctor Prist—the World's Leading Escapist. It sort of rhymes, you see."

"He escapes from places also?"

"Oh, yes. Not as good as Chardino perhaps, but very showy, with a great many flourishes. He's been trying to arrange an escape from the Tower of London for the past five years, but the authorities won't let him. Naturally he plays that for all it's worth. By now he's gotten almost as much publicity out of the fact that the authorities refuse to allow the escape as he would have from successfully accomplishing it."

Barnett wrote the name Prist down in his notebook. "Any others?" he asked.

"Well, if it's escapes you're particularly interested in, there's Walla and Bisby," Forbis said, pulling out another card. "You can see them at the Orion right now, as it happens. Their specialty is walking through a brick wall, which is constructed right on stage in full view of the audience."

Barnett sighed. "I can see that I'll need more detail about all of these people, if I'm to do my job right," he said. "I hate to impose on you like this. Have you some free time? Perhaps we could discuss this over a drink at the Croyden?"

Forbis grabbed for his hat. "Delighted," he said.

TWENTY-FOUR

INTERLUDE: THE EVENING

A Londoner can always be summed up by his clubs.
ARTHUR WILLIAM Á BECKETT

The purifying rain fell steadily, gently, caressingly, the drumming sound it made on the wet paving stones drowning out the casual noises of the surrounding city. He stood on the pavement on the corner of Montague Street and Upper Keating Place, awaiting his prey, his great cape wrapped around him against the rain. Not that he minded the rain; the cleansing rain, the obscuring rain, the protecting rain, the rain that washed away blood, that cleansed the hands, if not the mind. The rain that renewed everything in its wake, but could not bring forgetfulness. Memory was pain, but nepenthe would bring death, for he had nothing to keep him alive but memory. His actions now were the continuing result of the memories that went beyond pain and the mission that went beyond life. He was the wind.

He had been content for all the days since—since—the thoughts whirled as his conscious mind rejected the thought thrown up by his unconscious. That frightful image must, at any cost, be suppressed. That thing had not happened. Could not have happened. A red haze of grief and pain passed before his eyes, and then all was clear once more. He had been content, for all the timeless days that had passed since he had become the wind, to follow the same mindless progression. The details had fully occupied his conscious mind, had mercifully filled his thoughts, as he accomplished the deaths, one by one, of Those Who Must Die. He had always been very careful about details, even in his other life that had once been so important and was now so meaningless. Except that it had given him the skills he needed for his new tasks.

Like a man caught on the rim of a great wheel, fated to follow the same endless ellipse turn after turn, with only the scenery changing, he had traced, followed, located, entered, searched, killed, and silently departed.

This work, for a while, had so filled his conscious mind that further thought was unnecessary, and the attempt difficult. This cycle had served temporarily to suppress the pain, briefly dull the gnawing anguish that filled the well of his soul. But of late it had not been enough. The process was becoming too automatic, too easy; although he still took scrupulous care with each event, it no longer filled the whole of his conscious mind. Now the pain remained. The anguish grew.

Now the nameless gods that drove him demanded that he go further. He must risk himself, and yet win out. They must all die. He must track them to their lair and destroy them all. He must enter hell itself, in the guise of the devil, and terminate this corruption and all its foul, flagitious spawn.

A four-wheeler clattered and splashed down Montague Street and pulled to a stop in front of the house he watched. The jarvey jumped down from his seat and knocked on the front door. In a few seconds it opened a crack, and then closed again, and the jarvey resumed his soggy seat. Two minutes later a well-bundled-up gentleman left the house and secreted himself inside the cab, which promptly pulled away.

Lovely, lovely, thought the man who had become the wind. *The horse won't be in any hurry tonight. And the jarvey won't be peering about and getting rain in his face.* He retrieved a rubber-tired bicycle from the fence paling and set off through the rain in leisurely pursuit of the gentleman in the four-wheeler.

For the first twenty minutes the growler traveled vaguely northward through the empty streets, with the bicycle pedaling discreetly behind. Past Regent's Park and Marylebone to Camden Town the four-wheeler rumbled; and then it turned east and passed the Cattle Market and Pentonville Prison. In a few minutes it had entered an area of London with which the bicyclist was entirely unfamiliar. He looked about him as he pedaled with the simple pleasure of a child surveying a new playground. Ten minutes later, on a quiet residential street with well-separated houses, the four-wheeler clopped to a halt. The bicyclist stopped a respectable distance behind and pulled his machine out of sight behind a convenient hedge.

The passenger pushed open the carriage door and, after peering out and sourly observing the still-falling rain, gingerly climbed down, pulling up his collar and wrapping his overcoat closely around him for protection. He looked about him uncertainly, as though not quite sure what to do next. Then, signaling the jarvey to remain where he was, the man walked slowly down the street, peering at the houses on both sides as though trying to make out details of their gaslit interiors through the rain-fogged windows. Halfway down the block he found the one he wanted. By what sign he identified it, the watcher was too far away to determine. The man turned and waved the four-wheeler away, and then scurried down the short path to the doorway.

The watcher hurried up the street until he was close behind, and then he silently leaped over the low wall which bordered the path leading up to the house and concealed himself by crouching behind it. He watched as his quarry yanked the bellpull and impatiently shifted from foot to foot awaiting a response.

A panel in the woodwork to the left of the door slid open, exposing a four-inch-square gap at about waist level. The man removed what appeared to be a small gold coin or medallion from his pocket and, holding it between his thumb and forefinger, inserted it in the open panel for long enough for whoever was on the other side to get a good look at it. Then, as nothing happened immediately, he put the object back in his pocket and resumed his fidgeting.

A few moments later an arm extended from inside the panel, holding in its outstretched hand a piece of black cloth, which the waiting gentleman promptly snatched away. The arm was instantly withdrawn, and the panel closed. The man quickly removed his hat and pulled the black fabric over his head. It proved to be a face mask that covered the whole face down to the nose, leaving only the mouth and chin exposed.

When he had properly adjusted the mask, the man knocked a triplet on the door, and it swung open. He was surveyed and then promptly admitted to the house by a man dressed all in tight-fitting black, and wearing a similar mask. No sooner had the man disappeared inside and the door shut behind him than another man came up the path to the door, and the admittance process started anew. There must be a protocol, the watcher realized, discouraging one man from approaching the door before the man ahead was admitted.

The watcher remained crouched where he was while four more gentlemen donned masks and entered the house. It must, he decided, be the small medallion, the devil's mark, that was being displayed through the open panel. He took a leather wallet from a special pocket in his cape and carefully felt around inside one of the compartments. There it was, the gold medallion he had removed from the shoe of his last victim. He had not had occasion to dispose of it yet. Now he was glad. It would be his passport. It was now time for him to imitate the ones he had just watched, to don the devil mask and enter this hell.

The house was large and richly furnished, and had many rooms. The man who was the wind, having gained admittance, wandered from room to room, cloaked behind the ubiquitous mask. He was now as one with the servants of the devil, observing the operation of this special subdivision of hell. The men, even the servants, were all masked. The women, scantily clad hussies who wandered from room to room and made themselves available to any masked man who beckoned, were bawdyhouse women. They made the best of the hand fate had dealt them, selling the only skills they had.

He was familiar with these girls; the pattern of his life had brought him into contact with many such, and he had always been impressed by their stoic good cheer. But in this house, the gaiety seemed forced; beneath the pouting lips, deep in the flirting eyes, there lurked the shadow of fear.

The rooms were dedicated to various pleasures. In one a roulette wheel spun, surrounded by masked men and by women in dishabille; in another chemin-de-fer and vingt-et-un tables were kept busy separating masked men from their coins. All transactions were conducted in cash in this house, since credit could not easily be extended to masked men who made a point of not recognizing one another.

These childish games, where men hiding behind masks felt a special illicit thrill, were not the activities the watcher had been drawn here to see. The premise of this gentlemen's club, where the gentlemen hid behind masks and the devil peered out through the eye slits, must be that in the confines of this house, the minor vices were but a prelude to the most consummate evil.

Somewhere in this building that darker evil must exist. And he must find it. He went deeper into the building, up a flight of stairs, past several closed doors, and there he found what he had expected to find. And despite his foreknowledge, despite his own activities of the past six weeks, this once-gentle man who had become the wind was horrified.

To believe, even on the best evidence, that human beings can behave like imps from hell is an intellectual exercise; to be confronted with such behavior is a gut-wrenching truth. When the Executioner of Lille, a dedicated man, separated the head of Gilles de Rais from its slender body he was acting under orders of the court, and knew of the seigneur's crimes only secondhand. Perhaps if he had seen the twisted, tortured bodies of more than a hundred small children, victims of the mad baron, laid out before him, his hand might have trembled, the ax might have slipped, and the job would not have been so neat.

The man who had become the wind hardened his heart, and determined to keep his work professional, regardless of what he saw. He saw rooms dedicated to strange and terrible variants of the sexual appetites of man. He saw rooms equipped for bondage, and for torture. He saw instruments of pain of such delicate design and exquisite manufacture that it was clear that the artisans who made them regarded them as works of art. And he saw these rooms and these instruments in use.

A servant came down the halls, whispering, "An auction, an auction," to all whom he encountered. The man who was the wind drifted behind the others and followed them into the auction room. He had seen enough. He knew what he must do. He would pause in this room, surrounded by Those Who Must Die, long enough to see what they did here. Then he would leave and prepare. Then he would return.

The childish masks these imps of Satan hid behind to practice their perversions made it all too easy for this spy in their midst. But a spy would have to have the device—the gold medallion—to enter this house of the damned; this was their positive protection from the outside world. The medallions, in the hands of their owners, were carefully protected. The watcher smiled grimly at this thought. So was life itself carefully protected—and he took the one as easily as the other.

A short man climbed up on the low table in the center of the room, stepping up from a small stool that had been placed by one end for that purpose. He was garbed entirely in black like most of the others, and masked; but his cuffs were edged with crimson cord and his mask was crimson silk.

"Quiet!" a pudgy man standing near the watcher whispered to a companion. "It's the Master Incarnate!"

The watcher grimaced and his hands tightened involuntarily into fists. This then was the man! Here was the chief of the devilish clan. He must learn to recognize this man. Perhaps the so-called "Master" did not always wear the crimson; in pure black, surrounded by his vermin, he would be harder to single out. The watcher moved closer so that he could study the ears, and memorize the shape of the lobe. By this would he know the Devil Incarnate when next they met, no matter how he might be attired.

"Welcome," the Master Incarnate said, in a deep, commanding

voice. "There are three items today." He gestured, and three servants, each a giant man, entered the room. Each of them carried a woman over his broad shoulders. The three women were bound and gagged with silken cords, and each wore a white shift and, as far as the watcher could tell, nothing else. Two of the women were passive, and the third was twisting and kicking vigorously, but completely ineffectually, in the arms of the giant who carried her.

After an "examination" of the women that was as degrading as it was offensive, the auction began. There was an atmosphere of obscene gaiety in the room as the bidding on each of the handsome, terrified women in bondage progressed. The bidding remained spirited in this carnival of depravity, and the offers quickly ran up into hundreds of pounds for each of the women. The dearest was the spirited one, who kept up the fight, even while wrapped in the massive arms of the impassive servant. Bidding for her closed out at six hundred and twenty-five pounds. *And so*, the watcher thought, *my Annie must have been sold to one of these swine, in a room very much like this one.* And then he decided not to think about that anymore.

The three winners of this unholy auction did not carry a large enough purse with them to redeem their prizes. The understanding was that they were to return the next evening with the required cash. In order to identify the right masked gentleman, and ensure that he got the girl he had bought, each of them ripped a pound note in half and gave one half to the Master Incarnate to match up the next evening.

"Tomorrow," the Master Incarnate said, indicating the three terrified women with a wave of his hands.

Tomorrow, and tomorrow, and tomorrow, the watcher thought.

"Tomorrow you three fortunate men will claim your rewards!" The Master Incarnate clapped his hands, and the three trophies were carried off. "Tomorrow evening," he said. "You have much to look forward to."

And all our yesterdays have lighted fools the way to dusty death, the watcher said to himself as he took his leave. He had a day now to think, and to plan. Dusty death.

TWENTY-FIVE

AGONY

How then was the Devil dressed?
O, he was in his Sunday's best;
His coat was red, and his breeches were blue,
And there was a hole where his tail came through.

ROBERT SOUTHEY

Sherlock Holmes was not grateful. He awoke from his encounter with the poultry cart with a severe headache, a bruised hip and left leg, and a foul temper.

"How do you feel?" asked the portly man who was bending over him as he opened his eyes.

Holmes took a minute to focus on the man's face. "Rotten," he said. "Who the devil are you?"

"I am Dr. Breckstone," the man told him, enunciating carefully. "Professor Moriarty sent for me. You've been in a most serious accident. Do you remember anything about what happened?"

Holmes looked blurrily about, gathering his thoughts and his energy. Then he focused back on Breckstone. "Thank you, Doctor, for whatever you've done for me. I do remember what happened. I am fine now. I must be on my way."

"My dear man!" Dr. Breckstone said. "You must remain where you are for some hours at least. I'm not altogether sure yet that you've escaped serious internal injuries. And the head, my good man, is not the preferential site for internal injuries! You're lucky to be alive, and no more gravely injured than you appear to be. But I must really insist that you remain lying down here for a few more hours at least. Perhaps overnight."

"Nonsense," said Holmes, sitting up and swinging his spindly legs over the side of the bed. "Where are my clothes? And, incidentally, who undressed me?"

"I wouldn't know," the doctor said. "But your clothes are there, on that chair. Now at least sit still for a minute and let me take a look at you." He peered into Holmes's right eye, and then the left. "Look to each side," he said. "Very good. Pupils seem normal. Coordination is fine. Tell me, do you know where you are?"

"My dear doctor," Holmes said, pushing himself to his feet, "I am not suffering from mental confusion, or aphasia, or amnesia, or anything else save a severe headache and a powerful need to be on my way." He weaved back and forth, and almost fell forward, but was saved by Dr. Breckstone, who grabbed his arm and helped him sit back down on the bed. "Well, perhaps I *am* a bit wobbly," Holmes admitted. "But I'll be fine in a few minutes. Again, I thank you very much for your efforts. You may send me a bill, of course."

"There'll be no bill. Professor Moriarty is taking care of that," Breckstone said. "If you are determined to leave, then please dress yourself and walk about the house for fifteen or twenty minutes before you go. That will give a subdural hematoma, or whatever else may be lurking inside your skull, a chance to make itself known while I'm still here to do something about it."

Holmes rubbed his head above the left ear. "As you say, Doctor," he agreed grudgingly. "I need some time to think in any case. I'll find a room in which to pace back and forth for the next twenty minutes and smoke a pipeful of shag. I always do my best thinking when I'm pacing back and forth."

"I shall go tell Professor Moriarty that you're conscious," Breckstone said. "If you feel the slightest touch of vertigo or nausea, let me know immediately."

Half an hour later Holmes appeared in the doorway to Moriarty's study. "I apologize for any inconvenience, Professor," he said. "And I thank you for providing medical attention."

"Someone tried to kill you, Holmes," Moriarty said, peering down from the high shelf where he was sorting through a collection of large astronomical atlases. He selected one and climbed down from the stepladder with it under his arm.

"I am aware of that," Holmes said. "I must confess, Professor, that for a moment I was surprised to wake up in this house."

Moriarty regarded Holmes thoughtfully as he went over to his desk and set down the massive atlas. "Surprised that I took you in, or surprised that I allowed you to wake up?" He smiled. "A bit of both, I expect."

Holmes glared at him and walked stiffly over to the desk. "I am surprised that you didn't take the opportunity to dispose of this statuette," he said. "And now I'm afraid that both I and it must be on our way." He snatched the bronze statuette from the corner of the desk and stalked from the room.

"Take care, Holmes!" Moriarty called to the detective's retreating back. "There seems to be something about you that brings out murderous impulses in total strangers; so you can imagine how your friends feel." He chuckled at the sound of the front door slamming, and then went into the hall to make sure that Holmes had really left. Returning to his desk, Moriarty immersed himself in the dusty pleasures of the well-worn astronomical atlas, determined to get a few hours' research done before Barnett or one of Colonel Moran's minions returned with a report that would bring him back to this world.

While studying the columns of figures that interested him in the astronomical atlas, Moriarty was suddenly put in mind of another set of figures, and he pulled the Scotland Yard file from his desk and searched through it intently for the copy of the newspaper fragment that had been found on Lord Walbine's person when he was killed. Then he went over to a locked cabinet and removed a variety of maps, charts, and atlases of the London area and spread them open on his desk.

After performing cabalistic rituals over each of the maps with a ruler and a piece of string, Moriarty rang for Mr. Maws and had him go to the basement and retrieve the stack of daily papers for the last three months. Then he closed the door to the study and left word that he didn't want to be disturbed for anything but the most urgent news.

It was Barnett who disturbed him. At two o'clock in the morning Barnett burst through the front door, slammed into the study, and almost did a jig to Moriarty's desk. "I have your killer!" he announced, grinning broadly and waving an olive-colored envelope in front of him.

Moriarty looked up from the vast mound of books, charts, note pads, newspapers, and assorted drawing and measuring materials that now covered his desk top. "Where?" he asked.

"Well, I don't know *where* he is, yet, Professor; but I know *who* he is. And I have a pretty good idea of why he's doing it." The elated expression suddenly left Barnett's face, and he wearily shook his head. "Which is wonderful, I suppose, after all this time—a hell of a scoop, and all that. The only thing is, Cecily is still missing, and I don't see how this gets me any closer to finding her."

"I believe they are related problems," Moriarty said. He tapped the pile of charts and newspapers with a pencil. "And I believe I can find the young lady."

"You're jesting!" Barnett exclaimed.

"I assure you, I would never jest about a thing like that," Moriarty said. "I am quite serious. But first tell me about the murderer."

"He'll keep," Barnett said. "I mean—I'm sorry, Professor, but if you know where Cecily is—"

Moriarty laced his hands together and leaned back in his chair. "It is only a supposition at the moment," he said. "It remains to be confirmed."

"Well, if you think you know even where Cecily might be, if there's a one-in-ten chance, or a one-in-a-hundred chance, give me the address," Barnett said, leaning over the desk and speaking with an unaccustomed intensity. "I'll confirm it in very short order, believe me!"

Moriarty shook his head. "I'm sorry, Barnett. I didn't mean to raise your expectations to quite the fever pitch. It will take a bit more research and investigation before we can establish the present whereabouts of the young lady; and that depends upon my being right about who has taken her and where. But the logic is consistent, and I'm confident that we will find her, and before this newborn day is out. I have the key, but I'm not yet sure that I have the right lock."

Barnett sat back down in the chair facing the desk. "I don't follow that," he said.

"I shall explain," Moriarty assured him. "But first, tell me what you have found out about the murderer. Who is he, and why is he doing this? I assume by your attitude that you are fairly sure of your facts."

"I would say so," Barnett agreed. "You were right, Professor, which I'm sure doesn't surprise you. The man is a professional magician—an escape artist. Calls himself Professor Chardino—the Invisible Man."

"Very apt, considering what we know of his abilities," Moriarty commented. "What makes you pick out this one magician from the scores of performers that must be active on the stage today?"

Barnett tossed the olive envelope he was holding onto the large chart of Greater London covering one side of Moriarty's desk. "I won't bother telling you what attracted me to him in the first place," he said. "Let me just put it that his name quickly led to all the rest. And when I looked for confirmation, all the pieces fell into place as if they were waiting for me to stumble across them. First of all, he has disappeared from view, moved from his usual theatrical rooming house, and refused any offers of work for the past four months, even though he is in great demand. His daughter—"

"Ah!" Moriarty interrupted. "That's interesting. He has a daughter!"

"He *had* a daughter. Annie. About eighteen years old. She died on the seventh of January in mysterious circumstances."

"Fascinating!" Moriarty said. "Go on—in what way were these circumstances mysterious?"

"The death is officially listed as the result of 'injuries received in a street accident.' Supposedly, she was thrown from a carriage. But from the description of the attending physician, whom I happened to find on duty in the emergency room of St. Luke's, it appears the girl was probably tortured. And over a period of several days. The physician didn't want to come right out and say it, since he had no way to prove it, and he could get into considerable trouble if he was wrong. But that's clearly what he meant."

"You have indeed been busy, Barnett," Moriarty said. "Anything else?"

"On some obscure impulse, I went to the graveyard where the daughter is buried. I think the idea at the back of my mind was to see if I could get an address for the professor from the sexton—that's what the fellow who keeps the graves is called, isn't it?"

"Usually," Moriarty agreed. "It's also the name of a beetle of the genus *Necrophorus*. Go on."

"Yes, well, I was assuming that Professor Chardino might visit his daughter's grave occasionally."

"And leave his card?"

Barnett shrugged. "He might leave something. Perhaps flowers, which could then be traced back to the florist by someone with the deductive genius of a Professor James Moriarty."

"Did he?"

"As it happens, he did. Unfortunately, by the evidence of the sexton, who, come to think of it, did look a little like a beetle, they were always purchased from a florist right down the street. A little outdoor stand."

"Pity," Moriarty said. "And no card with the sexton?"

"No," Barnett said. "But"—he waved his hand at the olive envelope—"he did leave something else!"

Moriarty reached for the envelope and tore it open. "Well," he said, sliding the contents onto the one clear spot on the desk. "What's this?" He picked up the two small objects that had been in the envelope and examined them closely, comparing one with the other. "Identical medallions, except for such differences as one would expect from wear and handling, and for a tiny hole drilled at the top of one. Presumably for the link of a gold chain, as the medallions themselves would seem to be gold."

"That's it, Professor," Barnett said, smiling. "I think those are what you've been looking for."

"What Holmes had been looking for," Moriarty said. "I have no doubt. Exactly where did you find them?"

"At the gravesite, buried in the dirt."

"Ah. And what prompted you to look in the dirt?"

"The sexton. He told me that Chardino used to sit by the grave for long periods of time, talking to his daughter. And he thought that Chardino occasionally left things there besides the flowers. 'Trinkets,' he called them. So I looked, and I found two."

"You did indeed. Curious things, these." Moriarty hefted the two medallions in his hand. "They tell the whole story—and a horrible story it is."

"What do you mean?"

"This sigil has an interesting history," Moriarty said. "Oh, not these particular baubles, of course; but the design, the pattern, the notion behind it. It explains all to one who understands such things."

"And you do?"

"Indeed," Moriarty said. "As you know, I have always been interested in the obscure, the bizarre, the esoteric—the darker recesses of the human mind. I have seen you, on occasion, perusing my collection of books on these subjects."

"What has this to do with that?" Barnett asked.

"I will explain," Moriarty said. "Let us examine these medallions. On the obverse: a satanic figure, legs wide, arms akimbo, staring out at the observer. Around the figure, evenly spaced, the letters D C L X V I. On the reverse"—Moriarty flipped over the medallion—"a floral design twined about the tracery letters H C. Do you agree?"

Barnett, who had picked up the other medallion, examined it closely and nodded. "That's what it looks like to me," he said.

"Let us take it from front to back," said Moriarty, holding his medallion up to the light of the desk lamp and examining it through a small lens. "The pleasant-looking figure glaring out at you is a chap named Azazel, leader of the Sleepless Ones."

"The Sleepless Ones?"

"That's right. The symbolism is very interesting. The story is in Genesis, in an abbreviated form." Moriarty stretched his hand behind him for an old black leather-bound Bible, and opened it. "Here it is: Genesis Six: 'And it came to pass, when men began to multiply on the face of the earth, and daughters were born unto them, That the sons of God saw the daughters of men that they were fair; and they took them wives of all which they chose.

"'And the Lord said, My spirit shall not always strive with man, for that he also is flesh: yet his days shall be an hundred and twenty years.

"'There were giants in the earth in those days; and also after that, when the sons of God came in unto the daughters of men, and they bare children to them, the same became mighty men which were of old, men of renown.

"'And God saw that the wickedness of man was great in the earth, and that the whole imagination of the thoughts of his heart was only evil continually.'"

Moriarty closed the book. "Right after that God asks Noah to build himself an ark."

"I'm sorry, Professor, but I don't follow any of that," Barnett said. "I never really paid much attention in Sunday school."

"Let me expand on it for you," Moriarty said. "And I assure you, that they did not teach you this in Sunday school. The old myths sometimes tell us a surprising amount about the human unconscious. The 'sons of God' were angels; specifically in this tale a group of angels known as the Sleepless Ones, whose particular job it was to watch over men."

"Headed by this fellow," Barnett said, tapping the medallion. "Azazel."

"Correct. Now, these Sleepless Ones observed the 'daughters of men,' and they liked what they saw. They lusted after these beautiful human women, and so eventually they came down and married them."

"Naturally."

"Angels, I would imagine, can be very persuasive. But since they were angels, their children were not human children, but the Nephilim, or giants. And these giants were unruly children. Wait a second." Moriarty went over to a bookcase and ran his fingers along the spines of the books. "Here's the one. The whole story is in the

Book of Enoch. A different, and longer, version of the story from that in Genesis. 'And it came to pass when the children of men had multiplied that in those days were born unto them beautiful and comely daughters. And the angels, the children of heaven, saw and lusted after them, and said to one another: Come, let us choose wives from among the children of men and beget us children.'"

Moriarty ran his finger down the page. "Here's more; now we get to the giants: 'And when men could no longer sustain them, the giants turned against them and devoured mankind, and they began to sin against birds and beasts and reptiles and fish, and to devour one another's flesh and to drink the blood.'" Moriarty closed the book. "This, according to one legend, was the origin of evil on the earth."

Barnett thought this over. "That's interesting," he said, "even fascinating, but what relevance does an ancient legend have on what is happening today?"

"Think of it this way, Barnett. What sort of people would choose to use Azazel, the progenitor of evil, as their symbol? What do they say about themselves? They are either fools, or knaves, or—*they* are evil!"

"Evil." Barnett stared down at the medallion he held. "It is a term that doesn't seem to have direct relevance anymore, not to this day and age; but you make it seem to come alive."

"*They* make it come alive, not I. Any man who does not believe in the existence of evil—pure, deliberate, virgin evil—or who believes it to be a thing of the past is not truly aware of the world in which he lives. But the evil, my friend, is within us. We need no Azazel to bring it to life."

"What of these letters around the rim of the medallion?" Barnett asked.

"There is, indeed, the other half of the story," Moriarty said. "Think of the letters as Roman numbers: D C L X V I. Six hundred and sixty-six."

Barnett looked blank. "So?"

"The answer to that is, once again, in the Bible—this time in the Book of Revelation." Moriarty flipped through the last few pages of his Bible. "Here it is—Chapter Thirteen:

"'And I stood upon the sand of the sea, and saw a beast rise up out of the sea, having seven heads and ten horns, and upon his horns ten crowns, and upon his heads the name of blasphemy.'

"And then, at the end of the chapter, after describing how evil the beast is: 'Here is wisdom. Let him that hath understanding count the number of the beast:—for it is the number of a man; and his number is six hundred threescore and six.'"

"What does it mean?" Barnett asked.

"Nobody is sure," Moriarty said. "The Book of Revelation is by far the most obscure book of the Bible. The most usual belief is that it somehow represents the anti-Christ through some cabalistic numbering code."

Barnett leaned back and stared at his medallion, considering the sort of people who would favor this particular symbolism on their watch fobs. He found that he was weary from his day's exertions but still eager to go on. "What's on the back?" he asked.

Moriarty flipped over the medallion he was holding. "The flowers traced around the letters are *Veratrum*, commonly called hellebore. In ancient times it was believed to cure madness, and the soothsayer and physician Melampus is supposed to have used it to cure the mad daughters of Praetus, King of Argos."

"You seem to know an awful lot about these medallions, Professor," Barnett said. "I am aware that you have a most impressive store of esoteric knowledge. Many's the time you've told me that there is no bit of information that is not worth knowing. But this approaches prescience. Have you ever seen one of these trinkets before?"

"You suspect me of clairvoyance?" Moriarty asked. "No, I've never seen one exactly like these, but I've been expecting to run across something similar at any time over the past fifteen years. It seemed to me inevitable that someday I'd be staring at a sigil very much like this."

"It's new to me," Barnett commented. "I assume it has some specific meaning to you. What does it signify?"

"The letters HC on the reverse tell all," Moriarty said. "It is an example of the extreme conceit of those we're dealing with that they left the initials."

"HC?"

"Hellfire Club," Moriarty said. "A new incarnation of a three-hundred-year-old disgrace."

"The Hellfire Club?" Barnett looked thoughtful. "It rings a faint bell," he said. "Sometime in the past I have come across the name before, but for the life of me I can't recollect specifically where or when."

"There's usually a line or two in the history books," Moriarty said. "An amusing sidelight to the time of the Restoration. When Charles the Second returned to England, ten years after his father lost his head, and wondered why he'd been away so long. As a reaction to ten long years of rule by the stuffy old Puritans, a bunch of the young sprigs of the nobility went around raising hell. After all, they hadn't been allowed to so much as dance while the dour old Cromwells made the rules. So they called themselves the Hellfire Club. They drank, and they gambled, and they wenched, and they rode all over other people's fields, and they thoroughly enjoyed themselves."

"Boys will be boys," Barnett murmured.

Moriarty nodded. "And it seems that some boys will be boys at forty if they haven't been allowed to at twenty. But at forty, some of them have developed very advanced ideas of raising hell.

"Gradually the Hellfire Club became something other than it had been at the beginning. I imagine it happened as the 'boys' who just wanted a chance to run around a bit and sow an occasional wild oat had their fill of the missed excitement of youth and dropped out of the club to take up more serious pursuits. Those who remained were, let us say, more seriously dedicated to the single-minded pursuit of pleasure. And the pleasures they pursued gradually became more and more selfish, illegal, and sadistic. They went in for abduction, rape, torture, and murder."

"A lovely-sounding lot. Whatever happened to them?" Barnett asked.

"They were suppressed at the direct order of King Charles himself, who was never one to confuse freedom with license. They were suppressed again by a royal commission appointed by King William. It is believed that at this time they saw the wisdom of becoming a thoroughly secret society."

"That's it, then?" Barnett asked, when Moriarty paused.

"The club surfaced again briefly about sixty-five years ago, during the reign of George the Fourth. It was not identified by name at that time. A house in Cheswickshire burned to the ground, purely by accident as far as was known. In the burned rubble of the house, which was believed to be unoccupied, were found an exemplary collection of apparatus designed to restrain and torture human beings, along with the burned bodies of three young women. Subsequent investigation turned up the fact that several men, described as looking like gentlemen, were seen running away from the building at the time of the fire. One of the items rescued from the fire was an amulet with a strange design on it—a design much like that which you now hold in your hand."

"So that's what you meant when you said you've been expecting this?" Barnett asked.

"Indeed," Moriarty answered. "Ever since I learned of the events concerning the house in Cheswickshire, and realized the connection with the supposedly extinct Hellfire Club, I have expected someday to come across this medallion. There are some malignancies that do not die of their own accord, but have to be excised time and time again. I'm convinced that this is one such."

Barnett stared at the gold sigil he held, flipping it from back to front and peering closely at it as though he expected to read some great secret from its depths. What a catalog of horrors was represented by this small device. The devil on the front—Azazel, according to Moriarty—seemed to Barnett to be smirking at him in the gaslight. "It would seem," Barnett said, "that Chardino has been doing an efficient job of excising all by himself."

Moriarty nodded. "He has been going through the membership of the Hellfire Club like a scythe through wheat," he said. "In a way, it will seem a pity to stop him; in fact, I'm not altogether sure that there isn't a better solution."

"What would that be?" Barnett asked.

"I don't know yet," Moriarty admitted. "It is true that on humanist grounds our friend the magician should be discouraged from indiscriminate killing; but is his killing really that indiscriminate?

And is it not equally true that the gentlemen-members of the club in question should be discouraged from—whatever it is they are doing?"

"You think that the Hellfire Club is responsible for the death of Chardino's daughter?" Barnett asked.

"Don't you?" Moriarty replied.

"How do you suppose he knows who the members are and where to find them?"

Moriarty shook his head. "It is pointless to suppose," he said. "We must discover!"

Barnett nodded. "And just how are we going to do that?" he asked. "It doesn't seem to me that we're really much further forward. We know who the killer is, and who he's killing, and we can surmise why; but we don't know *where* he is, or where his victims can be found before they become his victims. I suppose we could always put an advertisement in the paper for members of the Hellfire Club to come forward and be saved, or put a twenty-four-hour watch on the churchyard, in hopes that Chardino will visit his daughter again before he kills too many more of these charming people."

"It's not really as bad as all that," Moriarty said. "I believe I can locate the Hellfire Club."

"You can?"

"Yes. I think so. The club's location is almost certainly transient, but I believe I have the key to their travels."

"The key—*that's* what you said about Cecily's location. My God! You don't mean you think they have her?"

"I'm sorry, I thought you had already guessed that," Moriarty said. "It is the only logical answer. Of course, I didn't know until you walked in that these people we are after are the newest incarnation of the Hellfire Club."

Barnett took a deep breath. "I didn't want to think about it," he said. "I mean, I knew *somebody* had to have her, as it's clear that she was abducted. If anything else had happened the authorities would have found her—or her body—by now. But I didn't want to think about by whom—or why—she was taken away. What do you suppose is happening to her?"

"It is just as pointless to suppose that as to suppose anything else," Moriarty said. "We will find her and take her away from her abductors. With any luck, we'll do it before the day is out. Now, since morning approaches rapidly, I am going to get some sleep."

"How do you know where Cecily is?" Barnett asked.

"I don't—not yet. But I shall. Join me in here after breakfast, say at nine-thirty."

"What about eight-thirty?" Barnett suggested.

"The most useful thing we could do with that extra hour," Moriarty told him, "is sleep. And I, for one, intend to do so."

Barnett had to be content with that, but he did not sleep well. Along about morning he finally did fall into a deep sleep, and then he had to drag himself out of bed a few hours later when Mrs. H pounded on his door and told him that breakfast was ready.

Moriarty was not at breakfast. Barnett could feel the tension rising in him while he ate, the tension he had become so familiar with in the past few days. Compounded of all the emotions that cramp the muscles and hit at the pit of the stomach: frustration, guilt, rage, fear, anxiety, and an increasing sense of helplessness. The feeling had by now become a permanent knot of pain, twisting away deep inside of him. Thoughts that he was not allowing himself to think were expressing themselves as sharp knives digging into his belly. He did not eat well.

As he was finishing, Moriarty entered the room. To Barnett's surprise, he could see that the professor had already been out of the house, and was evidently just returning. "A quick cup of coffee," Moriarty said. "We have work to do!"

Barnett rose. "What sort of work?"

"Sit down," Moriarty insisted. "I need my coffee." He dropped into his chair. "I have broken the code," he said. "I was just out checking my results and now I am sure."

"What code?" Barnett asked, fearful that Moriarty had gone off on some entirely new tack and had lost interest in the Hellfire Club and the missing Cecily. The professor's interest in any subject outside of mathematics and astronomy was all too likely to prove evanescent.

"Think back," Moriarty said. "Do you remember that among the effects of the late Lord Walbine there was a scrap of newsprint?"

"Vaguely," Barnett said.

"It was from the agony column of the *Morning Chronicle*," Moriarty reminded him, pouring himself a cup of coffee from the large silver urn in front of him. "On one side it said, 'Thank you St. Simon for remembering the knights.' On the other: 'Fourteen point four by six point thirteen, colon, three-four-seven.'"

"Something like that," Barnett agreed.

"I assure you, it was that, exactly," Moriarty said. "Now, on reading the report on the death of Quincy Hope—whose mysterious profession, by the way, turns out to have been quack doctor—"

"Quack?"

"Indeed. He cured people of any disease by placing bar magnets on various parts of their anatomy and taping them in place. At any rate, on reading the report of his death I noted that one of the items found in his room at the time of his death—some sort of anteroom or waiting room, I believe—was a morning newspaper. I procured a copy of that paper from our basement file and perused the agony column. I found no mention of St. Simon, or any of the knights, but I did find this: 'Nine point eleven by five point two, colon, red light.'"

Barnett nodded. "You think that's a code?"

"It is."

"How is the Count d'Hiver involved in this?" Barnett asked. "If he's the one who attacked Sherlock Holmes, he must know something."

"I have had people watching his house since yesterday," Moriarty said. "He has not yet returned home."

"Do you think he's one of them?" Barnett asked. "Is he a member of the Hellfire Club?"

Moriarty pursed his lips thoughtfully. "I believe he is," he said. "Moreover, I believe d'Hiver, himself, is the Master Incarnate."

"The what?"

"The Master Incarnate, which is what the leader of this devilish organization calls himself. You may wonder why I believe this of d'Hiver on so little apparent evidence. The inductive chain is a strong one, and the links are sound. The members—if I may call them that—of the Hellfire Club must wear masks when physically present at the club, and thus do not know one another's identities. It is one of the strictest of this despicable organization's rules. The only person who knows the name of a member, except for the one who proposed him, is their chief, the Master Incarnate."

"And so?" Barnett asked, feeling that he had lost one of the links of Moriarty's chain.

"And so, Mr. Barnett, the only person who could have known, by their names, that the victims of our mad magician were all members of the Hellfire Club is the Master Incarnate. Since none of the victims seems to have taken unusual precautions for his safety before he was killed, I think we can assume that the Master Incarnate did not pass on to his disciples the fact of their mortal danger. But he himself must have been at least intensely curious as to who was killing off his membership.

"If we assume the Master Incarnate to be d'Hiver, it would explain his passionate interest in the progress of Holmes's murder investigation, and his clandestine presence outside this house in response to my advertisement. From which he must have assumed greater knowledge on our part than we actually possessed. It would, therefore, explain his attack on poor Holmes. He must have panicked when he saw Holmes leave this house. Had he time for reflection, I am sure he would not have done so. Although he does seem to have come prepared to attack someone."

"Wasn't he afraid of being recognized, sitting out there?" Barnett asked.

"I would assume he was in disguise," Moriarty said. "Remember, the Mummer identified him by an overheard name, not by his appearance."

Barnett rose and refilled his own coffee cup. Then he resumed his seat and sipped quietly while he thought over Moriarty's notions. "What about this code?" he asked.

"Ah, yes," Moriarty said, removing a bulky object from his outside jacket pocket and passing it across the table to Barnett. "I wondered when you would ask. Please examine this; on it I base my case."

Barnett took the bulky object and found that it was the "Jarvis & Braff Compleat Map of the Great Metropolis of London & Its Environs, *Showing All Omnibus, Tramway, and Underground Lines As Well As Points of Interest,*" closed with its special "Patented Fold."

"What is this?" Barnett asked, after staring at it for a minute and extracting no meaning beyond that declaimed on the cover.

Moriarty sighed. "It is a map," he said. "It is also what we codebreakers call a 'key.'"

Barnett unfolded the map, which was closed with a sort of zigzag accordion pleat. It appeared to be no more than what it advertised: a map of London. "Is this the 'key' you were talking about last night?"

The professor nodded. "It is."

"That's wonderful," Barnett said, spreading the map out on the table. "Just what does it say?"

"It gives us the current location of the Hellfire Club," Moriarty explained. "They don't stay in any one place very long. They wouldn't want to take any chances on the neighbors getting too friendly. But then they have the problem of informing their membership of the new location of the, for want of a better term, clubhouse."

"This map," Barnett said, gesturing at the large five-color rectangle on the table before him, "gives the location of every place in London. But it isn't specific, that I can see."

"No," Moriarty agreed. "But the code message in the agony column pins it down."

"How does it work?"

"It is ingeniously simple." Moriarty rose and left the dining room for a second, returning with an eighteen-inch steel rule from his study. "I'll let you work it out for yourself." He tossed the rule to Barnett. "Let us start with the message found on the late Lord Walbine. 'Fourteen point four by six point thirteen.' What do you make of that?"

Barnett took out his pencil and jotted the numbers down on the margin of the map. "Measurements," he said.

"That's it," Moriarty agreed.

"Well, it wasn't very hard to figure that out after you handed me a ruler," Barnett said. "But just what do I measure?"

"There are several possibilities." Moriarty said. "Top, bottom, either side; or, for that matter, from some arbitrary point on the map—say the tip of the Tower, or the gate of the Middle Temple. Luckily for us, they were not that subtle. Measuring in from the left side and then down from the top will accomplish our purpose."

Barnett held the ruler uncertainly, staring down at the map. "I'm not sure—" he said.

"It's the lack of scientific training," Moriarty said. "Scientists are never at a loss as to how to mark up someone else's papers. I suggest you start by marking the first measurement along both the top and bottom margins of the map. Notice that the ruler is marked off in inches and sixteenths. I assumed those were the proper fractions, as it is the common marking for such rules, and I was proved to be right. So your first measurement is fourteen and four-sixteenth inches from the left-hand border."

Barnett marked this distance carefully along the top edge, and then again along the bottom, as Moriarty instructed. Then he laid the rule carefully between the two marks, and measured six and thirteen-sixteenths inches down from the top, marking the place with a small pencil dot. "I see you've been here ahead of me," he said, noting a second small dot almost directly under his.

"Babbington Gardens," Moriarty said. "Northwest corner."

"That's what I get," Barnett affirmed.

"Well, that was my first stop this morning," Moriarty said. "My assumption was that the final number—three-four-seven—was the identification of the proper building, and, therefore, almost certainly the house number. Two houses in from the corner, along the east side of the street, I found it. It is, at present, untenanted. Certainly strongly suggestive, if not proof positive."

"Didn't you break into the house to look around?" Barnett asked.

"Certainly not!" Moriarty said, looking faintly amused. "That would be illegal. But I did speak to the tenants in the houses to either side."

"You did?"

"In the guise of a water-meter inspector. It never ceases to amaze me what information people will gladly give to a water-meter inspector. I learned that the house was occupied until mid-March, that it would seem to have been used as some sort of club, that gentlemen came in carriages at all hours of the evening and through the night, and that on occasion strange noises were heard to emanate from somewhere inside. I also learned that neighbors who attempted neighborly visits were rudely rebuffed at the door."

"That sounds as if it must be the right place," Barnett said.

Moriarty nodded agreement. "It would be stretching the bounds of credulity to assume it to be a coincidence," he said. "But just to be sure, I then went to the location derived from the Hope Newspaper."

Barnett roughly measured off the distances indicated, and found Moriarty's pencil mark on the map. "Gage Street," he said. "How accurate is this system, Professor?"

"If you are careful in your measurements, it is sufficiently accurate for the needed purpose."

"Well, if that is so," Barnett asked, "then how secure is the code? If you found it this fast, why haven't others?"

"They have to know what to look for," Moriarty said. "Even if someone should guess that it is a map coordinate code he would have to know what map to use."

"You did," Barnett said.

"*I* had a list of the effects of the murdered men," Moriarty said. "Two of them had Jarvis & Braff maps close enough to their persons when killed to have them mentioned on the inventories."

"And the others didn't?"

"Presumably," Moriarty said, "the others had their copies of the map in an unremarkable place—the library, perhaps, or the hall table. That being so, the existence of the map was not remarked. Really, Barnett, I should have thought that was obvious."

"What is obvious to you, Professor, is not necessarily obvious to others. If that were not so, you might be in my employ instead of I in yours."

Moriarty began to frown, and then chose to smile instead. "A touch, Barnett, a distinct touch," he admitted.

Barnett retrieved his coffee cup from under the map. "What did you find on Gage Street?" he asked. "And, incidentally, why didn't you ask me to accompany you?"

"This was for reconnoitering purposes only," Moriarty said. "I knew the club was no longer there. The present whereabouts is indicated in the agony column of this past Wednesday's *Morning Chronicle*. And you needed your sleep." He laced his fingers together and stretched his arms out before him, palms forward. "I found the house almost immediately, despite the absence of the specified red light, because it, also, was still vacant. A lovely old manor house, set back on its own bit of land, surrounded by the ever-advancing squads of identical row houses. It was perfect for their purposes. Since the neighbors, in this case, could tell me nothing, I investigated the interior."

"You broke in?" Barnett asked. "For shame, Professor. That's against the law."

"I broke nothing," Moriarty insisted. "The front door was ajar, and so I walked in."

"There was, I assume, no one there," Barnett said.

"You assume correctly. The house was devoid of both inhabitants and furnishings. The only things I found to verify my theory were a pattern of screw and bolt holes in the floors, walls, and ceilings of certain of the rooms, suggestive of the apparatus that must have been fastened there. And this." Moriarty reached in his pocket and removed a small bit of knotted leather, which he held in the palm of his hand. "I found this—this artifact—by chance, in a crack in the baseboard in one of the rooms."

Barnett took it and examined it closely. To his eye it was nothing but a short, stiff, discolored strand of leather, tied in a knot. "What does it do?" he asked.

Moriarty took the object from Barnett's hand. "I remember once reading a description by Admiral Sturdy of life in the old sailing navy," he said, tossing the bit of leather from hand to hand like a magician about to do a conjuring trick. "He was a midshipman about the time of Nelson, and one of his clearest memories of that period was of the floggings he was forced to watch. The lash was tied with a little knot at the end to keep it from splitting. After each use—after some poor sailor had had his back laid open for some minor infraction—the ends of the lash were soaked in salt water to remove the blood. For if they allowed the blood to dry on, you see, the leather would get stiff; and the next time the lash was used, the tip, knot and all, might break off."

Barnett looked with sudden horror at the small leather knot. "You mean—"

"Whoever used this," said Moriarty, holding the tiny thing between thumb and forefinger, "didn't know about the salt water."

TWENTY-SIX

INTERLUDE: ECSTASY

Did ye not hear it?–No; 'twas but the wind.
GEORGE GORDON, LORD BYRON

He would get but one chance, and he must perform flawlessly to succeed, to live. But so it had been all his life, each escape more difficult, more critical than the last, each allowing no margin for error.

The notion had come to him the night before, while wearing the devil's mask and spying on the devil's entertainments. The satisfying pattern that he had been following–the stalking, the confrontations, the deaths of these devil's imps one by one–would no longer serve. It had filled his need, this singular obliteration, it had satisfied his soul. But ripping off the leaves would not kill the tree; he must strike deeper, and harder, and crush the root so that it could not spring to life again.

The plan he evolved was simple, but the details required much thought and preparation. All through the night he had thought, and all morning he had prepared. Shortly after noon he was ready to proceed.

It was almost one o'clock when he pulled up before the devil's house in his rented wagon. He climbed down from the driver's seat and carefully dusted off his green-and-brown-checked suit and meticulously adjusted his brown bowler before strutting up to the front door. With a conscious skill acquired over a lifetime of deluding people, both at stage distance and face to face, he had become the part he was playing. His face, indeed his entire character, wore an air of smugness that was proof against all casual inquiry.

The door opened at his insistent pounding, revealing a tall, hawk-nosed man garbed as a butler, wearing the noncommittal, disinterested air of the well-trained household servant.

This place has no need for such as a butler. It is clear that we are, the both of us, liars, he thought, glancing up cordially at the hawk-nosed man. *But I am the better.* "Afternoon," he said, touching the brim of his bowler. "I take it this is 204 Upper Pondbury Crescent?"

The hawk-nosed man thought the question over carefully before committing himself. "What if it is?" he asked finally.

"Delivery." He jerked his thumb over his shoulder, indicating the wagon. The man in the butler suit peered in that direction, reading the big, freshly painted sign hanging on the vehicle's side. GAITSKILL & SON, it said, WINE MERCHANTS.

"Brought 'em myself." Taking off the bowler, he wiped his forehead with a large almost-white handkerchief. "I'm Gaitskill. Needed in a hurry, they told me, so I brought 'em right along. Regular carter off this week. Mother quite ill. Streatham, or some such place. Damned inconvenient time. Bertie's on the Continent on a buying trip. That's the son. So here I am. Where do you want 'em?"

"What?" asked the hawk-nosed pseudo-butler.

The pseudo-Gaitskill pulled out a sheaf of consignment orders and shuffled through them. "Here it is," he said. "Twelve firkins of best claret. Where do you want 'em? My lad will help you take 'em in." He indicated the gangly youth sitting with his legs dangling over the back gate of the wagon. "Hired lad. Not too bright, but willing. A cool spot is best."

"How's that?" asked Hawk-nose. "Best for what?" A touch of confusion shaded his supercilious expression.

"The claret," Gaitskill explained impatiently. "Best in a cool spot. Keep for years that way. Decades. Best not moved around too much. Give each firkin a quarter turn every five years or so."

The hawk-nosed man stared at the two-foot-long casks neatly

stacked in the rear of the wagon. "I don't know," he said.

"Wine cellar is best," said the merchant. "As you might imagine from the name. Wine."

"I haven't been informed about this," the hawk-nosed man said.

The man who was the wind shrugged a merchant's shrug. "Someone forgot to tell you," he said. "Makes no difference to me. *I've* been paid. I'll take 'em away with me, or leave 'em here on the street, as you please. But I haven't all day, you know. Suppose me and the lad just stack the firkins neatly like on the pavement? Then you and yours can do as you like with 'em—at your leisure."

"No—well—" He paused to consider, to weigh the possibilities for error against each other. Obviously his master was not there to consult. "The cellar, you say?"

"Best place." The wind nodded.

"Well, come around back, then. There's an entrance to the cellar around back. No need to go through the house."

"No need indeed," the man who was the wind agreed, signaling to the lad he had hired to bring the first firkin around with him as they sought out the cellar door.

In half an hour they were unloaded, and the small casks were neatly stacked on an old shelf in the stone cellar. "This should keep 'em cool," the wine merchant told the butler. "I think your master will find that the vintage exceeds his expectations. Just let 'em settle for a day or so before you broach the first one."

"It's good quality, then?" the butler asked.

"Heavenly," the merchant assured him. "Ta, now. I must be on my way."

TWENTY-SEVEN

RESCUE

Here lovely boys; what death forbids my life,
That let your lives command in spite of death.
CHRISTOPHER MARLOWE

The rain began again in late afternoon, a cold rain falling through the gusts of a chill spring wind. By sunset it had fallen steadily for several hours, and promised to continue indefinitely. The overhanging clouds shut out what remained of the twilight, prematurely darkening the sky. The bay cob, for whom the rain was but one more indignity, plodded stolidly through the puddled streets, and the four-wheeler bounced and lurched behind. Barnett hunched forward in his damp leather-covered seat and stared through the mist-covered window at the shifting murky shadows of the passing scene: buildings, pavement, lamp poles, pillar boxes, occasional people scurrying to get out of the rain. It all had an unreal quality, as though it possessed no separate existence, but had been placed there, as a stage set might be, at the whim of some godlike director.

Barnett felt himself caught up in this world of unreality; for some reason he could not understand, he felt curiously divorced from himself, from where he was and what he was doing. He shook his head sharply to try to drive away the mental fog and turned to Professor Moriarty. "How much longer?" he asked.

Moriarty glanced outside for a moment, getting his bearings. "Ten more minutes should see us there," he said. "A bit early for our needs, I'm afraid. We may have to skulk in some doorway for a bit."

"I don't know if I can tolerate waiting once we're in sight of the house," Barnett said. "I feel as though I've already been waiting for centuries. Besides, I don't like to think of what might be happening inside that house while we are outside waiting."

"Practice patience," Moriarty instructed. "It is the one virtue that will stand you in good stead in almost any circumstance. In this case, it is essential. If we burst in before the time is ready, we will most assuredly do more harm than good. God only knows what these good citizens and accomplished clubmen we are planning to visit might do in a panic."

"I thought you were an atheist," Barnett commented.

"I am also a pragmatist," Moriarty said. "Therefore, what we must do is insinuate ourselves amongst them, and, at the propitious moment, effect a rescue of Miss Perrine."

"If she's there," Barnett said. He suddenly found that he was biting his lower lip, and consciously restrained himself.

"If she is not there," said Moriarty grimly, "we shall cause one of the gentlemen who is there to desire very strongly to tell us just where she is! You have my word, Barnett, before this night is out we shall have located and repatriated your lady."

"I pray that is so," Barnett said. "This is the fourth day she's been in their hands. It is not pleasant to contemplate what might have happened to her by now."

Moriarty looked at him. "That is self-defeating," he said. "Whatever has happened to Miss Perrine has already happened; there is nothing you can do to change it. And whatever it is, you must not blame her or yourself for it. You must accept it and go on."

"Are you saying one should do nothing about what is past?" Barnett asked.

"One can learn from the past," Moriarty said. Then, after a pause, he added softly, "Vengeance, occasionally, is acceptable."

A few minutes later the four-wheeler pulled to a stop, and the jarvey opened the tiny communicating hatch on the roof, cascading a small puddle of water onto the seat next to Barnett. "We're 'ere, Professor, just like you said," he yelled down. "Right around the corner from the 'ouse in question."

"Very good, Dermot," the professor replied. "Are any of our people in evidence?"

The jarvey put his ear to the small hole in order to hear the professor's question over the wind. "There's a couple of individuals what are loitering in doorways on the next block," he replied. "But as to 'oo they are, I can't rightly say from this distance, what with the inclement weather and all."

"Well, let's go see what we can see," Moriarty said, nodding to Barnett. "Wait here, Dermot. You might as well get inside the carriage and keep warm and dry until you are needed."

"Too late," Dermot yelled down, and he slid the hatch closed.

Barnett followed Moriarty across the street in front of them, which he noted from the corner sign was Upper Pondbury Crescent. The street, bordered by orderly rows of well-spaced houses, set comfortably back from the pavement, went off in either direction with only the slightest hint of a curve. "What do you suppose," Barnett asked the professor, "makes this a crescent?"

Moriarty glanced at his associate. "The vagaries of Lord Pondbury's business manager," he suggested. "A fondness for the term 'crescent' when he turned his lordship's private game preserve into sixty-five unattached town houses."

Mummer Tolliver appeared from behind a hedge and came trotting over. "Morning, chum," he said, nodding at Barnett. "Morning, Professor. That's the house over there." He pointed across the street at a house about halfway up the block. "The one with the chest-high stone wall running along the walk to the front door."

"Chest-high?" Barnett asked, peering through the gloom at the house Tolliver indicated.

The Mummer glared at him. "My chest," he explained. "Your arse."

Barnett looked down at the little man. "Don't be coarse," he said. "And what do you mean, 'morning'? It happens to be eight in the evening. Ten after, as a matter of fact."

"I 'ere tell as 'ow it's morning somewhere," the Mummer said coldly, dropping his aitches for emphasis. "Don't you know no science whatsoever?"

"Save your horological repartee for another time, Mummer," Moriarty said, staring suspiciously at the house across the street. "Are you certain that's the right place?"

"That is the place, Professor, no mistake," the Mummer said.

"Did you find a green cross?" Moriarty demanded. "That is the identification in this month's advertisement—a green cross," he explained to Barnett.

"There's a Maltese cross done in green glass set into the front window to the right of the door," the Mummer said. "You know, like them windows in a church."

"Stained glass?" Barnett suggested.

"You've got it," the Mummer agreed. "It shows up real good when you're right in front of it, 'cause of the light behind it; but you can't hardly see it from either side 'cause the window's inset quite a bit."

"Very good," Moriarty said. "This must, indeed, be the right place. Has there been much traffic while you've been watching?"

"Very little in-and-out," Tolliver said. "A cluster of gents went in shortly after I set myself and the other lads up here—that would be about six o'clock. Shortly after it started raining. Six in since then, and two out. They left together in a trap. And, o'course, one strange event."

"What's that?"

Tolliver led Moriarty and Barnett a few houses down from where they were standing and pointed out a bicycle which had been well concealed in the shrubbery to the side of the house. "A gent came pedaling up on this contraption and discarded it here, carefully out-of-sight like. Then he went over to the house what we're watching and immediately snuck off around the corner of the house. I can't say whether he went inside or not, but he didn't use the front door. That were about ten or fifteen minutes ago."

"Come now, that's fascinating!" Moriarty exclaimed.

"I would have merely assumed it was a servant, perhaps being a bit secretive on account of being late for work, feeling the necessity of using the back door," the Mummer said, "were it not for the peculiar circumstance of this here bicycle."

"That is, indeed, a peculiar circumstance," Moriarty agreed. "What do you make of it, Barnett?"

"You've got me," Barnett said. "Someone else watching the house?"

"Perhaps," Moriarty said. "But he must be myopic, indeed, to need to watch it from so intimate a distance. How many more of our people have we here, Mummer?"

"Fourteen, at present," Tolliver said. "Scattered up and down the street in places of concealment."

"Good, good," Moriarty said. "That should suffice. Now let us settle ourselves down and try to remain comparatively dry. The, ah, membership should start arriving any time now. Mummer, do you think you can insinuate yourself close enough to that door to enable you to get a good view? I want to know what the entrance procedure is."

"One of the few advantages of being small," Tolliver said. "I can hide in half the space it would take a person of standard stature. I'll give 'er a try."

"Good lad, Mummer," Moriarty said, patting him on the back. "Remember, discretion is the watchword. It is more important for you not to be seen than for you to see every detail."

"Don't worry, Professor," the Mummer said cheerfully. "I may be seen, but I won't be caught. And they won't nary suspect nothing, either. Here, watch this!" Tolliver shrugged his coat off and twisted his jacket around. Then, taking the dripping-wet bowler hat off his head, he removed a cloth cap from its inner recesses. He put the cap on and pulled it tightly down around his ears. Slouching and throwing his shoulders forward, he tilted his head a bit to the side, and allowed an innocent expression to wipe the usual sly grin off his face.

Barnett blinked. Before his eyes a miraculous transformation had taken place: the dapper little man had become a street urchin. Fifteen years had been wiped off his appearance, and no one seeing him now would believe he could possibly have anything more on his mind than retrieving a stray ball.

The Mummer wiped his nose with his sleeve and stared up at Moriarty. "Wat'cher think, gov?" he demanded in the nasal whine of the slum child. "Do yer 'pose I'll do?"

"Mummer, you're an artist!" Moriarty exclaimed.

"It's nuffink, Professor," the Mummer said. "Now, if you'll 'scuse me, I'll go practice me art." And with a skip and a slosh, he ran off down the street.

* * *

The man who was the wind was in the cellar of the devil's house. He had stealthily unlocked a small window over a long-disused storage bin when he had delivered the casks of wine. And now he was among the casks. He could hear footsteps, faintly, overhead, as the devil's imps arrived upstairs one by one. It was good. He took off his coat and rolled up his sleeves. There was plenty of time. Smiling a horrible smile, he reached for the nearest cask.

* * *

The Sons of Azazel began arriving at their clubhouse shortly after Moriarty and Barnett settled down to watch. One after another, at short intervals, the clatter of horses' hooves would sound over the rain, and a carriage would pull up somewhere along that block of Upper Pondbury Crescent. Two broughams, three hansoms, a quartet of four-wheelers, and an elegant barouche with a black canvas panel covering what must have been a crest on the ebony door—all arrived within the first half hour. From each vehicle one heavily cloaked man emerged and proceeded toward the front door of the Hellfire house. When one of these gentlemen arrived close on the heels of another, he would wait on the pavement, stamping his feet impatiently, while the first was received at the door.

Tolliver dashed back across the street as the latest hansom was disappearing around the corner. "I got a fix on 'er now, Professor," he said. "They goes up to the door and gives a pull on the bellpull. Then this little hole what is beside the door—over on the left—is opened from the inside. The gent what's outside sticks something in the hole for the gent what's inside to take a dekky at. I couldn't get a good look at the item, but I think it's one of them medals like you got. Then the gent what's inside hands the gent what's outside a mask, which he promptly sticks over his face. Then the door finally opens, and the gent what's outside goes inside. You got me, Professor?"

"I got you, Mummer." Moriarty turned to Barnett. "That explains one thing," he said. "I have been wondering why there have been no masks found in conjunction with any of the bodies, since they maintain the habit of going masked. A nice little solution to the problem. It means, also, that we won't have any trouble in entering the house."

"How are we going to do this, Professor?" Barnett asked. "I'm ready for whatever has to be done."

"It looks as though you and I will be the only ones entering directly," Moriarty said. "We each have a medallion, and we are, each, disguised as a gentleman. That should be enough to get us inside."

"Okay," Barnett said, raising the collar on his coat and adjusting his hat. "Let's go!"

"One at a time, remember," Moriarty cautioned him. "I shall go first, and await you in the inner corridor. If, for some reason, that should prove too conspicuous, I shall be in the first accessible room. Try not to speak."

"Excuse me, Professor, before you go," Tolliver said, "but when will you want me and the other lads to join in the festivities?"

"Keep close watch outside," Moriarty told him. "Here, take this; it's a police whistle. If I need you, I will signal by throwing something through one of the front windows. Then you blow the whistle to assemble our men and head right in through the front door. Otherwise, just be prepared to give support if we have to exit quickly."

"Right enough, Professor," Tolliver said. "I'll pass the word along to the lads to keep out of sight, but be ready to act if they hears the whistle."

"Who are these 'lads'?" Barnett asked.

"Colonel Moran," Tolliver told him, "and some of his pals from the Amateur Mendicant Society. The colonel 'as a look on him like he wants to hit something; and I'm sure squatting under a porch in the rain ain't doing his disposition no good, neither."

"Tell him how things stand," Moriarty said. "Tell him the answer to his problem is inside, and I shall bring it out. I'm depending on you, Mummer. Come along, Barnett, be right behind me now."

Barnett stood on the pavement in front of the house, fingering the small medallion and watching as Moriarty was admitted through the front door. Then it was his turn. His heart pounding loudly, he advanced to the door and pulled the wooden bell knob.

* * *

His preparations were just about complete now. One final check—couldn't have anything going wrong—and he would find his way upstairs and join the festivities. Festivities? He smiled. Eat, drink, and be merry, he thought, for it is almost tomorrow.

* * *

Moriarty waited for Barnett in a small room to the left of the entranceway, just out of earshot of the greeter at the door. Barnett looked around. "How prosaic," he whispered to the professor. "A cloakroom."

"The prosaic is ever intermingled with the bizarre and the frightful," Moriarty commented. "The Executioner of Nuremberg wears a dress suit and white gloves, and uses a double-bladed ax. The Mongol hordes invented the game of polo, but they used a human head in place of a ball. The castle of Vlad the Impaler was noted for its fine view of the Carpathian Mountains. I'll wager this place also has a washroom, and quite probably a kitchen."

Barnett shook his head slightly. "Has anything ever surprised you, Professor?" he asked.

"Everything constantly surprises me," Moriarty replied. "I think this is the direction we want to go."

They went down the hallway, peering into each room as they

passed it. Barnett tried to look nonchalant under his mask, but he kept having the feeling that every pair of eyes that turned his way would immediately see right through his disguise, and that any second one of the well-dressed masked men strutting about the hall was going to point a dramatic finger in the direction of his nose and exclaim, "That man in the wrinkled suit is obviously not one of us! Apprehend him!"

But the other masked men in the halls and rooms of this hellish club saw no difference between Moriarty, or Barnett, and themselves. And, Barnett was surprised to note, without seeing their faces he could detect no difference between them and other men. He wasn't sure what sort of difference he expected to see, but once he got used to seeing a mask instead of a face, these Hellfire men bore no stigmata visible to Barnett. In their dress and bearing they would not have looked out of place strutting down the halls of the Bagatelle, the Carlton, or the Diogenes. Perhaps on other evenings they did just that.

The rooms off the short entrance hall were dedicated to games of chance. There were three small rooms, fitted out for baccarat, whist, and vingt-et-un; and a large room with two roulette wheels and a piquet table. The action was spirited at these tables, and the stakes were high. The games were supervised by a pair of stewards in severe black garments, wearing identical papier-mâché masks modeled to look like smiling faces, painted porcelain white, with black eyebrows and a pencil-thin black mustache. The dealers and croupiers were all attractive women in their twenties; their colorful dress and easy manner placed them as belonging to that segment of society which the French called the *demi-monde*, the English having no polite term for it.

It was a bizarre scene that Barnett found himself wandering through; masked men and scarlet women playing at card games with a savage intensity under the actinic glare of the multiple gas fixtures that were scattered about the walls like perverted gargoyles. There was another game going on too, a subtler game played with nudges and winks and nods and indirect conversation, and blushes and giggles from the *demi-mondaines*. This was also being played with a fierce intensity, although Barnett could not, from what he overheard, clearly discern the rules, rewards, or penalties. The game, superficially sexual in content, had the flavor of evil and decay. Barnett noted a cynical hardness around the eyes of the women, and he thought he detected in some of their eyes the glitter of fear.

"What do you think?" he whispered to Moriarty, as the two of them stood in an isolated corner of the large room near the piquet table.

Moriarty looked at him for a long moment, as though debating which of the many ways to answer that question he would choose. "I think we are on the periphery of evil," he said. "We must proceed inward, toward the center. Prepare yourself for scenes that will not please you, and try not to give yourself away by reacting prematurely to whatever you see. Blend in with your surroundings, as distasteful as that may be."

Barnett looked around. "If I have to play, I'll play," he said. "I have had practice. Which way, do you suppose, is the center?"

"I have been watching," Moriarty said, "and as far as I can determine, the door in the opposite corner of this room would seem to be the portal to the netherworld of infinite and infernal delights. It leads to a corridor, and the corridor leads to—what, I wonder? I have seen several of the masked gentlemen go through it, but none of the, ah, ladies. Are you ready?"

"I hope so," Barnett whispered.

"Stiff upper lip!" Moriarty said. "Or, at least, *act* as though your upper lip is as stiff as an Englishman is supposed to keep his upper lip. You are going now into the *sanctum sanctorum* of this blessed club, the delights of which are the reason you pay the Master Incarnate his twenty guineas a month."

"I suspect I shall get more than my money's worth," Barnett murmured. "Lead on, Professor."

* * *

He was among them now. They smiled and laughed and played at their devilish games; and he smiled and laughed under his mask, and played well his own game. He took out his watch, a gift from the Burgermeister of Fürth after a successful escape from the ancient dungeons beneath the Rathaus: it was now quarter past ten. In one hundred and five minutes all games would cease. Midnight, the witching hour. He laughed again, aloud, but nobody noticed.

* * *

The house was divided into four sections, which, like the levels of hell in Dante's *Inferno*, were separated according to the sins favored by the inhabitants. Each level of greater sin was accessible at only one place, through the level of lesser sin. Moriarty and Barnett progressed from Level One, Gambling and Lechery; then to Level Two, Various Exotic Perversions with Willing—or Persuadable—Women. The room they entered, large, effusively ornate, and yet subtly tawdry, resembled nothing so much as the parlor in an expensive brothel. Which was certainly deliberate, and was in no way inaccurate.

Barnett ran his gaze over the flocked red plush wallpaper; the deeply cushioned chairs and couches, done in matching fabric; the elaborate and tasteless candelabrum, decorated with flowers and cherubim and remarkably voluptuous female angels; and the equally voluptuous ladies lounging on the couches, garbed in imaginative dishabille. "Aside from these idiotic masks," Barnett whispered, "this could be any one of fifty clubs in London, all catering to the same 'sporting' population."

"*Nemo repente fuit turpissimus,*" Moriarty murmured. "I find Juvenal quotable at the most unusual times."

"How's that?" Barnett asked quietly.

Moriarty shook his head slightly in mock annoyance. "Your American schools just don't believe in a classical education," he commented. "No wonder your English prose is so flat and unmellifluous; you are all innocent of Latin."

"Discuss my educational deficiencies some other time, Professor," Barnett requested firmly. "What did you say?"

"Roughly, 'No one ever mastered the heights of vice at the first try.' These chaps have to start somewhere, after all."

Suddenly a scream sounded from one of the nearby rooms—a high-pitched cry of unendurable agony. Barnett jerked his head around, seeking the source of the sound, but none of the others in the parlor reacted at all, except for a few of the women, who twitched nervously.

Barnett clutched at Moriarty's sleeve. "What was that?" he demanded.

"Casual, Mr. Barnett," Moriarty whispered intently. "Remain casual. This sort of thing must happen all the time. Remember the part you are playing. You are well used to such sounds. Indeed, it is why you are here."

Barnett stiffened his back and lifted his head into a parody of nonchalance. "What is it exactly that happens all the time," he asked, "which causes girls to scream in distant rooms?"

Moriarty leaned casually against a patch of flocked wallpaper. "You really don't want to know," he said. "Suffice it to say that other people's ideas of sexual pleasure may be far removed from your own."

"You mean—but why would they put up with it? The women, I mean?"

"These ladies are all imported from elsewhere for service in this house. This is a practice that is common in London houses of this sort, although these people take more advantage of it than others might. They serve for about two months, which is probably the length of time that the house stays in any one location, and then are sent back whence they came with a sum of money in hand. If necessary, as it frequently is, their, ah, wounds are first tended to in a hospital far from here, where the causes behind their injuries are overlooked by mutual agreement."

"Horrible!" Barnett said. "Much worse than any stories I've heard about the brothels in France."

"Your studies in depravity did not descend deep enough," Moriarty commented. "There are many similar places in Paris, as indeed in Berlin, Vienna, Prague, Warsaw, and every other European capital. With the possible exception of Rome—the Italians don't seem to be as prone to institutionalize their violence. As to what happens in such houses in the Osmanli Empire and the Arab world, they make our friends here look like dilettantes."

Barnett looked around him. "You make this place sound like a garden party," he commented.

"You are mistaken," Moriarty replied. "I said it was horrible, not unique. Besides, this is merely the, let us say, middle level of experience. The upper levels, for which they kidnap women off the street and throw dead bodies back onto the street, probably more nearly meet your requirements."

Barnett clutched convulsively at Moriarty's sleeve again, and then forced himself to let go. "If you can believe it, I had forgotten for an instant," he said. "Let us go on!"

"We must locate the door through which the initiates go to practice vices few others even know exist," Moriarty said.

"You expect to find Cecily at this next level?" Barnett demanded. "And yet you think she is still all right?"

"They must have cells," Moriarty said, "where women are held for, ah, future use. I expect to find the lady in one of these cells, and I expect to find the cells deep in the heart of the beast."

"Cells?"

"Yes. There were signs in the now-deserted houses that certain of their rooms had been used as cells."

"Well then—" Barnett began.

"Grab that man!" a harsh, commanding voice suddenly rang out from somewhere behind Barnett. "Don't let him escape! He is not one of us, he is a spy! Be sharp, now!"

Barnett started at the words, twisting around, and expecting to feel a heavy hand on his shoulder. To his amazement and relief, the short, imperious man who had barked out the commands was not pointing his accusing finger at Barnett, but at a slender man who had been quietly sitting by the piano.

"Here, now," the accused said, rising to his feet. "What's the meaning of this? Who are you, sir, and what do you mean by such an accusation?" He seemed amused, rather than alarmed. "Is this your idea of fun, little man?"

Several men who were dressed as servitors of the club appeared from different doorways, as though they had been awaiting the command, and moved closer to surround the tall, slender man.

"*I* am the Master Incarnate," the little man announced. "And you are a spy!"

"Whatever makes you think that?" the slender man asked, ignoring the surrounding servitors with a splendid nonchalance. "Are you absolutely sure you're right? Remember, Master, unveiling a member would be a very bad precedent to set, especially for you. Are you sure you wish to risk it, in front of all these fellow members?" With a wave of his hand, the slender man indicated the cluster of masked men, who had all stopped whatever they were doing and turned to watch the scene.

"I am sure," the Master Incarnate barked. "Especially as I can name you where you stand, and then prove it by unmasking you... Mr. Sherlock Holmes!" He reached for the mask and yanked it off, exposing the sharp features of the consulting detective.

"I must hand it to you, Count," Holmes said, edging toward the wall. "You have cleverly revealed my identity. But, after all, are you quite certain that I'm not a member?" He took a firm grasp on his stick and flicked it in the general direction of one of the servitors, who was approaching him from behind. The man jumped back with alacrity.

"Thought you could fool us this afternoon," the Master Incarnate said, grimacing his satisfaction, "grubbing about in the cellar."

"The cellar?" Holmes repeated, sounding surprised. "Whatever are you talking about, Count d'Hiver?"

The count ignored Holmes's use of his name. "I heard about it as soon as I returned this afternoon," he said, "and watched through a concealed peephole to see who would attempt to gain entrance this evening that shouldn't. And it was you, Mr. Holmes—it was *you*. I had a feeling during the course of this investigation that you were going to prove too clever for us."

"I suppose there would be no point in advising you that this house is surrounded?" Holmes inquired, backing the rest of the way to the nearest wall. The way to the entrance door was now blocked by two brutish-looking servitors of the house.

"There would be no point at all," the Master Incarnate declared savagely. "It isn't, and it wouldn't change things for you if it were. Take him!"

Five of the burly servitors leaped for Holmes, who lifted his walking stick and whirled it about him, fairly making it sing as he beat them off. In an instant two of them were down, and the remaining three were circling respectfully out of range of the lean detective and his three feet of ash.

Barnett gathered himself to rush to Holmes's aid, but he felt Moriarty's restraining hand on his shoulder. "To the other door!" Moriarty whispered urgently. "That door over there. I shall bring Holmes. Prepare to open it for us as we arrive, and close it firmly and promptly once we are through. Go now!"

Barnett sidled over to the door Moriarty had indicated and put his hand on the knob. Assuring himself that it opened easily, he nodded his readiness to the professor.

With a broad gesture, Professor Moriarty whipped his mask off and blew two sharp blasts on a police whistle. Everyone in the room froze in position for a second, forming a bizarre tableau that would remain forever etched on Barnett's memory.

"Over here, Mr. Holmes," Moriarty called. "I must ask the rest of you to remain where you are. You are all under arrest! Constables, take charge of these men!"

Without waiting to find out where these constables were, or where they might have come from, the masked Hellfires in the room made a dash, as one, for the far door. Count d'Hiver screamed at them to stop, yelling that Moriarty was a fraud, that it wasn't so; but they did not pause to listen. In a few seconds there was a plug of human bodies squeezing ever harder into the entrance door. Two men had already lost their footing, and were down under the pack, with little hope of getting up. As Barnett watched, another man was lifted bodily from the doorway by several others and hurried over many heads to the ground at the rear.

Holmes broke free and leaped across to where Moriarty stood, imposingly, belligerently firm, next to a couch. "This way," Moriarty said, and the two of them stalked across the room to the door Barnett was guarding for them. In a second they were through it, and Moriarty threw the two heavy bolts on the far side.

"This should hold them for a few minutes," the professor said. "Time enough for us to do what we have to, if we get to it."

"Glad to see you, Moriarty," Holmes gasped, leaning against the wall to catch his breath. "Never thought I'd hear myself saying that. You do show up in the oddest places, though."

"I didn't expect to find you here, either, Holmes," Moriarty commented. "And what on earth have you been doing in the cellar?"

"But I wasn't in the cellar, old man," Holmes replied. "I have no idea what that was about."

"Curious," the professor said, "very curious. But come now, there's work to be done. We can compare notes some other time."

"You realize there's almost certainly no way out of this unusual establishment from this side of this door?" Holmes asked. "We have managed to place ourselves one step deeper into the web. As soon as Count d'Hiver and his cohorts are over their momentary confusion, admirably contrived though it was, they will surely assault this door with a convincing show of strength."

"True," Moriarty admitted. "But what we have come here for is certainly up these stairs. I would not leave before accomplishing my goal, and I'm quite sure that Mr. Barnett would not allow it were I to attempt to do so."

Holmes glanced at the still-masked Barnett. "So that's who you are," he said. "Should have known. Glad you're here. And now, just what is it that we are after? Ah! Of course! Miss Perrine; I should have guessed."

They made their way cautiously up the narrow staircase, Moriarty in the lead, and found themselves about a third of the way along a hallway that ran down the middle of the upper floor. There were rooms off each side, and each of the rooms had been fitted with a heavy, solid door, with a strong bolt affixed to the outside.

Moriarty threw open the door to the nearest room, and found it empty; but there were a pair of posts fastened to the floor in the center of the room, with leather thongs running through eyebolts in the posts. Barnett did not like to contemplate what such an apparatus might be used for.

In the next room they tried there was a girl, clad only in a white shift, who shrank away from them in horror as they opened the door. The shift was in tatters, and they could see the strips across her back and thighs where she had been beaten. It was not Cecily Perrine.

"It's all right, miss," Sherlock Holmes said, advancing into the room. "We've come to get you out of here. It's all right, really it is. We won't hurt you." He continued talking to the girl and walking slowly toward her, as she, eyes wide, speechless with fear, retreated into the farthest corner of the room.

"See here, Holmes, there's no time for this," Moriarty said. He turned to the girl. "Any minute now there's going to be an awful row. Those people who have done this to you are going to try to stop us from freeing you and the others. You'd best come with us now, and help with the other girls as we release them. We'll see if we can find a room where *you* can bolt the door from the inside. When it's all over, I shall see that you and any other ladies up here are removed from this place and taken care of. Properly. Do you understand?"

"Yes, sir," the girl said, but her voice was heavy with doubt and fear.

Moriarty reached around inside his jacket, behind his back, and, after fumbling for a second, pulled out a long, flat leather truncheon. "Come here, girl," he said. "Take this. If anyone approaches you while we are otherwise occupied, hit them in the face with it. Aim for the nose. That will discourage them."

The girl came forward hesitantly and took the proffered instrument. "I shall," she said, slapping it tentatively against the palm of her hand. She winced, finding the device surprisingly painful. "I shall," she repeated, staring directly into Moriarty's eyes. Her voice gained strength. "I shall! Oh, indeed, I shall."

"Very good," Moriarty said. "Now, stay close behind us."

They returned to the hallway. "I doubt if we have much time," Moriarty said. "Each of you take a room. Dispose of any resident masked men in it as you see fit—as rapidly as you can. I suggest we open all these doors immediately, and release any more captive young ladies."

"I—think—so," Holmes said, staring back at the strange, dreadful equipment in the room they had just left. "How horrible. It is difficult to believe that these men are Englishmen."

"I occasionally find it difficult to believe that our Parliamentary representatives are Englishmen," Moriarty remarked dryly. "Let us proceed; I think I hear pounding from below. If either of you happen to notice a window facing the front of the house—which would be that side, there—kindly heave some article of furniture through it."

Holmes looked speculatively at Moriarty. "Some of your minions downstairs?" he asked. "Well, I shall be glad to see them. I fancy all the windows are boarded up; there seems to be a false wall across that side of all the rooms."

In the third room that Barnett entered he found himself staring at a scene that he would never forget. The floor was bare and covered with sawdust, and at its center was a six-foot oaken X which dominated the room. Cecily Perrine, clad only in a long white shift, had just been unchained from an eyelet bolted to the wall and, her hands bound with thick cord, was being dragged across the floor by a short, thickset, hooded man.

The man giggled inanely as he pulled Cecily toward the oaken torture device. He brandished a short, many-stranded whip which he flicked occasionally into the empty air as though to get in practice for the delights that would follow.

"My God!" Barnett screamed.

Cecily turned and stared impassively at this second hooded man who now stood in the doorway.

The man with the whip pushed Cecily aside and whirled around. "What are *you* doing in here?" he demanded petulantly. "Get out! Get out! This is my room. Mine! She is mine! Get out! You know better than this!" He bounced up and down with excitement and anger, and waved his whip at Barnett. "Leave!"

Barnett snatched at the whip, pulling it out of the man's grasp. "You bastard!" he yelled, scarcely aware of what he was saying. "You slime! What are you doing with this woman?"

"She's mine," the thickset man insisted in a shrill voice. "I paid for her, didn't I? Now you just get out of here, or I'll report you to the Master Incarnate. Get your own female!"

Barnett could feel the blood rising to his face, and the mantle of reason lifted itself from the primitive emotions beneath. Like a distant observer, cool and detached, he watched himself lift the short whip and bring its weighted handle down again and again on the head of the thickset man. The man fell to the floor, and Barnett stopped—not through compassion, but because the target of his rage was now out of reach.

Slowly the haze cleared from before his eyes and he looked at Cecily. Then he quickly looked away. He did not want to see her like this, he did not want ever to think of her like this, bound and helpless, and subject to the whims of evil men.

He crossed to where she lay and quickly, tenderly, untied her hands. "Cecily," he said, "what have they done to you?" To his surprise, he found that he was crying.

"Benjamin?" she whispered. "Is it you?"

He took his mask off—he had forgotten it was still on—and held her to him for a long moment. There was a robe in the corner which he used to cover her. "Can you walk?" he asked. "We must hurry."

"Yes," she said. "Get me away from here."

There were a total of seven women in the various rooms of this upper floor, and, at that moment, five men. Moriarty immobilized the men by tying their thumbs together behind their backs with short pieces of wire, which he produced from one of his innumerable pockets. By this time they could hear a steady pounding noise coming up from the door below.

"There is no other way out," Holmes said. "I have tried all the doors. Presumably we could find our way to the roof, but what then? It's a long way to the ground."

"I suggest we remove the false wall from one of the rooms facing the front of the house," Moriarty said. "If I can get to a window, I can get assistance."

"What good could your men do us now?" Holmes demanded. "They're down there and we're up here."

"A group of determined men assaulting the front door," Moriarty pointed out, "would at least provide a much-needed diversion. It would most probably complete the job of panicking the rank and file."

"Perhaps I can be of some assistance," a deep, well-modulated voice said from behind them.

They all turned. A tall man in elegant evening dress bowed to them politely before removing the mask that covered his face. "Allow me to introduce myself," he said, with just the slightest hint of a Middle European accent coloring his flawless English. "My name is Adolphus Chardino."

"Ah!" Moriarty said.

"Who are you?" Holmes demanded, shielding the seven young ladies behind him.

"That is of no moment at the present," Chardino said. "What is meaningful is that I can assist you in your efforts to leave." He removed a large pocket watch from his vest and glanced at it. "And I would earnestly suggest that you hurry; it would be wise to be gone within the next fourteen minutes."

"Why?" asked Holmes suspiciously.

"Well, you see, in fourteen minutes it will be midnight," Chardino told him earnestly. "And tomorrow—is another day."

"How do we get out?" Moriarty demanded.

"Follow me," Chardino said. He led them down the hallway to a small door.

They paused. "That," Holmes said, pointing to the door, "is a closet. I believe this man is in need of the services of an alienist."

"When these houses were built," Chardino said, opening the closet door, "some eighty years ago, the builders of the day separated the ceiling of one level from the floor of the next with a dead-air space to minimize the transmission of sound from one story to the next—a practice the architects of today would do well to emulate. In this building the space is two feet deep."

"How do you know about that?" Holmes asked.

"It is my profession to know such things," Chardino said. "It is such knowledge that enables me to perform miracles." He knelt down and searched with his fingers in a corner of the closet. "There is an access panel," he said. "Here!" He pulled up and the floor of the closet lifted out.

"How do you like that!" Barnett exclaimed.

"What sort of miracles?" asked Holmes.

"The usual sort," Chardino said. "Appearing, disappearing, escaping; what you might expect from a stage magician."

"Oh," Holmes said.

The sounds from the stairs increased. Now a chopping, cracking sound was added.

"They have found an ax," Moriarty said. "If we are going to leave, we should do so expeditiously."

"If one of you gentlemen would care to lead the way," Chardino said, "I would suggest that the ladies follow, and then the other two gentlemen. You will have to go single file."

"To where?" Barnett asked.

"There is no light," Chardino said. "I have placed a cord. Keep it to your left hand. It terminates at an access port leading to another closet on the floor below."

"Won't they see us coming out of the closet?" Barnett asked.

"It is in a seldom-used room," Chardino said. "And I shall do my best to distract them. Trust me. The art of misdirection is one I understand well. Now, hurry!"

Holmes looked doubtful, but he took the lead. It was a tight fit, but he managed to squeeze his lanky body into the small hole. "Here is the cord," came his voice from the black depths. "I shall proceed." A moment later he had disappeared into the narrow, pitch-black world under the floor.

Three of the rescued girls dropped into the space without comment, and crawled out of sight after Holmes; but the fourth balked.

"I can't!" she cried. "I just can't!"

"It's the only way out," Barnett said. "Come on, now, buck up."

"I have always been afraid of dark places," she said, backing away from the hole and shaking her head, her eyes wild. "Go without me if you must. I simply cannot crawl down there."

Chardino took her face in his hands and stared into her eyes. "You must go," he said clearly and simply. "You can do it; this one time you can. You will think of nothing. You will clear your mind of all thought. You will close your eyes and picture a bright meadow, as you crawl on your hands and knees, following the cord. There will be no other thoughts in your mind while you do this, and you will hear only the sound of my voice. I will be telling you that you *can* do it—you *can* do it. It is not hard, for you. Not this once. Not with my voice to guide you through the bright meadow which would be there if your eyes were opened. But they will stay closed. Do you hear me, girl?"

"Yes," she said, staring back into his eyes. "Yes, I hear you."

"Do you understand?"

"Yes, I understand."

"Then go! Remember, I am with you. You will hear my voice, as now, comforting you. For the sake of my daughter, go!"

The girl turned and lowered herself into the hole. In a second she was gone from sight.

Cecily Perrine was next. She dropped easily into the hole and crawled away.

The other two girls followed. As Barnett was about to go after them, he heard a splintering crash. "That's from the stairs; they must have chopped through!" he exclaimed.

"Go!" Moriarty commanded. "I wish to have a brief word with Professor Chardino, but I will follow right behind."

Barnett turned and lowered himself into the hole. He found the cord, a thin, very rough twine, and followed it into the dark. Ahead of him he could hear the sliding, thumping sound of the girl who had preceded him. Behind him, nothing.

It was not easy going; he found himself crossing over joists every few feet and ducking under beams the alternate feet. Once he got into the pattern of crawling, however, he found he could move steadily. But where was Moriarty? He should have been close behind him.

There was a sudden rattle from overhead, a stamping of feet, a banging of doors. If Moriarty wasn't on his way now, he would never make it. If the hatch in the closet wasn't closed, they would probably none of them make it. The Count d'Hiver would, assuredly, allow none of them to live.

There, ahead of him, was a glimmer of light from below. It rapidly grew clearer as he crawled, and then he found himself staring down into the illumination of one candle in an otherwise empty closet. He lowered himself down, carefully avoiding the candle. The door was open, and the others awaited him in the room beyond.

It seemed like an hour, although it could not have been more than a minute, before Moriarty's feet appeared at the trap, and the professor dropped into the closet. "Everyone made it safely?" he asked, looking around. "According to our friend, the front door is around to the left. We have no time to spare. Don't stop for anything! The masked men will have gone upstairs in response to d'Hiver's yells. They will be occupied for a time seeking us. We should have little interference down here. Stay close together."

"What of Chardino?" Barnett asked.

"He is keeping our opposition busy by flitting from room to room and drawing them deeper into the house," Moriarty told him. "Come!" He led the way from the little room and down a short corridor to the left, which terminated at a closed door. They met no one. Holmes, taking the lead, opened the door cautiously, peered through, and then closed it.

"As you thought, it is the entrance hall," Holmes whispered. "Front door to the right, gambling rooms to the left. There are six of them, that I could see, standing by the door and doing their best to look vicious. D'Hiver must have alerted them."

"Six?" Moriarty thought for a second. "No matter; we shall have to rush them." He grabbed a chair. "Keep the ladies back here. Put your masks on—it might gain us a second."

Barnett took a deep breath and prepared to follow Moriarty.

He was, he decided, becoming a fatalist.

"Now!" Moriarty whispered, and the three of them plunged through the door, Holmes in the center, Barnett hugging the wall on the left, and Moriarty—his chair held chest-high—on the right. The six by the door froze for a moment, staring at the oncoming trio. Perhaps it was the chair that puzzled them. But then, with an assortment of oaths that would have been out of place in any respectable men's club, they rushed to the defense. In a second Barnett found himself assaulted by several men larger than himself.

The area was too small for any effective punching, kicking, or gouging on either side, and there was no room for the use of sticks or canes. Barnett was finding it all he could do to remain where he was, while Holmes, with a flurry of brilliant boxing, was holding three men off and actually making a little progress.

Moriarty, parrying one gigantic door guard off with his chair, made a dash for the small cloakroom door to the right of the hall. Once inside, he heaved his chair through the small window facing the street, and then ran back to the hall in time to pull a guard off Barnett.

About twenty seconds after the chair went through the window, they heard battering sounds from outside the front door. A minute later Colonel Moran burst through, brass knuckles on each fist, at the head of a flying squad of Moriarty's minions. Colonel Moran scattered the resistance before him like a child scattering marbles, and in seconds the way was clear.

"Good!" Moriarty called. "Now out, quickly, all of you!"

"Let us clean the place out," Colonel Moran insisted.

"Trust me, Colonel," Moriarty told him. "It shall be done. But you get the boys out of here and away—now!"

The habits of a military lifetime were too ingrained to permit argument. Moran barely resisted saluting. "Yes, sir," he said, and gathered his troop before him on his way back out the door.

"Let us get the ladies, Barnett," Moriarty called. "Quickly now!" He went to the door behind which they waited and shooed them into the hall like a mother hen.

Barnett paused at the cloakroom door and grabbed an armful of capes and overcoats, wrapping one around the shoulders of each girl as she passed out into the rain. Moriarty, after seeing them start safely out, darted back to the door of the large gambling room. "Quick!" he called to the house girls who were lounging about awaiting the return of the masked men. "Out into the street! No time to explain! The police are coming! Move—move!"

The urgency in his voice must have communicated itself to the women, because they boiled out of the room and joined him in a mad dash through the outer door.

Barnett stopped on the pavement about one hundred feet from the house to gather the young ladies in his charge. "Around the corner," he told them. "There's a carriage. We won't all fit—"

"I have a four-wheeler on the next block," Holmes volunteered. "It's a rotten shame, isn't it?"

"What?" Barnett asked.

"Whistling for a policeman would accomplish nothing. One or two bobbies could not prevent that assemblage from dispersing all over London. We'll be lucky to apprehend more than a couple of them. There's no way I can get a raiding party here from Scotland Yard in time to do any good at all."

"I wouldn't worry about it," Moriarty said, coming up behind them. He had his watch out, and was staring at the face.

"Why?" Holmes demanded.

"There is no time," Moriarty said, closing the watch and putting it away. "Get down!" he ordered. "All of us. *Now!* I just hope we're far enough away." He dropped flat to the pavement, and the others followed. Barnett did his best to shield Cecily from whatever was to happen.

The Mummer came running over. "What's happening, Professor?" he demanded, staring down at the group.

Moriarty's hand came up, grabbed Tolliver by the lapel, and pulled him down to the pavement. A second later the earth lifted and heaved, and a sound that was beyond sound filled the air. It seemed to go on and on, and then, abruptly, it stopped. For a few seconds longer there was a new sound, coming from all about them—

the splattering, smacking noises of large objects hitting other large objects, or hitting the ground. And then that too died out.

Barnett lifted his head. Where the house had been there were now several fires. But—and this his mind did not grasp for a moment—there was no longer a house.

"Midnight," Moriarty said. "The start of a new day, and the end of the old. Let us go home."

TWENTY-EIGHT

THE GIFT

*So she went into the garden to cut a cabbage leaf to make an apple
pie; and at the same time a great she-bear, coming up the street,
pops its head into the shop. "What! no soap?" So he died, and she
very imprudently married the barber; and there were present the
Picninnies, and the Joblillies, and the Garyulies, and the Grand
Panjandrum himself, with the little round button at top, and they all
fell to playing the game of catch as catch can, till the gunpowder ran
out at the heels of their boots.*

SAMUEL FOOTE

B arnett spent the better part of a day composing the letter. It was as
short as possible, considering all he had to put into it. He rewrote
it fourteen times, and each time was convinced that he sounded just
as much like a stuff-shirted prig as the last time. Whenever he tried
to lighten the tone, it sounded frivolous to him; and he would not
sound frivolous.

Marry me, Cecily, the letter said. And then it went on to tell
why. It spoke of love and understanding and mutual aid and
trust. It touched on a woman's right to have a career, and how he
understood, and was willing to honor that. (*Prig!*) It skirted the issue
of complete independence for women by pointing out that although
he *most* assuredly believed in it himself, that would change neither

the laws nor the customs of Great Britain.

It was six pages long in his small script.

In the late afternoon he went over to Cecily Perrine's house. It was a week since the clubhouse had exploded, and Cecily had been confined to her bed for that time, tended by her father. The first three days of bed rest were for her health and recuperation. The last four were more for her father. The old man seemed to feel that her ordeal was somehow his fault, so Cecily stayed in for a few extra days to allow him to fuss over her.

Barnett came over every day, clutching some small idiotic present to his chest as he entered her room. This day he brought a potted plant, which he placed on the window ledge. Then he chatted politely with Cecily for two hours—afterward, he could not remember what they had talked about. As he got up to leave, he handed her the envelope.

"Read this at your leisure," he told her, "after I leave. It tells you how I feel. Somehow I'm afraid that if I try to do it in person, we will get sidetracked and have an argument, which is the last thing I want. Answer me when you are ready."

Then he shook her hand and left. The words that he had intended to add remained stillborn on his lips. He had practiced them, but he could not say them. He had planned to say that he, with this letter, was once more proposing marriage to her, and that if she turned him down this time he would have to stop coming by. Seeing her would become too painful.

That was what he had intended to tell her. But at the last moment he had lost his courage. Supposing she said no—she would probably say no—she had said no once before. Would he actually have the courage to walk away and no longer see the woman he loved? It was probably the wisest thing, but it sounded so final. Perhaps if he stayed around, someday he would ask her a third time, and that time she would say yes.

He shook his head as he walked away from the house. Never would he have believed that he could behave this way. Love, he thought, is an unstable, unkind, thoroughly demoralizing emotion.

* * *

Back at Russell Square, Moriarty was entertaining a guest. Barnett recognized the visitor as the Indian gentleman who had called himself Singh. "This house," the guest was saying as Barnett entered the study, "the explosion demolished it completely?"

"Utterly," Moriarty said. "My calculations indicate that there must have been at least two hundred pounds of gunpowder packed into the cellar. There was one fireplace standing complete from cellar to chimneypot, like an angry brick finger pointing at the sky, but all else was gone. Bits and pieces of the Hellfire Club were found a quarter mile away."

"How many bodies? The newspaper accounts varied."

"Twenty-six that they could be sure of."

Singh nodded. "Professor Chardino believed in a vengeful God. A fascinating case, indeed."

Barnett looked curiously at the slender, dapper Indian gentleman, who turned and extended his hand to him as Moriarty introduced them. "Mr. Singh," Moriarty explained, "has come to arrange for the transportation of the treasure. It is being returned to those from whom it was stolen—spiritually, if not actually."

"Ah, Mr. Barnett," Singh said, taking his hand and shaking it briskly, "it is a pleasure to meet you. Allow me to commend you on how well you perform under stress."

"Thank you," Barnett said. "I am grateful for any compliment, but to what occasion are you referring?"

"The incident of the loading of the treasure train," Singh explained. "Your little bit of misdirection was masterfully done!"

"Well, thank you again," Barnett said, smiling. "Were you there?"

"Ah, yes," Singh said. "You would not recognize me, of course, clad, as I was, in a *dhoti* and busily loading treasure chests. I was but scenery—a donkey laborer."

Barnett pointed a finger at him. "You—"

"Indeed," the Indian agreed. "Such is life."

Mr. Maws appeared at the study door. "Mr. Sherlock Holmes is here, and would speak with you," he informed the professor.

"Ah, yes, Holmes. He is expected," Moriarty said. "Send him in."

Holmes stalked through the door and up to Moriarty's desk without acknowledging the presence of anyone else in the room. "I have you now, Professor Moriarty!" he exclaimed. "Professor of thieves!"

Moriarty smiled. "Mr. Holmes," he said. "Allow me to introduce—"

"Your friends?" Holmes chuckled. "I shall shortly introduce *you* to a judge—and a good British jury. You have gone too far!"

"Of what do we speak?" Moriarty inquired mildly. "Have you a purpose behind this tirade, or is it merely something you've eaten that disagrees with you?"

"That statuette," Holmes said. "That bauble. A bronze statuette of the goddess Uma, one of Shiva's consorts. Worth thousands, according to Lord East. It is one of two identical pieces, over a thousand years old." Holmes consulted a scrap of paper he carried. "One belonged to Lord East, and the other to the Maharaja of Rajasthan." He looked up and glared at Moriarty. "And just how did one of these priceless pieces come into your hands?" He smiled and folded his arms across his chest.

"Allow me to introduce you," Moriarty said, indicating Singh, "to the Maharaja of Rajasthan. Your Highness, Mr. Sherlock Holmes. A bit impolite, but a good solid investigator. When his reach does not exceed his grasp."

The Indian extended his hand. "My pleasure, Mr. Holmes," he said. "I have, of course, heard of you."

Holmes glared at the Maharaja, and then back at Moriarty. He sighed, and a look of resignation crossed his face. "You have, I'm sure, some means of identifying yourself?" he asked the Maharaja.

"But of course," the Maharaja agreed, pulling out a passport. "If there is any doubt, I am known to Lord Pindhurst, her majesty's Minister of Imperial Affairs, as well as to her majesty, Queen Victoria. Indeed, I had lunch with her today."

"I am sure you did," Holmes said, handing the document back to the Maharaja. "And I am sure that you gave the statuette to Professor Moriarty. I won't even ask you what service the professor performed in return, your highness. It is a pleasure to meet you, despite the, ah, circumstances." He turned back to Moriarty. "There is a certain inevitability about this moment, Professor. I should have expected it, but I am ever the optimist."

"I am sorry to disappoint you," Moriarty murmured.

"I have not had a chance to properly thank you for coming to my assistance in that hellhouse," Holmes said. "It was very sporting of you."

"Think nothing of it," Moriarty said. "Whatever were you doing there, Holmes? It was an unexpected pleasure."

"You don't suppose you're the only one who reads the agony columns, do you?" Holmes asked. "I—borrowed—one of those pretty medals from someone who would not need it for a while, left him lying peacefully in a bush, and entered. By the by, Professor—that fellow Chardino; he was the killer, was he not?"

"He was," Moriarty agreed.

"I see." Holmes looked thoughtful for a moment. "One cannot justify murder under any circumstances, but there are some that come closer than others. Is there anything we should do—about his demise, I mean?"

"I am having a headstone erected for him next to his daughter's grave," Moriarty said. "You may contribute."

"What will it say?" Holmes asked.

"I think, 'A Loving Father,'" Moriarty answered.

"I will subscribe," Holmes said. "He certainly was that."

"A bit of news that you might want to pass on to your friends at the Yard," Moriarty said. "One of those Hellfire devils escaped the blast."

"Oh?" Holmes said.

"Yes. Colonel Moran saw him picking his way out of the rubble and recognized him, but he escaped in the confusion."

"Who was it?"

"Lord Crecy Darby. Colonel Moran knew him years ago in India."

"Plantagenet!" Holmes said.

"That's the chap," Moriarty agreed. "Colonel Moran calls him the most dangerous man he's ever known. Likes to cut up prostitutes. I would suggest you make an effort to find him, or we'll be hearing from him in a way we won't like."

"I shall pass the word on," Holmes said. "Well, *adieu*, gentlemen."

He clapped his hat on his head and turned to leave.

"Do come back and entertain us again sometime," Moriarty said. "*Au revoir*, Holmes."

"Beg pardon, sir," Mr. Maws said, as Holmes stalked by him. "A district messenger has just come with this." He held up an envelope. "It is addressed to Mr. Barnett."

Barnett grabbed it out of Mr. Maws's hand. It looked like—it was certainly Cecily's handwriting. He ripped it open.

One word only on the stiff paper inside: *Yes.*

"Catch him, someone!" Moriarty called. "Help him to a chair. Mr. Maws, bring the brandy. I think the poor man needs a drink!"

ABOUT THE AUTHOR

Michael Kurland is the author of more than thirty books, but is perhaps best known for his series of novels starring Professor Moriarty. The first volume, *The Infernal Device*, was nominated for an Edgar Award, and received stellar reviews, including this from Isaac Asimov: "Michael Kurland has made Moriarty more interesting than Doyle ever made Holmes." It was followed by *Death By Gaslight*, *The Great Game*, *The Empress of India* and *Who Thinks Evil*, published over a period of more than thirty years.

Kurland is also well known as a science fiction writer, and is the author of *The Unicorn Girl*, as well as the bestselling *Ten Little Wizards* and *A Study in Sorcery*, fair-play detective stories set in a world where magic works. He has edited several Sherlock Holmes anthologies and written non-fiction titles such as *How to Solve a Murder: The Forensic Handbook*. He lives in California.

THE PROFESSOR MORIARTY NOVELS
MICHAEL KURLAND

A sweeping and eloquent detective series featuring
Sherlock Holmes's nemesis, Professor James Moriarty.
Aided by an American journalist, Benjamin Barnett,
and his infamous network of informers, criminals and
'specialists', Moriarty reveals himself to be far more than
just "The Napoleon of Crime", working for both sides of
the law, but always for his own ends.

The Infernal Device
Death By Gaslight
The Great Game (July 2014)
The Empress of India (September 2014)
Who Thinks Evil

PRAISE FOR THE MORIARTY NOVELS

"Michael Kurland has made Moriarty more interesting than Doyle ever made Holmes." Isaac Asimov

"As successful as its predecessors at bringing fin de siècle Europe to brilliant life... the action veers and twists like that in a contemporary spy thriller." *Booklist*

"A deliciously complex and abundantly rewarding novel... Surprises abound... This is no ordinary Holmes pastiche... Uncommon are the pleasures such writing affords." *Publishers Weekly*

"Kurland writes in a style that can only win praise from the Baker Street Irregulars... From whatever celestial outpost he now occupies, Conan Doyle must be beaming his approval." *West Coast Review of Books*

"In a world that sometimes seems overrun by pastiches, it is indeed pleasant to find an author with a new idea that is presented with some ingenuity." *Baker Street Journal*

"For readers who like Sherlock Holmes, and for those who like Victorian mystery thrillers, *Death By Gaslight* is a fine bouillabaisse to be savored bit by bit." *The Armchair Detective*

"Kurland's novels are a fascinating new look into the world of Sherlock Holmes." *Duncan (Oklahoma) Banner*

SHERLOCK HOLMES
Gods of War

JAMES LOVEGROVE

1913. The clouds of war are gathering. The world's great empires vie for supremacy. Europe is in turmoil, a powder keg awaiting a spark. A body is discovered on the shore below Beachy Head, just a mile from Sherlock Holmes's retirement cottage. The local police are satisfied that it's a suicide. The victim, a young man, recently suffered a disappointment in love, and Beachy Head is notorious as a place where the desperate leap to their deaths. But Holmes suspects murder. As he and Watson investigate, they uncover a conspiracy with shocking ramifications. There are some men, it seems, who not only actively welcome the idea of a world war but are seeking divine aid to make it a reality...

AVAILABLE JUNE 2014

SHERLOCK HOLMES
The Will of the Dead

GEORGE MANN

A rich elderly man has fallen to his death, and his will is nowhere to be found. A tragic accident or something more sinister? The dead man's nephew comes to Baker Street to beg for Sherlock Holmes's help. Without the will he fears he will be left penniless, the entire inheritance passing to his cousin. But just as Holmes and Watson start their investigation, a mysterious new claimant to the estate appears. Does this prove that the old man was murdered? Meanwhile Inspector Charles Bainbridge is trying to solve the case of the "iron men", mechanical steam-powered giants carrying out daring jewellery robberies. But how do you stop a machine that feels no pain and needs no rest? He too may need to call on the expertise of Sherlock Holmes.

SHERLOCK HOLMES
The Spirit Box

GEORGE MANN

Summer, 1915. As Zeppelins rain death upon the rooftops of London, eminent members of society begin to behave erratically: a Member of Parliament throws himself naked into the Thames after giving a pro-German speech to the House; a senior military advisor suggests surrender before feeding himself to a tiger at London Zoo; a famed suffragette suddenly renounces the women's liberation movement and throws herself under a train.

AVAILABLE AUGUST 2014

SHERLOCK HOLMES
The Army of Dr Moreau

GUY ADAMS

Dead bodies are found on the streets of London with wounds that can only be explained as the work of ferocious creatures not native to the city. Sherlock Holmes is visited by his brother, Mycroft, who is only too aware that the bodies are the calling card of Dr Moreau, a vivisectionist who was working for the British Government, following in the footsteps of Charles Darwin, before his experiments attracted negative attention and the work was halted. Mycroft believes that Moreau's experiments continue and he charges his brother with tracking the rogue scientist down before matters escalate any further.

SHERLOCK HOLMES
The Breath of God

GUY ADAMS

A body is found crushed to death in the snow. There are no footprints anywhere near it, almost as if the man was killed by the air itself. This is the first in a series of attacks that sees a handful of London's most prominent occultists murdered. While pursuing the case, Sherlock Holmes and Dr. Watson find themselves traveling to Scotland to meet with the one person they have been told can help: Aleister Crowley. As dark powers encircle them, Holmes's rationalist beliefs begin to be questioned. The unbelievable and unholy are on their trail as they gather a group of the most accomplished occult minds in the country: Doctor John Silence, the so-called "Psychic Doctor"; supernatural investigator Thomas Carnacki; runic expert and demonologist Julian Karswell.

PROFESSOR MORIARTY
The Hound of the D'Urbervilles

KIM NEWMAN

Imagine the twisted evil twins of Holmes and Watson
and you have the dangerous duo of Professor James
Moriarty—wily, snake-like, fiercely intelligent, terrifyingly
unpredictable—and Colonel Sebastian 'Basher' Moran—
violent, politically incorrect, debauched. Together they run
London crime, owning police and criminals alike.

A one-stop shop for all things illegal, from murder to high-
class heists, Moriarty and Moran have a stream of nefarious
visitors to their Conduit Street rooms, from the Christian
zealots of the American West, to the bloodthirsty Si Fan and
Les Vampires of Paris, as well as a certain Miss Irene Adler...

"It's witty, often hilarious stuff. The author portrays the
scurrilous flipside of Holmes's civil ordered world, pokes
fun at 'guest stars' from contemporary novels and ventures
into more outré territory than Conan Doyle even dared."
Financial Times

"[A] clever, funny mash-up of a whole range of literary
sources... It is extravagantly gruesome, gothic and
grotesque." *The Independent*

TITANBOOKS.COM